The Secret in the Forest

Other books by Carol Grier

How to Recognize a Good Man When You Meet Him,
and How to Treat Him

Choices, a Memoir

Secrets, a Memoir

The Secret in the Forest

CAROL GRIER

Renaissance Print
Portland, Oregon

Published 2015 by Renaissance Print, Portland, Oregon
Printed in the United States of America

ISBN: 978-0-9836295-0-4 (paperback)
ISBN: 978-0-9836295-2-8 (e-book)

This a a work of fiction. The characters, incidents, and dialogue are products of the author's imagination. Any resemblance to actual persons, living or dead, is coincidental.

Editor: J. Gale Frank
Book design: Jennifer Omner

To Jim, who has been gone for many years,
but will always be remembered with love.

What is past is prologue.
—William Shakespeare

Contents

CHAPTER 1

Pine Bluff — 1969

My first sight of Jimmy Tuttle was a shock. I had agreed to take on this fifteen-year-old kid for the summer, but actually seeing him made me wish I had thought twice before agreeing.

"Good God Almighty!" George, one of my hired men, muttered as he stared at the young kid on the other end of the train platform.

I had to admit the boy was an awful sight. Shoulder length blond hair, a shirt that looked like it had about five shades of paint smeared all over it, dirty leather thongs on dirty bare feet, and darned if he wasn't wearing beads. I smiled at the thought of what my fashionable niece, Marie, must think about her grandson. It would be a hard pill for her to swallow.

"Folks will run him out of town if they catch sight of him," George muttered.

It was true that Pine Bluff didn't tolerate hippies very well. There'd been too much trouble with them and their marijuana. "There won't be a problem if I'm with him," I said. "Now let's get a move on. We can't just stand here gawking at the kid."

George trailed behind me as I walked the length of the train platform to where the kid stood by the station house entrance. Normally, I don't go near this place. Too many sad memories. The Clearwater River had washed it away in 1916. Jacob Jacobsen, my husband, and twelve other poor souls were washed away with it. He was only twenty-six. I was twenty-three. We'd been married just four years. Some losses never stop hurting.

But there stood the kid. He hadn't moved an inch. His eyes had the apprehensive look of a deer that had been shot but hadn't yet fallen. A rebellious spoiled brat, his dad had called him, along with some other worrisome things.

It hadn't been too many days before that I was in the kitchen kneading bread dough and cursing my aching hands, when the phone rang. It was Bob Tuttle, my great niece's husband, wanting me to take on their boy for the summer — me, a 76-year-old woman. But my age wasn't the point right then. Jimmy looked like he was capable of making the summer miserable for everyone around him. Well, we'd just see about that.

"I know I'm asking a lot," Bob had said, "but you and your ranch could be the making of him. He's been spoiled rotten by his mother and grandmother and all their money. And they don't believe he can do anything wrong, no matter what he does. He's going to be a worthless bum if things don't change."

"How does Jessica feel about sending him up here?" I couldn't believe his mother would be in favor of it. From what I'd seen, she'd done her best to smother the kid. The one time I visited them, the little guy was shiny clean and mouse quiet.

"Being up there with you would be the best thing that could happen to him," Bob said. "That doesn't answer my question, Bob. I think I'm entitled to know how Jessica feels about it." I could hear him sigh.

"Well, the truth is, I need Jimmy to be away for the summer, not only because you and your ranch would be good for him, but also because I want Jessica to get some marriage counseling with me. If she refuses, I'm going to divorce her and sue for custody of Jimmy. He shouldn't be here when I bring the whole thing to a head."

I didn't want to be involved in their marital problems. But then Bob told me how the kid had been caught shoplifting and using drugs.

"He's too eager to go along with the things that his so-called friends are doing."

"His friends are hippies?"

"Yes, they are, but Jimmy's no more a hippie than I am," Bob said. "Oh, sure, he looks the part, and tries to act like one, but he's too fond of the finer things in life. He's doing it just to bug us."

Sounded to me like the boy could use a summer of good hard work. I'd never had any kids, but I didn't have to be a mother to discipline a spoiled brat. Just ask my hired hands. Yet, I still had doubts about taking on such a responsibility.

"Bob, what's to keep him from running away?"

He sighed. "There's more to it, Matilda. Jimmy got his girl-friend pregnant. It was a helluva shock to both sets of parents. She had an abortion, so of course he didn't have to suffer a bit."

"I see." Sounded like the kid needed to learn a few things, quite a few things, in fact. But Bob wasn't through yet.

"And then Jimmy had the guts to want us to buy him a car

for his sixteenth birthday, which will be September tenth. I said no, but Jessica ignored my wishes and told him she'd buy him one."

"Oops. You must've been pretty upset."

"Yeah, you could say that. I really blew my stack. I guess it made an impression, because Jessica backed down."

That's when Bob told me about the bargain he'd struck with Jimmy. Seemed that if the boy made it through the summer working on my ranch, Bob would buy him the car.

"But he could run away, you know." I wanted Bob to really think about that.

"Then he wouldn't get the car. I honestly don't think he would like being on his own, especially up there in the woods."

"Before I make up my mind, how did you get Jessica to agree to this?"

"Uh . . . I was afraid you'd ask me that. Well, you know what a motivating force money has been in her mother's life."

"Yes."

He hesitated. "And Jessica is her mother's daughter."

"Of course." What was he trying not to say?

He chuckled. "Please forgive me, Matilda. I reminded her that you don't have an heir."

I couldn't help but laugh. "Pretty smart." I liked Bob Tuttle, what little I'd seen of him. I thought my great-niece, Jessica, was darned lucky to get him. Surprised me that she had. At any rate, I was just curious enough about the boy to take up the challenge. So, like a fool, I agreed to take him on.

And then Bob had to go and open his mouth again. "I have another favor to ask, Matilda. Tell Jimmy the truth. Show him

Pine Bluff, and the shack where his grandmother grew up. Tell him what really happened."

I couldn't help but groan. "What's the point, Bob? It was a long time ago. Maybe it's too bad that my dimwitted brother told you the truth."

"No, I'm glad Daniel did."

I started to ask him why he couldn't tell Jimmy himself, but I already knew that would be a mess, with Mommy and Grandma right there to deny it all. So I agreed to the whole thing. I can't believe I did that. One of these days I'm going to have to practice saying no. Seemed like I'd forgotten how.

But I had to admit I looked forward to a little summer diversion. Don't get much of that at my age. And I really felt old when I looked at Jimmy in that ridiculous getup of his. Times had sure changed. He wasn't a clean little mouse anymore.

"You must be Jimmy Tuttle. I'm your great-aunt Matilda, and this is George. He works for me at the ranch."

It tickled me when the kid had to crane his neck to look up at me. Times like this I almost enjoy being a tall string bean. It was easy to see he was scared, but he tried to hide it with an insolent glare. The way he looked me over from boot to hat let me know in a hurry that he didn't think I looked any better than he did. I glared right back at him, just to let him know I didn't like snot-nosed kids.

When he saw the jeep, he looked like he'd swallowed a dead fly. "We're going to ride in this piece of junk?"

"Yeah, if it runs, otherwise we walk," I said. "You can sit on the floor in back, but hang on."

You could see the kid's brain grind on that one, but after a bit he threw his duffel bag, along with what looked like a new pair of boots, in the back of the jeep and clambered over the tailgate, which was comical, since the kid didn't realize he could lower it. George and me, we didn't dare look at each other. Out of the corner of my eye I could see that the kid was mad as hell sitting back there swallowing dust.

"Some freeway system you've got here in Idaho," he yelled. "This isn't even a road."

"Nope." I looked straight ahead.

"It's just one big pothole with monster rocks in it."

"That's about right," I said.

Just then we hit a bump and he flew up in the air, then landed hard on his butt. "Ow!"

"Better hang on. It gets pretty steep up here a ways. You could fly right out over the tailgate."

George gave me a look that said, plain as anything, "No great loss."

George doesn't believe in wasting words. When he does talk, he comes straight to the point. He's tall, about six four, and skinny, except for his wide shoulders. Though he's close to sixty, his hair is still dark brown. He wears bib overalls over a plaid flannel shirt, summer or winter, and he wouldn't change clothes at all if I didn't yell at him about it.

I couldn't look back to check on the boy until I had quit grinning, but when I did turn around, the kid had commenced to hang on, all right. He was hanging on so hard I figured he'd have blisters when we got to the ranch, but they'd get a lot worse before we were through with him.

The jeep wallowed at the bottom of a dry creek-bed. Just like always, it came close to tipping over before it ground up the other side.

"What the hell was that?" he yelled.

"Just a dry creek-bed. Nothing we can't handle. You should see it when it's full of water."

"Right. Groovy."

I might not have understood the language, but I recognized sarcasm when I heard it. "You've been thrashing around some back there. You sure you're hanging on?"

"Yes, dammit."

"Good. I hope you're enjoying the view. This is God's country, you know."

"He can have it."

He wasn't doing too well. Poor little scared city kid. I doubted he'd make it through the summer. I wondered what Emma and Daniel would think about their great-grandson if they could see him. Well, Emma would love him, she couldn't help that, but I knew she'd be a bit sad that he had turned out the way he has. And Daniel? It would be fun to see his reaction to this kid, since he didn't grow up himself, until he ran into a lot of pain and sorrow.

The view of the canyons and their forested walls is the prettiest sight you can imagine. If you look closely, you can count at least seven different shades of green in those trees. Sure the road is just a couple of dirt ruts with potholes and rocks. That's all a self-centered kid like Jimmy would notice. He wouldn't see the beauty around us if I rubbed his face in it.

We climbed over the mountain, without more than a gasp

or two from the jeep, then back down the other side into the beautiful valley where my ranch is. Every time I come back here from town, I remember the day Jacob and I stood here, knowing we'd just bought a piece of heaven. We accomplished a lot in those few years before the flood. Jacob would be proud of his spread and proud to know that the house and barn are still as sturdy as the day we, and our family and neighbors, built them.

The mountains around us are covered with both white and yellow pine, as well as fir trees. Maples and poplars grow down by the river. And the pasture is lush with alfalfa. I've had a few offers to buy me out, but what would a seventy-six-year-old woman do with all that money? Bob was right. I've no kids to leave it to. I hate to think what will happen to the place when I'm gone.

I looked back at the kid. "They didn't have scenery like this in Frisco when I was there."

His eyes popped open, indignant. "It's not Frisco. It's either San Francisco or The City."

"That depends on who's talking about it, son."

"I'm not your son," he snarled.

"No, thank God."

When George stopped the jeep by the house, old Roscoe came out to meet us. He's one of those no-breed, even-tempered, rust-colored dogs. About that time, Jimmy unfastened the tailgate. At least he had figured that out. He got out of the jeep and gave the dog a wary eye. "He's smiling."

"Yep," I said. "That's his one talent."

Then George, who hadn't said a word the whole trip, piped up with, "Roscoe smiles just before he bites."

Jimmy froze, and slowly took his duffel bag out of the jeep. He didn't make another move, neither did Roscoe, who just kept on smiling.

Figuring the boy was having a hard enough time, I said, "Welcome to the J-Bar-J. You don't need to pay much heed to old Roscoe. He wouldn't harm you if you came at him with an axe. He does give the deer fits when they come near the house, but apart from that, he's not much use around here except for laughs."

"Some entertainment." Jimmy glared at George's back.

I aimed the boy toward the house and asked him if he knew how to ride a horse.

"Yeah," he grunted.

I could just imagine the sissy type of riding he'd been taught, but maybe he at least knew which end of the horse was which. We stepped onto the back porch and went in the kitchen door. My kitchen is large, with a big stone fireplace on one wall. On the other end of the room there's a mess of cupboards, plus the sink and counters. Along the other walls are a refrigerator, two stoves, one wood, one electric. I use the electric one during the summer heat, but I hate the thing. Over the sink is a window that looks out over what I call the front yard, where my sweet gum tree and two apple trees stand healthy and green. Lost the third apple tree last winter to a nasty storm.

"Want a glass of lemonade?" I asked.

"Huh-uh."

That kid was determined to be unhappy.

"When we're in the house, we're generally sitting over there." I pointed at the big oak table and chairs in the center of the room. "Or we're upstairs in bed."

"Cool, man."

I ignored the little turkey's nasty tone of voice. "The door over there on that wall leads to the storeroom. You'll keep your outdoor gear in there." I grabbed his boots out of his hand, thankful that his father had thought to buy them for him. I opened the door to the storeroom and tossed them in, then turned back to him. "I don't imagine you give shucks about seeing the parlor, so let's go put your things in your bedroom."

I led him into the hall and up the stairs. "Your room's the first one on the left." Jimmy lagged behind me. I figured he was getting pretty homesick about now.

When he walked into the bedroom, he let his duffel bag drop to the floor and went over to the bed. Now, that bed is a comfortable one. I had put one of my prize quilts on it, but he didn't even see it. He just sneered at the walnut chiffonier, the dresser, and the leather rocker. Then he pounded the bed with his fist. Seemed the room didn't please him any more than the jeep had. Right in front of me, he said, "Shit. Three whole months."

I just told him I'd yell when dinner was ready and left him there. When I got to the kitchen, Oscar was sitting in the rocker by the fireplace. He's my headman, has been for years. I always think of Oscar as one big muscle. The man is built so square a charging bull couldn't knock him over. His steely blue eyes narrowed when he saw me. "Understand you got yourself a real prize."

Oh, Lord. He was mad at me for taking on the kid. I hadn't expected that, but I was pretty sure he'd come around soon. I hoped so. "Prepare yourself, Oscar. Making a man out of this boy will take some doing."

His wide face flushed bright red. "We don't have enough to do during the summer, now we've got to baby-sit a spoiled city kid?"

I didn't think the boy would give Oscar much guff, but how much guff would Oscar give the boy? My summer diversion began to feel like a winter chill.

When Jimmy came down for dinner, I showed him where to sit and introduced him to the men. "You've met George, and this is Oscar. He's headman here. And over there is Buck, so named because his father bagged a five-pointer the day he was born, or so he claims. You want to take everything these hooligans say with a grain of salt."

"I've already learned that." Jimmy didn't bother to look up, much less say hello.

Now that I think of it, Buck didn't look up either. He's not one to show his emotions. He seldom says two words in a row, in fact. He's about six-foot-six and skinny, with a long morose face to match. His hair, once a muddy brown, is now a muddy gray. He looks a lot older than his 56 years. He's a natural born grump if there ever was one, but he's also a hard worker.

I turned to Jimmy. "You might as well meet the indoor animals, while I'm at it. You've already met Roscoe. That Australian Shepherd over there, gulping down his food like it was his last meal, is Aussie. You'll get to see the way he works cattle one of these days. And that black cat there on the window sill, his name is Lucifer."

Jimmy just grunted and sat down at the table. When he took a look at my fried chicken dinner with all the trimmings, his mouth curled in a sneer. "I don't eat chicken."

Well, he was asking for it, wasn't he? Did he really think

I'd cook special meals just for him? "I guess you won't eat, then. This is a working ranch, not a hotel, and I'm the owner, not a short-order cook."

He just sat there while the rest of us got on with the meal.

"You don't eat? No wonder you look so puny," Oscar said.

The kid sneered in Oscar's face. "You're really out of it, you know that?"

Oscar looked at the boy, from his hair down to his bare feet. "You look a lot like your grandma, especially your pretty hair."

Buck and George, in unison, raised their heads, looked at Jimmy's long curly hair, then went right back to eating. I about busted my gut trying not to laugh. That poor fool boy was up against some real experts.

But then Jimmy sneered at Oscar's shiny bald head. "At least I have hair."

I held my breath. Oscar's real sensitive about being bald. Seemed like a good time to change the subject.

"Speaking of your grandmother, have you ever heard the story of your Pine Bluff family? I'll have to take you to town one day and show you the cafe. It's still there. Your great-grandma Emma did the cooking, and your aunt Valina was their waitress."

"What kind of dumb name is Valina, anyway?" he said. "I bet the kids all called her Vaselina."

"I don't believe they did. But maybe kids were kinder back then than they are now."

He swallowed hard. That Adam's apple of his would give him away every time. And to think this spoiled greenhorn brat had made a baby. His nasty crack about Oscar's lack of hair gave me a sudden itch to send him packing, but, by golly, I had promised to take him for the whole summer. I went right on with my story.

"I guess you'd say it all began there in the cafe. That's where the family met a man named Timothy O'Callahan, a city person like you, only they dressed differently in those days."

He looked at me like I was dumber than a stump. "I know Timothy O'Callahan was my grandfather, if that's what you're getting at. And I know he died right before my mother was born."

I cleared off the dinner plates and passed around the bowls of apple cobbler. After seeing the boy's attitude, I was tempted to go ahead and get that story out in the open. He needed it, God knows.

"That's right. Your grandfather came to Pine Bluff in the summer of '29, to do a little fishing, he claimed. Seems he was quite the ladies' man. Most of the women in town were swooning over him."

I watched Buck and George inhale the cobbler then push their chairs back and leave the room. They usually didn't eat that fast. The cowards just wanted to leave.

Jimmy shifted in his chair and glared at me. "Look, I'm not interested. Okay?"

I smiled. "You will be."

I had just opened my mouth to continue the story, when I saw Jimmy's eyes droop. Of course he wasn't interested in family history, no more than I was in ladies' fashions. "Better go up to bed, Jimmy. We ranchers get up early."

He groaned, struggled out of his chair, and headed for the hall, but Oscar stayed planted at the table, his mouth set in a grim line.

"That kid's a real corker," he said.

That's when it really dawned on me that I hadn't even bothered to talk to Oscar about taking on the kid, yet he was the one who'd have to teach him how to do most of the chores. "Well, I'd like to try this, but how do you feel about it?"

He glared at me, his arms firmly crossed over his wide chest. "How do you think I feel? He's a pain in the butt."

I couldn't argue with that. "He sure is."

"You expect me to teach that miserable brat how to work on a ranch?"

"I hope you will." Oscar had never been this mad at me before. That glare of his hadn't eased up a bit.

"Well, since the boy is already here, would you like to tell me what job we start him on tomorrow?"

I could hardly blame Oscar for being angry. I had always been able to count on him when things got rough. I sure didn't want to lose the best ranch hand I'd ever had over a stupid kid. I'd give Jimmy a few weeks, and if Oscar was still this angry, I'd have to send the kid home. "I'll introduce him to the cow and the chickens, first. Show him how to milk Daisy."

Oscar snorted. "Hope we won't be drinking sour milk for the next three months. After you've taught him how to terrorize the chickens when he tries to take their eggs, and how to yank on poor Daisy's teats, then what?"

"I need to see how well he handles a horse. He claims he knows how to ride, so we'll saddle up. After lunch he can chop up that apple tree the lightning split last winter."

Oscar groaned. "Then I'd better show him how to use an axe tomorrow morning before I leave to check the fences. Hope to hell the kid brought boots with him. I'm not handing him an axe if he's wearing those stupid sandals."

"He has boots. His dad saw to that." I didn't tell Oscar how relieved I'd been when I saw Jimmy toss those boots into the jeep. The way the kid acted, I was surprised he hadn't thrown them off the train.

When I rapped on Jimmy's door at five-thirty the next morning, the only response I got was total silence. He had to get up, so I kept hammering away at the door until I heard him mumble some of that crude language he liked. I pretended I hadn't heard him. "Get your butt downstairs. Breakfast's ready. And wear your jeans and boots. You're going to be riding and chopping wood."

"Son of a bitch."

I left when I heard him call me a crazy old bat. Little jerk didn't have good sense. When he came downstairs, he looked almost like a normal kid in his jeans and tee shirt. He'd even tied his hair back with a piece of string, and he wasn't wearing those silly beads. He got his boots out of the storeroom and put them on, but I had to look away when he got all tangled up in the laces. The men just looked at their plates.

"What were those animals that howled most of the night?" He sat down at the kitchen table and leaned on his elbows, like his load was too heavy to carry.

"Those were coyotes," I said. "Lots of them around here."

"Bastards kept me awake."

"You'll get so you don't even hear them."

He just glared at me.

I scooped two eggs out of the frying pan, and started to put them on his plate, but he raised his arm to fend them off. They damned near landed in his hair.

"I don't eat breakfast," he snarled.

Stubborn? That kid sat there like he was daring us to urge a slice of bacon or a piece of toast on him. We ignored him while we ate. Then Buck and George headed out.

Oscar stood up and gave Jimmy a hard look. "Come on, I'm in a hurry, and I need to show you how to use an axe."

"And after that, Jimmy, come back here." I said. "I'm going to teach you how to milk a cow and feed chickens."

"I can hardly wait." He didn't move an inch. I knew Oscar wouldn't take that for long. Well, neither would I.

"Move it, Jimmy. There's work to be done." I held my breath as I took the dirty dishes over to the sink. He finally stood up and shuffled after Oscar with a comical looking gait. Didn't know how to walk in his new boots yet.

Later, through the kitchen window I watched Oscar teach the boy how to cut into the edge instead of the middle of a bolt of wood. Every time Jimmy swung the axe overhead I got nervous. Hate to admit it, but up to then I hadn't fully comprehended what a responsibility I'd taken on. I could order men around, or deal with a mean bull, and once I'd shot a cougar before it could kill me. Not much got to me. But I'd never had children. What on earth had possessed me when I told Bob I'd take on the kid? And what right did I have to disillusion him about his family? If he actually believed me, it might scar him for life.

When the lesson was over, I took the boy out to meet

Daisy. She's a beauty . . . fawn colored, fine-boned, and gives the richest cream I've ever had from a cow. She even lives in her own special shed.

"We use a Jersey," I said, "because they're medium-sized and docile." I sat down on the milk stool and demonstrated how to milk her. Then I stood up and pointed at the stool. After a bit of cussing and groaning, Jimmy commenced to squeeze the teats. Poor Daisy kept looking around at him, alarm in her eyes. I petted and soothed her into putting up with him. When he finally got some squirts of milk out of her, I took over and finished the job. I could tell we weren't going to have a miracle on the first day. Next, I took him to the chicken yard and showed him the coop and the watering can.

"Ever seen live chickens before?"

"Nope," he said, boredom oozing out of his every pore.

"Well, it's time you met some." I pointed at the coop. "There are fifteen of them in there. It will be your chore every morning and evening to see to their feed and water, and to gather the eggs."

I ignored his pitiful groan, then showed him where the mash and grit were and told him about the scratch, "Its cracked corn and wheat. You throw it out over the chicken yard. If you don't, chickens are so dumb they'll peck at each other if they get bored."

He was busy yawning. I knew he wouldn't remember a thing I said. No sense wasting my time, so I took him to the barn so we could saddle up. I gave him Sunny, an older gelding, and I rode the Arabian. The kid seemed to warm right up to Sunny, even reached out to let the horse blow on his hand, but he had a struggle getting into the saddle. Sunny is a quarter horse, big, sixteen hands. Jimmy wasn't much over five feet.

"Are all your horses this big?" he muttered, his face red from the effort of clambering up on Sunny.

"Most of them. They're work horses, after all."

His awkward scramble up into the saddle had convinced me he was a real greenhorn, so I was surprised to see he had a soft hand with the reins. You can ruin a horse by yanking on its mouth. Maybe he knew more about horses than I'd thought. But, just in case I was wrong about that, I kept our tour down to a slow jaunt across the field and over to the river. Then I gave him a quick look at the corral. He sat a horse well, but I didn't know if I could trust him with one when he was out of my sight.

"The cattle are up in the high country for the summer," I said. "We've already castrated and branded the calves. Too bad you missed that."

He rolled his eyes. "Right."

One thing for sure, he had sarcasm down pat. "Better get you back to the house so you can chop up that apple tree." From the glower on his face, you'd have thought I'd said we were going to the hanging tree.

I spent the rest of the morning keeping an eye on him through the kitchen window. Anything could happen with him flinging that axe around, but I'd be damned if I'd try to protect him. Jessica had already done too much of that. And I'd been asked to make a man out of him. Dear Lord, he did sweat. At least I figured it was sweat he kept wiping out of his eyes. 'Course he was carrying a heavy load of self-pity, too.

When he finally got the hang of using the axe, I took him a glass of milk and two fresh-baked cinnamon rolls. Didn't want him cutting his foot off because he was weak from hunger. He inhaled those rolls so fast I almost got him two more, but that kid didn't need any pampering. I was pretty sure there wouldn't be any more trouble with him about the food I served. Nothing like hard work to whet one's appetite.

He smiled at me as if he'd been pardoned from a death sentence. Probably figured he was through chopping for the day. He drank his milk slowly, and cut me a look that let me know he was up to something.

He kept peering at me and then shook his head. "Aren't you a little old to be running this ranch?"

"Well, I obviously am running it."

"The man next door to us in San Francisco is 85," he said. "His mind is gone, and when he walks he shuffles like a wooden puppet. His daughter takes care of him. Mom feels sorry for her, but my dad feels sorry for him."

"I see." Did he know how much he'd given away about his folks? "I wonder how the old man feels about it?" I started back to the house.

"Wait a minute. I thought you were going to tell me about the family."

I almost laughed out loud. What he really thought was that he'd get me to talking and he wouldn't have to chop wood. Well two could play at that game. "Oh, it's nothing but old-time news. Young person like you wouldn't want to hear all that."

"Sure I would. After all, Timothy O'Callahan was my grandfather. Mom says it's a pity that such a talented man had to die so young."

I just about lost my upper plate. What kind of lies had Mary told Jessica, for God's sake? No wonder Bob wanted me to tell him the truth. I didn't relish it, but I knew I had to do it, and do it right now, while he was begging for it. Besides, we had plenty of wood chopped any way.

I sat down on the stump next to him, real slow, dragging out the suspense as long as I could. "How much do you know about your mother's side of the family?"

He thought a moment, then shrugged. "Well, not much, I guess."

"During the depression in 1929 none of us had very much money, but your family had less than most. They lived in a two-room shack with no running water. They didn't starve, but they came close to it a few times."

The kid scowled. "You're lying. My grandmother is rich."

"She is now, but the family sure wasn't back then."

"You're wrong. My grandfather had money, lots of it."

This wasn't going to be easy. "Where did you get that idea?"

"Grandmother told me."

I shook my head. I hadn't realized how twisted Mary's thinking was. And Bob expected me to tell her grandson that his grandmother was a liar? "That's interesting, but would you like the hear the real story?"

"What would you know about them?" He gave me that sneer of his again.

"What would I know? I was there."

"You were?"

"Dammed right I was. Figure it out. I'm your grandmother's aunt. Her father, Daniel, was my brother. You got that clear in your head?"

That stopped him cold. He got a kind of wistful look on his face. "Did you know my grandfather?"

"Of course I did. The whole town did."

He leaned forward eagerly. "What was he like?"

I wasn't so sure that the truth would undo the lies Jimmy had been told. And why would he believe me? And if he did, what might it do to him? Well, I didn't have to hurry this. There was the whole summer, that is if the kid lasted that long.

I stood up. "I forgot that I have something in the oven. We can talk about this later. Go ahead and finish chopping up that tree." I walked back to the house.

When I went downstairs the next morning, I found Oscar frying bacon. "Aren't you up earlier than usual?"

"I've got to go up in the high country today to check on the cattle," he muttered.

"Well since the kid knows which end of a horse is which, why don't you take him with you?"

He turned his back to me and fussed with the bacon. "If you say so."

I didn't like the surly growl in his voice. "I'll come along too," I said.

He turned to me and scowled. Before he could object, the way he usually does because he thinks I'm too old to be riding my own land, I said, "I'm still capable of riding up my own mountain. Besides, if it turns out Jimmy can't hack it, you can stay up there, and I'll bring him back to the ranch."

Oscar's jaw started working, but he turned back to the stove and fussed with the bacon again.

Because he's only 58, he thinks I'm too old to do a lot of things around here. Wait until he's 76. I hope people give him a bad time just the way he does me. And I know him. He'll do whatever he damned well pleases, exactly the way I do.

Later in the morning, we headed up the mountain. Jimmy rode the Arabian, Oscar the Morgan, and I rode Sally, one of my quarter horses. Now don't get the idea it was a pleasant ride. Far from it. Nothing pleased the kid. And not much pleased Oscar either.

"Why in hell do we have to get up so early?" Jimmy groaned.

"Because there's never enough daylight for all we have to do, not even in summer." I waved my arm at the country around us. "Besides, it's a beautiful morning."

Jimmy snorted. "The hell you say."

Oscar turned in his saddle and glared at Jimmy. With those two along, snarling at each other, I knew the day was doomed. Jimmy was a handful, all right, but from the way he held himself in the saddle, you'd have thought he'd spent all his life riding horses up steep mountain trails. It tickled me that we at least had that much in common.

At the next curve in the trail, we could see the ranch down below. From up there the pasture looks like green velvet. Jimmy swept his eyes over the scene, then sneered and turned his back on it. Looked like he wasn't going to allow himself to have one positive thought about the ranch.

When we stopped in the first meadow, three cows were watering at the stream. They looked at us with blank faces.

Jimmy let out a disgusted sigh. "So what are we supposed to do up here?"

"Check the cattle. All kinds of things can go wrong. For

instance, a cow might have a broken leg and we'd have to shoot it."

"I thought Oscar brought that rifle because we might run into a wild animal," Jimmy said.

"Sometimes we do see deer or elk, or a bear, even a cougar or bobcat," I said, "but they avoid us as much as they can. They're a lot smarter than cows. Smarter than a lot of people I know, too."

We started up to the next meadow riding single file, Oscar first, then Jimmy, and me bringing up the rear. We hadn't gone far when Oscar reined in his horse so fast that Jimmy nearly collided with him. I soon found out why he'd stopped. A dead cow lay on the grass next to the trail. Oscar, rifle in hand, got off his horse and knelt beside it. "We interrupted a cougar's lunch." He pointed at the teeth marks on the cow's flank.

I got down to have a look. "Damn. What killed it? It wasn't the cougar." Just the thought of possible disease made my blood run cold.

Oscar scowled and walked around a bit, scanning the ground nearby.

Jimmy got off his horse and stood beside me. "How can you tell it wasn't the cougar?"

"No bleeding. Rigor mortis had already set in before that cougar took his first bite."

Jimmy kept looking around, probably afraid the cougar might leap out of the trees at any moment.

Oscar pointed at the weeds off the trail. "Looks like these have been stomped on by a human, not by this cow. Jimmy, help me turn the cow over on its other side." Oscar took the front legs, Jimmy the back ones. They had a bit of a struggle turning it, but when they did, we could see a dark red spot on the ground.

Oscar pointed at a bullet hole just below its shoulder. "This cow's been shot."

Now that made me furious. "Who'd do a thing like that? It sure as hell isn't hunting season."

"Well, someone was hunting, season or not." Oscar shook his head. "Probably thought it was a deer." He squatted down and scowled at the cow's head. "Well, this beats all. The son of a bitch cut off one of the cow's ears."

"What?" I bent over to look at it. There was only a small bit of dried blood where the ear had been. "What kind of nut . . . ?"

Oscar stood up. "The kind that wants a trophy, I expect."

Jimmy frowned. "That's sick. Once he killed the cow, why didn't he take the whole thing?"

I set him straight. "Because if he got caught with one of my cows, he wouldn't just be fined, he'd go to jail, if I let the bastard live. I don't take kindly to people who kill my livestock. We live off the income these cattle bring."

Jimmy rolled his eyes. "Okay, okay."

Oscar stood up and slung his rifle over his shoulder. "I'll go on up and check the salt lick and the rest of the cows. You got your thirty-eight with you?"

"You bet. It's in the saddlebag. We'll start down and wait for you by the stream. Want a sandwich to take with you?"

"Nope. See you down below." He got on his horse and started up the mountain. As soon as we started down, Jimmy said, "You know how to shoot a gun?"

"Of course I do. Only way I've managed to live this long."

"Did you ever shoot a person?"

"Sure."

He was quiet for a moment. "Did you ever kill anyone?"

"Yep. Had to."

He gulped. "Why?"

I reined in Sally and waited until Jimmy's horse came up beside mine. "Some years ago a man worked for me who turned out to be a mean, hard-drinking son of a bitch. He beat one of my horses so bad I had to put it out of its misery. Then the bastard decided to beat on me. I shot him between the eyes."

"Gawd! I bet he was surprised." Jimmy sat limp in his saddle, his mouth agape, eyes fairly bugging out of his head.

When I grinned at the sight of him, he straightened up real fast, trying to look like a tough guy. Fool kid.

"Oscar must've thought we might run into the guy who shot the cow," Jimmy said. His eyes darted from one side to the other.

Pretty obvious he was scared. "Not much chance that scum would stick around."

Jimmy just grunted.

By the time we got down to the stream, I was mighty happy to get off that horse. My hips and back were giving me fits. The day had heated up. We splashed the cool water of the stream on our faces and sat down on the mossy bank to eat lunch.

After we finished, Jimmy lay back on the grass and went to sleep. He was kind of cute when he was asleep.

Jacob and I had planned to have at least three or four children, but we wanted to finish the house first, and buy some cattle and horses. We had just finished doing that when the river took him away from me. We thought we were being sensible waiting like that. But if only I had been pregnant I would have a grown child now with both Jacob's blood and mine. And Jacob would have left a part of him behind for me. After all these years the grief can still slap me. Grief. It never completely goes away. It just burrows into a body's heart and soul and waits to be brought out again.

Well, I've got a child now, at least for the summer.

Wasn't long before Oscar rode into the meadow. After he'd gulped down a sandwich and a cup of coffee, he said, "Everything's all right up above. Think we ought to let Cal Lewis know about the cow?"

"I'd planned on it." I turned to Jimmie. "Cal is the game warden," I explained.

"And how about the sheriff?" Oscar said. "That ear thing doesn't set right with me."

"Same here. But first we'll see what Cal has to say."

As soon as we got back to the ranch, I called Cal Lewis. If someone was hunting out of season, he needed to know. He wasn't in his office, so I left a message, though I didn't mention the cow's missing ear.

Just before noon the next day, I took two pans of bread out of the oven and poured myself the last dregs of the breakfast coffee. No sooner tasted it, than I poured it down the sink. My brother, Daniel, had liked coffee that strong but to me it tasted like bitter glue. Come to think of it, Daniel and I had rarely agreed on anything. I thought he was lazy and he thought I was a nag. I suspect we were both right.

The men were haying in the south pasture with my neighbor, Sandy Hill, and Orville Adams, a fellow from Pine Bluff who helped us out in the summer. When I drove up in the jeep with their lunch, the kid clomped over to meet me, still having a hard time operating his boots.

"I hope to hell you brought something to drink," he growled. "I'm dying in all these clothes." He had on his jeans and a long-sleeved flannel shirt buttoned up tight. He'd put up such a fuss about having to wear them I was surprised to see he hadn't at least rolled up his sleeves.

"You figured out yet why you have to wear those clothes?"

He rolled his eyes, held up two scratched, bloody hands, and imitated Oscar's voice. "Hay eats your skin."

"That's right. So put on your gloves."

He bristled right away. "After I eat, damn it!"

I turned my back to him and went over to talk to Oscar. "How'd it go?"

"Kid was in the way every time we turned around. The men complained about him all morning."

"I suppose they came out of the womb already knowing how to hay?" We glared at each other for a moment, but then I looked around at what they'd done that morning. "The kid couldn't have slowed you down very much. I see you've already finished cutting the field."

"Just the windrows to rake," he muttered. "Sure sorry you missed the snarling match between Sandy and the kid."

Lord in heaven. Oscar sounded as nasty as the boy did.

"I'm just as happy to have missed it. You'd better get something to eat before the kid inhales the whole mess."

Jimmy stood at the tailgate shoving food in his face so fast that he looked like a scene in a jerky old-time movie I'd seen years ago. I watched as Orville Adams walked over and helped himself to some lunch. There's nothing really ugly about his appearance, but he isn't somebody you'd want to look at for too long. His eyes are almost colorless, and they're jammed together so close they make him look sneaky. Worse, his jaw is always loose, as if its hinges don't work right. 'Course he can't help what he got at birth. Orville's not stupid, but he isn't bright either. Folks in Pine Bluff call him a casual laborer, their polite term for just plain lazy. Oh, he works hard when he's helping us with our haying, but he can't keep up that pace for long. He leaned against the jeep and said something I couldn't hear to Jimmy. They both laughed. Well, at least Orville was trying to be friendly with the kid, and that was a lot more than Oscar and George and Buck were doing.

I went over to talk to Sandy. He's not my favorite person, but he's a neighbor and alone. I looked at him and shook my head. Same old Sandy, wearing the same old coveralls. Had to be at least five years since they'd been washed. And that grizzled face of his. He always looked as if he was trying to grow a beard, but never quite made it.

"Want to stay for dinner?" I asked.

"Nah. I've got to get on back home," he said. "I don't have hired men to do all my work for me the way you do."

"That's because I'm not as tight as you are," I said.

His ranch is next to ours, on the west side of the valley. He helps us with our haying and we help him with his. He gets a helluva lot more help than he gives, though. He glared at me but he knew I could out-talk him, so he didn't try to start anything.

"Your hay about ready?" I asked.

"Yep."

"We'll be over to help you with it. Just give me a call."

He turned his head to spit and took a tin of chewing tobacco and a knife out of his pocket. "Have something to show you when you come over. You've got a problem with one of your fences."

"Nothing new about that."

"More to it than you think. There's mischief going on."

I sighed. Sandy could always find something to fret about. "Well, don't you worry, Sandy, we'll take care of it." I didn't bother to hide the impatience I felt.

He scowled at me, then sliced off a piece of the tobacco and slid it into his mouth. That's his way of getting back at me. He knows darned good and well I hate tobacco chewers.

"That kid's got a mighty peculiar attitude," he said.

I chuckled. "Understand it's a lot like yours." That did it. He snorted, turned on his heel, and started toward the jeep for some lunch. As he walked away, the bastard spit out the tobacco. Now, he knew he was about to eat lunch. He put that nasty stuff in his mouth just to give me a hard time.

When I got back to the house, I called Bob Tuttle at his office.

"Have you killed him yet?" he asked.

I laughed. "No, but my head man might've had the urge

a time or two. As you can imagine, Jimmy feels badly mistreated. But so far, he's learned how to milk a cow and feed chickens, chop wood, shovel manure in the barn, and right now he's helping with the haying."

Bob chuckled. "I can't believe it. He's never had to work hard in his whole life. And are you filling him in on the family history?"

"I wanted to talk to you about that. Jimmy's been told some mighty fancy lies about Timothy. You sure you want me to reveal that his mother and grandmother are liars? He won't thank you or me for this. I started talking about the family and it's pretty clear that he's not going to believe me, Bob."

"Please try, Matilda. You're the only one in the family who has a realistic grasp of the whole thing. He needs to know the truth instead of the crap his grandmother and Jessica have him believing."

"And what about Jessica? She may never forgive you."

Silence.

"You haven't told her about this plan of yours, have you? You'd better, because Jimmy is sure to bring up the subject as soon as he gets home. He'll have a lot of questions to ask his mother."

"Jessica didn't hear the truth until we were married. Your brother Daniel told her when he and Emma were here for a visit. Marie was furious. She hadn't wanted her baby to ever find out." Bob sighed. "And it's almost as if Marie got her way, because Jessica's blanked it out of her mind."

I always forget that Mary changed her name to Marie when she left for San Francisco. I suppose Marie does sound a little more fashionable. "Too bad Marie handled it the way she did. She had a rough time, but it doesn't pay to pretend it didn't happen."

"That's what I'm concerned about. Marie's not too pleased with Jimmy right now, but she won't admit it. Not that Jimmy cares. He knows she'll give him money no matter what he does. You're the perfect person to show him what real life is all about."

"I'm not sure the boy can understand what happened. I'll start by taking him down to Pine Bluff, show him around, sort of introduce him to the town's characters. I'll see how it goes."

"I'll keep in touch, Matilda. And thanks again."

Later that day, the men straggled in from the hayfield, a grimy bunch. I met them outside. "Don't go in my house until I've hosed you off." Jimmy yipped when the cold water first hit him, but when the men laughed at him, he shut up quick. When I'd finished hosing off all four of them, Oscar told the kid to take off his clothes.

"I'll be damned if I will."

Oscar grabbed his collar and looked him square in the eye. "If you don't, she'll come over here and do it for you, and then we'll all be as nude as plucked jaybirds, dangling right here in front of her. And it will be your fault."

Both George and Buck grunted in agreement. Orville snickered. The four men took off their boots and socks, then started unbuttoning their shirts. Jimmy looked at me, panic in his eyes.

"If I see you're cooperating, I'll turn my back, and you can all go upstairs and get some dry clothes," I said.

Jimmy finally started to strip. I turned my back. What the men don't know is that I always turn around when I hear the creak of their footsteps on the porch. An old woman has to get her jollies any way she can. And I do like the sight of a man's bare butt.

After dinner, I took Jimmy to the barn so he could clean it out while I checked on Mattie's Lady, my pregnant mare. I heard the kid groan when he picked up the shovel. "Got blisters on those hands, Jimmy? Come here and let me see them."

He shuffled over and held up his palms. My God they were raw. I lied, and said, "Not too bad. You'll have working-man's calluses before you know it."

"Just what I've always wanted," he growled.

"I've got some leaf lard down at the other end of the barn. Come on, let's go put some on your hands."

He didn't move. "What's leaf lard?"

"It's a salve we use on the horses when they get a raw spot, like when a harness rubs the hair off. Great stuff. Your hands will be better in no time."

He wrinkled his nose. "But you use it on the horses."

"Well if it's good enough for my horses, it's sure as hell good enough for you. Now get your city-boy butt over here."

He followed me and held out his hands. Though he flinched when I put the salve on his raw palms, he didn't utter a sound.

"Next time keep your damned gloves on. Now George or Buck will have to clean out the barn."

I walked back to my pregnant mare's stall and went in to

check her out. "How's Mattie's Lady today?" I felt her belly and stroked her sides. "Got a bit of misery?"

Jimmy walked up and leaned his elbows on the stall, hands in the air. "Something wrong with her?" He blew on his hands.

"She's pregnant and overdue." I took a big carrot out of my pocket and broke it into pieces, then fed it to the mare, one piece at a time. "I'd rather cater to the whims of a horse than a human any day." I left Jimmy there and went back to the house.

It wasn't fifteen minutes later that Oscar came in the back door. "The kid's smokin' pot. I could smell it. He's out behind your sweet gum tree. What do you want me to do about it?"

"I'll take care of it. Bob Tuttle warned me this might happen."

It's easy to sneak up on a city kid. He was sitting behind that tree, all right, puffing away on a funny looking pipe. Couldn't even roll his own. A leather pouch sat on the ground beside him. I scooped it up in my hand as I came around the tree at him.

"Hey," he said. "What . . ."

I grabbed the pipe out of his hand while I still had the advantage of surprise. "There'll be no marijuana on this ranch," I said. "You've got to be alert to work here. Besides, it's illegal and I don't cotton to that sort of thing. And I especially hate the idea of you smoking by this particular tree."

"I don't know what's so damned important about this tree." He sprang up from the ground and tried to grab the pipe and pouch out of my hands. "That's my private property. You can't take it."

"The hell I can't." He stood there glaring at me. I glared right back.

"I don't have to put up with this," he bellered.

"Stop and think, little city boy, neither do I. You can go home any time you want. Don't flatter yourself that I'd stop you. But if you stay, you abide by my rules." I walked away as he swore at me. My Jacob had planted that tree as a surprise for me shortly after the house was finished. He knew I loved sweet gum trees. We didn't know if it would like our climate, but it had grown and thrived. Each time I look at it, I swear I feel Jacob near me.

When Jimmy finally came back to the house, I made him sit down next to me on the porch. Neither of us said a word for some little time, until he finally broke the silence.

"My grandfather came from New York, didn't he?"

Wait a minute. All of a sudden his voice was sugar sweet, his face all smiles. Well, I wasn't as easy to con as his grand-mother was. But it might take him a while to figure that out.

"That's right," I said. "But Timothy left home when he was only ten. Seems when his father drank, and that was often, he beat up on Timothy's mother. One time he beat up on his ten-year-old kid. That's when Timothy decided to leave home."

Jimmy stared at me. "That's a lie."

"Maybe so, but it was Timothy himself who told my brother, Daniel, about it."

"I don't believe it."

I shrugged. "Suit yourself." This was going to be quite a summer.

CHAPTER 2

Pine Bluff — June 1929

Valina Addison dropped the plate of flapjacks onto the table in front of Spike Washburn and glared at him. He always tried his best to pat her bottom or peer at her breasts. She despised him.

"More coffee?" She spat the words at him.

"Now, honey, you shouldn't be nasty to a good customer like me." Spike grinned at her breasts and a narrow stream of tobacco juice slid down his chin.

She yearned to tell him exactly what she thought of him; instead, she turned to a stranger standing at the counter. He wore knickers, just like the ritzy people in the magazines at Palmer's Drug & Sundries. Such a handsome man. The regular customers would be talking about him for days on end.

"Got any tailor-mades here?" he asked.

She'd never seen eyes the color of his, so light blue they were almost slate-colored. They reminded her of wolves' eyes. She shivered.

"Miss?" He tilted his head and smiled at her. "Got any Avalons or Lucky Strikes?"

"Pardon?" She could feel her face flush. "Oh. Yes, we do."

"Then I'll take a pack of Avalons, please."

She opened the glass door of a cupboard at the end of the counter, pulled out a pack, and put it in front of the stranger. He paid for the pack and sat on the stool next to old Lester. Valina almost laughed at the contrast between the two men. Old Lester always wore ragged coveralls, and his dirty gray beard straggled clear down to the middle of his chest. He wasn't much to look at but at least he wasn't as nasty as Spike was. Lester was just old.

"I'll have a cup of coffee." The stranger thumped a cigarette out of the pack and lit it with a shiny gold lighter. She'd never seen one of those before. But she'd never seen anyone like him before, either. Fascinated, Valina watched him as she poured his coffee. Most of the men who came in the Pine Cone Cafe rolled their own and used wooden matches. The cafe carried tailor-mades mainly for the travelers.

Not a big place, the restaurant had only eight tables covered with red and white checked oilcloth, and six stools at the counter with red leatherette seats. Valina liked the homey feeling of the room. Everything was spotless, except the wooden floors. The owners, Tillie and Ben, tried hard to keep them clean, but loggers' boots left a lot of mud and scars in their wake.

Just then Valina's father walked in. She sighed. He had time to drop in only because he didn't have a job. Once in a while, when the family was almost out of food, he'd work for a week or two. But then the work would dry up, or he'd quit and go fishing. Yes, he was a handsome man, tall and lanky with brown hair and warm brown eyes to match. And Valina was proud of the fact that he wasn't a lady's man like some of the other men in town. She watched as he joked with the regulars. He'd been her hero when she was little. His easy laugh still made her giggle. When he sat on his favorite stool at the counter, she poured him a cup of coffee.

"Just one cup, Valina. I'm going fishing."

She sighed again. The worst of it was he really believed he was providing for his family with those darned fish.

The stranger looked at him. "I've heard the Clearwater River has the biggest trout in the whole state of Idaho. Is that true?"

"Sure is. Fellow caught a twenty-inch rainbow yesterday," her father said, "right behind that seed store across the street. There's an even better hole about a hundred yards upriver. I've caught my limit there every time. If you'd like I could show you where it is. Only take a minute."

The stranger eyed Valina's father for a second, then smiled. "Sure. I'd like to see the place."

"Well, then let's go." Papa stood up and headed for the door. The stranger started to follow him, but Old Lester put his arm out to stop him.

"Don't be smokin' in the woods around here. This is the driest summer we've had in years. Things are tinder dry, just waitin' to burn."

"Yeah," Spike said, "and we've had more than our share of fires."

"You might have noticed that Pine Bluff is walled in by forested mountains," Old Lester said. "Makes the town a target for fire."

Valina's father scowled at him. "Ah, Lester, you've always been a worry wart."

Old Lester sneered but kept his mouth shut.

The stranger didn't say a word, just headed for the door.

"Papa, couldn't you let him finish his coffee first?" Valina asked.

The stranger turned and looked at Valina. "This pretty girl is your daughter?" He winked at her. "You can pour me another cup when we get back."

She felt her face flush. No one else had ever said she was pretty, only this handsome stranger.

Then Papa spoke. "I'm Daniel Addison. And your name?"

"Timothy O'Callahan."

When the door shut behind them, everyone started talking at once. "He's a handsome dandy." . . . "Did you see those snazzy knickers? . . . "Wonder where he's from?" . . . "That's a brand new '29 Model A Ford he has out there."

Old Lester raised his voice. "With a name like O'Callahan, he's got to be an Irishman. Watch out for that one, Valina. I saw the way he looked at you. They're all full of blarney." He shook his head. "And they're too fond of their hootch."

Herb Johnson, the mayor, a heavy-set man whose trousers hung below his ample pot, yelled from across the room, "And you're not a drinker, of course."

Everyone snickered. They all knew Old Lester's drinking habits.

"Wonder if Mister O'Callahan's goin' fishin' in those fancy clothes of his." Dogie Hanks had a self-satisfied smirk on his face. All the other customers laughed at his remark.

Valina didn't laugh with the rest of them. Dogie was an old cowboy who hadn't worn decent clothes since he left his diapers. No one in Pine Bluff knew beans about style, except maybe her older sister, Mary. She worked at Osborne's, Pine Bluff's best, and only, clothing store. Mr. O'Callahan probably thought they all looked like country hicks. Which they were.

After work she went out the front door of the cafe, and stood there sucking in the clear mountain air. What a relief after the odors inside. Her hair, her clothes, even her shoes smelled of grease. No wonder. Most of the food they served floated in it, especially the fried potatoes and eggs. Her feet hurt so bad she took off her shoes. She'd walk home barefoot. But just then she realized that Mr. O'Callahan was sitting there in his car, and her father was sitting on the passenger side. Her father? In that beautiful, shiny black car? Mr. O'Callahan nodded at her and honked the horn. It made a funny sound, sort of like ahooga. He motioned for her to get in. Quickly she slipped on her shoes. With all the regulars watching, she stepped into the snazzy automobile and waved at the gawkers in the cafe. A ukulele lay beside her on the seat. She knew that would really impress her little sister, Rachel.

"I'm sure looking forward to a home-cooked meal," Mr. O'Callahan said.

"Won't be fancy," her Papa said, "but my Emma's the best cook in the whole county."

Valina cringed. Would Mama have enough food for company? Leave it to Papa to not even think about that.

They drove through the town up to where the road began to climb. Dense clumps of morning glory, blackberry and thistle narrowed the road, but it didn't faze Mr. O'Callahan. Neither did the rocks and potholes. Valina bounced up and down in the back seat. She hoped the car would still be in one piece when they got to the cabin.

"Beautiful country," Mr. O'Callahan said. "I envy you, Daniel, living here."

Valina gnawed on her lip. Would he still be envious when he saw their cabin? It was just a large kitchen with a bedroom. No electricity or running water. Thank goodness he wouldn't see the tiny attic where she and Mary and Rachel slept.

As soon as the car stopped, she got out and ran to warn Mama. "Papa's brought company for dinner."

"Oh, dear. Thank goodness I made a big pot of stew. Quick. Go get a jar of peaches from the cellar. I'll make a cobbler. Then go get Rachel. She's down by the creek."

Valina hurried down into the cellar. It was chilly and musty smelling in there. With the light from the open door she could see the row of peaches. She clutched one jar, ran up the dirt steps of the cellar, then over to the steps into the cabin. She put the jar on the table, and hurried back out the door.

The path to the creek was one of the few places where her father had kept the underbrush trimmed back, there and at the garbage pit. If he didn't, the nettles and wild blackberry vines would grow right up to the cabin. Some unknown family, long before the Addison's time, had cleared out the pines around the cabin and tried to grow fruit trees. Only one gnarled apple tree remained. Each year her mother made applesauce out of the stunted, worm-eaten apples it bore. Alders and cedars had overgrown the rest of the small orchard.

"Rachel. Where are you?" Was she off in the woods some-where? Drat. "Rachel? Answer me. We have company for dinner." Where was the little scamp?

Just as Valina walked by the apple tree, Rachel jumped out of the woods and yelled, "Boo!"

Startled, Valina glared at her little sister. "When are you going to grow up?"

"You jumped a foot. And I'm not supposed to grow up yet. Who's the company?"

"Mr. Timothy O'Callahan. I rode home in his new Model A car. He plays the ukulele. I saw it on the backseat."

"Copacetic! This oughta be fun." Rachel started for the cabin, running.

When Valina got to the clearing, Rachel was standing near them, her eyes bugging out at the sight of the car. The men were comparing the big trout they'd caught. She had to force a smile when they held them up for her to admire. Why were men so fascinated with fish? She was relieved when they all started for the cabin, but was mortified when Mr. O'Cal-lahan stumbled on the foot worn spot at the front door. She looked around the room and cringed. The straight-backed chairs beside the scarred dining table looked like they should be cut up for kindling. Two of them didn't even have backs any more, just wobbly seats. Papa had tied wires between the legs but they still wobbled. Even the oilcloth on the table was cracked. A big piece of it had peeled away right in the center.

"Emma, this is Timothy O'Callahan," Papa said. "He's come for dinner."

"How do you do, Mr. O'Callahan."

Mr. O'Callahan took off his hat, held it in his hand, and gave her mama a big smile. "There's no treat like a home-cooked meal for a man who travels all the time, Mrs. Addison."

Valina marveled at his good manners. But where could a gentleman sit in this cabin? There was just the rocker, which was thankfully still in one piece, or the camp-cot, padded with an old army blanket. What must Mr. O'Callahan think of them?

The door opened and Mary sauntered in. Valina watched as Mr. O'Callahan stared at Mary. His reaction didn't surprise her. All the men acted that way when they saw her older sister.

"What a beautiful young woman you are," he said.

Mary gave him a Mona Lisa smile, one Valina had seen her practice in the chipped mirror on the wall in the attic. Valina thought it made her look silly, maybe even a bit strange. And then Mary posed in front of the door, making sure he had a good look at her slim figure enhanced by her blue silk pongee dress. Valina almost gagged. Mary probably thought she looked like a movie star, with one hand at her waist and the other fondling her phony pearl necklace. And wouldn't you know, Mary was quite the seamstress, as well. She wouldn't have that pretty dress, otherwise.

"Our eldest daughter, Mary," Papa said.

Mr. O'Callahan just mumbled something and kept looking at Mary as if he'd like to have her for dinner. Valina wanted to scream. Yes, Mary was gorgeous, but couldn't he see how cold and conceited she was?

Then Mary gave him her most dazzling smile, and said, "I didn't catch your name."

"Timothy O'Callahan." His voice was suddenly hoarse.

Mary sat down in the best of the chairs and slowly crossed her legs. "You must be a stranger in town."

He smiled at her. "Yes, but I won't be a stranger for long."

When Mary looked down, demurely, her long eyelashes almost resting on her cheeks, Valina clenched her fists at her sides. Everybody knew that Mary and Paul Bradford would get married. So why was she flirting with Mr. O'Callahan? Valina glanced at her mother. Hadn't she noticed the shameless way Mary was acting? Well, she was scowling at Mary, but Mary sure wasn't looking at Mama.

Later, after the dinner dishes had been cleared, Mama asked Mary to dish up dessert.

"I have on a good dress, Mama. Valina will do it." Mary raised her eyebrows at Valina. "Won't you, little sister?"

Valina glared at Mary as she went to get the cobbler and got a self-satisfied smirk in return. Mary had sat across from Mr. O'Callahan where he'd have to look at her. And she was posing again. The Queen of Sheba surrounded by her adoring court.

Later, when Mr. O'Callahan had finished his cobbler, Papa said, "We'd all enjoy hearing about your travels, Timothy."

"Well, if you insist."

And, by turn, the room became San Francisco's Chinatown, with violent tong wars and gambling dens, where Mr. O'Callahan had barely escaped with his life. Or New York's Harlem, where he'd played trumpet in the bands with famous musicians. And, even better, Hollywood, where he'd been involved in making movies.

"Mr. O'Callahan, would you play your ukulele before I have to go to bed?" Rachel pleaded.

"Be happy to," he said. And he played "Five-foot two, eyes of blue, oh, what those five feet could do" . . . "Chinatown my Chinatown, when the lights are low." Then Papa chimed in with his harmonica. And they all sang, harmonizing, laughing, begging for more . . . "Alexander's Ragtime Band" . . . "Ramona."

At nine o'clock Mama asked them to sing Rock of Ages. Valina got goosebumps on her arms when she heard Mr. O'Callahan's rich baritone voice. Then Mr. O'Callahan politely thanked Mama for the dinner, said goodbye to one and all, and drove off in his Model A.

Valina sighed. She'd probably never see him again.

A narrow slit of blinding sunlight woke her the next morning. She turned her head away from it and tried to go back to sleep, but the sticky heat in the attic made it impossible. The cracks between the logs in the walls allowed the winter wind to fill the room with icy misery, but in summer the air hung, sullen and still, a wilted ghost refusing to move.

Valina slipped out of bed. Someday she'd have a bed all to herself, with smooth percale sheets instead of threadbare flannel ones. And it wouldn't be in a hot attic, either. She could hear Mama building the fire in the stove downstairs. The attic wouldn't be so blasted hot if they had an electric stove. Most everyone in town had one, but the Addisons didn't even have electricity. Oh, why couldn't Papa be more ambitious? She backed out of the open door of the attic, her bare feet groping for the first rung of the ladder. When she married and had children she'd make sure they never had to use a ladder to get in or out of their bedroom. She'd have a regular stairway. Maybe even have carpet on it. She climbed down, avoiding the rough places that had the biggest slivers.

Mama was adding more wood to the fire. Her face, round and dimpled, glowed with perspiration, and wet gray wisps of hair curled at her temples. Valina watched her brush the wood dust off her hands and move the big granite coffee pot over the firebox. Poor Mama had to work so hard.

"You're up early, Valina."

"It's too hot to sleep. Can I go down to the creek for a minute and cool off?"

"Yes, but I'll need you to hang up some new flypaper when you get back." Mama pointed at the long sticky coil, black with flies, hanging near the back door.

Valina hurried out the door and walked quickly down the path to the creek. Its mossy bank tickled her bare feet. She stepped into the cold stream and sat down, watching her nightgown surrender to the weight of the water. Then she lay back into the water and let the coolness cover her whole body. Even the bed of flat round rocks felt good. At least they were cold. She moved as a fish would move, undulating, turning slowly as the water swirled around her body. A vine maple overhead kept the morning sun at bay. Only the smallest fingers of light penetrated its green canopy. The early morning chatter of the birds had ceased. The soothing voice of the creek was the only sound. Valina stretched her arms and wiggled her toes.

Remembering Mr. O'Callahan's visit, she smiled. Mr. O'Callahan. Timothy O'Callahan. His name had a wonderful lilt to it, just as an Irish name should. Valina O'Callahan. That sounded spiffy. Being married to him would be exciting. He had been so many places, done so many things, and he was ever so handsome. Not only that, he must have ambition. His car and clothes were expensive.

Her reverie ended abruptly. Rachel stood on the bank watching her.

"Well aren't you a sight? Wait till Mama sees how wet you are. You need to come help with breakfast." Rachel crossed her arms over her chest and looked down her nose at Valina.

"Sometimes you're too uppity for your own good, Rachel." Valina got out of the creek and tried to wring the water out of her nightgown and hair. "You're only nine years old and I'm seventeen. There's a big difference. Besides, I haven't been here that long."

"You sure have. Papa's awake and chomping at the bit. You know how he gets when he's hungry."

"Mm-hmm. He acts like a big baby."

"Mama wouldn't like it if she heard you say that." Rachel crossed her arms over her chest. "Besides, I like Papa just the way he is."

"Of course you do. You're the youngest and he spoils you."

"Me spoiled? I don't lie in the creek while Mama works, like some people I know."

Rachel gave Valina a triumphant glance and started toward the cabin. Dejected and wet, Valina followed her.

"Daydreaming again, Valina?" Mama was so busy cooking breakfast she didn't notice her sodden appearance. "Need I mention the flypaper?"

"No, Mama." Valina stood on a chair and unhooked the

flypaper, holding it as far from her body as her arm would allow. If Papa would only bury the garbage more often they wouldn't have so many flies. She carried the nasty thing outside and hurried to the garbage pit. At least Papa had dug it as far away from the cabin as he could get.

She heard a car. She gasped. Mr. O'Callahan? No one should see her looking like this. She ran to the pit, tossed the coil into it, and raced back toward the cabin only to come face-to-face with him there in the yard. Oh, no! Her nightgown was plastered to every part of her body and he was taking in every inch of it. The amused challenge in his eyes made her heart pound. For a moment she thought he was going to touch her. She wished she could turn to stone, but then the thought of herself as a statue, her body forever revealed made her stomach lurch.

"Good morning." She didn't wait for him to answer, just hurried to the door.

"Mama, quick ... Mr. O'Callahan's out there."

"I thought I heard his car, but what's he doing here at this hour?"

"I don't know, but don't let him in until I get up the ladder."

"Good heavens, child, did he see you like that?"

Valina didn't answer. She was too busy scrambling into the attic. Mary and Rachel were still up there, Mary primping, Rachel struggling with a knotted shoelace.

Valina knew the minute Mary saw her she would make some nasty comment.

Sure enough, Mary looked at Valina and shook her head. "Rachel said you'd been wallowing in the creek. I never heard of anything so stupid."

Valina sighed. "I just wanted to cool off. What's so stupid about that?" She wished she had a towel so she could at least dry her hair.

"Girls," Mama called. "Mr. O'Callahan's here. Come help with breakfast."

Mary glared at Valina. "Don't tell me he saw you like that. He certainly wouldn't be attracted to anyone looking so vulgar. You're not his type anyway."

Valina frowned at Mary's nasty assumption. "I managed to get up the ladder before he came in." Darned if she'd admit the truth. Reverend Howard would call that lying by omission but Valina didn't care. Mr. O'Callahan wouldn't say anything about it. He was a gentleman, after all. She waited until Mary and Rachel had gone down the ladder, then stripped off her wet nightgown and got dressed.

When she climbed down the ladder, he was sitting at the table drinking coffee. He winked at her and said, "Good morning." She nodded, and avoided looking at him, though she could feel his eyes following her.

"Isn't breakfast ready yet, Emma?" Papa called from the bedroom.

"It won't be long." Mama put another chunk of wood in the stove. "In the meantime, we need some more wood cut." She pulled a sliver out of her thumb and adjusted the damper.

"Oh, the plight of a man with three daughters and no sons." Papa crept up behind Mama and kissed her on the neck. She jumped and they all laughed. "I'm doomed to work hard for the rest of my days, Emma." He put his arms around her waist. "Now, I ask you, who's going to take care of me when I'm old and feeble?"

"God will. You can count on that." She gave him a playful shove. "Please go cut some more wood." She pointed at the wood box by the stove. "The pile in there is getting low."

"I'll help you, Daniel," Mr. O'Callahan said.

"Fine. Looks like a good day for fishing, doesn't it?"

Fishing? So that's why Mr. O'Callahan was here so early. Would've been nice if Papa had let everyone know. Valina glanced up just in time to see Mr. O'Callahan's eyes sweep up and down her body before he followed Papa out the door. She shivered and rubbed her arms. How could she be cold when the room was so hot?

The regulars at the Pine Cone Cafe spent the better part of the next morning talking about Mr. O'Callahan. When Bertha Wilcox came in for coffee, Valina knew the word had gotten around town, because Bertha didn't even like coffee. The fat old gossip always told anyone who'd listen that it gave her gas.

"Had the stranger for dinner, I hear," Bertha said. Her beady brown eyes gleamed with curiosity.

Valina had a wild urge to say, "No, we had stew," but she knew Bertha wouldn't see the humor in it.

"That's right." She filled Bertha's cup.

"What's he do for a living?"

"I don't know." Even if there wasn't gossip, Bertha was the kind of woman who would make some up.

Bertha scooped three heaping teaspoons of sugar into her coffee and scowled. "Well, where's he from?"

"New York, originally." Valina turned her back and started washing cups in the small sink Tillie and Ben had put in last month. A great idea, since it saved her steps and left the big kitchen sink available for the plates, and the pots and pans. She didn't mind doing dishes at the café. The novelty of a sink and running water made it almost fun. Besides, Bertha might stop prying, since she'd have to talk to her waitress's back.

But Bertha kept right on. "New York, huh? A real city slicker from what I hear. Have to watch out for that kind. 'Course your folks don't have any money, so they don't have to worry about losing it to a fast talker. But you girls had best be careful."

Valina clenched her fists in the dishwater. Damn her.

Herb Johnson spoke up. "Bertha, you should've seen his Model A. Mighty handsome car."

"And you should've seen our pretty little Valina when she rode off in it," Spike said. "Good thing her papa was with them, that's all I can say."

Valina fumed. And damn Spike Washburn, too.

"Now, that's exactly what I was talking about, Valina." Bertha stopped short when Minnie Higgins, Doc Bradford's nurse, dashed in and slammed the door behind her. Her white uniform was so starched it looked like it would crack if she sat down. So did her tall skinny body. She strode quickly over to the counter where Valina stood.

"I need a ham sandwich for Doc," she said, in a voice that brooked no nonsense. "He didn't get breakfast. Been up since four this morning delivering the Anderson baby."

"What'd Thelma have, this time? Boy or girl?" Bertha asked.

"Boy. Their sixth you know. They were hoping for a girl." Minnie shook her head. "About time to quit filling up their back yard with boys, I'd say. 'Course, it's none of my business, thank God. But six boys, that's a handful."

Valina liked Minnie. You could count on her to be free with her opinions, but she wasn't malicious like Bertha.

"Understand you Addisons had a handsome stranger in for dinner last night," Minnie said.

"Yes, we did."

"And he has a fancy car, too, I hear."

"Mm-hm."

"In that case, maybe you'd better tell Mary that Paul's coming home from college tomorrow on the four o'clock train. Doc and Catherine got a call from him last night."

"Okay, I'll tell her." She hurried into the kitchen to make the sandwich. So Paul was coming home. Now, wasn't that the cat's meow? Valina wished Mary would marry him and get it over with, since everyone was so set on it. They would move to Portland, where he'd take over his dead parents' business, and then maybe the men in town would forget about Mary.

She put Doc's sandwich in a sack, took it out to the counter and handed it to Minnie. "Here's your order. I put in some of Doc's favorite pickles, too. Want anything else?"

"Nope," Minnie said. "It'll be hard enough to get him to sit down for ten minutes to eat this." She hurried out the door.

"Doc's lucky to have Minnie working for him." Bertha said. "He takes care of everyone but himself. Don't imagine a woman like Catherine could train him. Good thing Minnie's there to ride herd on him."

Dogie Hanks cackled. "She makes a damned funny lookin' cowpoke."

"Oh, shut up, Dogie." Bertha slid her cup toward Valina for a refill.

Valina filled it, hoping Bertha's gas would kick in pretty

soon. Bertha had made Catherine Bradford sound like a rotten wife, and that wasn't true at all.

The front door flew open and Valina's boss, Ben Hillyard, dashed into the room. "There's a fire roaring up Dead Man's Canyon," he yelled.

In spite of his large size, Herb Johnson moved quickly. "They'll need all the men they can get," he said. "Come on, Dogie, Spike."

"I don't fight fires," Spike growled.

Herb glared at him but Spike didn't move. Herb gave a disgusted grunt and hustled Dogie out the door.

"Valina. I'm going with them," Ben said. "Tillie will be here for the dinner shift." He hurried out the door.

A few minutes later, Mr. O'Callahan walked in with Papa right behind him, holding up two large trout for everyone to see. All Valina could think to say was whoopee, but she didn't dare say it.

"Well, good morning, Valina." Mr. O'Callahan smiled and doffed his canvas fishing hat. "You're looking exceptionally pretty this morning."

She blushed and smiled at him, then remembered . . . "Papa, there's a forest fire up in Dead Man's Canyon. Some of the men have gone to fight it."

Just then Herb Johnson threw the door open so hard Papa had to jump out of the way. "The wind's blowing the fire toward us," Herb said. "We need all the men we can get to help build backfires. We've got to get it under control or the town could burn."

Papa thrust the two fish at Valina, and he and Mr.

O'Callahan hurried out the door with Herb. Even Spike stood up and followed them.

Valina held the two fish by the gills, one in each hand. She hated the slimy feel of them and the little spiny things inside the gills felt like needles piercing her fingers. She hurried into the kitchen and put them in the big refrigerator. "These are here temporarily, Margaret, while Papa's fighting the fire."

"What fire?"

"I forgot you can't hear anything back here in the kitchen. The fire's in Dead Man's Canyon, heading this way. All the men have gone to help fight it."

Margaret paled and dropped the butcher knife she'd been holding. It clattered in the sink. "That's near Whiskey Creek."

Why was Margaret so upset? "You know someone who lives up there?"

"My intended."

"Intended? You mean you're going to get married? That's wonderful." At thirty-eight, Margaret Black, was one of the town's spinsters. A big-boned woman, she had legs that looked like sturdy oaks, and feet to match. She'd been the cook at the Pine Cone Cafe for the last twenty years.

"It won't be wonderful if the fire gets him." Margaret took a hankie out of her apron pocket and wiped her eyes.

"There's just Bertha and me out there. Why don't you come sit with us for a while?"

"Not Bertha. Please don't tell that old windbag."

"Don't worry. I won't tell a soul. Come on. We'll say your eyes are red from chopping onions."

"No. I'll stay here. She can ferret out secrets like no one

I've ever known, then tell the whole world within the next ten minutes."

"Yes, I know." Bertha had spread the word about Papa each time he'd been fired. She went back into the restaurant. Bertha was gone, thank goodness. She made a fresh pot of coffee and put it on the hot plate.

The front door banged open and that brat Roy Bailey came in carrying his slingshot, his gray cap pulled so low on his head it rested on his ears. What kind of mischief had he been up to now? Probably shooting at defenseless birds.

"Minnie said to tell you that Mrs. Bradford went to your cabin and brought your mama and Rachel back to stay at her house," Roy said. "And I'm supposed to go tell your sister, Mary, at Osborne's the same thing." He flipped his slingshot around in the air, then remembered there was more to the message. "And you're supposed to go there, too."

Surprised that he'd remembered to tell her, Valina said, "Thanks for letting me know, Roy."

"Aw, that's all right." He climbed up on one of the stools and grinned at Valina. "Minnie said you should give me a creme soda and put it on Doc's bill."

"Coming right up." She smiled. Minnie had known that Roy wouldn't forget to deliver the message if she promised him a crème soda.

She liked to use the bottle opener that was fastened under the counter. The lids came off easily and fell into an empty coffee can she'd put right under it. The neatness of it pleased her. Mr. Hillyard had liked her idea for the bottle opener, too. In spite of sore feet and certain unpleasant customers, she enjoyed her job. The Hillyard's treated her like a grownup, even took some of her suggestions.

A movement outside the window caught her eye. Oh, no. Rachel bounced in the front door and headed for the counter. "Does Mama know where you are?" Valina asked.

"Of course she does. She sent me to tell you to come to Catherine's house." Rachel made a face when she saw Roy, and sat on a stool as far away from him as she could get.

At many a dinner hour, too many as far as Valina was concerned, Rachel had complained about Roy's latest prank, what a brat he was. But Roy wasn't one bit worse than Rachel. Mama and Papa couldn't see that, any more than they could see how stuck up Mary was.

"Want a creme soda, Rachel?" She'd never hear the end of it if she let Rachel sit there while Roy drank one.

Rachel beamed. "Sure."

Valina handed her a bottle and a straw. Now that the door had been opened the smell of smoke filled the room. She went over to the window and peered out. Her heart began to pound. How close was the fire? But she mustn't get panicky. Someone would warn her if it came near the town.

She fixed herself a tuna sandwich and sat down next to her little sister. Rachel started blowing through her straw into the creme soda. Roy soon started blowing in his.

Valina sighed. "Cut that out, you two."

But the blowing escalated into a contest of who could make the most noise. Valina glared at them, then stood up and took her sandwich into the kitchen. Those two brats weren't one bit concerned about the fire.

When she came back to the counter, sticky creme soda was all over the counter, the stools, even the floor.

"That's it. See if I ever treat you to one again, Rachel." She wet two rags and slapped them down on the counter. "You two brats clean up this mess you made. Start in on the stools. And they'd better be spotless when you're done."

"You can't tell me what to do," Roy said, his arms folded across his chest.

"No, but I can tell your mother what you did, can't I? And I'm just itching to, believe me."

Roy muttered a lot but he kept working.

Rachel wouldn't look at Valina. "Are you going to tell Mama?"

"You two disgust me, horsing around like this. Don't you realize that fire could sweep right through this town? Why do you think the men have all gone to fight it? Our homes could burn, with everything in them, including us."

Both of them stood gaping at her, their eyes wide. She threw two clean rags at them. "Keep scrubbing."

Fortunately, by the time Tillie Hillyard came in, the cafe was clean again and the subdued culprits had fled.

When Valina saw the worried frown on Tillie's usually sunny face, it scared her. "Have you heard anything more about the fire?"

"No, but I'm closing the cafe. You go home right away. I'll tell Margaret."

Valina followed Tillie into the kitchen. "I have to get Papa's fish out of the refrigerator."

"Margaret, I'm closing the café." Tillie said, "But if the men don't come back tonight, we'll need to fix food to send up to them."

"What time do you want me to come in?"

"Early. I'll be here at 4:30."

"So will I." Margaret washed her hands, took off her huge apron, and hung it on a hook by the back door.

"I'll come too. And Mama will want to help." Valina put the two fish in a gunnysack she found under the sink, then went out the back door. A wall of acrid smoke stopped her for a second. She took a quick breath and pushed on toward Catherine's house. By the time she had walked just a short way, her eyes burned and her throat felt raw. The smoke was an eerie color, a muddy orange. The fire must be awfully close.

She shifted the heavy gunnysack to her other hand and hurried toward the Bradford place. A substantial home, Mama called it. Two-storied, it had a big veranda with eight wicker chairs on it. And inside there were carpets, elegant furniture, even electric lights and plumbing.

One day, about a year ago, Valina had asked Catherine how she and Mama had become friends. Catherine said, "When I married Doc and moved to Pine Bluff, I was never so lonely in my life. I was about ready to give up and go back to San Francisco, and that would have been the end of our marriage. But just in time, here came your mother with an apple pie, welcoming me to Pine Bluff. I've loved her every day of my life since then."

The dense smoke had blotted out the sun and the lights were on in the house. Mama met her at the door, a worried frown on her face. "Thank heaven you got off early."

"If the men don't come back tonight, Mrs. Hillyard wants us to come in at 4:30. We'll fix food to send up to them."

"That's a good idea. Catherine's calling Dottie right now to see if there's been any word from the men yet." Dottie Harper was the town's telephone operator, and any news went to her first.

"What'll I do with these fish?" Valina held up the gunny-sack. "Papa and Mr. O'Callahan left them with me."

"Good. Now we can contribute something to dinner. Catherine insists that we spend the night. We'll put them in her refrigerator."

Rachel didn't look up from the piano, where she was one-fingering her way through "Rock of Ages." Valina rolled her eyes. Rachel was trying to impress Mama with that song, just in case someone told on her.

It disgusted Valina to find Mary sitting at the kitchen table filing her nails. If she wasn't careful, someone might ask her to help cook dinner.

Catherine was on the phone, listening. Valina yearned to look like Catherine, tall and willowy, with dark hair held back in a smooth chignon.

Catherine said, "Thanks, Dottie," and hung up. "She says the phone up on Whisky Creek still rings, but no one answers. Probably Harry Jensen and his men are off fighting the fire. No one's called to report anything yet, but at least that phone line's still working. It's the closest one to the fire, so that's a good sign."

Valina hoped Harry Jensen's silent phone line didn't mean that he'd been hurt, or worse. She glanced at Mary, still calmly filing her nails. Wasn't she scared? Not even a little bit?

"By the way, Mary, did Catherine tell you Paul is coming in tomorrow on the four o'clock train?"

"Yes, she did." Mary shrugged. "But the train might not come in, what with the fire."

Well, at least she knew there was a fire. Valina rubbed her eyes, but that made them burn even worse.

The phone rang, three longs and a short, the Bradford's ring. Catherine answered it, listened for a moment and said, "Thanks again, Dottie," and hung up. She turned to the others. "Reverend Howard has called a meeting at the church tonight. Prayer first and then we'll plan for emergency conditions. Let's start dinner, Emma. With luck, my busy husband will be home soon. He needs to be at that meeting."

That night, though she lay in a comfortable bed made with smooth percale sheets, Valina couldn't sleep. The smoke in the room made her cough. Was the fire closer? Had any of the men been burned or hurt? Maybe even killed? Oh, Papa. She tried to drag her mind away from the worry, but the town would be trapped if the fire overtook it. Would they all die of burns? She'd heard it was a horrible way to go. Or would the smoke choke them to death? There was the Clearwater River, but there were only a few rowboats in town, and they weren't really in good shape. At the meeting, Doc had said that if the fire came into town, they should each go lie in the river and breathe through a wet cloth. But the river was deep and the current strong. Perhaps drowning would be easier, though, than burning. She shuddered. When the grandfather clock downstairs struck four, she got out of bed and dressed, glad she'd be working hard at the cafe. It might help keep her mind off the fire.

Both Mama and Catherine helped. Margaret baked cookies while the others made sandwiches. At one point, Mrs. Hillyard said, "You can call me Tillie from now on, Valina. Your folks must be really proud of you. You're a good worker."

Valina could feel herself blushing. "Thank you, uh, Tillie." She looked at Mama who was beaming.

A subdued Rachel volunteered, "Can I help, too?"

"You can go to the general store and get some more sandwich meat." Tillie said. "Tell Mrs. Edgerton to charge it to our account."

At 7:30 that morning, Old Lester and Bill Palmer, the only men left in town, except Doc Bradley and Reverend Howard, showed up with two horses and three mules. Two of the mules were loaded down with axes and shovels wrapped in old army blankets. The men loaded the food, along with jugs of water and coffee, on the other mule and headed for Dead Man's Canyon. It usually took about three hours to get up there by way of the dirt road. The town settled down to wait.

Their work done, Valina and the four women sat down at one of the big tables in the other room and drank coffee. Rachel had a dish of ice cream.

"At least we'll know something when they get back," Valina said, looking at Margaret. Margaret just nodded.

Tired and worried, they all sat, staring at nothing, sipping their coffee. Finally, Rachel said, "Wonder how Mary's doing at work over at Osborne's." At a signal from Mama, she wiped ice cream off her mouth, "Want me to go see?"

"All right," Mama said. "But you come right back. You need to stay with me today."

When Rachel left, Mama said, "I've never seen her like this before. So quiet. The poor little thing is really frightened."

Valina knew she should feel guilty for scaring Rachel. But Rachel behaving herself? What a treat.

Late that afternoon, news spread that Bill and Lester were on the outskirts of town. A crowd waited for them out in front of the cafe. But there were three men riding in, not two.

CHAPTER 3

J-Bar-J Ranch — 1969

The next day, just before noon, I got a phone call.

"Your line's been busy for the last hour." The woman's voice was brusque, to say the least. She hadn't even said hello, but I had a good idea who it might be.

"Is that you, Jessica Marie?" She hates it when I call her that.

She huffed a bit. "Of course it is."

I wondered if she thought all I had to do was sit and talk on the phone. "Sorry my line was busy, but it's a ten-party line, and right now about fifty percent of those parties are listening in. Is there a problem?" I swear I could hear her grinding her teeth.

"Why, no. I would simply like to speak to my son." She'd put on her uppity airs for the benefit of the eavesdroppers.

"He's out mending fences with Oscar." I knew that would go over just dandy.

"Can't you call him to the telephone?"

Her childish whine grated on my nerves. "That'd be a bit impractical," I said. "He's a couple hundred acres away from the house."

I heard an angry gasp on the other end of the line, but I broke in before she could get all wound up. "Jimmy's doing real well. He's learned how to clean out a barn, and chop wood, and eat a decent meal . . ." I never did know when to shut my mouth.

"Are you inferring that I haven't fed my son properly?" She'd gone from whine to ice.

"Not at all. But right now I have to take the lunches out to the men. I'll tell him you called. Talk to you later." I hung up on her. Can't stand the silly woman, even if she is my great niece.

When I carried the food out to the jeep, Roscoe was asleep on the porch. He opened one eye, but decided I wasn't worth the effort. When he was younger, he liked to sit beside me in the jeep and help me drive.

I took the rickety jeep, the one that's falling apart even faster than the other one. We don't use it much anymore. Had it since the beginning of creation. Before I headed out, I tied up the tailgate with a rope to keep the food from bouncing out. Some of the ruts in the field are pretty deep.

When I found Jimmy and Oscar out in the pasture, I was glad I'd brought three jugs of water. Their shirts were pasted to their backs with sweat. Fencing is hot, dirty work, second in misery only to haying. Oscar had said there was a five-foot section of fence down, post and all, but from what I could see they'd already mended it. "Looks like you're done," I said.

"Just finished." Oscar wiped his hands on a rag he'd taken out of his pocket. Jimmy hot-footed it over to the jeep where the food was.

"Wait just one damned minute, boy," Oscar said. "Pick up that fence tool and put it in its carrying case. We don't leave tools scattered all to hell and gone."

"For pete's sake, I'm just going to eat lunch."

"Hey." I glared at the boy. "Do as Oscar says."

He grumbled, but he put the fence tool back in its case, then made a big point of tying it on the saddle where it belonged. "Now can I have lunch?" he snarled.

Oscar took a step forward as if he meant to hit the kid, but I grabbed his arm and he stayed put.

"Jimmy, go eat," I said. "Oh, by the way, your mother called just before I came out." He didn't respond to that piece of news. He'd already headed for the food.

Oscar jerked his arm away from my hand. "That kid . . ." He shut his mouth in a tight line. Then he took a deep breath and cleared his throat. "Somebody took wire cutters to the fence."

"You're saying it was deliberate?"

"That's right."

"Are you sure? It could've rusted out."

He turned his head and spat on the ground. "You don't believe me, come look at it." With that, he stomped over to the fence.

I followed him and checked out the piece he held up in front of me. That fence had been cut. "You're right. But why would anyone do that? We don't keep cattle down here this time of year."

He shrugged. "Didn't happen 'til the kid came here."

I almost whacked him one. "You've made it perfectly clear

in the last few days that your nose is out of joint. Don't know which is worse, you or the kid. Now, I'm going to pretend I didn't hear that nasty remark of yours." I glared at him. "And you'll forget you ever thought it, won't you?"

He scowled at me. "If you say so, boss."

I went right on. "Sandy mentioned there was mischief going on with our fences . . ."

"Its deliberate." He scowled at me. "That's worse than just mischief."

"We'll have to ask Sandy what he knew about this when we help with his haying."

Oscar gave me a curt nod and headed for the jeep. I followed him. Jimmy stood at the tailgate stuffing his face with the last of a beef sandwich.

When he saw me, he grumbled, "I'd rather shovel shit than mend fences."

Had there been one decent word from him about anything since he'd arrived at the ranch? If there had, I sure couldn't bring it to mind. I turned my back to him and watched Oscar drink about a half gallon of water, then tear into the sandwiches.

"You turned over the windrows on your way out here?"

"With Oscar dogging my every step?" Jimmy growled. "Damned right I did."

I turned to him. "I wasn't talking to you, smart mouth."

Jimmy just shrugged and studied his sandwich. When I glanced back at Oscar, he was stifling a smile.

"I think we'd better spend tomorrow haying over at Sandy's," I said. I wanted to talk to Sandy about the fences, but

I hated to leave Mattie's Lady. Someone would have to stay home with her. If she got in trouble, the vet couldn't get there in time. "You'd better stay here tomorrow, Oscar. Mattie's Lady might need you."

"Okay by me." He sounded relieved. He wouldn't have to be plagued by Sandy or the boy. Maybe a day of peace would sweeten his disposition.

I waited until the two of them were through eating, which didn't take long. Then I got in the jeep and drove back toward the house, with Oscar and Jimmy right behind me in the other jeep.

When we drove up to the barn, Cal Lewis, the game warden, was riding in from the other direction. He's a big chunky man with rust-colored hair and a ready grin. Riding beside him was a young Indian man. Downright handsome he was, with a strong wide jaw and warm brown eyes like those of my childhood Indian friend, Joe. There aren't many Indians left around here. Most of them live on those blasted reservations.

Cal and the Indian got off their horses. "This is Buddy Fast Buffalo Horse," Cal said. "He's a first-rate tracker. Often helps the sheriff or me find the lawbreakers around these parts."

I glared at Jimmy before he could open his big smart mouth. If he made one crack about Buddy's name, I'd kick his butt right there in front of everyone. But Jimmy seemed fascinated by Buddy. Probably never seen an Indian before.

Roscoe walked over to Buddy and sniffed his boot. Buddy held the back of his hand out for the dog to smell. Damned if Roscoe didn't grin at him. Buddy laughed and knelt down beside the dog. "You're a funny old boy." He petted Roscoe's head and rubbed his ears. If that dog had been a cat, he'd have purred.

Then Cal said, "You left a message that someone had shot a cow. Where did it happen?"

"Up in the third meadow."

"No evidence or tracks, I suppose," he said.

"Nope. Hard to tell how long the cow had been dead. One odd thing though . . . the S.O.B. cut off one of the cow's ears."

Cal nodded, a disgusted look on his face. "Yep. I've been aware of this creep for some time. He's no game-happy tourist. You got any idea who he might be?"

"Not a one. Neither does Oscar."

"Well, I think I do, but I have to prove it first," Cal said.

My curiosity punched me a good one. "Come on. Out with it. Who do you think it is?"

He shook his head. "I can't say just yet."

"Cal Lewis, I think I'm entitled to know what's going on. That creep shot one of my cows."

He grinned. "Just like a woman. Can't stand not knowing. Matilda, it's my duty to keep my mouth shut until I have proof."

Jimmy was sitting on the porch step, his back to us. Every little bit I'd hear him sputter. Getting a big kick out of his great-aunt Matilda being told to shut up, wasn't he?

"Well, when you have proof, please let me know so I can visit him in jail."

"Oh, no. No visitors. Family only."

"Better start praying it isn't some shirttail relative of mine. I'd show no mercy."

"Don't I know it?"

Jimmy snickered. "It'd look great in the papers: 'Seventy-six-year-old woman shoots poacher right between the eyes'."

I walked over and poked his butt with the toe of my boot. "Watch it, smartass."

I looked back at Cal, "A couple of days ago Sandy told me some of our fence was down, and that there was some mischief going on. Why don't we ride over there and find out what he has to say."

Before Cal could even nod in agreement, George and Buck went to the barn and brought back horses for Jimmy and me. They were obviously eager to get rid of the boy. And maybe me, too. Who knows. Jimmy mounted Sultan, that Arabian he liked so much. Now Oscar could have a nice rest without the kid around for a while.

When we rode up to Sandy's place, the door was wide open. His dog, Angus, stood next to it, whining.

"Sandy must be in there," Jimmy whispered, his eyes wide.

We got off our horses real fast. I took my first aid kit out of the saddlebag and we went in the house. Angus stuck so close to us he almost stepped on our feet. In the dim light of the front room, we could see Sandy sprawled on the floor next to the couch, his left leg splayed out at an awful angle. Angus went over and lay down right next to him.

Jimmy squawked and backed up a step. "Jesus. Is he dead?"

I walked over to Sandy, knelt on the floor, and felt his neck for a pulse. "He's still alive, barely. "Sandy, it's Matilda."

His eyelids fluttered and he moaned.

"Lord, you must've had a helluva fall."

Jimmy tugged at my sleeve and whispered, "Did you see his arm?"

I nodded. The break was so bad you could see the bones poking out of the skin.

Buddy walked over to the end of the couch. "The phone's been knocked off this table. He must've tried to call for help." He picked it up and put it back on the table. "What can I do?" he asked.

I pointed at the door to the bedroom. "You and Jimmy can go get the blankets and pillows off his bed." From the way Sandy was struggling for breath, I was sure he'd punctured a lung. I took the syringe and morphine tablets out of the first aid kit. The doctor in town had given them to me in case of an emergency like this. It's not legal but it's humane.

When Jimmy and Buddy came back with the bedding, I covered Sandy with a blanket and gently eased a pillow under his head. Then I turned to Buddy and the kid. "You'll need to stay with Sandy for a little bit. I have to dilute a tablet of morphine in boiling water before I can give him a shot. I'll be in the kitchen if you need me." Buddy nodded and knelt beside Sandy.

Jimmy looked pale, but he didn't say a word. He backed up and sat down in the worn leather chair Sandy loved so much, and kept his eyes on the pitiful old man.

It took a while to find a spoon and pan that I could scrub clean enough to boil. After what seemed like an age, I got some water boiling and dissolved the tablet in it.

When I went back in the front room with the loaded syringe, Jimmy sprang out of the chair like he thought I was going to poke him with the thing. Out of the corner of my eye I could see him turn his head away while I gave Sandy the shot. Buddy held Sandy's arm for me.

And then Sandy moaned again "ams . . . ams." What was he trying to say? Poor man. The pain had to be godawful.

"You want me to go get George and have him bring over the pickup so we can take Sandy to a hospital?" Jimmy asked.

I took his arm and walked him outside. "I want you and Buddy to get George, but not to take Sandy to the hospital. He'd never make it. Think about the pain he'd be in on that rock bed of a road. No. We'll need George and the pickup so he can take his body to the mortuary, when the time comes."

Jimmy looked at me like I was Satan himself. "You're going to just let him die?"

"He is dying. No way we can stop it. And Sandy told me more than once that he wanted to die here on his own land. I have to abide by his wishes. I'll send Buddy out so you can get started."

He didn't say a word, just turned and walked toward the horses. As he started to mount Sultan, he gave me an uneasy glance then quickly looked away.

I went in the cabin and explained to Buddy. "The kid could go by himself to get George, but I think he'd be a lot better off if you went with him."

Buddy stared at me for a moment. "What about you?"

"I'll be okay."

He hesitated. "If that's what you want." He looked at Sandy. "We'll hurry." He was gone before I could blink.

I sat down by Sandy. Had his horse thrown him? No, I

could hardly believe that. Sandy was an excellent rider. We'd probably never know what happened. A miracle that he'd managed to get back to the house. I couldn't even imagine the agony he must have been in, dragging himself here. So like Sandy.

By the time I heard the pickup and the horses, Sandy's breathing was even more shallow. It hurt to listen to him.

George came in and stood beside me, just watching Sandy. "Why don't you go outside for a little while? I'll sit with him."

"No. He needs someone to be holding his hand when the time comes. I don't think you'd feel comfortable doing that, but you could make us some coffee. Wash the cups first, though." I'd never seen George like this, wanting to help me.

Jimmy didn't say a word, just eased himself down into the leather chair. I figured he'd been through quite a bit more than anyone bargained for when he came to my ranch, maybe too much for a fifteen-year-old city kid.

We didn't have long to wait. Sandy's last breath was a long easy sigh. I bent over and kissed his grizzled cheek. "Goodbye, Sandy."

That's when Angus pointed his nose at heaven and let out a mournful howl. Even George had tears in his eyes.

Nothing we could do but load the body into the bed of the pickup. After we finished, who should show up but Sandy's horse? He still wore a saddle. Buddy walked over to him and patted his neck, then peered at the horse's side. "He has cuts on his flank. Must've gotten into some barbed wire. I could stay here and take care of him and feed the livestock until other arrangements are made."

"Aren't you working for Cal Lewis?"

"Not really. I just went along to keep him company. He's a good friend. He'll understand."

"But the cabin is filthy. You couldn't sleep in there."

"I'll sleep in the barn till I get the place cleaned up."

Had I heard him right? "You'd clean up that mess?"

"Sure. Somebody has to."

"I'll be damned." I looked closely at the handsome young man. "Didn't know they made them like you anymore. It would be a great help to everyone concerned if you would stay, and I do thank you."

I almost laughed when I saw Jimmy's face. He was actually gaping at Buddy with a look of admiration. Had the snotty city kid found someone he could look up to? Buddy being an Indian was probably a novelty to the boy. And Buddy was also a tracker, and young . . . generations closer to Jimmy's age than the rest of us.

To Buddy, I said, "Sandy has a daughter who lives in Pine Bluff. I'll get in touch with her and see what she wants done with the property. But right now, we'd better get going so George can take the body to the mortuary."

We all stared as Angus jumped into the back of the pickup and curled down right next to Sandy's body. Dogs can sure break your heart.

Jimmy and I rode behind the pickup. It was hard to concentrate on anything but the body in the flatbed, and the awful angles of the blanket covering it, that, and the dog beside it. We didn't talk for about a mile, until Jimmy finally spoke up.

"You kissed him goodbye."

"Yeah."

"Why? I thought you didn't like him."

"He was my second husband."

The way the kid looked, sort of green around the mouth, I was afraid he'd had one too many shocks.

"You're kidding."

"Our marriage didn't take. After our divorce I took back Jacob's last name."

It was obvious that Jimmy was having a hard time accepting the idea of marriage between Sandy and me. Quite a few people had that same problem.

"I was sorry that Sandy was alone again, but he could've hired someone and had company on the place. He wouldn't do it, though. Stubborn old coot. And the longer he lived, the worse he got. Poor Sandy."

"Is that why you always helped him hay?"

"Well, that's usually a custom between ranchers. We help each other. And once in a while I'd bring him some decent food, just so I could check up on him."

"He was a lot older than you wasn't he?"

I laughed. "Lord, no. He was seven years younger. That's what happens to people when they stop living life. You've got to grab each day and wrestle it to the ground."

Jimmy stared at me for a moment, but then his eyes veered back to Sandy and the dog. I thought I'd better try to get him to talk about it. "Ever seen someone die before?" I asked.

"Nope."

"It's really something, isn't it?"

"Yep."

"It always amazes me how quickly the soul departs. It takes the body a while to get cold, but the eyes . . . the soul is there one instant, gone the next."

"Yeah. Unreal. What's going to happen to Angus now?"

Obviously, he didn't want to talk about death. "I expect we'll keep Angus if he'll stay. But you never know what a dog in mourning will do. He's been alone with Sandy ever since he was a tiny pup. Of course, Sandy's daughter might want him, but Angus is a country dog. They wouldn't be able to keep him in town."

"Did his daughter ever come to see him?"

"He wouldn't let her on the place. She married Tom Lewis, who is a good man, but Sandy hated his guts. Tom had a job in his dad's store. When he made it clear to Sandy that he wasn't interested in ranching, Sandy accused him of being a sissy. Tom took offense at that, and things were never the same. As far as Sandy was concerned, he no longer had a daughter. Hannah Lewis has spent thirty years praying for reconciliation with her papa, but it never came. He had no damned reason in the world to treat her that way. She's a nice woman with a fine husband and children. Like I said, the older he was, the worse he became. As rigid as frozen earth."

When we got to the ranch, Angus let us know that he had no intention of leaving Sandy's body, nor would he let anyone else near it. I told Jimmy to go get one of the tarps in the barn.

But when Oscar and Buck climbed into the bed of the pickup with the tarp, Angus snarled at them. Seemed to know their plan. It was a pitiful sight. They managed to throw the tarp over him, but not without pain to all concerned. How that dog did struggle. We chained him to the sweet gum tree and he commenced to bark, non-stop. When George drove away with Sandy's body, I admit I got tears in my eyes watching that poor dog suffer. Jimmy hustled over to the barn. I went in the kitchen to use the phone. It was busy. Big surprise.

"Clara, get off the phone. We have an emergency here. You can find out about it when you listen in. Just get off the damned phone." I hung up and waited a few seconds, then picked up the receiver and dialed. Someone answered on the third ring. It was Hannah.

"Hannah Lewis . . . This is Matilda Jacobsen. I have bad news. Your father had a terrible fall. He died a couple of hours ago." I heard a gasp on the other end. "Hannah, is someone there with you?"

She managed to say, "Yes," but she was crying too hard to talk, so I didn't force conversation. "George is taking his body to the mortuary. He should be there in about an hour. We'll be happy to help you any way we can. And please let me know when the funeral will be. Hannah, I'm sure sorry." I hung up so she could get on with her grieving.

I started to fix some ham sandwiches, but Oscar stopped me. "I'll fix them, Mattie. You must be exhausted."

That was his way of apologizing for his rotten attitude. I handed him the bread and butter. "You're right, Oscar, I'm bone weary." I went out on the porch and sat down. Wasn't long before Jimmy came back from the barn. Angus was still barking. Roscoe sat at a respectful distance, watching him.

"That Roscoe's a good guy. He knows Angus is hurting.

Don't ever let anyone tell you that animals don't have feelings, Jimmy."

"Too bad Sandy didn't have some."

"People are more complex than animals. Sometimes they hurt each other pretty bad."

"That tree Angus is tied to. Isn't it too special to you for a dog to be tied to it? He could damage it couldn't he? At least that chain might."

Wondered when he'd get around to that. "Jacob and I planted our first vegetable garden in this plot of ground here between the porch and that tree. One morning I looked out, and damned if the cucumber plant hadn't twined itself around the trunk. Jacob kidded me about growing pickles on a tree. But pretty soon, if he had a problem he needed to think about, I'd find him sitting under that same tree. Then I started sitting under it whenever I was in a pickle. You'd be surprised at the powers that tree has."

With his usual sarcastic snarl, Jimmy said, "God, that's corny."

I poked him in the ribs. "Watch yourself. It's just a family joke, but it means a lot to me."

He rolled his eyes.

Only fifteen people showed up at Sandy's funeral. Oscar and Jimmy and I were three of them. The service was short. The minister hadn't known Sandy. Neither had his daughter, Hannah, for that matter, so there wasn't much of a eulogy. What could they say about him? That he was a stubborn son of a bitch? That could have been real interesting.

I've never had much regard for church. Thing about it

that bothers me most is that you can't be yourself. Everyone puts on their holy airs. They're about as holy as I am, which is not at all. The funeral service was a good example. It had nothing in the world to do with Sandy. Seemed hypocritical to me. Would've been better to say a prayer for him up there on his little part of the world, the part he loved. Instead, we listened to the usual Bible verses and prayers, and gritted our teeth through the wobbly-voiced soprano's version of Abide With Me. Why, Sandy would've had a fit.

Naturally, my mind wandered. I knew Sandy better than anyone else in the church did. I still get embarrassed remembering I actually married him. Loneliness can make you act like a damned fool. A big mistake, that marriage. It lasted only six interminable months. We couldn't stand each other. I kept comparing him to Jacob. Sandy didn't have Jacob's capacity for love, or his sense of humor, or his sexual prowess, for that matter. And Sandy was jealous of my ranch. It was bigger than his. Poor Sandy. What a disappointment I was to him. He wanted a meek and dependent wife, like the one he'd had. I didn't fit the pattern.

When the service was over, Hannah came back to where I was sitting. She's a large motherly woman, the kind of person who makes life run smoothly for everyone around her. She could've been a joy and comfort to that noodle-headed Sandy. Now he'd never know what he missed.

"Thank you for helping my father, Matilda," she said.

"I was just glad I had my first aid kit with me so I could ease his pain. His dog, Angus, wouldn't do very well in town. Would you mind if we kept him? If he'll let us, that is."

"Why, of course. Please do."

"We have him tied up at the ranch. We had quite a time getting him away from Sandy's body."

"Oh, dear." Hannah wiped her eyes. "Poor dog."

I changed the subject, fast. "Since your husband's brother is Cal Lewis, I assume you know Buddy Fast Buffalo Horse."

"Yes. He quite often works with Cal." She looked puzzled.

"Well, he was with us the day your father died. He offered to stay there and take care of the livestock until you decide what to do with the place. I hope that's all right."

"Of course. Buddy's a fine person. It was very kind of him. But I can't imagine that Dad would leave the place to me."

"I'm sure he did. When we were divorced, he signed everything over to you in his will." I didn't tell her that I'd threatened to take him for everything he had if he didn't. "The will should've been filed in the courthouse, since it was part of the divorce agreement. Perhaps you'd better look into it."

After the graveside service, I took Jimmy over to show him where Daniel and Emma's headstones were. He didn't have much to say. I figured he'd had just about enough, thanks.

Oscar had gone to pick up some supplies, so I took Jimmy over to the courthouse. It's still a mighty handsome building, stone from Idaho mountains on the outside, and Italian marble floors on the inside.

"This is where your great-grandfather held down his one and only steady job." I laughed. "He'd brain me if he could hear that."

Jimmy gawked at the sign over the water fountain. "Don't

spit tobacco juice in this fountain." Astounded, he read it again. "You mean people would actually do that?"

"Believe it. Tobacco chewers are a miserable lot."

We went outside and I pointed at the brick building across the street. "That was the hotel where Timothy stayed. Lots of salesmen and travelers stopped here because of our fine hotel. It's a bank now, with offices upstairs where the guestrooms were." He didn't seem impressed, so I walked him over to the Pine Cone Cafe. It isn't called that anymore, but I think it should be.

"This is the cafe I told you about, where Emma did the cooking and Valina waited on tables." We looked in the window and I pointed at the counter. "That's where Valina and Daniel first laid eyes on Timothy."

He perked up a bit. "Is this the way it was back then?"

"Pretty much." I pointed at the red and white sign right over our heads. "Of course, some damned fool changed the name to Barby's Place. I don't know about you, but that makes me want to puke."

He grinned. "Yeah, man, that's bad."

I pointed at the river on the other side of the road. "At least the Clearwater River looks the same. Remarkable how clear it still is." He didn't even look at it. What did I expect, anyway? He didn't care shucks about that country town or its river.

"Did Emma and Daniel live in this town all their lives?" he asked.

"Yes, they did."

"Why? They could've moved to the city and been near Mom and Grandmother."

I sure as hell wasn't going to get into that can of worms. "They wanted to live here."

"You're kidding. Who'd want to live in a hick town like this?"

"We don't all want to live the same way. To you, The City is an array of choices; to me, it's a prison."

He just shrugged.

Still trying to impress him with the memories in the town, I said, "Up at the end of the street is the house Mary lived in when she and Timothy got married." I led him up the road, determined to give him the flavor of the place if it killed him. Suffocating heat rose form the pavement. The weeds next to the road had dried up long ago. The houses lining the road were all the same — clapboard, small, and weathered.

I pointed at the big gray house on the left. "That's the place where Mary and Timothy set up housekeeping."

He scuffed his feet in the dirt shoulder of the road and gave the house a quick glance.

"It looks shabby now, but it was a showplace back then. Mary thought she'd moved into heaven. You'll see why when we get to the cabin."

I started through the woods. He followed, grumbling with every step. The brush had almost overgrown the road. We fought with the nettles and blackberry bushes that kept reaching out to plague us. I'd soon have to hire someone to cut it back.

Jimmy commenced to act like a fussy baby. "Shit," he snarled, scratching his arms, "I itch all over."

"For God's sake, what's a little itching?"

We glared at each other for a bit, then walked on. I stopped when we came to the clearing. "Here we are."

Jimmy looked at the cabin, then at the grounds around it. "Is someone living here?"

"No."

"But all the bushes and vines have been cut, and the weeds around the cabin have been mowed."

"That's because I own it. I hire someone to keep the underbrush from taking over the cabin."

Jimmy screwed up his face in a disgusted sneer. "Why would you do that? It's a wreck."

"Because . . ." Oh, hell, he wouldn't understand. "Just because."

I gestured for him to follow me and went into the cabin. It smelled musty, but the wood stove was still there, along with the table and broken-down chairs. Jimmy looked around, then slowly went into the bedroom. I followed him. Neither of us said a word. He went back into the other room, saw the ladder to the attic, and began to climb it. I started to warn him about the old wood, but decided to keep my mouth shut.

He stuck his head into the attic, looked around, and said, "This is where the three girls slept, isn't it?"

"Yep."

He climbed back down and walked to the door. "Is the creek still there?"

"Sure. Follow me."

When we stood in the woods by the gurgling stream, Jimmy said, "Man, this is groovy. Valina stretched out in this creek to get cool that time, didn't she?"

"Mm-hmm. On a hot day just like today." Those words of his had just made that miserable damned walk into the cabin worthwhile.

He stretched out on the mossy bank, his head resting on his arms. I sat down near him. We didn't speak for some little time. Memories crowded me . . . Emma standing at the hot stove, her face flushed. Daniel coming in with a string of trout, a big grin on his face. Lord, how I missed them.

Jimmy stood up, went over to the creek, and splashed its cool water on his face. "Is it all right to drink this water?"

I shook my head. "Not anymore. Let's start back. We're due to meet Oscar at the cafe. You can have something to drink there."

I hated to leave the cool peace of the clearing. I felt closer to Daniel and Emma there. Seemed like they were sitting on the bank with us, taking it all in, admiring their great-grandson. Ah, well, it was time to go.

Later, when we got back to the ranch, I went straight to the barn. Oscar was in there with Mattie's Lady.

"How's she doing?" I asked.

"About the same. I don't think it'll be tonight."

"Well, then maybe you'll get the hay baled before she needs us."

"With any luck."

I gave the crew leftovers for dinner and some chocolate cake. Oscar volunteered himself and Jimmy to do the dishes. Jimmy didn't even whine. So I went out and sat on the porch. My back and hips ached something fierce from riding in the jeep on that miserable road.

Later, Jimmy came out and sat down in the chair next to mine. "You always sit out here just before dark," he said.

"Evening's my favorite time of day in summer." The crickets began to play their cheerful tune and the sky turned that eerie blue shade it gets just before dark. The green trees of the mountains had already turned black.

"What are those flickering lights?" Jimmy asked.

"Lightning bugs." I expected a derisive comment, but it didn't come. We watched the sun sink behind the mountain, its quiet shadow turning the green pasture gray. "See those bats darting around up there?"

"Bats?" He scrunched down into his chair and hunched his shoulders.

"They keep the bug populations down," I said. "They're not at all interested in you."

"But they carry rabies."

"Rarely. You ever been acquainted with a rabid bat?"

He rolled his eyes and shook his head.

"Well, let's see . . . you don't like cows, or chickens, or bats, so I doubt you'll go into animal husbandry for a career. What are you interested in?"

"I'm not sure yet. But I won't be a corporate man like my dad."

"Oh? Why not?"

"Because his office is like a cell in a prison. He even wears a uniform: gray suit, white shirt, maroon tie. And he has to answer to a jillion people. I'd go nuts in a place like that."

"I'm sure I would, too."

He looked at me out of the corner of his eye. "Yeah, you would. Look at all the freedom you have here."

Hadn't he learned anything? "Did you happen to notice all the hard work that goes along with that freedom?"

"Well, at least you're your own boss."

"Oh, no. You've got that wrong. The weather is our boss. Nature is ruthless. Why, one winter we had such a freeze that it killed half my cattle. It took five years to make up for that loss. And then there was the year of the big flood. You remember that platform where you got off the train in Pine Bluff?"

"Yeah."

"One year the river flooded and carried the station house away. My husband, Jacob, was one of the people carried away with it."

"Oh." He was quiet for a minute. "When was that?"

"Several years before your Grandmother Mary was born."

The way he looked at me I knew he was thinking that nobody could be as old as I was and still be alive. I often think that myself. We sat on the porch for a while longer, just watching the evening fade. After a bit, I heard Oscar behind me at the screen door. "We're going to play some poker, if you're interested."

"You ever played poker?" I asked Jimmy.

"Isn't that the card game they play in the old western movies where the bad guy always cheats and gets killed?"

He surprised me. "You like westerns?"

"Naw. My dad's the one who's nuts about them. He watches them on TV."

"I had a TV once, but I gave it away."

He moaned. "Why'd you do a thing like that? It sure would've helped break the monotony around here."

"We couldn't get reception worth a damn. Besides, after I saw what was offered on the fool thing, I couldn't see the point in having it."

But Jimmy's remark had set me to thinking. He was awfully young to be stuck in the mountains with four old people. A lot to ask of a kid his age, especially a city kid. For the first time, I realized that the boredom might be harder for him than all the work. I stood up and started for the kitchen door. "Come on. Let's see if you can learn to play poker."

When we'd all settled in at the kitchen table, I told the boy that we played for high stakes. "White chips are worth a penny, the red a nickel, and the blue a dime."

Buck and George stared when Jimmy took a twenty dollar bill out of his pocket and slapped it on the table and asked for change. I knew they felt dead certain that they were playing with a high roller.

Two hours later Jimmy won his first pot and we shut down the game. He'd spent the whole time looking bored, but I was on to him. A bright kid, that one. The men all went up to bed, but Jimmy stayed at the kitchen table putting away the chips and counting his money.

"That was fun," he said.

Well, well. His first sweet words.

When I woke up early the next morning, I knew a storm was brewing. My corns were giving me fits. I got into my clothes as fast as my aching bones would let me, and went out in the hall and yelled for the men to get their butts in gear.

"Got to bale the hay quick. A storm's coming."

The men hit the kitchen within ten minutes, and my

special omelet, the one with onion and dillweed, was waiting for them, along with buttered toast and coffee.

Jimmy, who groaned every morning when he had to get up, finally dragged himself downstairs after the men were almost finished with breakfast. He stomped into the kitchen, buttoning his shirt in the wrong holes. His uncombed hair reminded me of a patch of tall grass that had gone to seed. When he tripped on his untied shoelaces, his disposition went from bad to worse.

"What the hell storm are you talking about?" he growled. "Look at all that blue sky out there."

"Matilda knows," Oscar said, "so keep a civil tongue in your head."

"She knows what?" Jimmy sneered at Oscar, then turned a glare on me. "She just wanted to get us out of bed earlier than usual."

I opened my mouth to give the kid the devil, but I didn't get a chance. Just then, George spoke up. Everyone pays attention when that happens.

"Matilda knows when her corns ache we'll have a storm," he said. "She's never been wrong."

"Bullshit." Jimmy stuck out his jaw. "That's the stupidest thing I ever heard."

"Sit down and eat," Oscar roared. "When we go out that door you're going with us, breakfast or no breakfast."

Jimmy, wide-eyed and speechless, sat, and gulped down his breakfast. When the men stood up to leave, Jimmy stuffed a piece of toast in his shirt pocket and followed them out the door, nearly stepping on Oscar's heels.

I put some cool wet rags on my toes to ease the pain and fretted a bit while I drank a second cup of coffee. I felt bad for Oscar. I had expected way too much of him. Why should he be saddled with the boy?

The telephone rang and I figured, what with the way the morning had started, it had to be Jessica. She'd been so riled up when she called before she was bound to call again. Sure enough, I was right.

"I thought all night about the hard work you're expecting Jimmy to do," she said, getting right to the point. "It's inhumane. He's just a boy."

I wanted to tell her she was full of crap, but if I did, she'd yank the kid right back home, and Bob wouldn't have a chance in hell of stopping her. So I just said, "Jessica, you need to talk to your husband about that."

A mighty chilly silence followed, then, "Let me speak to Jimmy, please."

"He's out baling hay."

"And I suppose he's too far away to come to the telephone." Her voice was tight with sarcasm.

"That's right."

"Ask him to call me as soon as he gets back, please." She was as mad as a hornet-stung bull. Darned fool woman was out to undermine her own husband, to say nothing of her son. Nothing I could do about it, either. The kid would just have to figure it out for himself.

I went out to put Mattie's Lady in the pasture near the barn. She needed a little grazing time before the storm hit. She was happy to see me, so I petted her for a while and told her how great she was. That foal of hers was sure taking its sweet time coming into the world.

The men had already stopped baling hay when I drove up with their lunch. I knew the baler had broken down again, because Oscar's face was purple.

"Goddamn thing breaks down every time we hay," he snarled.

I knew better than to say a word. So did Buck and George, not that they would anyway. They came over to the jeep and started pawing through the box of food.

Jimmy sidled up to me and said, "Not a cloud in the sky, is there?"

Orville, who'd showed up just as the men were going out to the field, walked by on his way to the food. He shook his head as he went by Jimmy. Was he agreeing with him, or feeling sorry for him? I couldn't tell, and the kid sure didn't notice.

"Just pray that you get through haying before the storm starts," I said.

He smirked. Little brat knew he'd riled me. He strutted over to the back of my jeep to get some lunch. I turned just in time to see the shock on his face when he saw the heat lightening off to the west.

That's when Oscar got the baler going again. "Forget lunch," he yelled. "We haven't much time."

I had a good laugh, driving home.

An hour later, here came Oscar driving the baler, Buck and Jimmy in the jeep, and George and Orville on the loaded hayrack. By God, they'd finished before the storm hit. They parked the hayrack in the barn just as the rain started. I was about to go put Mattie's Lady in the barn, when Oscar saw her and did it for me. He even rounded up Aussie and shut him in the barn, too.

I hate to think about how much I need Oscar on the ranch. There's so much I can't do anymore. He's been with me ever since he was seventeen. Only two years older than Jimmy is now, but what a difference. Oscar was a country boy. He knew all about hard work.

I watched him go over to the sweet gum tree and untie Angus. He led him over to me. "Want me to put him in the kitchen?" he asked.

"Might be a good idea. No telling how he feels about thunderstorms." The poor dog had given up barking, but he still hadn't eaten much.

We all sat on the porch, the men wolfing down ham sandwiches and drinking a big pitcher of lemonade I'd just mixed up. Jimmy gave his crusts to Roscoe, who'd spent the whole day on the porch.

Oscar glanced at Jimmy, then said, "That wet stuff out there can't be rain, can it George?"

"Nope. Can't be rain." George said.

Buck grunted and Orville brayed that awful laugh of his.

Jimmy squirmed in his chair. "Okaaay . . . so I was wrong, so what?"

Oscar glared at the kid. "So you owe your Aunt Matilda an apology."

Out of the corner of my eye I could see Jimmy dart a quick look at me, like he was hoping I'd say he didn't need to bother, but I kept my mouth shut. He looked at Oscar again, then back at me. He ducked his head, his eyes aimed at the floor.

"Oh, all right. I'm sorry, Aunt Matilda."

"I accept your apology. But some opinions are better kept to ourselves, aren't they?"

"If you say so."

Lightning crackled over by the barn. No other sight or sound like that in the world. Always makes the hair on my arms stand straight up. I looked over to see how Jimmy had reacted.

"Wow," he said.

The thunder rolled and thumped a good one. A big grin lit up his face. "This is cool."

"Maybe so, but lightning is mean stuff," I said.

"You think I'm stupid?" Jimmy's mouth curled in disgust. "I know lightning's dangerous."

He had the nastiest way of saying things. Oscar caught my eye and gave his head a little shake, like he couldn't stand to hear another word from the kid. I nodded to let him know I agreed with him. God, I felt guilty, foisting that brat off on those poor men.

We sat there and watched a wall of water stream down from the roof of the porch. Couldn't see a blessed thing out in the yard. Not even the porch steps. A godawful crack of thunder rolled right over our heads, so loud it hurt my ears. And a bit later it sounded like the house had been split in two by the loudest screaming shriek of lightning I'd ever heard. We all sat, frozen, except for poor old Roscoe. He bolted under my chair, whining and shaking as if he'd seen the devil himself.

I looked over at Jimmy. He was staring straight ahead, his mouth slightly ajar.

Too bad I didn't have a camera with me right then.

Oscar stood up. "It hit something, Mattie. I'd better go see . . ."

"Don't even try," I snapped. "If something's on fire, this rain will control it better than we could. Wait until the storm has passed."

After a bit we could hear the storm move over the mountain. The smell of scorched wood filled the air. We all saw it at the same time, the jagged black scar winding around a big oak tree. A large part of the tree lay sprawled on the ground like a twisted body. I mourned for the oak, though I was glad the sweet gum tree had been spared. But that oak tree wasn't more than forty feet from the porch.

"If it'd been just a bit closer, we'd have been fried," I said.

In all the excitement, I'd almost forgotten Jessica's phone call. She'd have a tizzy fit if she didn't hear from her little boy. "Your mother phoned again this morning," I said. "She wants you to call her."

He didn't act too happy about it, but he started into the kitchen. I stopped him. "Not a good idea to be on the phone during a lightning storm. Might wait a few more minutes."

From the way he rolled his eyes, I guess he thought that was just another stupid superstition, but he came back out on the porch and sat down fast enough. When we could barely hear the next roll of thunder, Jimmy asked, "Can I call her now and get it over with?"

"Go ahead."

The line wasn't busy for a change. He got long distance right away. We could hear him say, "I'm fine. How are you?"

He'd gotten his mother all right. Seemed like a full minute before he could get a word in, though.

"Mom, I made a bargain with Dad."

Oscar raised his eyebrows at me and we waited another long spell.

"I said I made a bargain."

Looked like we might have the kid through the summer, after all. But did we really want him?

He didn't wait long to break into her next tirade. "Dinner's ready, Mom. I have to say goodbye now. Talk to you later."

Dinner? It was the middle of the afternoon. I wondered if Jessica Marie had figured that out yet.

When Jimmy came back to the porch, Oscar and George and Buck went into the house. Orville lingered.

"If you don't need me anymore, I'll head back to town," he said.

"You got work somewhere else?"

"Huh-uh. Why?" he asked.

"Sandy's hay never did get cut. Bet we could salvage some of it, in spite of the rain. You interested?"

His eyes lit up. "I'm always interested in money."

"I'll go call Buddy, see if he can help out." I stood up, waited for my hips to get the idea I was about to walk, then headed into the kitchen.

By God, the party line still wasn't busy. I let the phone

ring about fifteen times. I was ready to hang up, when Buddy answered the thing. He agreed to help with the haying the next day.

I went back out on the porch. "Buddy will help you. And I'll send along Buck and Jimmy. With the four of you, that'd be enough help for the amount of hay you'll find."

"Good deal," Orville said.

"I'll pay you for both jobs when you're done."

Orville nodded and headed for the bunkhouse.

Out of the corner of my eye, I could see Jimmy glaring at me, but I ignored the kid. Don't suppose he was too thrilled about doing some more haying. Too bad. I leaned back in my chair, let the cool air soak into my skin, and admired the bright green of the wet pasture. Nothing like a summer rain. And my corns had stopped aching. But, wouldn't you know, when I was all set to relax, Jimmy started talking. "You said there were times when the family almost starved. If you're so great, why didn't you help them?"

Swear to God, every time I got the idea the kid might be coming around, he'd revert to his nasty little self. Made me damned mad to have a snot nosed, marijuana smoking brat judging me.

"Emma and my brother were too proud to ask for help, a quality that's missing in your generation, I'm afraid. Little Rachel let it slip once, but even then, Emma absolutely wouldn't take any help. Of course, I found ways to get around that once in a while."

He started to say something, but changed his mind.

"Besides," I said, "helping isn't always a good idea. I got Daniel a job once. Turned out to be a big mistake."

"You? Made a mistake?"

There was that damned tone of voice again, "I've been wrong in my life. Quite a few times." And one of my worst mistakes was sitting right there beside me.

CHAPTER 4

Pine Bluff—1929

The women waiting in front of the cafe stared at the third man who'd come back from the fire with Bill and Lester. There on the horse with Bill Palmer sat Mr. O'Callahan, blood all over his face and shirt, his arms hanging limp, his head lolling to one side. Bill had tied a rope around both their waists. Valina thought it was a good thing he had, or Mr. O'Callahan would have fallen off. She shuddered.

Without a word, Bill and Lester rode on past the cafe to Doc's office on the next block. Valina and a sober group of women and children followed them. When the two men helped Mr. O'Callahan off the horse and into Doc's office, the group waited in silence in front of the building. It wasn't long before Bill and Lester came back outside.

"I know you're anxious for news," Bill said. "Mr. O'Callahan's the only man who's been hurt. Emma, your Daniel saved him not once, but twice. First, he shoved him out of the way of a falling tree, and just in time, too. The tree was on fire. Would've burned Mr. O'Callahan to a crisp."

Mama squeezed Valina's hand so hard it brought tears to her eyes.

"Then, not long after that, Mr. O'Callahan lost his footing and fell down the face of the mountain," Bill said. "All that stopped him was scrub brush and a rock ledge. He's a mighty lucky man."

The women gasped and Lester broke in. "The men said Daniel tied a rope around one of the trees and went down that cliff just like a mountain goat. He wrapped a rope sling around Timothy and damned if Daniel didn't start climbing back up, while the men above pulled the rope. No one could believe the way he scaled that mountain, and he was guiding Timothy's body at the same time."

Valina heard Mama whisper. "Thank you God."

Then Bill Palmer said, "They've got the fire at bay but it's still far from out. The best news is that the wind isn't blowing our way right now."

A collective sigh of relief followed his words, but Valina wondered how badly Mr. O'Callahan was hurt. His face had looked pasty white and sort of blank, as if he wasn't really conscious even though his eyes were open. She realized that everyone was waiting to hear how badly injured he was. But would anyone let them know?

Catherine seemed to read her mind. "I'm going in and find out the extent of Mr. O'Callahan's injuries."

Even the children kept quiet until she came back, and then everyone clustered around her.

"He's very badly bruised and he has deep gashes on his head and left arm, but he'll be all right. He'll stay in the infirmary at least overnight."

Valina relaxed. It felt good to have something to smile

about for a change, even though the smoke from the fire was still hovering over them like an evil veil.

· · ·

At noon the next day, when Ben and Tillie came in to pick up the week's cash, Tillie sent Valina to the infirmary with some lunch for Mr. O'Callahan.

"You don't need to hurry, Valina," Tillie said. "I'll take over the counter while Ben goes to the bank."

Tillie had covered the tray with a clean dish towel. The town was so dry that the dust flew in the air from just a footstep or two. The shrubs along the road were covered with the dust and hard to identify. It was even hard to see the hawthorn and mock orange, which grew higher than the flat kinnikinnick. Valina coughed. She was weary of the heat and the dust and the smoke.

At the infirmary's front stoop, she balanced the tray on her left arm and opened the door with her right hand. The building was an old store that Doc had remodeled years ago. The outside still looked like a store, but on the inside it was a small hospital. You could even get an X-ray in there. The walls and woodwork were white, with beige linoleum on the floors. And Catherine had made white curtains for the windows, which looked meticulously clean.

Minnie rushed over to take the tray from Valina and set it on a table next to Timothy's bed.

Valina whispered. "How's he doing?"

Minnie kept her voice low. "He's asleep."

"No, I'm not." He sounded like he'd swallowed sandpaper. He opened his eyes and looked around the room. "What is this place?"

"Its the town's hospital, such as it is. Lucky for you it's here," Minnie said. "You lost a lot of blood."

"Every time I doze off, I dream I'm falling down a mountain."

"That's exactly what you did," Valina said.

He stared at her. "Is that a fact?"

She nodded. "Bill Palmer and Lester said you fell down the face of the mountain. You landed on a rocky ledge. Papa climbed down and brought you back up."

"Your Papa did that for me, Valina?"

"That's what they said."

Minnie interrupted. "Time for lunch." When she helped him sit up he winced from the pain. "Hurt all over don't you? It's no wonder," Minnie said. "You've bruised every blessed inch of yourself. Doc couldn't believe you didn't break a bone or two. What you need is some nourishment, and then a long nap."

"Can I stay while he eats?" Valina asked.

"Sure. See to it that he eats every bite of it. I've got to go help Doc. Be back in a minute."

Valina sat on one of the other beds and watched him wolf down the food. He caught her eye and they both laughed.

"Think my manners are poor? Have a little mercy. I'm a starving man."

"I'm just glad you're feeling well enough to eat. My stomach did a flip-flop when I saw you covered with all that blood." She cringed at her lack of tact. Not exactly the right thing to say to him, especially when he was eating.

He looked up at her. "You're sweet to care about me, Valina. I'm not used to that."

Not used to it? Even with a bandaged head and bruised face, he was handsome. What woman wouldn't care? And certainly Papa had cared about him enough to risk his own life to save him.

After he finished eating, she took the tray from him and put it by the front door. He groaned as he struggled to lie down.

She hurried over to him. "Here, let me help you."

He sighed, "Gladly."

"Just lean against me," she said.

He groaned again and put his arm around her waist as she lowered him. His arm stayed there, even after his head settled onto the pillow. His eyes didn't leave hers. "You can help me lie down any time, Valina, any time at all."

She pulled away, flustered. Better get back to work before she made a fool of herself. When she left she could still feel the warmth of his arm around her waist.

It took four more days of battling the fire before all the men could leave Dead Man's Canyon. When they finally got home, most of them slept for twenty-four hours straight through. Then the pace of life went back to normal. Papa went fishing and the regulars at the cafe talked about the fire. Valina was sure a topic like that would be good for at least a year. And each time Mr. O'Callahan came in, just looking at him reminded them of Papa's heroism.

"Yes, sir," Herb Johnson would say each time, "when Daniel started skipping down that mountain, I thought he was a goner, for sure."

Then Dogie would shake his head and say, "But the way he climbed back up while pulling Mr. O'Callahan with him. I still can't believe it."

It pleased Valina that Papa had been an-honest-to-goodness hero, but he was still out of a job. And right now, anybody in town would hire him. She was pretty sure this was the first time people had ever had a good opinion of him. Papa could make use of that. She hoped he would.

About then, Bertha Wilcox got in one of her nasty little digs. "Your papa's a big hero, now, huh? Hard to believe he'd go to all that trouble, since he's not exactly an ambitious sort."

Valina couldn't stand it. "Mrs. Wilcox, my father's a good man. I'd really appreciate it if you'd quit talking about him the way you do." She thought Bertha's eyes would pop right out of her head.

"Well. I'm sure I don't know what you mean by that sassy remark, young lady."

Valina stared Bertha down. "More coffee, Mrs. Wilcox? Oh, that's right. It gives you gas, doesn't it?"

The instant Bertha slammed the door behind her, the regulars began to hoot.

"Good for you, Valina," Herb said. "It's about time someone stood up to that old biddy." Everyone else smiled and nodded agreement.

On Monday morning, Mr. O'Callahan came into the cafe. When he sat down on a stool at the counter Valina poured him a cup of coffee. She tried to avoid looking at the long angry scar on his forehead.

"Came in to say goodbye," he said.

"Do you feel well enough to travel yet? You still look pale."

"I've got to get to work, but I should be back in about a week or ten days."

Well, at least she'd get to see him one more time. "I've decided to make Pine Bluff my home base," he said.

"You mean it?"

He grinned at her. "Sure do. Not every town has a man in it who would risk his life for me. Thought maybe your papa and I could go hunting in the fall."

"I'm sure he'd like that." It didn't look like Papa would have a job anyway.

Mr. O'Callahan put a quarter on the counter and stood up. "And Valina, you keep the riff-raff out of here until I get back." He winked at her, then turned and walked out the door.

At noon, Paul Bradford came in and sat at the counter. Valina hadn't seen him since he'd come home. An unruly lock of dark hair on his forehead made her smile. Seemed like it was always hanging there just above his eyes, brown eyes a person could trust. He wasn't a fancy dresser like Timothy, but she thought his plaid shirt and cotton slacks suited his tall lanky frame.

"You expecting Mary?" she asked. The strange look on his face puzzled her.

"No," he said, "are you?"

"Not really." She handed him a menu and got him a glass of water, then waited for his order.

"I'll have a bacon and tomato sandwich and a cup of coffee." He closed the menu and handed it to her. "Understand you got the best of Bertha Wilcox."

"Nobody ever gets the best of her. I did get in a few good licks, but how did you hear about it?"

"Oh, you know how this town is. Word gets around fast."

"Too true." She smiled at him and went to place his order. When she was five, Mama had told her that Catherine and Doc would finish raising Paul, who had just turned nine, because his parents had died in an accident. It became Valina's project to cheer him up. For starters, she took him some wild daisies she'd picked. They probably embarrassed him, but he was gracious about it. Once in a while, she took him one of Mama's cinnamon rolls. No matter how messy it looked from being clutched in her hand, he always thanked her and ate it right away.

But one time she found him crying. She patted his hand, told him everything would be all right, and that they all loved him. Most boys would have been mortified, but not Paul. He thanked her. Even at the tender age of nine, he had been a gentleman. Later on when everyone, even Mama, said he was bound to marry her older sister, Valina reluctantly gave up her romantic fantasies about him. Maybe if there'd never been a Mary, things might have been different. She poured him a cup of coffee. "How does it feel, being a college graduate?"

"Feels great. Doc and Aunt Catherine want me to take a couple of months off before I move to Portland."

"You're going that soon? We'll all miss you." He must be planning on proposing to Mary right away.

"Oh, I'll be back every so often. I couldn't abandon Aunt Catherine and Doc. Not only that." He looked up at Valina. "I'll miss . . ." He looked at her as if he were sending her a special message. "I'll miss everybody."

He looked as if he cared about her, especially. If only he did. Embarrassed, she looked around the room. "Oops. I've forgotten some of my customers." She went over to give menus to Miss Furman and Mrs. Sampson, Mary's supervisor over at Osborne's.

"I see Paul over there at the counter," Mrs. Sampson said. "Too bad I'm taking lunch now instead of Mary. Not wishing Paul and Mary don't get together, but I'll hate to lose that girl. She's a genius with a needle and thread."

Oh, goodie. Now, Mary wasn't just beautiful, she was a genius. Valina bit her tongue. If Mama knew how she felt about Mary she'd be upset.

When she went into the kitchen to place the orders for the two women, Margaret looked up from her pie dough, and said, "If you see Ben before I do, would you tell him I need to talk to him right away?"

"Sure." Valina started to make a crack about wedding bells, but thought maybe since Margaret had waited so long to get married, that she might not appreciate any flip remarks.

Valina went back into the other room, poured Paul some more coffee and went over to see if Spike wanted any. He grinned at her. The sight of his tobacco stained teeth always turned her stomach. Just as she started filling his cup, he patted her bottom and some of the coffee spilled onto his leg.

"Ow," he roared. "Be careful where you pour that stuff."

"Then you'd better be careful where you put your hands, Mr. Washburn." She held the coffee pot over his head.

Suddenly, Paul stood beside her, his jaw rigid. "You're not to touch Valina again, ever."

From the other side of the room, Herb yelled. "That's right, Spike. You leave that girl alone."

"I didn't mean anything by it."

Herb walked over to the table, grabbed Spike's elbow and pushed him toward the door. "Let me explain what trouble . . ."

Paul, still looking like he wanted to bash in Spike's face, went back to his coffee. Valina pulled herself together and served the orders for the now speechless women.

"Can I get you anything else?" she asked.

They shook their heads, still mute, so she went over and sat on a stool by Paul.

"Thank you. It was nice of you to stick up for me."

"You didn't think I'd let Spike get away with that, did you? No one should treat you that way, and they won't if I'm around."

She didn't know what to say. Why was she so tongue-tied?

"I'd better get going," Paul drank the last of his coffee. "I promised to do some yard work for Aunt Catherine. See you later."

"Yes. Thanks, again."

He smiled and left. Wistfully, she watched him until he was out of sight. Paul Bradford was such a fine person. Mary would be a half-baked fool to turn him down. She rubbed her eyes. Even though the fire had been out for several days, the stench hadn't left the cafe. The foul air of smoke and old grease didn't seem to bother the regulars, but they didn't have to stay in there all day. She went over to the sink behind the counter and splashed some cold water on her face.

The afternoon dragged on. At three, Ben Hillyard came in.

"Margaret said to tell you that she needs to talk to you right away," Valina told him.

"Oh? Wonder what that's about?" He headed for the kitchen. And just as Valina thought seriously about eavesdropping, that darned little brat, Roy Bailey, came in for a creme soda. She didn't dare let him out of her sight.

Early the next morning, Valina heard Aunt Matilda downstairs talking to Mama. Curious, she got out of bed and got dressed. No need to waken Mary and Rachel. Especially Mary. She wasn't fond of Aunt Matilda. Didn't like anything about her, in fact.

Whenever Aunt Matilda came to town, she wore buckskin culottes, high-laced boots, a man's plaid shirt, and a wide-brimmed man's hat. Her appearance embarrassed Mary, but Valina thought the outfit suited Aunt Matilda very well. Besides, their widowed aunt was a remarkable woman. She ran a ranch up in the high country. Papa always said he was sure his sister could terrify a hungry cougar into submission. Valina didn't doubt it a bit. Aunt Matilda wasn't just any ordinary woman. She also wasn't the kind of person you hugged. No sir. Not a woman who owned a big two-story house on all those thousands of acres and bossed three hired men around.

When Valina climbed down the ladder, Mama was pouring a cup of coffee for Aunt Matilda. "This is a nice surprise, Mattie," she said.

Valina knew Mama was waiting for Aunt Matilda to explain why she was there.

"I need to talk to Daniel."

"Oh."

Papa got cross if anyone woke him too early, but Valina knew Aunt Matilda wouldn't put up with that sort of nonsense.

"Good morning, Aunt Matilda." Valina thought she'd better get that in before the fur started to fly.

Aunt Matilda looked at her and said, "Nice to see that some members of this family get up at a decent hour."

Mama sighed and went in the bedroom to wake up Papa.

"What in the blazes does she want at this ungodly hour?"

His voice sounded muffled. Did Mama have her hand over his mouth? Would she do that? Aunt Matilda settled herself in a chair, crossed her arms over her chest, and grinned.

Papa, feet bare, hair mussed, eyes snapping, stalked into the room. Valina had a cup of coffee ready for him. He scowled at her, but took the coffee and sat down across from Aunt Matilda. "Well, my dear sister, what brings you down off the mountain at this ungodly time of day?"

"I heard about a job you could have cooking in the logging camp upriver from my place." She leaned back in her chair, long legs sprawled out in front of her.

Papa took a large gulp of coffee. "And how long would this job last, dear sister?" he asked through clenched teeth.

"Till the season's over, of course. Why do you ask?"

Papa took another gulp of coffee and cleared his throat. "Well, I have a few other possibilities for permanent work here in town."

"If anything else turned up we could get word to you." Mama said. "At least there'd be money coming in, Daniel."

Papa stared at her. Valina could tell he hadn't expected Mama to side with Aunt Matilda. It made Valina furious that he could even consider not taking the job. "Papa, you're a good cook. I bet they'd hire you in a minute."

Aunt Matilda hooted. "He doesn't even have to be a good cook. They're desperate."

Papa looked over at Mama. "Well, I could look into it, I guess."

Aunt Matilda stood up. "Good. Get your things together, Daniel. I brought one of the mares with me. You can ride her."

"In heaven's name, woman. I can't leave that soon."

"Of course you can. They need you right now."

"Valina, go get Papa's clothes ready," Mama said, "while I pack them a lunch."

Valina dashed into the bedroom, got out the worn canvas bag, and started packing. She could hear every word Papa said.

"What is this, a conspiracy? You, Emma. Seems like you're pushing me right out the door. Even Valina is. What's going on here?"

Valina held her breath.

"Daniel, you know how desperately we need the money."

Thank goodness, Valina thought. For once, Mama held her ground.

In a more subdued voice, Papa said, "But how will you manage?"

"We'll be fine, just fine. Really we will."

After a long silence, Papa said, "Very well, my dear, if you say so. Satisfied, Matilda?" His voice sounded ugly. "I'll go water the horses."

"Good idea," Aunt Matilda said. "They could stand a little care before we go back up the mountain. Here, Emma, let me give you a hand with that lunch."

"Thank you for helping us, Mattie." Mama's voice sounded shaky. "You're a good woman."

"And you are the best. But that lazy brother of mine is another story. I hate seeing you living in this hand-to-mouth existence. Look at this place. Some of those chairs don't even have backs on them. What the hell does your family sit on? It's not fair. You know darned well your girls don't have the things they need."

"I know," Mama said. "I worry about it a lot. But at least they have love. And Daniel's a good man. You know that."

Valina could tell that Mama was crying.

"I'm sorry, Emma," Aunt Matilda said. "I never can keep my mouth shut. But, honestly now, are you going to have enough food?"

"We'll be fine. Mary and Valina have jobs. They don't get paid much, but at least it's something. And I'm sewing and ironing for some folks."

Valina went into the kitchen when she heard Papa come back into the cabin. "The horses are ready," he growled. "We can leave any time."

"I'll take those things, Valina," Aunt Matilda took the canvas bag and Papa's boots. "Take good care of your mother. Daniel, get the lunch."

Mama gave the sack to Papa, then kissed him goodbye and walked with him to the door.

When Papa reached out his arm to Valina, a sad, hollow feeling came over her and she went to him.

Aunt Matilda turned her horse toward the mountains and yelled, "Come on, Daniel. Got to get up that mountain before it gets too darned hot."

Papa mounted the mare and waved at them. Valina put her arm around Mama. They watched as Papa and Aunt Matilda disappeared into the woods. The early morning air felt cool on Valina's bare arms. Suddenly she realized that the awful smoke was truly gone.

"Mama, can I go down to the creek for a bit? The smoke's gone and I want to be in the woods and just breathe for a few minutes."

Mama nodded. "Go ahead, but don't be gone long."

Valina thought that Mama might want a few minutes alone, too. As she walked, she heard the usual rustling in the surrounding undergrowth of the woods. A startled blackbird flew out of the clump of hawthorn next to the path, and a squirrel darted in front of her then flipped back into the woods. When she got to the creek she sat on a rock beside it. She could breathe again, and it smelled like a delicious mixture of pine and cedar and warm brown earth.

In the alterations room at Osborne's, Mary finished shortening a red satin dress, a dress as flashy as the woman who'd bought it, Zoe Adams. Zoe, with her questionable reputation, had walked into Osborne's just as if she belonged there.

Though aghast at having to wait on a woman like her, Mrs. Sampson had been pleased when she bought the dress.

"At least we've sold the horrid thing," she said, as she handed it to Mary to be hemmed.

Zoe had insisted that she wanted it shorter, above her knees. Mary knew the styles were short, but a dress that short on a thirty-year-old woman? Disgusting. And red with Zoe's orange-red hair? Just thinking about it made Mary nauseous. Mrs. Sampson had laughed and said, "She claims that her father, Cooley, gave her the money for the dress. Why, everyone in town knows how Zoe makes a living. Besides, Cooley is nothing but a drunk who never has a cent, though he certainly manages to get hold of his liquor somehow."

Mary thought prohibition was a joke. People who wanted liquor either made their own or bought it at the Spar Pole, while the sheriff just turned his back. Those who obeyed the law didn't drink anyway. She wouldn't go near a place like the Spar Pole, but she would like to go to one of those swanky gin mills in New York where the women wore expensive furs and jewels, and the men were handsome and rich.

Lost in thought, Mary jumped at the sound of footsteps on the stairs. Mrs. Sampson again. "There's a gentleman here to see you, Mary. He's waiting over by men's overcoats."

"A gentleman?" Mary asked.

"Indeed he is." Mrs. Sampson raised her eyebrows and winked at Mary.

"Thank you, Mrs. Sampson." Who on earth? It couldn't be Papa. Maybe Paul? He was sure to ask her to marry him any day now, but she hadn't made up her mind yet. Not handsome, but nice looking, Paul did have money. Still, she didn't want to live in Portland, Oregon. She wanted to live in a real city like New York or San Francisco. Of course, Paul was the best choice of the men in Pine Bluff. He was the only choice. Loggers certainly didn't interest her, and she would never consider being a rancher's wife. Everyone said she looked like Mary Pickford, and she didn't intend to waste her looks in Pine Bluff, or Portland either, for that matter.

When she saw Mr. O'Callahan standing next to overcoats, it occurred to her that she might have another choice after all. He'd made it obvious that he was attracted to her. No surprise there. My, he did look stylish. She couldn't imagine Paul in knickers and a V-necked sweater. He was so tall he'd look ridiculous, but Mr. O'Callahan's build looked perfect in them.

His eyes skimmed her body. "Good afternoon, Mary."

"Why Mr. O'Callahan. I didn't think we'd ever see you again, considering the awful experience you had here. How are you feeling?"

"Fine, now that I've seen you."

His glazed expression amused her. She gave him one of her radiant smiles and gloated over the obvious effect it had on him. She'd made a sophisticated man from New York blush. How interesting. What else could she make him do?

"What time do you get off work, Mary?"

"Six o'clock. Why?"

"Could I give you a ride home?"

She paused, as if she needed to give his request careful consideration. "Why, I guess so. Yes, that would be nice."

"Six o'clock it is, then. I'll be outside in my car."

She would put Paul off for a while and see how it went with Mr. O'Callahan. He obviously had money. Maybe she could even talk him into going back to New York to live. Besides, he was attractive, and he stirred something in her, something she needed to explore. A girl had to look out for herself, after all.

Not five minutes later, Mr. O'Callahan, greeted warmly by the usual crowd at the Pine Cone Cafe, found a stool at the counter. "Hi, there, Valina," he said. "How about a cup of coffee?"

She poured the coffee as she peered at the scar on his head. "Looks better. You're back sooner than I expected."

He brushed her hand as he reached for the sugar. "Your papa gone fishing?"

"No. He has a job cooking in a logging camp. Started a few days ago."

"Is that right? Will he be home this weekend?"

"I doubt it. He's probably stuck up there for a while." She missed Papa. Other than fighting the fire, he'd never been away before, except when he went hunting, and then only overnight. She could tell that Mama missed him too, something fierce, though she tried not to let on.

"Well, in that case, do the Addison women need any masculine assistance?" he asked.

"Thank you, but we're managing okay." Without Papa in the house, Valina knew Mama wouldn't think it was a good idea to have Mr. O'Callahan there.

"You get off at four, don't you? That's just half-an-hour

from now. Why don't you let me take you home? Maybe there's something I could do to help out."

"Well . . . okay." How could she turn down such a kind offer? But what would Mama say?

Later, when Timothy helped her into the car, his hand brushed against her breast. She jerked away, shocked. The touch of his fingers had made her nipple harden. She could have died right then and there. Did it show? She glanced down quickly at her blouse. It didn't. She forced herself to breathe slowly.

He didn't say a word until he drove through town and stopped the car in the woods. "I'm sorry I touched you," he said. "It was an accident. Still, I'm feeling guilty, and I'm sure you know why."

"What do you mean?"

"I want you. You do things to me. Unfortunately, I'm too old for you. But if I were younger . . ."

"You're not too old. I am seventeen, after all." Why had she said that? Now he'd think she was bold. "Oh, dear. I shouldn't have said that. I'm so embarrassed."

"Don't be, please." He patted her hand, then looked at her and sighed. "I'd better get you home."

She tried to calm down. Mama would be unhappy enough when she saw one of her daughters in Mr. O'Callahan's car, to say nothing of how she'd feel if her daughter looked all red and flustered.

When they drove up to the cabin, Mama was out by the woodpile, gathering wood for the fire.

"Here, let me do that." Mr. O'Callahan was at Mama's side before Valina could get out of the car. "I understand Daniel has a job up in the woods. Looks like you could use a little help here. Tell you what. I'll pick up some steaks for dinner, then come back and chop a pile of wood for you."

Mama had a hard time taking it all in. "Really, Mr. O'Callahan, we can manage."

He stood firm. "Ma'am, I'd consider it a great favor if you'd allow me to help you. Your husband saved my life."

Valina put her hand over her mouth to hide her smile. She didn't think Mama had much choice after what Timothy had said.

Mama's tentative smile was all he needed. "Great. I'll wait to come back until Mary gets off, if that's all right? So she can have a ride home. What's her quitting time?"

"Well." Mama's eyes blinked fast when she got nervous. "Six o'clock."

"Swell." He took the armload of wood into the house, then bounded back down the steps and went over to his car. "See you later."

Mama opened her mouth to say something, but it was too late. He'd already started the car.

When Timothy picked her up at six, Mary knew that her blonde hair and ecru dress looked elegant against the dark upholstery of his car. She crossed her legs, slowly, pleased with the luster of her silk hose. She smiled when he had a hard time dragging his eyes away from her legs.

"Aren't you going to start the car?" she said. When he looked up she teased him with her eyes.

He grinned at her. "You really have sex appeal, girl. Maybe more than your share."

She laughed. "That's a fine thing to say."

"Is there a possibility you'd share it with me?" He put his hand on her knee.

She uncrossed her legs and his hand fell to the seat. "Mr. O'Callahan, I'm not easy, if that's what you mean." She turned her face to the window at her side. Well, the hook had been set. This could be her way out of this awful hick town. A glorious thought.

"I didn't mean to insult you."

"You must admit we hardly know each other." She kept her face toward the window.

"Well, how do I get to know you better, Mary?"

She turned toward him, her whole body a gesture of decorum, her practiced glance just the opposite. "Why, I suppose you should tell me more about yourself, to begin with."

He leaned toward her. "We'd need to be alone."

"That might be difficult." She edged away from him. "I don't think my mother would approve."

"I don't think she would either, but you have a break for lunch, don't you?"

"Of course."

"Tomorrow's Sunday, so that's out. But I'll be back Friday morning. What time do you get off for lunch?"

"One o'clock, but we certainly couldn't eat at the cafe."

"Meet me at the foot of the bridge, right underneath it on the grass. No one will see us there. I'll bring a lunch from the hotel."

"I'd have to bring my own lunch or Mama would be suspicious," she said.

"If that's the case, I'll just feast my eyes on you." He ran his hand along her arm. "You're the most beautiful thing I've ever seen."

She moved closer to the car door. "I'm not a thing, Mr. O'Callahan, and I must warn you, I don't intend to become any man's toy."

"Yes, I understand. I like that about you. We both know exactly what we want, don't we?"

"But is it the same thing?"

"Let's find out. Will you meet me?"

She looked straight ahead, her face composed. "I'll give your invitation some thought, but now we'd better get home. Mama will be worried."

Mr. O'Callahan not only had dinner with them that night, he came back the next day to finish cutting wood. He was stacking the woodpile when the family got home from church.

"Dinner's on the stove," he said. "I'll be through here pretty quick."

Mama herded the girls inside. "What in the world is he talking about?"

"Mama, look." Rachel pointed at a large pot sitting on the stove, one they'd never seen before.

Valina took the lid off and peered inside. "It's a pot roast, with carrots and potatoes. Where do you suppose he got it?"

"At the hotel, silly." Mary started setting the table.

"Oh, my goodness," Mama said. "Somebody go get a jar of peaches. I'll make another cobbler."

Rachel, climbing the ladder to the attic, yelled, "I've got to change out of my good clothes."

Valina rolled her eyes and went to get the peaches.

The afternoon sun, sketching soft designs through the pine trees and underbrush, reminded Valina of the Rembrandt prints in the art book at school. The dark green background, the musty brown earth in the clearing, the contrast of light and shadow. The luminous glow of Mr. O'Callahan's naked back. The axe thumped, a hollow throb.

His voice broke the spell. "Would you please bring me a dipper of water, Valina."

She hurried to the galvanized tub by the door, lifted the covering slab of oak, scooped out a ladle of water, and carried it to him in both hands. His reddish hair had turned brown at the temples from sweat. The metal dipper caught the light as she handed it to him and she could see its reflection in his eyes. Odors of pine and sweat hung in the air.

"Thank you, Valina." His eyes probed hers. She forced herself to look away.

"I need to get Mama something from the cellar." She could feel him watching her as she walked away. When she finally heard the axe fall again, she took a long shaky breath.

The wooden cellar door, heavy, partially rotted, opened onto crude dirt steps. Jars of home-canned venison, fruits, and vegetables stood in neat rows on thick wooden shelves. The damp air cooled Valina's flushed skin. She stood still, letting it soothe her body. But she couldn't force the picture of his naked chest and arms out of her mind. She picked up a jar of peaches, and turned back toward the steps, only to find them blocked by Mr. O'Callahan.

"Need some help?" he asked.

"No thanks. I can manage." She couldn't see his face against the light, just the outline of his body.

"Mr. O'Callahan. Did you bring your ukulele?" Rachel's voice.

It startled him. He turned away and Valina climbed out of the cellar.

"Well? Did you bring it?" Rachel asked.

"Sure did." He walked over to get his shirt and put it on. "As a matter of fact, I figured you'd probably play a selection or two for us after dinner. How about it?"

"You know I can't play the ukulele," Rachel said.

"Want me to teach you how?"

Rachel gasped. "Would you?"

"You bet. We'll start the lesson this very night."

"Oh, Valina, did you hear? The ukulele."

Mama, coming out of the cabin, tried to calm Rachel. "Stop jumping up and down, child. What is it you're trying to say?"

"He's gonna teach me the ukulele. Isn't that the cat's meow?"

Mama sighed. "Sometimes your exuberance is wearing, Rachel. But if it makes you this happy, I guess it's all right with me." She looked at the large stack of wood that had been cut. "Mr. O'Callahan, we'll be forever in your debt. How can we ever repay such kindness?"

"You could start by calling me Timothy. I'd feel more at home if you did."

Mama hesitated, then smiled. "Why, of course, Timothy."

He persisted. "And the girls, too. I'd like very much for them to call me Timothy."

Valina could tell that Mama thought he was taking undue liberties.

"The girls? Oh, I hardly think so. It's not . . . well, I guess there's really nothing wrong with it."

"Timothy it is, then. I'll take in some of this wood." He stacked a pile on one arm and headed for the cabin. Rachel rushed to open the door for him.

"We're beholden to him," Mama whispered.

"You don't you like him, do you Mama?" Valina said.

Mama stared at the large pile of wood. "I'm afraid he's too good to be true."

As she followed Mama into the cabin, Valina puzzled over what her mother had said about Timothy. Too good to be true? Hardly.

Dinner was again filled with more tales of far-off places. Timothy's adventures seemed endless.

"You look quite young, Timothy, yet you've had enough experience for a man of sixty," Mama said.

"If you're asking my age, Emma, I'm twenty-six. Left home at ten. Had sixteen years to sow my wild oats and figure out what I really wanted from life was a home, a good wife and children. But, first, I have to find the right woman."

Valina bit her lower lip when she saw Mary practicing her Theda Bara smile on Timothy. Dear God she looked stupid. But Timothy hadn't even noticed Mary making goo-goo eyes at him. He was looking at the empty bowl in front of him. "Say, do you suppose I could have a little more cobbler? It's mighty good, and a man sure works up an appetite chopping wood."

"I'm sorry. Of course." Mama started to rise, but Valina had already hurried to get the cobbler.

"Now, there's a girl who'll make a man a good wife someday," he said. "Thank you, Valina."

Valina's face flushed. "You're welcome, Mr. O'Callahan."

"You're supposed to call me Timothy from now on, remember?"

Valina beamed at him. He thought she'd make a good wife. And nine year's difference in age wasn't that much. But her delight soured when she caught sight of Mary posed on the edge of her chair like a movie queen, a scornful sneer on her face.

"Timothy, tell us more about New York. "Mary said.

CHAPTER 5

J-Bar-J Ranch — 1969

By four in the morning, all hell had broken loose. I went downstairs and pounded on Jimmy's bedroom door.

"Wake up." I yelled. "We need your help." I could hear him thrashing around in there like a spooked turkey. Couldn't he find the door, for God's sake? "Hurry up."

He opened the door just wide enough so he could yawn in my face. "What the hell's going on now?" His fierce scowl didn't impress me the way he hoped it would.

"Lightning started a fire over on Mohaten Ridge," I said.

That woke him up. He opened the door wider. "How far away is it?"

"Not far enough. Only fifteen miles. Fortunately, the wind isn't blowing our way, yet. Buck and George have gone to help fight it, and Mattie's Lady picked this time to go into labor. Come on. We've got to get over to the barn right away."

"Can I get dressed first?" He gave me a real smart-aleck look.

"Only if you hurry, and I mean hurry." I had to yell that through the door he'd just shut in my face. But for once, he got into his pants and boots real fast. The fire must've scared him.

He was still putting his shirt on as he came out the bedroom door.

He started to follow me down the stairs, but stopped in his tracks. "Hey. You're not counting on me to help with the birth, are you?"

I had started back down the stairs, but I stopped and turned to emphasize my next words. "Damned right I am. Now get a move on."

"But what about Oscar? Why can't he do it? Heck. He knows all about it." He had panic written all over his face.

"Won't hurt you to learn."

"What for?" he bellered. "We don't raise horses at home."

"Don't worry. You won't have to deliver the foal. But we'll need your help. Now move it."

He grumbled and swore all the way to the barn. When we got there, Mattie's Lady was lying on the floor having a contraction. Oscar was squatted down beside her. "We've got a problem, Mattie," he said. "All I can see is the head. The foals not in the right position."

I could hardly stand to look at the mare. Her eyes . . . I swear she knew.

"Soon as this contraction passes we have to get her to stand up and stay up." Oscar patted her flank and waited.

When I saw her relax, I said, "Come on, girl, you've got to stand up so we can help you." I urged her with all the love I could muster, while Oscar pulled on her harness. She finally stood up. I patted her neck and rested my head against hers.

"That's my girl."

"I think we'd better take her outside," Oscar said.

I glanced through the open door. Would there be enough light? Well, the big spotlight was still on, and dawn would break soon. I led her outside and talked to her until she seemed calmer.

"Okay, Oscar, go ahead." Lord, that was hard to say.

One at a time, Oscar shoved both his arms inside the mare. Blood began to spurt out of her.

"Stop it. You're hurting her something awful," Jimmy yelled.

"Can't be helped," Oscar said. "If I don't find those legs and get them turned the way they should be we're going to lose both the mare and the foal. We might anyway."

The mare's tail, a bloody broom, kept swishing across Oscar's face. "Damn it!"

And then he yelled, "I can't see."

"Jimmy, go back to the stall and get the towels," I said. "You've got to keep Oscar's face wiped. Hurry, now. I've got to stay up at this end to keep her from lying down."

I could see the whites of my Lady's eyes, the only sign of her pain and fear, that, and the way she was breathing. Of all the fine horses I've had over the years, none could ever compare to Mattie's Lady. And now all I could do to help her was pat and stroke and talk to her. Hell.

In just seconds, Jimmy came flying out of the barn with an armload of towels. He wiped off Oscar's face, all right, but you could see how squeamish he was about the blood.

Just then, the mare snorted and moved her head. The pain must've been unbearable. I patted her neck and crooned in her ear. "You know you're my very favorite horse. There's never

been a better one than you." I remembered the wonder I had
felt when I trained her. She had immediately responded to my
slightest movement. When I rode her, we were one creature,
extensions of each other, moving across the land.

"The legs are under the foal, Mattie. I'll have to move
them." The mare's tail hit Oscar's face again. "Pay attention,
boy. Wipe my face."

"Sorry."

Jimmy worried me. I hoped to God he wouldn't faint. He
had nearly as much blood on him as Oscar did.

It seemed like forever before Oscar finally said, "I got one
leg turned." I could hear him trying to catch his breath. "Now
for the other one."

It didn't take as long for him to turn the other leg, but now
even more blood was gushing out of the mare.

"My God," Jimmy said, "the poor thing." He sounded like
he was about to cry.

"Okay, look here, Jimmy," Oscar said, "see that hoof there?
You've got to pull on that as hard as you can, while I pull on
the other one. I'm about wore out." He took another deep
breath. "Now, pull. That's the way, son."

I couldn't see very well from up by the mare's head, but I
could sure hear the grunting and heavy breathing. My Lady
quivered but she endured. Born with heart and courage, that
mare.

"It's coming," Oscar gasped. "Keep pulling. That's the way.
It's a colt, Mattie."

"Look at the way its tongue is hanging out." Jimmy
sounded frantic. "Is it dead?"

I heard Oscar give the foal a sharp whack on the chest. "It's breathing, Mattie."

Exhausted, Mattie's Lady slowly lowered herself to the ground, then lifted her head and looked at her foal. When her head fell back to the ground, I knew she was gone.

I sank down beside her, patted her and kissed her on the forehead. Another damned goodbye.

When I stood up, Oscar was milking the mare. Jimmy turned to me, indignant. "Why in hell is he doing that? The poor thing's dead, isn't she?" There were tears in his eyes.

I had to swallow my own tears before I could answer. "Yes, she's dead. But the foal needs that first fluid for immunity. Take one of those clean towels and dry the little fellow's face while I go get the iodine and scissors."

When I came back from the barn, I cut the umbilical cord, dotted the stump with iodine, then gave the foal an immunization shot. Jimmy's face had turned a baby-poo green. He'd never forget this experience, that's for sure. Neither would I. The little foal kept trying to get up, a good sign.

"Is there something wrong with him?" Jimmy said. "Isn't he going to be able to stand up?"

"Oh, they all have to struggle, at first. We sure have our work cut out for us now. This foal will need feeding every two hours. Hope Buck and George get back soon."

I watched Oscar pick up the awkward little foal. What on earth would I have done without him? Jimmy and I followed him, as he carried the little guy into the barn.

When we got the colt settled, I said. "You two go get cleaned up. I'll feed him while you're gone."

I'd brought a bottle of formula with me when we came out of the house, just in case we'd need it. Oh, hell, I knew we'd need it. I'd known all along there was something wrong with the way my Lady had carried that foal.

Oscar hesitated. "You okay?"

"Yeah, I'm fine." Frankly, I needed a few minutes alone. Funny how one's losses never get any easier. You'd think I'd be used to it by now.

The foal took right to the bottle, tugged hard. Another good sign. When he finished, he wobbled around the stall, while I followed him with a towel trying to finish cleaning him off. And then, abruptly, just the way a human baby would, the little guy fell asleep.

As I went to the house, I didn't let myself look back at Mattie's Lady. I craved a cup of coffee, and Jimmy had already made a pot. I took a small sip. "Well, I'll be damned. It's good."

He grinned. "Sure it is."

When I went out to the porch, he followed me. The minute I sat in the rocker, Lucifer jumped up in my lap. His warm body cuddled up against mine. Animals know when you're hurting. I stroked his soft fur and drank my coffee.

Jimmy sat down in the chair beside mine. "Oscar showed me how to make formula for the colt. I'll take the first shift."

"Okay. Two hours from now."

"And I heard on the radio that the fire is under control."

"Good."

"Aren't you going to take a rest? Oscar is."

"He worked harder than I did. I've got too much on my mind just now to be able to sleep."

His face turned solemn. "Mattie's Lady."

"She was the finest horse I've ever owned, and I've had a good many in my time. Damned shame."

"Maybe the colt will be just like her."

"Let's hope so." Bob would have been proud if he could have seen his son right then. The boy was actually trying to comfort me.

"What are you going to name it?" Jimmy asked.

"You have to know them for a while before you pick out a name. He'll probably tell us himself in a day or two. I remember one colt we had when Daniel and I were kids. That colt started right out just full of the devil. He'd sneak up behind Daniel and bite him. Got him every time. Daniel wanted to name him Satan, but Papa wouldn't hear of it. Said it wouldn't be fitting. So Daniel came up with Lucifer."

I pointed at the cat on my lap, "When this little guy was born, he had the same kind of mischief in his heart. Couldn't resist calling him Lucifer. I never did figure out why Papa thought the name Lucifer was any better than Satan. Do you know, though, that colt acted up every day of its life, until our hired man started calling it Luke?"

"Ah, horse pucky."

I chuckled. He'd gotten that expression from Oscar, sure as fate. "It's true. Why, all God's creatures deserve respect."

We didn't say anything for a bit, just sat there, at ease with each other for a change. I liked that. Maybe the boy was coming around. I leaned back in my chair and let the freshness of the new morning sink into my skin.

Two days later, my shoulder woke me up before sunrise.

Wretched thing has pained me off and on ever since I broke it in '42. I knew I wouldn't go back to sleep, so I got dressed and went downstairs. The light was on in the kitchen. Oscar had just come in from the barn.

"Last of the two-hour feedings," he said, yawning while he poured himself a cup of coffee.

"Good. Let's have Buck and George start on the four-hour feedings." Just then my conscience gave me a nudge. "You're doing a good job with Jimmy. I want to thank you for that, and for your help when the colt was born. Don't know what I'd do without you." He got all flustered and red in the face. I'd embarrassed him. "Can't you take a compliment, for God's sake?"

He shrugged. "Didn't sound like you, that's all." He gave me a sly grin. "I'm used to rougher language, I guess."

"Well, God forbid that I should change my ways, but my mother did try hard to put a little polish on me." I gave him a whack on the arm with my fist. "You old fart."

"Now that sounds more like the Matilda Jacobsen I know." He was relishing every minute of this.

"Seriously," I said. "I think the boy's attitude has changed for the better, don't you?"

"Yeah. The birth of the foal and the mare's death did it, I think." Oscar put up a warning hand. "But don't go expecting too much. He's just a kid, and a boy, at that."

"Boys are worse than girls, huh? Lord, I wish Daniel could hear you say that. He thought I was awful." Before Oscar could agree with Daniel's opinion, I said, "Don't you dare say it."

He just laughed and headed on out to the barn.

Buck and George had already eaten and left for the barn when Jimmy finally came down to breakfast. He shuffled into the kitchen his eyes still filled with sleep. I took a good look at him. Darned if he hadn't put the buttons of his plaid shirt in the wrong buttonholes again. I almost gave him a bad time, but he looked so pitiful I decided to keep my mouth shut. I waited to see if he even knew I was in the room. He mumbled something, then slouched down into a chair. I didn't say a word. No sense talking to someone in a coma. He didn't eat, just moved the scrambled eggs around on his plate with his fork. When he didn't even glance at the cinnamon rolls, I began to wonder if he'd turned finicky on me again. But I soon found out what he had on his mind.

"How'd you know I was smoking marijuana that day?"

So that was it. "Marijuana has an odor like a pile of dirty socks that have been dipped in sugar water. First time I smelled it was on a hippie sitting next to me at the cafe. I about upchucked my lunch."

Jimmy's eyes popped open and he stared at me for a moment. "Oh. How do you know I might not have smoked some more of it since then?"

"I thought I just told you. It's the godawful smell. Those hippies think we don't know marijuana from rose water. Hell, their hair and clothes reek of the stuff."

Abruptly, he changed the subject. "Did you mean it when you said I could name the foal?"

"Sure did. You picked one out yet?"

He took a big swallow of coffee and cleared his throat. "How about Mattie's Boy?"

He really got to me with that. I couldn't say a word.

"Well? Don't you like it?" He sounded anxious.

Somehow, I found my voice. "Damned right I do. It's perfect."

He grinned. "Cool." Wasn't long before he started cramming food in his mouth.

I followed him out onto the porch when he'd finished breakfast. The sun broke over the mountain right at that moment with such glory that even the boy seemed impressed.

"You'd never sell this place, would you?"

"If I ever had to leave my ranch I wouldn't last long. My soul would stay right here where it belongs."

He blinked a couple of times and cleared his throat. "Better get Daisy milked."

"When you're done with that, go help Buck shoe the Arabian."

About an hour later, I looked out the window and saw Jimmy walking toward the house from the barn. By golly, he'd finally learned how to walk in those boots. He even looked like he belonged here. Well, almost.

He came in and headed straight for the kitchen table where he grabbed an apple out of the fruit bowl. Mouth full, as usual, he said, "Can't Buck talk?"

"I've heard a few words over the years." I got busy hulling strawberries. "Shortcake for dinner," I said, knowing it was his favorite dessert. But he didn't even hear me.

"All Buck did was grunt and point," he said. "The horse communicated better than he did. I don't even know if I did it right."

"You did."

"How would you know?" Jimmy tossed his apple core into the sink and started eating another apple. You'd think I hadn't fed him breakfast.

"He'd tell you if you'd done it wrong."

"You mean I'd have to make a mistake in order to get him to talk?"

"That's about it."

"Weird."

I got a pitcher of lemonade out of the fridge and put it on a tray, along with some glasses. I handed it to Jimmy.

"What am I supposed to do with this?" he asked.

"Follow me." I held the back door open for him and pointed at the table on the porch by my rocker. "Put it there and help yourself." I sat down in the rocker. "Time for a break."

But Jimmy wiggled in his chair. Just couldn't sit still. All that energy boiling inside of him made me envious. I remembered how that felt.

The dogs began to set up a ruckus. When Jimmy saw the rider coming up to the house, his face lit up like the summer sun. "It's Buddy."

When Buddy got to the house, he dismounted and bounded up onto the porch. Jimmy poured him a glass of lemonade before I could even get out of my chair.

Buddy grinned at him. "Thanks," he said. He drank the lemonade in one long gulp, then put the glass on the table and turned to me. "I have a proposition to discuss with you, Mrs. Jacobsen."

"For God's sake, call me Matilda. So, what's your proposition all about?"

He got right down to cases. "My girl, Linette, says she
won't marry me until I settle down. I've been kind of drifting
for the past few years, ever since I got out of the Army, doing
some tracking, some ranch work, odd jobs."

"You're mighty young to have done all that." I'd thought he
was about twenty-one.

He chuckled. "I'll be twenty-six next month. The point is,
I think Linette's right. I'd like to buy Sandy's ranch, if you'd
want to have me as a neighbor, that is."

"Why, I'd be overjoyed," I said.

Jimmy beamed.

But Buddy wasn't finished yet. "There's just one problem.
I called the county and found out Sandy's ranch is only a
hundred acres." He shook his head. "We couldn't make it on
that. We'd need another two hundred."

"And you want to buy that other two hundred acres from
me. Is that it?"

He smiled. "That's what I had in mind."

"Do you have the money for it?"

He chuckled. "I think so, but that would depend on what
your price is."

"I need to ponder that a bit and go over the plat of the land.
Suppose I call you in a few days?" He had such a hopeful look
on his face when he nodded that I pretty much knew I'd say
yes.

"And there's another thing I wanted to mention," he said.
"I found a piece of barbed wire a couple hundred feet from

Sandy's cabin, a piece about three feet long. I couldn't figure out why it was there. Sure not near any fence. When I took a closer look, I saw there was dried blood on it. "Thought it might be what cut Sandy's horse."

A chill rippled up my back, but I shook it off. "No telling what Sandy may have used it for," I said. "He wasn't the neatest person in the world."

Buddy nodded. "You're probably right."

But after Buddy rode off, I wondered if Sandy had had trouble with someone. Was that what he'd wanted to tell me? Oh, hell. I was beginning to think like a fretting old woman.

"What was that all about?" Jimmy asked.

"Don't really know."

When Jimmy and the men headed upstairs for the night, I went to the roll top desk in the parlor and got out the plat of my land. Then I fixed myself some hot chocolate. Jacob and I often sat in the kitchen talking about our dreams for the place. And I sure needed to talk to him right then.

"How would you feel if I sold some of our land to Buddy Fast Buffalo Horse, Jacob? He wants to buy Sandy's place, but he can't make a living on just one hundred acres. Not these days. Buddy's a nice young man. I'd like to help him out by selling him a few hundred acres. Besides, he'd be a whole lot better neighbor than some mangy hippie who'd grow marijuana on Sandy's place." If the men could hear me they'd think I was nuts. Some things are just too hard to explain.

"But I can't give up a piece of our land unless you approve, Jacob. Remember how we felt when we bought it? So proud. Our piece of heaven, we called it. And it still is. But you aren't here, and I'm getting old and achy and tired. I was thinking of offering Buddy two hundred acres, with an option to buy another hundred when he gets settled in. How would you feel about that, Jacob?"

It wasn't that I expected his voice to boom down from heaven, it was just easier to make big decisions if I said it as if Jacob were here in the room with me. I let it simmer in my head a bit. Seemed like it would work out well for all concerned. I felt good about selling to Buddy, but I still had to give some thought to what price I'd ask.

The next morning Jimmy hurried so fast that he almost fell down the stairs getting to breakfast. He sat down at the table, grabbed the milk pitcher and a glass, then looked up at me and grinned. "I made it," he said.

Now, I never knew what kind of mood to expect from the kid, but this was a new one. He was too happy. Made me suspicious. "Don't get carried away with that milk. You haven't been out to milk Daisy yet. What's going on, anyway? You trying to give me a heart attack, getting down here so early?"

"Oscar's going to teach me how to drive the jeep today. My dad will sure be surprised when he gives me my first driving lesson, won't he?"

He sounded much too smug. I turned to look at him. "Just how do you mean, surprised?"

He rolled his eyes as if he hadn't really expected a retarded old woman to understand. "I'll already know how to drive." He said it slowly, so I couldn't miss his point.

"Well, now, there's a big difference between driving in The City and driving up here. On the other hand, driving your dad's car will be easier than driving a jeep. Evens out, I guess."

"Maybe I could talk Grandmother Marie into buying me a jeep."

Jimmy's remark about Marie buying him a jeep had soured my disposition in a hurry. I gave him a look that would wither a cactus. "Nothing I hate worse than a sponger."

He blinked. "What the hell's a sponger?"

"It's a person who takes from others rather than do for himself. I'm going to be damned disappointed if you turn out to be one of those lowlifes."

"So my grandmother's rich and likes to give me stuff. I don't see anything wrong with that. Why should you?"

"You're not stupid. Figure it out for yourself." I ladled some oatmeal into his bowl and went over to the sink. Damn that woman and her money. Hell, yes, she'd buy him a jeep. And that silly Jessica was no better. Every week since he's been here, Jimmy'd had a letter from her with a twenty-dollar bill in it. All that money for a snot-nosed kid. And for what? He had no need for it up here. The woman was an idiot.

Good thing the men came downstairs just then, or I might've told Jimmy what I really thought of those two women.

Jimmy commenced buttering up Oscar, oblivious to the fact that Oscar could see right through him. It got so bad that even Buck and George took to rolling their eyes at the ceiling. I had to admire Oscar's patience with the boy. He'd sure need a lot of it when Jimmy got behind the wheel of that jeep.

They were just about through with breakfast, so I said,

"While Jimmy milks Daisy and feeds the chickens, I need to talk to you, Oscar."

He glanced at me, nodded. When Buck and George and Jimmy left, Oscar poured himself another cup of coffee.

"What's on your mind, Mattie?"

"Buddy wants to buy Sandy's place, but he'll need more land in order to make a go of it. He'd like to buy some of mine. How would you feel if I sold him two hundred acres, with an option to buy another hundred when he gets on his feet?"

"But are you going to cut down on the number of cattle we have? Some of the cattle feed on that land."

"We've had several good years in a row. I think we could manage with fewer cattle now. Might be easier on you three men."

Oscar gazed absently out the kitchen window. "I suppose."

"And Buddy would be a good neighbor."

"Yeah."

Why was he dragging his feet? "The sale wouldn't bring down your share of the profits, if that's what's troubling you. I'd planned on raising your percentage."

His face turned a bright scarlet. "I hadn't even thought about that."

I grinned at him. Boy, had I hit a nerve. Well, I couldn't blame him. He runs the place, and he's entitled to profit from it. All three men deserve something for their old age. 'Course Buck and George don't get as much as Oscar does.

"So what do you think of the idea?" I asked.

"I think we could do with a little less acreage. You going to sell him some of the cattle, too?"

"I might, but it would depend on what his plans are."

About then I saw Jimmy in the doorway, standing on first one foot and then the other.

"Your student has arrived, Oscar. Better take him out to the jeep before he explodes."

Jimmy led the way to the jeep, just as if Oscar couldn't find it. I went out and brought Angus into the house while I did the dishes. He was more comfortable with us now, but I didn't feel easy about turning him loose just yet. When I got through cleaning up the kitchen, I took him outside and put him on a rope so I could teach him to sit and come. That's when Bob called. I got there on the sixth ring.

"Hope I'm not bothering you, Matilda."

"No. Just out training the dog."

"How's Jimmy doing?"

"Fine, though he's had an experience I'm sure you hadn't counted on when you sent him up here. My neighbor, Sandy, had a bad fall. Jimmy was there with me when Sandy died."

I could tell that he was sort of absorbing the news. But pretty soon, he said. "How did he take it?"

"Better than I thought he would, though I can't say I know what's going on inside the boy's head. We took him to the funeral, too. That gave me a chance to show him the town and the family places. He wasn't much interested until I took him down to Emma and Daniel's old cabin. Still sure you want the boy to hear all this?"

"Damned right I'm sure."

"Okay. But you don't really think it'll help you win out against all that indulgent money, do you?"

He sighed. "Maybe not, but I have to try."

"I can appreciate that."

"You sound discouraged," he said. "That's not like you. What happened?"

"It's just that Jimmy knows his grandmother will buy him any blessed thing he wants."

"I've been depressed by that ever since Jimmy was born," Bob said. "If only he could mature enough to see what's going on."

"You want him to be more grown up than the grownups around him? That's a lot to expect of a kid, isn't it?"

Bob groaned. "You're right, but please keep trying."

"I will, but remember one thing. I give guarantees to people only for the way my horses are trained, not for teenage kids."

"I know," he said. "I didn't mean to put pressure on you. I'd better let you get back to work. Talk to you later."

I had no more than hung up, when Hannah Lewis called.

"You were right," she said. "Dad left his ranch to me. I'm having a hard time getting used to the idea."

"In his black little heart, Sandy did love you, Hannah."

She was quiet for a spell. I'm not known for my tact, that's for sure.

But then she started up again. "We got a call from Buddy Fast Buffalo Horse. Did you know he wants to buy Dad's place?"

"Yes."

"Tom and I had decided to put it up for sale just before Buddy called. Buddy's like a gift from God."

"Well, you deserve something good to happen. You'll have no trouble with Buddy. And I'm going to sell him two hundred adjoining acres, so he can make a go of the place."

"That's so nice of you, Matilda."

"No, not nice, selfish. I want a good neighbor over there."

She chuckled. "You're the most honest person I know."

"Honesty is seldom welcome, but I seem to be stuck with a big chunk of the stuff."

She giggled. "Tom and I will be up soon to clear out Dad's things. We'll see you then, Matilda."

"Look forward to it."

We hung up and I went to my desk to look up my tax assessment. Time to figure out the price for those acres Buddy wanted. When I settled on an amount, I called him and told him my terms. He jumped at the whole idea. It surprised me that he had a sizeable amount of money to put down. And he must've heard the surprise in my voice.

"I was in the army for four years, Matilda. I put every cent I could in savings bonds. Then last year, the government gave all the Indians from my reservation a monetary settlement. That's their term, not mine. And then my brother died, and I inherited his share. I've been looking for a place ever since."

"You're pretty sharp," I said. "I like people who know what they want and plan how to get it." This was one smart young man.

"Well, I plan to learn a lot from you about ranching."

"Any time. You'll need to have the new property lines surveyed. I'll pay half the cost. Tom Lewis has done some surveying. I'm sure he'd be glad to help out."

"Okay. Thanks."

"And afterward, I want to ride with you along the new property line."

"Sure. I'll let you know when it's been done."

"Fine. After that we can deed you the land."

"I'm sure looking forward to that."

I could tell he was grinning. So was I. It was such a relief to know that he cared about that property right next door. What a good neighbor he would be.

Late that afternoon, I asked Jimmy to help me pick apples. "There's a three-legged ladder in the shed. I'll bring the baskets."

The old tree had outdone itself. I had propped up several of the branches for fear they'd break from the weight of all the fruit. I showed Jimmy how to use an orchard ladder. It took him a little time and a lot of swearing but he finally got the hang of it. When his basket was heaped high with apples, we sat on the porch while I peeled them for sauce.

"Doesn't Buddy Fast Buffalo Horse live on one of those Indian reservations?" he asked.

Have to admit that surprised me. "You didn't know that there are some native Americans who manage to make a living off the reservation? As far as I know, there is no law that says they can't do that. Buddy's tribe is the Nez Perce. Their remarkable leader was Chief Joseph. In 1877, he and his people were given thirty days notice to leave their beautiful home-land in Oregon's Wallowa Valley and relocate in an Idaho reservation. Chief Joseph never gave up trying for the right to take his people back to their homeland. He died in 1904. He was a fine man, but the white men didn't recognize the dignity and intelligence of the native people in this land. Buddy is a good example of and for his tribe."

"Yeah. There's a lot we aren't taught in school about the bad stuff our people have done. Like that war in Vietnam."

"Human nature is mighty hard to understand sometimes."

We were both quiet for a while, until I said, "This is a good opportunity to get back to the family history lesson."

Jimmy groaned, but he settled back in his chair, his feet propped up on the railing.

"When Timothy came along and romanced Valina, she was convinced that he loved her. He really got her all stirred up. But, hells bells, she didn't know beans about her own biological urges."

He gave me a disgusted look. "You talking about sex?"

I nodded. "And Valina knew even less about the kind of urges Timothy was having."

"They must've been pretty stupid in the olden days. Me and my friends know all about sex, for Pete's sake. It's no big deal."

"That's right. I keep forgetting you're one of the enlightened generation." Knowing what I did about him, I had to ask, "But supposing a girl gets pregnant. What happens then?"

His eyes darted to my face, while his Adam's apple bounced up and down. He cleared his throat, but it didn't help. His voice came out high and croaky, like a little kid's. "Well, I suppose the girl has an abortion."

How I wanted to tell him I knew what he'd done to his poor little girlfriend. Abortion. It sure let him off the hook, didn't it? But it wasn't likely that she'd ever be the same.

He deliberately yawned in my face. Had to get his macho image back in shape.

I ignored the little creep, but it was all I could do to sit there beside him.

CHAPTER 6

Pine Bluff—1929

After work, Valina ran home so fast she could hardly talk when she got to the cabin. "Margaret Black's quitting," she gasped. "She's going to marry Harry Jensen."

Mama put the last of the potatoes she'd just peeled into the Dutch oven and wiped her hands on her apron. "That widower from up on Whiskey Creek? I didn't know they were seeing each other."

"She told Mr. Hillyard he should offer you her job." Valina grinned.

Mama stared at her. "I've never cooked in a restaurant. I wouldn't know how."

"Margaret would be there for a week to help you."

Mama poured a large saucepan of water into the Dutch oven, then shook in a handful of salt and pepper. "I couldn't leave Rachel here alone all day."

"He said you could have Rachel there any time you wanted. Besides, he's sort of desperate, I think. Tillie can't be there all day and night, too."

"No, not with her little ones." Mama scowled at the stove. "Hmm . . ."

"We'd all help." Why wasn't Mama more excited?

"But Rachel needs me, especially with Papa gone."

"She could help in the cafe. It would make her feel important and she'd have less time to make trouble."

"Maybe. We certainly need the money."

"Mr. Hillyard asked if you would come in with me tomorrow. He wants to talk to you about it. Rachel can come along too." Valina watched as her mother stared off into space. "Mama, wouldn't it be wonderful to have enough money for something nice now and then?"

Mama gave her a sharp look. "Well, all right. I know I could count on you and Mary to help out here at home."

Valina didn't think Mary would be much help. She always managed to get out of work by sitting down at the sewing machine.

It turned out that Mama fit right in at the Pine Cone Cafe. The customers couldn't get enough of her cooking, and Spike turned into a gentleman overnight, though Valina kept the coffee pot handy, just in case.

Rachel posed the only problem. At first, Mama would keep her busy helping in the kitchen, but Rachel soon began to grumble and pout, so Mama sent her in to work with Valina.

But Rachel broke too many dishes. So Valina decided to have her just keep the coffee cups full. But Rachel dripped coffee all over the tables, sometimes even on the customers.

When Herb Johnson complained, Rachel shrugged and said, "Well, wipe it up with your napkin."

Valina decided she'd better talk to Mama. "Something has

to be done about Rachel. Herb Johnson just told her she was mouthy, and she was. She told him he shouldn't eat so much."

"Oh, my land! What am I going to do with her?" Mama closed her eyes and massaged her temples. "With that attitude, she might turn away customers, and that wouldn't be fair to the Hillyards. Send her in here and I'll have a talk with her."

Valina kept track of her customers from the door into the kitchen while she eavesdropped.

"Mr. Johnson was cross with me." Rachel whined.

"You get sassy with people, and then expect them not to be cross with you?" Mama said.

Rachel's whine turned into a forced whimper. "I didn't mean to be sassy, Mama."

"You are plenty old enough to know that you can't just say whatever comes into your head, especially the things that come into yours. I can't risk having you drive away customers."

When Mama sighed, Rachel began to sob. Mama sighed again and said, "Play until lunch. We'll have to try something different," Mama said. "From now on you'll come to town in the mornings with Mary. She goes to work later than I do. You'll work an hour with me and you can help us clean up after lunch, and then you'll have from two to four to play again."

"Oh, boy!"

Valina shook her head. It sure hadn't taken long for Rachel to stop crying. Couldn't Mama see that?

"Hold on a minute," Mama said. "Two conditions. First, you don't even go near the river bank. And second, you cause no trouble for anyone or any creature. Do you understand?"

"Yes, Mama."

"All right. Run and play, but be back right at four."

Valina didn't believe Rachel would take Mama's terms seriously. She never did. The new schedule worked fine for three days. Then Mrs. Bailey came in and, without saying a word, marched right into the kitchen. Valina kept a nervous dialogue going with the customers until she heard the back door slam. She peered into the kitchen, but she could tell by the scowl on Mama's face that she was in no mood to talk.

When Tillie Hillyard came in to replace Valina at four, a dirty-faced Rachel came in right behind her. Valina got ready to leave, frustrated that she hadn't found out why Mrs. Bailey was so upset. She'd planned to ask Mama, but now with Rachel there she couldn't.

"I'll be a little late coming home, Valina," Mama said. "You girls go ahead and eat. I want to stop off at Catherine's after work."

While they walked home, Rachel kept up her usual chatter, until Valina said, "Have you any idea why Roy Bailey's mother came to talk to Mama this afternoon?"

"Mrs. Bailey?" Rachel wouldn't look at Valina.

"Uh-huh. She stayed quite a while, and slammed the door when she left, too."

Rachel didn't say another word all the way home.

Emma, weary and discouraged, climbed up the front steps of the Bradford house. She knocked on the door and waited. She hated to bother Catherine. She was probably right in the middle of fixing dinner.

But when Catherine opened the door she greeted Emma

with a big hug. "Oh, how I've missed you since you started working. Sit down and relax for a bit. How are things going? Do you like your job?"

"Yes, I like it all right," Emma said. "Oh, my feet and back get tired, but the money will make life a lot easier. On the other hand, Rachel's become a problem."

Catherine frowned. "Sounds like you could use a cup of tea."

While Catherine was in the kitchen, Emma felt an unfamiliar stab of jealousy. The lush carpets, the over-stuffed sofa and chairs, the lace curtains at the windows were all luxuries to Emma, but necessities to Catherine. And why not? Catherine's family had money, and though a doctor didn't earn much in a mountain community, Charles' family wasn't poor, either. Emma and Daniel, on the other hand, came from people who'd had to struggle all their lives to make ends meet. Sometimes Emma felt Daniel was fanatically committed to poverty. Only recently, had she admitted to herself that her marriage wasn't as happy as it should be. She felt old before her time, tired of the fight to feed and clothe her family, tired of pretending that she didn't mind Daniel's irresponsible ways.

Emma rubbed her neck. She had to get hold of herself. Wallowing in self-pity wouldn't help. Daniel had a job now and so did she. Maybe things would get better.

When Catherine came back, she handed Emma a cup of tea and pushed a footstool under her feet. "Now then, what's wrong?"

"Confining Rachel in the restaurant didn't work out, so I decided to let her have several free hours to play each day. But

Mrs. Bailey came into the cafe this afternoon in a rage. Seems Rachel slipped into their chicken coop and took some eggs. Then she climbed the tree next to Roy's bedroom and threw the eggs through the open window."

Catherine chuckled. "Rachel's too bright for her own good."

"Bright? Don't you mean brat? It's not funny, Catherine. Not at all. I'm worried to death about her. And frankly, Daniel's not much help."

"I'm sorry, Emma. It's just that I think Rachel's bored. And at her age she'd be bored even if you weren't working. She needs something to challenge her, some way to work off steam. Let me help you."

"I can't put the burden on you."

"It won't be a burden. Let me give her piano lessons. You told me, yourself, that she picks out tunes on the piano at church. She does it here, too."

"Yes, that's true. She has a good ear." Tears welled in Emma's eyes. She took a sip of tea and swallowed hard, then set her mouth in a firm line.

"Don't let her talent go to waste," Catherine pleaded. "Let me give her the lessons."

Emma's pride wouldn't allow it. "I can't do that."

"Why not?" Catherine put her hands on her hips. "Emma Addison, are you so proud you won't let a friend help you? Shame on you."

"But she's a handful, and you have a busy life of your own."

"Busy? Not since Paul grew up. He doesn't need me anymore. Having Rachel here each afternoon would make this empty house less painful for me. Couldn't you find it in your heart to loan her to me now and then?"

Emma bit her lip. Poor Catherine. Of course she'd feel lost without Paul. Why not let her try to civilize Rachel? It might be good for all concerned. "All right. But I'll pay for the lessons."

"You certainly will not. I don't need the money. Besides, I'm fond of the little imp. Send her here tomorrow morning. Just send her. Don't say why. Agreed?"

"All right. Agreed." Emma relaxed for the first time since her session with Mrs. Bailey. She leaned back in her chair and enjoyed her tea.

"Can you stay for dinner?" Catherine asked.

"I'd love to, but I'd better get home."

"Well, could Paul drive you home and chop some wood for you."

Emma grimaced. "Timothy O'Callahan spent the weekend chopping a mountain of wood for us."

"You don't like him, do you?"

"No. Daniel does, but I don't trust the man. And I don't like him hanging around my girls. He's too experienced." She sighed. "Oh, I'm probably just borrowing trouble."

Later, when Emma got home, she announced, "Family meeting."

The three girls took their seats at the table.

Emma looked at the two older girls. "Today Rachel stole eggs and threw them into Roy Bailey's bedroom. As you all know, Rachel, this family doesn't tolerate that kind of behavior."

Mary turned on Rachel. "Why would you do such a stupid thing? The people in town already make fun of us. We don't need you making things worse."

"Mary," Mama said, "That's enough. We have things to discuss other than gossip."

Mary pursed her mouth and glared at Rachel.

Emma rubbed her forehead. Her head ached. She wished she could go lie down. "You'll all need to pitch in and help with the chores. And you two older girls will be supervising Rachel, as well. Rachel, you've had dinner?"

"Yes, Mama."

"Then get ready for bed. Tomorrow you and I will go to the Bailey's first thing in the morning. You will apologize and offer to work for Mrs. Bailey to make up for what you did. The type of work will be up to her."

"Mama . . ."

"And then you'll go to Catherine's."

Rachel started to speak, but Emma stopped her. "You heard me. Now go to bed." Good thing Rachel had been her third child, Emma thought. If she'd been the first one, there might not have been any others.

The next day, Mrs. Bailey accepted Rachel's apology, though she was barely civil. When Rachel offered to work for her, Mrs. Bailey bristled and said, "Absolutely not," and slammed the door in Rachel's face.

As they walked away, Rachel said, "I don't think Mrs. Bailey likes me."

"What on earth do you expect, child? You've been a constant problem to the poor woman."

Rachel kicked the dirt and pouted, an act that didn't

impress Emma. Secretly, she thought Mrs. Bailey was no dummy. At least she'd had the good sense to turn down Rachel's offer of work.

Much to Emma's surprise, Rachel didn't balk at Catherine's plan for piano lessons. Instead, she devoured each lesson and begged to go back in the afternoons to practice.

A week later, Catherine sat on a stool in the cafe kitchen visiting with Emma.

"I'm sure she could be a professional musician. She has amazing talent. If not a performer, then at least a teacher."

Catherine's words upset Emma. She yearned to see her littlest one succeed, but Rachel's talent would require an education for which there was no money. But maybe, now that she and Daniel were both working, they could start saving money.

When they all walked home after Mama's shift, Valina marveled at the change in Rachel's disposition, though she still babbled. And then dear intolerant Mary raved on and on about that awful Zoe Adams and the horrid red dress. Mary was such a snob.

"Could you cast the first stone, Mary?" Mama asked.

"Why, Mama, everyone knows about Zoe Adams."

Mama's back stiffened. "Your holier than thou attitude doesn't become you, Mary."

No one spoke again until they got home, where two horses stood in the clearing by the cabin.

"It must be Papa and Aunt Matilda." Rachel said, and ran on ahead. Papa opened the door just as she got there.

"Papa!" Rachel threw her arms around him. "How long can you stay?"

"Oh, for a while," he said.

Aunt Matilda stood behind him in the doorway, a stern scowl on her face. Valina couldn't look at Mama. Papa was out of a job again.

"What happened, Daniel?" Mama's voice was quiet, too quiet.

"I'm sure my dear sister will be very happy to fill you in on the details." Papa glared at Aunt Matilda. "So I shall defer to her."

"Oh, no you don't, Daniel. I'm not the one to tell her, you are." Aunt Matilda stood, feet apart, arms folded across her chest.

Papa's eyes fairly snapped. "Have it your way, Matilda. You always do." He turned to face Mama. "I was fired."

"Why?"

Mama's voice sounded stern, maybe even angry, and Papa's face didn't look normal, either. He had to clear his throat twice before he could answer. "The foreman called me a nigger-lover because I stuck up for the Negro race. I got angry and hit him in the jaw. That's when he fired me."

"Surely that didn't surprise you." Now Mama's voice was kind of nasty. Mama never spoke to Papa that way. So sarcastic. Even Aunt Matilda looked shocked.

Papa blinked. "Emma, you know my principles. I won't take orders from a bigot."

"Oh, my God!" Aunt Matilda's face turned bright red.

Mama put up her hand for silence. "Matilda tried to help us, Daniel. You've embarrassed her with the people at the logging camp." Mama sounded furious. "Isn't it fortunate that I now have a job cooking at the Pine Cone Cafe?"

Valina couldn't believe Mama would talk to Papa in that tone of voice.

Mama turned to Mary. "See that Rachel gets to bed. And, Valina, fix something for Aunt Matilda to eat. Daniel, you and I are going for a walk."

"A walk? It's dark out there."

"Then get a lantern."

Both Mary and Rachel stared wide-eyed at Mama. When Valina saw Aunt Matilda's satisfied smirk, she had to suppress the chuckle that rose in her throat. No one said a word. They simply watched Mama march out the door, with Papa right behind her.

Emma didn't speak until they were a good distance from the cabin. "First of all, I don't like Timothy O'Callahan hanging around our girls. He tried to ingratiate himself with me from the moment you left. Unfortunately, he was indispensible. He chopped wood, and bought food for us."

"How can you object to that, Emma? He's a fine person. I don't understand your uncharitable attitude."

How could Daniel be so stupid? "And I don't understand your lack of common sense. What do we really know about him? Only what he tells us, and most of the things he tells us are outrageous."

"I'm sorry you feel that way, but he is my friend. I will not turn him away, no matter what you say."

Emma gritted her teeth. Daniel could be so frustrating. "I see. Well, mark my words. You're making a terrible mistake."

"I seriously doubt that. Now, can we go back to the cabin?"

"Absolutely not. I have more to say."

"Emma . . ."

"As to your unwillingness to work for a bigot, since nearly everyone in this area is a bigot about Negroes, even though there isn't a Negro to be found within miles, just how do you expect to find a job, much less keep one?"

"I'll manage."

"Oh, yes, just like you always have. Damn poorly."

"I don't think it's necessary for you to talk to me in that tone of voice, or to swear, either. What is wrong with you?"

"Wrong?" She stood up as tall as she could, straining to look him in the eye. "Let me tell you something. It's time for you to get a job and keep it. You and your self-imposed poverty. You've cheated your children. Yes, and me, as well. And I'm disgusted to say that I've let you."

"I take offense at that," Daniel said.

"You take offense? I wish that could be as humorous as it sounds. I don't care what kind of job you get, but just remember that there are things I don't like about my job either. Do you think I enjoy working ten hours a day in that blistering hot kitchen?"

Daniel's mouth opened but nothing came out.

"Do you think I don't have pains in my back and legs and feet? Do you think I'd hit my boss and get fired? Never, no matter what he might say. We have children to support. Now, have I made myself clear?"

He blinked and gasped, "Abundantly so."

"Good. Then let's go back to the cabin."

When Paul came to the cafe for lunch again the next day, it surprised Valina. But maybe it was Mama's cooking that brought him in. He'd always liked it. He threw one of his long legs over a stool at the counter and sat down. "Hi. I'll take the daily special. Doesn't matter what it is, as long as your mother cooked it."

So it was Mama's cooking.

"Going to the dance Saturday night?" he asked.

"Sure. The whole family is."

Just then, Valina saw Bertha come up to the counter. Had the word about Papa gotten around so soon?

"Good afternoon, Valina."

Valina grimaced. Bertha's voice always set her teeth on edge. She nodded at Bertha and poured Paul some coffee. When she looked up again, Bertha was still standing there.

"Did you want something, Mrs. Wilcox?"

Bertha just smiled. Valina braced herself.

"I understand your father's out of a job again," Bertha said. "Fired, I hear."

Valina couldn't stand it another second. "Would you please turn your head sideways, Mrs. Wilcox? I'd like to take a look at your ears. I've heard they're the biggest ones in town."

The cafe was silent for a moment, until Paul chuckled, then the regulars all laughed.

Bertha glared at all of them. "I don't see anything funny about this." She turned back to Valina, "You're still mighty sassy, I see."

"At least I'm not vicious like some people I know," Valina said.

Bertha's eyes bulged with anger. "The Hillyards will hear about this." She stalked out of the room as the customers clapped and stomped their feet.

"You really set her on her ear." Paul grinned. "No one else

has ever had the courage to cross her." His dark eyes held hers for a moment. "You're quite a gal, you know that?"

Valina blushed. She rested her hands on the counter. "I wasn't very polite, but I don't think anyone should have to put up with her nasty remarks."

Paul stood up to leave, but before he left he reached out and lightly covered both of her hands with his. She didn't know where to look, but she could feel the blush that rose on her face. As soon as he left, she turned her back to the rest of the people in the room.

Late that morning, Mary caught her breath when she saw Timothy saunter into Osborne's Ready-To-Wear. He stood directly across the table from her, a sly grin on his face. "Just got into town," he said.

So he'd come back, had he? She kept folding the socks on the table. He wasn't the only one who could play the game. "May I help you?" she said. She pretended to look right through him. As a rule, she didn't like working the floor when Mrs. Sampson was at lunch, but today it couldn't have worked out better. The other clerks would think he had come in just to buy something.

He grinned at her. "I'd like a pair of those socks you're folding." His eyes challenged her. He walked around the table and stood beside her. "You going to meet me under the bridge?" he asked.

"What size do you wear?" She kept her eyes on the socks. His cocky attitude made her nervous but she didn't dare let him know that.

"Size ten," he said. "I'll take that brown pair." He reached into his back pocket and took out his wallet.

"That'll be fifty cents," she said. His hand caressed hers as he gave her a dollar bill. She pulled away, turned to the register, put the socks in a paper bag, and handed it to him with his change. "Here you are."

He took hold of her hand. "Well? Are you meeting me?"

"Yes, but please take your change and let go of my hand. I don't want gossip about us, and you're a great object of interest around here." She glanced quickly at the other two clerks on the floor, but they were busy with stock, thank heaven.

"You're the only object I'm interested in. What time can you meet me?" His eyes swept over her.

She felt a thrill of amusement. She'd worn her silk georgette with the pleated skirt. Its creamy color matched the color of her hair. She looked ritzy and she knew it. He didn't have a chance. "It shouldn't be more than forty-five minutes. Now leave, please." Her plan was working, but she knew he'd be hard to manage. She'd have to be very careful.

Instead of walking on the street, Mary used the alley behind the store. It led straight to the river and there would be less chance of being seen that way. She paused at the dirt road that ran along the river. No one in sight.

When she stepped off the road into the grass, it tugged at her new silk hose and the heels of her shoes sank into the ground. A grasshopper jumped on her skirt. She swore under her breath at the stain it left. God, how she hated living in the country.

He had spread out a blanket behind some bushes underneath the place where the bridge joined the bank. She sat down beside him and calmly began to eat her sandwich. "I made extra. Would you like one? It's ham."

"No thanks. I'd rather talk about us." His fingers tickled her arm. "You know how much I want you, Mary. What must I do to have you?"

"I won't give myself away, Timothy. I thought I made that clear." She moved away from him an inch or two. He probably thought he was irresistible. What man didn't?

He rolled over on his back and looked up at the bridge. "So you're talking about marriage, is that it?"

"Not only marriage but the conditions of the marriage. I don't want children right away." She checked his reaction. His expression hadn't changed.

"What else?"

"I want to live in New York, or, at the very least, in San Francisco."

Timothy grinned at her. "You're honest, I'll say that for you, but I hope you're as warm-blooded as you are cold-hearted. I want sex with you first, to make sure you're not frigid."

"Oh, really? And are you a good lover?" Men were so conceited. She put the rest of her sandwich back in the sack. Hardly a time to be eating.

"That's something you'd find out, if you'd let me make love to you, isn't it?" he said.

"No doubt. But then you wouldn't marry me, would you?" The look in his eyes unnerved her, but she wouldn't let it get to her. No. If he wanted her, he had to marry her. But she needed to reel him in with care. "Timothy, I don't mean to be unkind or cold. I'm more attracted to you than I've ever been to any man. But I have to look out for myself. No one else can or will. Look at this town, then look at me. Do I belong here?"

"No, you don't. But we'd have to live here for a while. Business keeps me in this area, and it's a very lucrative business. You'd like the money, wouldn't you?"

"Of course." No sense pretending she wouldn't. That's what marriage was supposed to do for a woman.

"I might be able to get situated in San Francisco, but it couldn't be done overnight. It might take a year, or more. What do I do in the meantime, sleep with whores?"

"That's a ridiculous thing to say."

"Is it?" he said.

"I have to get back to work." Disgusted with his threat, she started to get up. Whores, indeed.

"Not before you kiss me."

His arms pinned her down on the blanket and he moved until his body was on top of hers. His lips brushed hers with a gentleness that caught her off guard, and when his mouth opened, her own response frightened her. She had to stop him.

But he broke away first. "You are passionate, my love." He rose and pulled her up onto her feet. "You didn't know that, did you?"

"It doesn't change my conditions, so don't get your hopes up." She straightened her dress and patted her hair.

He laughed. "We are so much alike it just might work. Your family goes to church on Sundays, right?"

"You know we do."

"Pretend you're sick this Sunday so we can be together."

"I don't think that's a good idea. Now I need to get back to work. I'll leave first. You stay here for a while, please." It wouldn't do for them to be seen together coming out of the weeds. A ruined reputation would kill any further chances she might have. She thought he looked as if he could read her mind.

"I'll pick you up after work tonight," he said. "In the meantime, you think about what it would be like, making love with me, and I'll think about your conditions."

Would he agree to them? Well, if he didn't, there was always Paul. But could Paul ever arouse her as easily as Timothy had? She doubted it. By the time she got back to Osborne's she had barely calmed down. She didn't dare be alone with Timothy for very long. He'd eventually break down her resistance. God, his body had felt good on top of hers. But she had to be the winner. Her whole future depended on it.

A few minutes later Timothy walked into the Pine Cone Cafe. He hailed the regulars, but he didn't sit with them. He sat at the counter and winked at Valina.

"Any of the daily special left?" he asked.

"I'm sure there is. I'll bring you an order."

"Say hello to Mama, and tell her I'll take you home at four and chop her some more wood."

"Uh . . ." Valina leaned toward him and lowered her voice. "Thanks, but you won't need to chop wood. Papa's home. I'll explain later."

"Well, I'll still take you home so I can see your father. I've missed him."

Valina knew she should ask Mama about riding home with him, but she thought it was time to start making her own decisions. After all, she'd be eighteen in November.

When he came to pick up Valina, Timothy reached across the front seat of the car to help her in. Her eyes widened at the strength of his hand, the bulge of his shoulder straining at the seams of his shirt. His sleeves were rolled up and she had a wild urge to touch the reddish-gold hair on his forearm. She forced herself to look at the road.

"Before I left last week I rented a cabin back in the woods." Timothy said. "It's down the road that branches off this one just before you get to your cabin."

"It must be the old Carter place."

"I believe that's what the man called it. Want to drive in and see what it looks like?"

Valina was nervous about going there with him, way back in the woods. Mama wouldn't approve. "I should probably get home."

"Oh. If you don't want to, that's fine."

He looked so disappointed she couldn't stand it. "Well, I guess it wouldn't take too long to just look at it."

He grinned and started to whistle a song she'd never heard before.

The road into the cabin, two dirt ruts, was almost over-grown with grass and underbrush. He looked like he wanted to cuss at the bushes that scraped his car.

Valina shook her head and giggled. "It would be easier to walk into here, you know."

He frowned. "It's too far to walk."

Valina laughed. "Do realize how few cars there are in Pine Bluff? There are only two of them. Everybody walks. That's the way we get from one place to another."

He grinned at her. "Not me. Not when I have this car, by golly."

The woods opened onto a small clearing where blackened stones of a crude fireplace stood, the stark remains of a former cabin that had burned years before. Beyond the clearing, the road disappeared under thick layers of pine needles. Timothy drove on about half a mile, until they reached the old cabin.

"Come have a look," he said.

The cabin smelled of mildew and mice. A wooden table, two chairs, and a narrow cot had been left behind. Fireplace ashes had drifted out onto the floor. A powdery mist floated with each of their footsteps.

"It's creepy," Valina said. "You're not really going to stay here, are you?"

"Just till I settle down with the right woman. I hired the hotel maid to clean this up. She said she'd do it on Monday. But it'll need a woman's touch. Curtains, dishes, bed linens, that sort of thing." He handed her five ten dollar bills. "I've been watching you, and I've noticed that you're not only lovely, you're very capable. Would you make this place homey for me? I'd really be pleased if you would."

She hesitated, astounded at his request, to say nothing of the amount of money she held in her hand.

"If you don't want to, I can have the maid do it. But I especially wanted you." He paused, his eyes fastened on hers. "I don't think you even know it, but you're the sort of girl men want to marry."

Valina's heart pounded. Timothy O'Callahan wanted her to make this place a home for him. And that was the second time he'd brought up the subject of marriage. She put the bills in her apron pocket. "I'll be very happy to fix up your cabin."

"You're a darling."

He pulled her to him and kissed her. His hands stroking her back sent chills clear through her. And his mouth . . .

He backed away. "I shouldn't do this. Not to you." He took her hand and walked her out to the car. "I'd better take you home."

They rode in silence. Valina's mind kept going over the things he'd said, and his kiss. He certainly acted like he was in love with her. And she knew beyond a doubt that she loved him. It thrilled her that he'd chosen her to fix up his cabin. When she got through with it, he'd know for sure what a good wife she'd be.

• • •

Almost everyone in town turned out for the Saturday night dances. Babies wrapped in blankets slept on the floor next to the walls; long tables sagged under the weight of the women's special recipes; and the Clearwater County Fiddler's Society played its traditional first number. "Turkey in the Straw".

After Timothy danced two dances with Mary, Valina began to think he wasn't interested in her, after all. But then he asked her, and his lead, strong and sure, made her feel like part of him. While they danced, he teased her with his eyes. She smiled, floating in his arms. She hated for the music to stop, but she knew she had to share him. She was shocked, however, when he asked Mama to dance the next set. She glanced at Mary. The outrage on her face told Valina exactly how upset her sister was.

"Would you like to dance, Valina?" She looked up at the sound of Paul's voice.

"I'd love to." They whirled into a fast waltz. She'd forgotten what a good dancer he was. Not as good as Timothy, though.

"You're having a nice time, aren't you?" Paul said.

"I always have a nice time." She smiled up at him but he didn't smile back.

He looked so serious. "Is something wrong?"

"No, not really. It's just that I'm moving to Portland. Early tomorrow morning, in fact."

"Tomorrow? I thought you planned to be here for the rest of the summer."

He shook his head. "I have to get over there and get started. But I'll miss watching you have a good time, Valina, whether it's here at the dances, or when you're pinning Bertha's ears back."

They both laughed.

It would be strange having him gone for good. When he'd been away at college he had at least been home for the holidays and summers. Portland was so far away. "You'll come home for the holidays, won't you?" she asked.

"Yes, for Thanksgiving and Christmas."

"Thanksgiving isn't very far off."

"I guess not, though it seems like it is, right now."

Valina thought he looked sad. Mary hadn't said a word about him leaving. Strange. Neither had Mama. Did they even know? "When did you decide to leave?"

"About an hour ago. You're the first person I've told."

"Oh."

They danced to the end of the set. When the music stopped, Paul stood there in the middle of the floor, looking at her like he wanted to say something.

"That's the end of the set," she said.

"Could we dance another one, since I'm leaving?"

"Well, sure. I'd like that."

They didn't talk while they danced. He already seemed far away, and his eyes looked so sad. She had a strange feeling she might never see him again.

As soon as the second set was over, Paul walked her to the front door. "I've got to go home and pack. I only came because I wanted to say goodbye to you."

She walked with him out to the front stoop. "Have a wonderful time with your new job. I know you'll do well. See you on Thanksgiving."

"You keep Bertha in line while I'm gone." He kissed her cheek, then quickly walked away.

What did that kiss mean, for goodness sake? And why did she have a lump in her throat? She had always known he would leave one day. After the dance, Valina didn't tell the family about Paul leaving. She knew Mary would have a royal fit when she found out.

Sure enough, when Mary heard the news the next day as the family walked home from church, she went into a rage.

"Mama, what do you mean, Paul's left? He can't do that."

"Catherine told me right after the service," Mama said. "He's already gone."

"Yes, he told me last night that he was leaving," Valina said. Mary would be infuriated by that piece of news.

Mary stopped in the road and grabbed Valina's arm. "Just what did you think you were doing last night, making a big play for Paul? Didn't you think I'd see what you were trying to do?"

Valina yanked her arm away. "I didn't ask him to dance, he asked me. And why are you so upset, anyway? You've avoided Paul ever since he came home from college."

"That's true, Mary," Mama said. "You haven't gone out of your way to see him, so why should he tell you? And why shouldn't he tell your sister, or anyone else he chose?"

"But Valina was flaunting . . ."

"That's enough, young lady. You are not to harass your sister about this. I don't want to hear another word about it." Mama gave Mary a stern look. "I mean that."

Mary sputtered, but she finally shut up.

The following Thursday at Osborne's, Mary was swamped with alterations. It seemed that every fat woman in town had tried on her fall clothes, only to find that they needed letting out. Mary hated working with heavy wools in the summer heat.

Besides, there was precious little to be happy about. Timothy hadn't been near her since that lunch under the bridge. Well, he'd taken her home after work, but he'd hardly said a word, much less made a pass at her. And only two dances with her on Saturday night. The nerve of him. He acted like nothing had ever happened between them. But he was due back tomorrow. Would he even come back? If only Paul had danced with her, Timothy would've been jealous, she was sure of that. But that wretched Valina had monopolized Paul.

And to think Paul left town without so much as a word to her, now of all times, when she needed him most. Was he carrying a torch for someone else? She should've played up to him more. Well, he'd be home for Thanksgiving. If Timothy hadn't proposed by then, Paul would. She'd make sure of it.

Timothy came into the cafe on Friday at three-thirty and took his usual seat at the counter. "Thought I'd sit here and have some coffee until it's time to take you home." He grinned and winked at Valina.

She leaned close to him when she poured his coffee, her voice low. "Maybe you'd better meet me where the street ends, just before we go through the woods to our cabin."

"Sure. Good idea." He looked around at the customers, then got up and went over to join the regulars.

Valina glanced at Bertha sitting over at the corner table. Wouldn't you know she'd be there when Timothy came in? Her nasty little eyes hadn't left him since he'd walked in the door. Timothy had stayed at the counter for just a few seconds, but Bertha's mind could conjure up all sorts of things.

Valina couldn't wait to see if Timothy liked what she'd done to his cabin. She'd bought the items at three different stores, afraid that one of the owners would be so amazed at an Addison with money that Mama might hear about it. Fortunately, Mama and Mary had to work later than she did. Rachel had been out of the way, too, practicing piano at Catherine's after school. And Papa was always gone, or too preoccupied to notice what time she came home.

The hardest part had been the watercolor. She had had to paint it at Timothy's cabin because Mama and the girls would've seen it. Besides, the subject, a gnarled pine tree, stood near his cabin. Would he like it? Would four o'clock never come?

Later, when she walked up to the edge of town, Timothy was waiting there in his Model A. She slid quickly into the car, eager for him to see how much she'd accomplished.

"Well, pretty girl, how's the cabin coming along?"

"It's all done."

"I should've known." He looked at her as if he knew everything about her, as if he could see into her mind and liked what he saw. She smiled. Yes, she was a responsible, efficient woman. He'd see.

When he stopped the car, he put his hand on her thigh. Goose bumps rose on her arms. "We're here," he said. "Let's go see what it looks like. He opened the door and she went in first, turning to see his reaction.

"Good Lord, you've made a miracle, Valina. Look at this place. I hardly recognize it. It's beautiful." He took in every detail: the colorful chintz curtains at the windows, the matching spread on the cot, the pillows she'd made, the table with the checkered tablecloth, the little pitcher with wild roses in it, the braided rugs on the floor. And then he stopped in front of her watercolor.

"Did you paint this?" He turned to look at her. "You did, didn't you?"

"Yes. It's my housewarming gift to you."

"You have warmed my heart as well as my house, Valina. Come here." He reached for her hand, turned it palm up and kissed it. "I can see your love in the painting, and in everything else you did. You do love me, don't you?"

"Yes," she whispered.

"My precious darling." He kissed her neck, her chin, her mouth. His tongue wound around hers. She felt him unbutton her blouse. When he'd found her nipple, he tugged at it and her back arched at the sensory assault. She loved him, oh yes. But the sudden thought of Mama shook her. It would break her heart if she knew. "Timothy, I mustn't."

"Ah, my little love, don't be afraid. We were meant for each other. I'll take care of you, I promise."

She started to tell him . . . what was it? His other hand had crept under her skirt, exploring the place between her thighs. His fingers started moving in a steady rhythm and an urgent burning started in her groin.

"I love your sexy little body," he whispered in her ear.

She tried to push away the thought of Mama. Timothy loved her and she loved him. It wasn't a matter of if she should, it was a matter of their love. He wanted her. Someone actually wanted her and that someone was a man, not a boy.

He slowly stripped off her blouse and skirt, then stood back and pulled the straps of her teddie down. It skimmed her body as it fell to the floor. Embarrassed, she covered her breasts with her hands but he shook his head and pulled them away.

"You mustn't hide. You have a gorgeous body, and I want it desperately."

Quickly he took off his own clothes. Her hands, of their own volition, began stroking the muscles of his chest and shoulders, her fingers sifting through the curly red hair on his chest. She looked down and stared, fascinated. Was he going to put that big thing in her? Dear heaven, she shouldn't be standing here naked, staring at him like this.

He smiled. "You've never seen one before, have you?"

"No," she gasped. "It's so big."

He grinned and pushed his pelvis toward her. "Yeah, I'm well-hung. Wait till you feel what it can do to you, baby."

Before she could say a word, he picked her up and carried her to the cot. "This will hurt a little the first time, sweetheart, but you'll love it just the same. I'll make sure you do."

Wait . . . this was wrong. "I shouldn't." She forced herself to sit up.

He put his hands on her breasts and pushed her back down on the cot. "Too late. You want me. You're mine now."

It did hurt, but the pulsing rhythm of his body moving in and out of hers stirred a wild, uncontrollable throbbing within her whole being. She was the drum on which he beat, a beat that grew louder, louder, until she screamed, and his cries matched hers, until the movement slowed, and the sound died, and only their shallow breathing remained.

"I told you you'd like it, little love."

She couldn't speak. Tears rolled down her cheeks.

"Aw, now, don't cry." He wiped the tears away and held her close. "I didn't hurt you that much, did I?"

She shook her head. "I didn't know it would be like that, so overwhelming."

He laughed. "You've just had it with the master. And it'll get better each time we do it." He kissed her, then leaned away from her. "I wish we could do it again right now, but we don't have time, do we?"

"No, I'd better get home." She rolled off the cot and slipped into her clothes, suddenly feeling cold and ashamed. "I don't like sneaking around like this, Timothy."

"We won't sneak for long, believe me." He stood up and took her chin in his hand. "Tell me you love me. You haven't said it in so many words. I want to hear it."

"Oh, I do love you, Timothy." She leaned against his bare shoulder, but moved away when, against her thigh, she felt him start to get big again. There wasn't time. She wanted to ask him when they'd be married, but she was afraid he'd think she was pushy. Besides, she knew he'd mention it soon.

But later that night, when she was getting into bed, she realized that Timothy had never told her he loved her.

The following Thursday, Valina had just finished preparing dinner for the family, when Mary got home an hour earlier than usual. Mary had been underfoot all week, raving like a maniac. She had even come into the cafe for lunch every day, something she never did, just so she could sit at the counter and hiss accusations at Valina, like a stupid goose.

Wearily, Valina braced herself. "You're home early."

"Mrs. Sampson told me to go ahead and leave, since I didn't feel well," Mary snarled.

Valina didn't think Mary had used a civil tone of voice since the day Paul left. And she didn't look very sick, either.

Mary flounced over to where Valina stood by the table. "I'm sure you wouldn't feel very well if your sister had tried to take away your beau."

"Once and for all, I did not try to take away your beau. Have you taken leave of your senses?"

When Valina tried to put the plates on the table, Mary stood in her way. Valina moved around her, but Mary outmaneuvered her. Valina sighed. "Will you please get out of my way?"

"No," Mary yelled. "I hate you for what you've done to me."

Valina couldn't stand it. "I haven't done anything to you, do you hear me? Nothing. Nothing. Nothing." She could hear herself yelling. She shoved Mary out of her way, and headed for the stove, but Mary managed to block her before she got there.

"Leave me alone," Valina yelled.

"You're the reason he didn't tell me," Mary screamed.

"You know you don't care a fig about Paul, at least you don't act like it. Besides, all I did was dance with him."

"You didn't just dance with him. You danced with him all evening."

"I did not. I only danced two sets with him. What in heaven's name do you expect me to do about it? I don't know why he didn't tell you he was leaving. Why don't you ask him when he comes home for Thanksgiving?"

"I will, believe me. And you're to keep your hands off him. You hear me?"

"I never had my hands on him." Valina wished she could tell Mary it was Timothy she loved, not Paul. But Mary would be jealous of that, too, and try to take Timothy away from her. Just the thought of it gave her a chill.

No matter what Mary said, she couldn't stop daydreaming about Timothy, and the way he made love to her. She tried not to think about Mama and how disappointed she'd be. But after all, she and Timothy were going to be married, so why should she feel guilty?

Valina turned away from Mary and started toward the door.

"Where do you think you're going?" Mary demanded.

"To the outhouse. I prefer the smell out there to the noise in here. And don't you dare follow me. I've had enough of you. You've said all of this a thousand times."

Just as Valina reached for the doorknob, the door opened and Mama and Rachel walked in.

"What's going on in here?" Mama said. "We could hear you halfway into town."

"Mary's still mad because Paul told me, instead of her, that he was leaving." So there. It felt good to tell on her.

Mama scowled at Mary. "I told you to leave your sister alone."

But the scowl had no effect on Mary. She just drew herself up to her full height and looked down at Mama. "I'm nineteen years old, and I can say anything I please."

"You certainly can, but you'll do it in your own home, not in this one." Mama's mouth clamped shut in a tight line.

Valina looked at Rachel and raised her eyebrows. The spoiled princess of the family had just been reduced to a humble peasant. Rachel grinned and fluttered her eyelashes, a perfect imitation of Mary when she was in one of her la-de-da moods. Valina had to put her hand over her mouth to hide her silent laughter.

Mary's jaw fell open and stayed that way until she could speak. "Mama, you know I can't support myself yet."

"Precisely my point," Mama said.

Their eyes locked, until Mary finally gave in and looked down at the floor. No one said a word, but Valina wanted to cheer. Having a job sure made a big difference in Mama.

Just then the door opened a crack. "Is it safe to come in yet?"

Papa's voice. Valina laughed. Leave it to Papa to break up a perfectly good fight.

When he came into the room, he gave them a radiant smile. "Emma," he said, "you'll be happy to know that I got a job today."

His grand announcement hovered in the air, then sagged like a wounded bird.

Silence.

His smile faded. "Well, doesn't anyone want to hear about it?"

"I do, Papa." Rachel took hold of his hand. "Tell me."

"Emma? How about you?"

"Go ahead," Mama said, though she didn't look very enthusiastic.

He looked at each of them and beamed. "Starting tomorrow I'll be the new janitor at the Clearwater County Courthouse."

"Oh, Papa, that's swell," Rachel said.

"For how long?" Mama's voice sounded hard.

Papa, crestfallen, said, "It's a permanent job, Emma. I thought you'd be pleased."

"I will be, once I know it's permanent."

The two of them stood in the middle of the floor staring at each other. And then Papa took five candy bars out of his pocket and put them on the table. They'd never had candy bars before.

Rachel pounced on one. "Look, Mama, Hershey bars!"

"Not before dinner, Rachel," Mama said.

"Well, lets eat fast, then. Please?"

Rachel's eager face broke the tension. Papa went over and put his arm around Mama's waist. His eyes danced. "And maybe later we could celebrate my new job."

Mama ducked her head, her face pink. "Daniel, you're incorrigible."

After school the next day, Rachel came into the cafe and settled herself on a stool at the counter. "Mama's different lately," she said.

Valina stopped wiping the counter. "What makes you say that?" She already knew, but she wanted to hear Rachel's version.

"The way she talked to Mary last night. Mama's never done that before."

"That's true." Valina knew Mama wouldn't approve of them talking about it, but they'd both been shocked when Mary had kept her mouth shut even after they'd gone to bed. At first, Valina hadn't been able to sleep, waiting for the whine to start again, but Mama's invitation to move out must've given Mary laryngitis.

"And . . . there's something else," Rachel said. "Do you think Mama still likes Papa?"

"Why, of course she does. She doesn't just like him, she loves him."

"But she's been awful cross with Papa lately."

"Well, I get cross with you sometimes, but that doesn't mean I don't love you."

Rachel stared at the counter for a few seconds. When she

looked up again, she pushed a nickel across the counter. "Papa gave me money for a creme soda."

As Valina got the soda, she remembered a certain visitor who'd been in that morning. "I think you should know that Mrs. Bailey came in today. Seems Roy came home yesterday with raw marks around his wrists. He wouldn't tell her how they got there, but she was plenty curious about your recent activities."

"Oh?" The straw in Rachel's mouth muffled her voice. "Did she talk to Mama?"

"I don't think so. What did you do to him?"

Rachel yanked the straw out of her mouth. "Why does everyone always suspect me?"

"That's easy. You're always guilty. Now, how did you scare him so bad that he wouldn't even tell his own mother?"

Rachel peered up at Valina. "You won't tell Mama?"

"You know I don't make promises like that." Rachel would tell her, anyway. The little scamp loved to brag when she'd put one over on Roy.

"If you really want to know, I tied him to a tree back in the woods."

"Rachel, that's dreadful."

Rachel just shrugged. "He got loose, anyway, so why should he tell his mother?"

"You didn't threaten him with some dire consequence, by any chance?"

Rachel's face creased into a mischievous grin. "Only that I'd tell Miss Langdon that he cheated on the arithmetic test yesterday."

"He did?"

"Yeah. I saw him do it. Copied answers right out of the book. He's such a sap to think I wouldn't see him. He sits right in front of me."

"You know, I've been thinking about you and Roy. I bet you two will get married when you grow up."

Rachel choked on her creme soda. "You're crazy."

"No, I'm not. After all, you must think a lot of each other to spend so much time figuring out ways to get the other one's goat."

"Why, I wouldn't marry that stupid Roy Bailey if he had a million dollars. In fact, I don't plan on ever getting married," Rachel said.

"Then you won't have any children, will you? But maybe that would be best. Think what it would be like if you had a child just like you."

Rachel stood up, huffy as an insulted old maid. "You're as batty as Mary is. I'm getting out of here. It must be catching."

Valina thought the world would be a lesser place without Rachel in it. She was a pain in the neck, but she was always so blithely cheerful about her own transgressions. No guilt in her makeup, but no guile either. Valina giggled. Rachel was a lot like Aunt Matilda. Poor Roy was doomed.

CHAPTER 7

J-Bar-J Ranch — 1969

Early the next morning, I told Jimmy to go out to the barn and help reset a shoe on one of the thoroughbreds. "Buck's there waiting for you. He'll supervise."

"With ESP, right? All he does is grunt, remember?"

"Why don't you try grunting right back at him?"

The kid scowled. "What the hell kind of conversation would that be?"

"Buck's kind."

"Oh, crap." Jimmy ambled out the door, not exactly the picture of enthusiasm.

I'd finished peeling the apples and was sifting flour for pie dough, when he came back.

"That didn't take long," I said.

"Buck grunted, so I must've done it right."

"You did. And right now Oscar's waiting for you in the south pasture. He found a broken fence this morning."

Jimmy glowered at me and stomped out the door.

Wasn't a half hour later that Oscar and Jimmy drove up in the jeep. I went out on the porch. "Where's Jimmy's horse?" I asked.

"You know Sunny," Oscar said. "He'll be along in a minute."

Sunny always knew his way home, but I thought it was strange Jimmy hadn't ridden him. "The fence mended already?"

"We started in, all right," Oscar said, "but the kid cut his hand on some barbed wire."

Jimmy got out of the jeep and came up on the porch, clutching his left hand in a rag. I peeled it off as gently as I could. The heel of his hand was cut long and deep.

"You gave it one helluva a yank, didn't you? I'll need to clean that out and take a couple of stitches in it."

Jimmy almost fell off the porch. "You aren't a doctor."

"I'm the doctor on this ranch." I took his arm and led him into the kitchen. "You had a tetanus shot lately?"

"What's that?" He sounded mighty uneasy.

"A shot to keep you from getting lockjaw."

"Lockjaw?" His eyes got big and his skin turned a bit sallow. "Is that what it does to you, locks your jaw?"

"Mm-hmm. But the shot will take care of it. Nothing to worry about." He got downright pale. I sent Oscar away in case the kid fainted. No sense humiliating him in front of Oscar.

"Okay. First, I'll put some Novocain in that hand so I can scrub the wound. Got to get it good and clean before I sew it up. The shot will sting, but once it takes effect, you won't feel a thing." He turned his head and squeezed his eyes shut, then pulled away so hard I had to use a half-nelson on his arm. Good thing I'd been wrestling horses and cattle all my life. Not that I didn't pay dearly for my efforts. That no-good shoulder of mine can really hold a grudge. After I gave him the shot, I said, "Now that didn't hurt much."

"The hell it didn't," he growled.

"Come over to the sink. And don't panic. This brush is soft."

"You're gonna scrub it with a brush?" He started to edge his way to the back door.

"You don't need to watch, you know, but you do need to keep breathing or you might faint." I waited for a few seconds. "You won't even feel it."

He fearfully poked his hand near the wound, then raised his eyebrows. "Yeah, it is numb."

When he finally came over to me, I cleaned out the wound, put in three stitches, and bandaged the hand before he knew what happened. "Okay, it's all done." I turned my back to him and filled the syringe while he examined his bandage. Then I swabbed his arm and stuck the needle in before he had a chance to get all excited about it.

"Ow!"

"Tetanus shots do smart a bit."

He rubbed his arm and glared at me.

"I feel like having a mess of trout for dinner," I said. "Let's go fishing." I didn't give him a chance to say yes or no. "I'll fix a lunch to take with us. Want a cup of tea while I'm doing it?"

"Tea? Men don't drink tea." He stomped out onto the porch and slammed the screen door behind him. The old wicker chair out there squeaked when he sat in it.

A cool breeze started as we walked across the pasture to the river. Jimmy kept stumbling. Either his foot sank into a hole, or his toe stubbed up against a lump of dirt.

Guess you have to be born to the pasture to know how to walk in it. I didn't let him carry the can of worms for fear he'd dump them on the ground. Just carrying his pole seemed precarious enough. 'Course, he was favoring his wounded hand. Very dramatic about it, too. Until I'd spent time with Jimmy, I hadn't realized what a handicap it was to be raised in a city. When we got to the river, I led him upstream a ways to a grove of poplar trees. One of the trees had fallen along the river's edge. We stopped by it.

"There's a deep hole right here where I can usually catch a few. If we're lucky, we'll snag us a whole dinner's worth. You know how to put a worm on the hook?"

He gave me a disgusted look. "Sure. Me and my dad go fishing every summer. Where'd you get the worms?"

"I picked them before I went to bed last night. Planned to do a little fishing today."

His eyes narrowed. "Picked?"

"Worms surface in the lawn at night when you shine a flashlight on them. But they're fast little devils. The grass has to be fresh cut or you'll be grabbing air."

He snorted. "Yeah, sure."

Poor dumb kid.

We each put a worm on our hooks, though he had a hard time doing it one-handed. Then we propped the poles up on the log and put rocks against them to hold them down. Wouldn't like to hook a big one and see the pole swim off behind it. We sat on the grass, leaned back against a large rock, and ate our lunch, glancing at the poles now and then. The river slid lazily along, gleaming in the sunlight.

"Betcha a dollar I get the first fish," Jimmy said.

"You're on. I'll take your money any day."

We were silent for quite a while, waiting to see a pole jiggle. Then, out of nowhere, he said, "Do you believe in God?"

The kid threw me a curve with that one. Religion? I thought it over for a minute before I answered. "When you look around at this world, you have to believe in something. A power, a God. It's too complex to be an accident."

"If there is a God do you think he looks like us?"

We were getting pretty serious here. Sandy's death must've started him thinking.

"Who should he look like? The Bible says we were created in God's image, but the Bible was written by fallible men. We have no concept of a higher form of life than ourselves, a natural conceit, but a foolish one. God could be a faceless, sexless intellect, a power the likes of which we can't even begin to imagine."

He studied that for a bit, then said, "I'd never thought of it that way."

Why couldn't I keep my mouth shut? I didn't want him to go home and quote me. "What do your parents believe?"

"Mom goes to church once in a while, but I don't know what she believes. Dad's never said anything about it, either."

"Why don't you ask them sometime?"

He shrugged and lapsed into silence. I leaned back and gave my eyes a rest. But he had another question. "Would you go to church if you lived in town?"

My eyes popped open. "No. For one thing, I wouldn't live

in town. Besides, I believe that organized religion is a crime against God."

He frowned. "I don't get what you mean."

"Too much harm's been done by religious groups. Some have killed in order to prove their way is the only way. Talk about sin! My religion, if you can call it that, is my reverence for what's here around me. The land, the things that grow on it, the creatures that live on it. But that's just my view. You're entitled to your own."

"Whatever it is you believe, you call it God."

"More convenient to say God or Him, than any of the other things I've heard. What about you? Do you believe in God?"

"I don't know. I've been trying to figure it out."

"Religion is a great comfort to some people. Your great-grandmother Emma's religion went clear through her character. She was one of the pure ones, always doing for others, always forgiving, though she certainly had her human side."

Something caught my eye. Jimmy's pole was bobbing up and down. "Fish on."

He grabbed the pole. "I told you I'd get the first fish!" By golly, he got so busy reeling in his line, he forgot all about that cut on his hand.

Hannah and Tom Lewis arrived at the ranch early Saturday morning on their way to her father's place. Hannah walked up onto the porch where I was standing. "Matilda, the lawyer told us we had to have a witness present when Buddy signs the papers for the ranch. I hate to impose on you."

"Why, I'll be glad to. I'd like to see Buddy, anyway." I turned to Jimmy. "Go saddle up Sally for me." He didn't even breathe until I added, "And the Arabian for you. And tell Oscar where we're going."

Jimmy grinned and hustled out the door.

I made Hannah and Tom come in the house and sit down. "Have a cup of coffee before we start off."

Hannah took a sip of hers, and said, "We called Buddy this morning, to be sure he'd be at the house when we got there. And we brought along cleaning supplies. Doubt that Dad did much to keep up the house."

I didn't tell her that Buddy had already cleaned the place. Let her be surprised.

Tom spoke up. "Buddy asked me to survey a new property line for you two. Do you have your plat handy? I need to see if it matches the one at the courthouse."

"I'll get it right now. It's on my desk." I came back and handed the plat to Tom. Out of the window, I saw Jimmy riding up to the house on the Arabian, Sally right behind them. Not ten seconds later, the kid yanked open the screen door. "Horses are ready, Aunt Matilda." Before I could say a word, he was back sitting on the Arabian.

I just shook my head and explained. "That kid is chomping at the bit to get over to Buddy's place. He flat out idolizes the man."

"He could do worse," Tom said. "Buddy's real people." He took Hannah's arm and led her to the door. "If you're ready to go, we are too, Matilda."

"Might as well." They took off in their truck, while Jimmy and I rode behind swallowing their dust, grateful when they moved clear out of sight.

They were still sitting in their truck when we got to Sandy's place. Hannah's eyes were red and puffy. "I thought we'd wait for you before we went in," she said.

She held her body stiff, like she dreaded going in the house. Couldn't blame her. She hadn't been allowed in the place for years.

When we walked into the front room, there stood the most beautiful Indian girl I'd ever seen. She was tall, with skin the color of maple nut ice cream. Her face, with its high cheekbones, was framed with long thick black hair. She wore a soft white shirt and creamy cotton slacks. Mary, or Marie, now that she was our family's successful fashion expert, would probably say that her outfit complemented her coloring. I'd say the girl looked like an Indian princess.

Jimmy stared at her, open mouthed. Well, she was a sight to behold. No wonder Buddy's face lit up whenever he looked at her.

"You must be Linette," I said.

She smiled. "That's right, and you must be Matilda Jacobsen." Her voice had a peaceful sound, like the soft ripple of water in a brook.

"Call me Matilda."

Right after Buddy made the rest of the introductions, a younger version of Linette came in the front door. The girl had thick black hair like Linette's, but it was pulled into one long braid down her back. Her face was fuller and her skin a little darker. And there was a soft, innocent look in her eyes, that sweet look young girls have before some SOB disillusions them. Looked to me like she might be fourteen or fifteen.

Maybe that was because she wore denim jeans and one of those damned tie-dyed shirts like Jimmy had worn when he got off the train.

When Jimmy caught sight of her, you'd have thought he'd been punched in his gut. God. I hoped she lived at least a hundred miles from here.

"Take a breath, boy," I whispered. Oh, he did give me a nasty glare.

"This is Anika, Linette's younger sister," Buddy said. He gestured to her. "Come meet Matilda Jacobsen and her nephew, Jimmy."

When Anika smiled at us, and said, "How do you do," Jimmy sucked in his breath. I gave him a look I hoped would cool him off, but he wasn't even aware I was in the room, much less standing right beside him. I swear to God, if she'd patted him on the head he'd have wagged his tail.

"Anika is quite a horsewoman, Matilda." Buddy grinned at the pretty young girl. "I bet Jimmy would like to see your horse, Anika."

She smiled at Jimmy. "Want to?"

Jimmy came back to normal with a grin that almost split his face. "Sure." He hung back and let Anika go out the door first, then followed her, strutting exactly like that silly rooster of mine.

As I watched him leave with her, a shiver crawled between my shoulder blades. I hadn't counted on him meeting a girl his own age, especially one as beautiful as Anika. Even worse, she would soon be Buddy's sister-in-law. Should I warn Buddy about Jimmy and his hormones? Nope, I couldn't do that.

Buddy put his arm around Linette's waist and pointed at the cardboard boxes lined up in the room. "Linette took every box the grocer had so we could pack up Sandy's things."

"You've already packed for us?" Tom said.

"Oh, dear, that was our job, not yours." Hannah looked around the room. "And you've cleaned the place, too."

"It wasn't any trouble," Buddy said. "We'd like to buy some of the furniture, if you'd be willing to sell it."

I went into the kitchen with Linette, so Buddy and the Lewises could discuss their deal in peace. A delicious spicy aroma filled the room. The kitchen was spotless. The walls were a pale yellow instead of the faded dirty green they'd been before. "Buddy not only cleaned the place, he's painted the kitchen. Looks like a real home now."

"He did a good job, didn't he?" Linette took a pan of gingerbread out of the oven. So that's what smelled so good.

I could see Hannah walking slowly around the living room, touching a table or a chair now and then, lost in her memories. She was having a hard time. Lord, I was glad she hadn't seen the pitiful way her father died. The poor woman had enough heartache without that.

Linette went over to the kitchen door and announced. "If you're ready, I'm serving gingerbread. Buddy, will you let the kids know?"

Buddy went to the open front door and yelled, "Dessert."

Didn't take long for Jimmy to escort Anika to the kitchen table. The little turkey pulled out a chair for her, then grabbed the one next to it and sat down before anyone had a chance to split them up, not that we would have tried.

When we were all seated, we savored warm gingerbread topped with applesauce and sweet whipped cream. It tasted even better than it smelled.

Anika favored Jimmy with a shy smile. "I've never been to San Francisco."

So he'd been bragging to her about being a sophisticated city man, had he?

"If you ever make it there, I could show you around," he said. "There's a lot to see and do . . . a lot more than up here. Theaters, Golden Gate Park, the beach, all kinds of things. You'd like it."

Her breath came out in a soft sigh. "Oh, I know I would. I've heard they have great stores, too."

"Yeah, the best." He tilted his chin up, looking for all the world as if he owned those stores. The little snot.

Buddy leaned across the table toward Jimmy, trying to get his attention. Finally, he reached over and poked Jimmy's arm. Still trying to be a man of the world, Jimmy turned to Buddy and said, "Did you want something?"

"Yes," Buddy said, trying hard to control the grin on his face. "How would you like to come over tomorrow morning and help Anika and me paint the outside of the house?"

Jimmy beamed. "Sure. What time?"

"Six," Buddy said.

Jimmy looked too damned happy. I could picture him making an ass of himself tomorrow trying to impress Anika. Bet he wouldn't have any trouble getting out of bed at five, either. Well, at least I wouldn't have to watch his asinine performance.

Jimmy tossed a glance in my direction. "Is that okay with you, Aunt Matilda?"

About time he thought of that. Little turkey was pretty smart. "Fine," I said, knowing how nice it would be for Oscar to have a day without him.

After we finished eating, Buddy signed the papers for the purchase of Sandy's ranch and I witnessed them, a joyful moment for Buddy and Linette, but a glance at Hannah's wistful face told me how hard it was for her.

Then Buddy took me aside. "Anything strange going on at your place?"

"Oh, just another cut fence. Why?"

"Well, a couple of tools I know were here, are missing."

"Sure you didn't mislay them?" But I knew he was too tidy to lose things. Besides, he didn't have holes in his memory like some of us do.

"I'm sure." Buddy said. "And a few other things were out of place."

"Sandy tried to warn me there was mischief going on. Could be kids with more nerve than brains."

"Maybe, but I don't think so."

"Oh?"He started to tell me something, but just then we heard a truck drive up and stop. Pretty soon, a tall handsome Indian man, about Buddy's age, walked in the front door.

"This is my new foreman," Buddy said. "Linette's twin brother, Lance."

I took another look at the young man. Same oval face, same large dark eyes. "Yes, I can see the resemblance, all right." They were a mighty handsome family, the twins and Anika.

Some dogs started barking, and Buddy turned to Lance. "You brought the dogs with you. Glad you did. Thanks."

"They're out in the cab of the truck," Lance said. "We'd better let them out before they tear the seat to shreds."

Next thing I knew, there were two Dobermans slobbering all over my hands and stepping on my feet. Now, Dobermans are usually classy dogs, but these two were klutzes.

Buddy shook his head and laughed. "I got them for watch dogs, but they need a little training."

I grinned at him. "They'll sure let you know if someone comes snooping around, won't they?"

"That's the idea."

On the way back to the ranch, Jimmy had a question. "Why didn't Sandy like Tom? He's okay."

"I don't know why Sandy reacted to their marriage the way he did. He was such a poop. I think most of the problem was stubborn male pride. He would never tell me what his problem was with Tom, even though just a few words could have changed everything."

When we got back to my place, Mattie's Boy trotted over to greet us.

"He isn't as frisky as he was," Jimmy said.

"No. Sunny's been a good influence on him."

Jimmy patted the colt's neck. "Yeah, but I kind of miss all that."

"Young critters grow up too fast, don't they?"

I watched him poke his fingers in the colt's mouth and pick up one of its hooves. He and Mattie's boy had both learned a lot in a few short weeks.

That evening, while Jimmy and the men finished their chores, Oscar helped me get dinner. Once in a while he likes to show off what a good cook he is. I don't discourage him. I washed the spinach and set the table, while he broiled the steaks, sliced some tomatoes, and cooked the ears of corn.

"I'm glad we're alone," he said. "I went back and finished mending that fence today. It was deliberately cut. No two ways about it. I don't like this one bit."

"Neither do I, but how can we put a stop to it?"

He scowled. "There has to be some way to catch the bastard."

"We sure can't guard all the fences twenty-four hours a day."

"No," he said, "but the two sections of fence he cut were in adjoining fields. Why couldn't I spend the night watching the field on the south side, while George watched the one on the north?"

"For how many nights? You don't know when he'll come back, or even if he will. And there's an awful lot of fencing along those fields, some parts hidden by trees. Besides, he could cut them in the daylight."

"Well, hell's fire, we've got to do something." He stopped slicing and held the knife in mid-air. "Wonder why this guy has such a grudge against us?"

"It isn't just us. Buddy said a couple of tools were missing out of Sandy's barn, and some other things had been moved."

"Damn," Oscar growled. "I hate to see the creep get away with this. We should call the sheriff."

"He couldn't do any more than we can to stop the miserable wretch."

"Well, at least he'd know what's going on."

Oscar sure didn't like hearing me reject his plan. I knew he'd stew until he came up with another idea. Well, I wished him luck.

The next day, Jimmy took off for Buddy's before I got downstairs to make breakfast. I'd told him the night before that he'd better be back by dinner time or I'd send out a posse for him. And I emphasized, in case he hadn't noticed before, that dinner time was six o'clock. The idea of him being away for the whole day bothered me a bit. The little turkey was my responsibility, mine alone. I kept myself busy so I wouldn't have time to fret. I baked bread, made an apple pie, did a load of wash, ironed, picked cucumbers and put them in a crock of brine, and made lunch for the men. By that time my butt was dragging, but damned if there wasn't still part of the day left.

So I picked a mess of green beans and sat under the pickle tree to snap them. Next thing I knew, my head jerked as I woke up. Damn, I hate nodding off like that. Sure makes a body feel old.

As you might've guessed, six o'clock came and went, but no Jimmy. I fretted and kept the food warm until six-thirty, then dished it up. One minute I'd be furious with the kid, the next minute I'd be scared limp. Where the hell was he? I didn't want to call Buddy just yet. Maybe after dinner.

Oscar couldn't resist needling me. His face as innocent as a babe's, he looked around the room. "Where's Jimmy?"

Damned if I'd rise to his bait. He knew Jimmy was over at Buddy's, at least I hoped he was there.

But Oscar had more to say. "From what you told me about

that cute girl over there, if the kid had his way, he'd move in with Buddy."

"Maybe he's already moved in," George said.

"Umm," Buck said, through a mouthful of potatoes.

"Course, he could've fallen off his horse," Oscar said.

"Yup," George nodded. "Might've broken his leg."

Don't know what got into me, but I stood up, picked up my plate and took it out to the porch. I sat down in the rocker, set on finishing my dinner in peace. If one of those half-baked men followed me, I'd throw the plate at him. Fortunately for them, they left me alone.

At seven-thirty, I had just decided to call Buddy, when the phone rang. My stomach lurched when I heard his voice.

"Matilda, I'm very unhappy with Jimmy," he said. "It was about three when we finished painting. Jimmy asked if he and Anika could go for a short ride. I said they could, but to be back by five. They didn't come back until a half hour ago."

I glanced at the clock. It was 7:35.

"I gave him hell, Matilda." He cleared his throat. "I hope that doesn't offend you."

"Offend me? He'll be the one who's offended when he gets back here. I'm real sorry about this."

"Not your fault. Just wanted you to know about it."

"I think I hear his horse off in the distance. Thanks for calling, Buddy."

I waited on the back porch with blood in my eye. If he had touched that girl, I'd break his neck. He saw me when he rode up to the house and his face got pale. He knew I was in a rage. "Get off that horse before I drag you off," I yelled.

"Buddy . . . ?" He dismounted and stood by the horse.

"Yeah, he called. Seems you took Anika off and stayed away quite a bit too long."

He grabbed the halter and clutched it until his knuckles went white. "We didn't know how late it was."

"You didn't give a damn how late it was. If you laid a hand on her . . ."

"Nothing happened, I swear."

"Ah, but you tried, didn't you?"

He concentrated on the toes of his boots. "She wouldn't let me get near her."

"Sounds like she has her head on straight. Too bad you don't."

He looked up at me. "But nothing happened!"

"Shut up and listen to me. I know about your little girl-friend in The City."

He gulped, his Adam's apple fairly waving up and down. "Dad told you?"

"Of course."

He gulped again.

"Wonder what that girl will go through for the rest of her life because of what you did? It can't be easy to know you aborted a baby."

He hung his head, and in a low voice said, "She doesn't want to see me anymore."

"Good for her. Does your Dad know that?"

"No. He didn't want to hear me talk, right then."

"Can't say I blame him."

He still couldn't look at me.

"You had a nice thing going with Buddy. Why'd you mess it up?" For a moment there, I thought he was going to bawl, but he got hold of himself.

"I didn't mean to." His voice sounded like he'd just swallowed a cotton ball.

"Think about that while you do your chores." I turned my back on him and went inside the house.

CHAPTER 8

Pine Bluff—1929

On Friday morning Mary was glad she could work alone in the alterations room. She was too nervous to be around other people. She'd brought her lunch in case Timothy came to town and wanted her to meet him. If he didn't at least stop by, she'd just fly apart.

But at noon, nervous or not, she had to take Mrs. Sampson's place on the floor. She'd arranged and rearranged the table of men's sweaters twice before she heard the door open. Timothy stood there, grinning.

"Oh, it's you. You startled me," she said.

He smiled. "No, I didn't. You've been waiting for me."

He was so sure of himself. Normally, she would hate someone like him, but no one had ever challenged her this way. Appalled, she realized that it made her want him. "It's a good thing we're alone in here. What would people think, hearing you?"

"I don't care what people think. Did you bring your lunch?"

"Yes." Damn, she should've said no. He had her and he knew it. She wanted to slap the smirk right off his handsome face.

"Meet me at the same place under the bridge." Without another word, he wheeled around and walked out the door.

The nerve of him. She caught herself clutching one of the sweaters and quickly smoothed it out and put it where it belonged.

Later, when she walked under the bridge, he was stretched out on his back on a blanket. Hardly asleep, though. She could see he was hard just waiting for her. She wanted to cover him with her own body. Instead, she clenched her fists until her fingernails bit into her palms. She had to keep her head.

She sat as far away from him as she could. Dried weeds, poking through the blanket, felt like needles piercing her thighs. How could she appear cool and collected when she was sitting on the scratchy things?

He watched her closely as she ate her sandwich, his concentration on her every bite, while she got indigestion. She wanted to toss the sandwich into the river, but then he'd know she was nervous. He'd love that.

His hand crept under her dress and worked its way up her thigh. She tried to shove him away, but he suddenly reached up and grabbed both of her arms. Her sandwich fell to the grass beside her.

"How would you like to be raped?"

"Timothy!" A cold shiver swept over her.

"That's the only way I'll get you isn't it?" He took her face in his hands and forced her to look at him, his eyes boring into hers. "Isn't it?" His face was so close she could taste the tobacco on his breath. Suddenly he let go, stood up, and turned his back to her. "Unless I marry you."

She couldn't say a word, couldn't breathe.

He knelt beside her. "So, I'll marry you. God help me, I have to have you." His kiss hurt her mouth. When he pulled away, his eyes glittered. With triumph or anger? She couldn't tell.

"You know we'll have to elope," he said.

She'd always wanted a big wedding so she could design her own beautiful wedding dress, but no one in Pine Bluff had formal weddings. Besides, Mama and Papa didn't have money even for the essentials, much less a wedding. And Mama wouldn't pay for it if she did have the money. She'd be very upset about this marriage.

"When?" she asked.

"We'll make a good pair, you and I. We're so much alike. How about next Friday?"

Could she get her clothes ready in just a week? Maybe she could sneak a few things to Osborne's each day. And what she couldn't take, Timothy would have to buy for her.

She smiled. "You mean not show up for work after lunch, or would you be in town earlier in the day?"

"I'll be here just before noon. Leave your boss a note saying you went home sick. You won't be working there again, anyway."

"What about Mama and Papa?"

"Leave a note for your mother. Something about how we had to elope because she didn't approve. And before I leave on Sunday, I'll give you a note for your father. He'll be all right."

Mary remembered how Mama had threatened to kick her out. Well, now she'd find out what it was like to have her gone.

After work that day, Valina walked past the edge of town and found Timothy waiting for her. She had planned to bring up the subject of marriage. She'd even rehearsed what she'd say. Now the time had come to say it.

But he was quiet on the drive to his cabin, and she found herself tongue-tied. He must be tired. Or maybe he didn't feel well. When they walked in the cabin, he clutched her to his body, his face so fierce that she drew back.

"I'm sorry, Valina, I can't be patient this time. I can't. Forgive me, darling, but I need you desperately."

He ripped his clothes off, then pawed at hers, his hands clumsy, not gentle and sweet like before.

"Timothy, wait . . ." She pushed his hands away. What on earth was wrong with him? While she took her clothes off, for fear he'd tear them, he grabbed a rubber out of his slacks pocket and put it on.

Suddenly, he picked her up, dropped her on the cot, and lay on top of her. No caresses, no kisses, just his thrust and it was all over. She felt dirty and violated, and she hurt, he'd been so rough.

Mortified, she hurried to get dressed. When he put his arm around her, she shrank away.

"Sorry, baby. I shouldn't have spent all day thinking about you. I got too worked up. Once that happens a man can't hold back."

She watched his face. A shudder rippled down her back. Would he have treated her that way if he really loved her? She walked over to the door and opened it. "I'll walk home from here."

"You don't have to do that. Let me at least take you out to the road."

"No thanks." She left him standing in the middle of the room.

When she had walked clear to the road and there'd been no sound of the car behind her, she couldn't hold the tears back any longer.

The following Friday when Valina got home from work, she saw two envelopes on the table, one addressed to Mama in Mary's handwriting, the other to Papa, but in an unfamiliar hand.

Strange that Mary would leave a letter for Mama. She could've come to the cafe and told her whatever she had to say. Of course, she was furious with Mama right now. Maybe that's what it was about. But who wrote the letter to Papa?

She built a fire in the stove. No use whipping herself up over Mary. She had her own problems. She'd dragged herself through the week, depressed and confused, not sure she ever wanted to see Timothy again. Yet, she'd found herself hoping there was a reason for what he'd done, praying he'd explain and apologize. But by Friday, he hadn't come to the cafe. She knew it was over. Just like that.

Valina tried to blot him out of her mind while she scrubbed four potatoes and put them in the oven. By the time Rachel came home after her piano lesson, she had dinner ready and waiting in the warming oven.

Rachel pounced on the two letters and peered at them. "That's funny. Why would Mary write to Mama?"

"I don't know."

Rachel pointed at the letter for Papa. "Who's this one from?"

"I don't know that, either."

"Well, why don't we open them and see?"

"Rachel, you know we can't open someone else's mail. Now set the table. We'll find out what's going on when they get here."

"Yeah, if they'll tell us."

"Never mind. Just set the table."

Rachel pouted. "Set the table. That's all I ever hear."

Later, when Mama and Papa came home, Rachel grabbed the letters. "This letter's for you, Mama. It's from Mary." She handed it to Mama. "And this one's for you, Papa."

When Mama read the letter her stricken face made it clear that something awful had happened. Suddenly, she crumpled to the floor.

"Emma!" Papa dropped his letter and knelt beside her. "Oh, God, Emma." He picked her up and carried her to the bedroom. Valina and Rachel followed him and stood in the doorway.

Valina could hardly breathe. Mary must've done something terrible.

Rachel began to cry. "What's wrong with Mama?"

"She fainted. But I'm sure she'll be all right," Papa said.

"But, Papa, why did she faint?"

He paused for a moment, his eyes on Mama. "Mary and Timothy have eloped."

"Eloped? No!" Valina bolted out of the cabin and ran into the woods. It couldn't be true. How could he have done what he did to her? She doubled over from the pain in her stomach and vomited until only bile came up, until her knees shook so hard she could hardly stand.

She had been so stupid. Timothy didn't love her. He had just used her to satisfy his lust. Mary was the smart one, too smart to give him sex until she got him to marry her, while Valina was the world's biggest fool. And now she'd carry shame with her, heavy as an iron weight, for the rest of her life. She was no better than Zoe Adams. She slowly walked back to the cabin. She needed to see if Mama was all right.

"Emma. Wake up, darling, please," Daniel said.

The constant tap of his hand on her face annoyed her. "Stop that. I'm awake." Emma dreaded opening her eyes, afraid that he'd find some reason to defend Timothy and they'd quarrel. But nothing he said could ever justify Timothy's actions. Mary, married to that horrid man. And the wicked note. "We had to do it this way, Mama. Because you don't like Timothy."

It was true. She didn't like him. She never had and never would, nor would she ever feel quite the same about her oldest daughter. Mary had always been self-centered, and there'd been painful times because of it. But this time the rift might be too deep for things to ever be the same.

"Emma, are you all right?"

"Yes, dear." Emma sat up on the edge of the bed. "I'll be fine."

Rachel stood next to the bed. "Mary was mean to you, wasn't she?"

Emma glanced at Daniel. "I'm afraid both Mary and Timothy were very thoughtless."

Valina bit her lip to keep from spewing out how she felt about the two of them.

"Mama, if Mary loved Timothy, why'd she kick up such a fuss about Paul?" Rachel asked.

Trust Rachel to get straight to the point, Valina thought.

Slowly, Emma stood up and put her arm around her youngest daughter. "I hadn't thought of that, yet. Why, indeed? Doesn't make a lot of sense, does it? I don't know the answer, dear." She took Rachel's hand. "Let's go eat dinner now."

When they went into the kitchen, Valina was already there dishing up the food.

After dinner, Emma went outside. She needed to be alone. She started toward the creek. The sound of its soft gurgling and the pungent odor of the pines usually had a soothing effect on her.

She sat down on the bank next to the creek and looked up through the trees at the dark blue sky, "Dear Lord, I don't know if I can welcome this awful man into our family. Please give me the strength I'll need." Tears welled up in her eyes. "And please forgive me for what is in my heart. Amen." She bathed her face with the cool water. It would be dark soon. She should go back.

"Emma?"

"Over here by the creek, Daniel."

He walked up to her and put his hand on her shoulder. "I was worried about you. Are you all right?"

"Yes." She patted the ground beside her and he sat down. "This is a good opportunity for us to talk."

"I thought it might be," he said. "I don't believe Timothy

did the right thing any more than you do." He took her hand in his. "And for Mary to run off was bad enough, but to deliberately hurt you was unforgivable."

"Oh, Daniel, how are we going to handle this? Mary is our daughter."

"And like it or not, by now Timothy is part of our family, too."

Emma groaned. How could she be civil to that man? "It hurts to realize how badly we failed with Mary."

"Let's not blame ourselves, darling." He put his arm around her. "We still have Valina and Rachel."

"Yes." Emma relaxed into the comfort of his arms.

Soon, in the gray minutes before dark, a doe and her fawn came out of the woods several yards upstream. Emma and Daniel kept still as the deer drank from the creek. How simple it was for animals, Emma thought. Human parenthood was so complex, full of challenges and defeats.

As soon as the doe led her fawn away, Daniel pulled Emma to her feet. "It's almost dark. Let's go talk to the girls about it."

When they went into the cabin, Emma said, "Come sit at the table with us, girls. We need to talk."

Valina sat down on one of the chairs. Rachel plopped down on the chair beside her.

Emma'd never seen Valina look so angry. It worried her. "Do you have anything to say about the elopement, Valina?"

"Yes I do. They should've thought about the people they'd hurt before they decided to sneak off."

"Yeah," Rachel said. "Mama, I know he shouldn't have done it, but I like Timothy. I wish I liked Mary." She hesitated, her eyes flitting first to Emma, then to Daniel. "That was a bad thing to say, wasn't it?"

Daniel spoke up. "I don't think so."

"Neither do I," Emma said. "We love Mary, but sometimes it's very difficult to like her. Still, she is part of our family, isn't she?"

"Yes, Mama," Rachel said.

"And now Timothy is also part of our family. I'm not going to lie and say I'm happy about it, but I will be civil to him because he's our daughter's husband, and I hope you girls will be civil, too."

Rachel nodded and smiled.

"I can't promise," Valina said.

Emma gnawed on her lip. This grim-faced girl didn't even resemble her sweet Valina. Well, maybe it was just the shock. And it had been a terrible shock.

The next day, Valina went to Timothy's cabin and burned her watercolor in the fireplace. She cringed at the thought of how he must've snickered at her crude little gift. She wanted to burn the whole cabin down, but that wouldn't erase what had happened. He knew she'd never be able to say a word about it. And he could hold it over her head for the rest of her life. He'd do it, too. She shuddered. What if they stayed here? How could she stand it? When she walked out to the road, she remembered the last time she'd walked out of there. Her temples pounded. Timothy. She hated the very sound of his name.

Two weeks later, as the family finished dinner, the door opened. Mary and Timothy walked in. Mary looked radiant, of course, wearing a stunning light blue dress that Valina had never seen before. Her hair was different, too — shorter and curlier.

"Well, aren't you going to congratulate us?" Mary smiled as if they should all be delighted.

Valina bit her tongue. Oh, the things she could say. She didn't dare open her mouth or all the hate and bitterness would fly out.

But Mama spoke right up. "We're still getting used to the idea. It's a bit hard, though, since we didn't have the slightest inkling that you two were interested in each other." Mama kept her eyes on her coffee cup while she spoke, her hand clenched on the handle.

Mary's eyes flashed with anger.

Quickly, Timothy said, "I apologize for that, Emma, but your beautiful daughter swept me right off my feet."

Bile rose in Valina's mouth. She had to swallow hard to keep from vomiting again. She'd prayed every night for forgiveness, but how could God forgive her? She kept her eyes lowered so the others wouldn't see the shame in her eyes.

"Are you going to live in our town?" Papa asked.

Valina drew in a quick breath and looked up.

"For a while." Timothy said. He grinned at Mary and squeezed her hand. "I rented the Zimmerman house today. We'll be at the hotel until we get it furnished."

Oh, how Valina wanted to ask him why they couldn't live in his cabin. She'd made it so beautiful. He'd said so himself.

"What does 'for a while' mean?" Mama asked.

Mary moved closer to Timothy, a smug look on her face.

He put his arm around her. "My little bride would like to live in San Francisco, but it will take some time to make the arrangements. Can't say exactly how long."

The sooner, the better, Valina thought. She hated him now as much as she had once loved him. Why hadn't she seen through him before? What a fool she was.

Mary cleared her throat and looked at Mama. "Timothy and I thought you might have a reception for us."

Mama, cool as anything, looked right back at Mary. "It wouldn't be appropriate, under the circumstances. Not at all appropriate."

Mary's eyes narrowed. She opened her mouth to say something, but Timothy put his hand on her arm. "We're mighty tired from the long drive. I think we'd better go."

Valina could feel Timothy's eyes on her. "Goodnight, Valina." She didn't answer him.

"And you, too Rachel," he said.

Out of the corner of her eye, Valina saw Rachel smile at him.

An awkward silence hung in the air after they left. Then Mama went into the bedroom and Papa went outside, and though Mama shut the door, Valina and Rachel could hear her crying. Rachel's eyes got so big and scared looking that Valina swallowed the lump in her own throat and said, "Want to play Tic-Tac-Toe, Rachel?"

"Sure."

Valina couldn't keep her mind on the game. There would never be a way to avoid seeing Timothy, not as long as they lived in Pine Bluff. If only she had someone she could talk to.

When Rachel had won three games, she sat back in her chair and glared at Valina. "You're letting me win, aren't you?"

"Not deliberately."

When Papa came back inside, he went into the bedroom. Despite the closed door, Valina could hear the murmur of their voices, and Mama had stopped crying.

"I'm tired, Rachel. It's time for bed. I have to get up early and you have to go to school tomorrow."

Rachel glanced at the bedroom door. "Do you think Mama's all right?"

"Yes. Papa's with her. Come on, let's go to bed."

Rachel sighed. "Okay."

The next morning all of the regulars came into the cafe, even old Lester, who'd been visiting his daughter in Lewiston. Valina could hear Herb and Dogie telling him all the latest news, including the elopement, which just might be the biggest item of the whole year.

Then Bertha came in. "I hear the newlyweds are back." She peered at Valina to see what kind of reaction she'd get.

But Valina just smiled and said, "That's right. You want your usual oatmeal and toast, Mrs. Wilcox?"

Bertha scowled. "No. I'll have flapjacks and sausage."

"Coming right up."

Valina hurried to the kitchen before Bertha could say anything else. Catherine was there talking to Mama.

"I don't understand," Catherine said.

"All we heard from Mary was Paul, Paul, Paul. She was furious that he'd told Valina he was leaving, instead of telling her," Mama said. "And then the very next week she eloped with Timothy."

"But that doesn't make sense."

"It certainly doesn't."

Valina interrupted. "An order of pancakes and sausage for Bertha, Mama." She turned to Catherine. "Have you told Paul about the elopement?"

"Yes. He was surprised, but he confessed that he wasn't planning to propose to Mary."

"Mary will regret this marriage for the rest of her life." The minute Valina said it, she wondered if she'd gone too far. Catherine and Mama were staring at her. "I'd better go see to the customers." She hurried out of the room.

What would she do if Timothy and Mary came into the cafe? How could she hide the way she felt? Old eagle-eye Bertha would smell a rat right away.

And then she realized that she would have to put on an act for the rest of her life. How awful. She looked around the room. Surely she wasn't the only sinner in town. How many others were doing the same thing?

She took her time pouring coffee into the half-empty cups of the customers, thinking about each person as she moved around the room. Bertha was bound to have some awful secret. Be like her to poison the neighbor's dog. And Dogie, he could have rustled cattle. Spike? Maybe murder. For only a moment, she felt better, but then the depression that haunted her came back even stronger. She went into the kitchen to pick up Bertha's order.

"Thanksgiving is only two months away," Catherine said.

"Paul's going to stay a whole week. I can hardly wait to see him."

Valina delivered Bertha's order, then went back to the kitchen to see if the hash browns for old Lester were ready.

"I won't take no for an answer, Emma." Catherine looked at Valina as she walked in the kitchen. "Use your influence on your mother."

"My influence? About what?"

"I want your family, including Mary and Timothy, to come to our house for Thanksgiving dinner. It would make things easier, wouldn't it?"

Valina thought everyone would behave better at Catherine and Doc's house, especially with Paul there. "Yes, it would. I think it's a great idea, Mama."

"Ha. So it's settled, Emma." Catherine stood up and headed for the door.

"All right, but I'll cook the turkey," Mama said.

"You'll do nothing of the sort. You'll bring two pies, and I don't want to hear another word about it." Catherine waved and went out the door before Mama could reply.

"That Catherine. What a dear friend she is." Mama had tears in her eyes.

Just as Valina started back through the doorway into the restaurant, she heard Bertha's voice and she stayed out of sight.

"Marry in haste, repent at leisure, I always say. Of course, we all know the usual reason for hasty marriages."

"Wash your mouth out, Bertha, and your mind, too, what there is of it."

It was Minnie's voice. Valina grinned and went into the

room. No one ever got the best of Minnie, least of all Bertha Wilcox. "Hi, Minnie. What can I do for you?"

"Give me a half-dozen of Emma's apple muffins. Thanks to your mother's cooking, Doc is eating like a pig."

It took Mary only a few days to settle into her home. Two-stories, it could have held three cabins the size of Mama and Papa's, and it had plumbing, electricity, a huge stone fireplace, even a telephone.

Timothy had insisted on furnishing all four of the bedrooms upstairs. She didn't think it was necessary, but he had the money, so she didn't object.

The bathroom, off the kitchen with its pedestal sink, its claw-footed bathtub, and its chain-pull toilet was the room she adored. She bought the very best towels and put a braided rug on the floor and a little table with a crisp white doily on it by the sink.

The kitchen was a marvel, too. A sink with running water and an electric stove. She still couldn't believe it.

Her soprano voice filled each room as she scrubbed woodwork, floors, windows. Her very own place. Something she'd dreamed about all of her life. Mama would die of envy when she saw it. No, she wouldn't. She smiled. But Valina would.

Mary was singing "Black Is The Color of My True Love's Hair" when Timothy came back from the store. He handed her a sack of groceries and scowled.

"My hair isn't black but Paul Bradford's is."

Who'd been telling him about Paul? Damned gossipy town. "Why, Timothy O'Callahan. I've never been interested in Paul. The old biddies in town tried to pair us off but it didn't work, did it?" She put her arms around his waist and nibbled on his chin. He was so easy to distract.

He groaned. "You're going to kill me off, you passionate little bitch."

She spun away from him and flounced into the kitchen. "Now you'll have to beg for it."

Grinning, he followed her into the room. "Pretty sure of yourself, aren't you?" He started sifting his fingers through her hair.

It aroused her, but he could do that by just walking into the room. She was surprised that she enjoyed sex. She hadn't expected to. Was it was because he'd had plenty of experience? Funny that didn't bother her.

She curled her arms around his neck. "Maybe I could travel with you."

"Not when I'm working." His jaw tightened. "We've been over this before."

Angry with herself, she moved away from him. Why hadn't she waited until after sex? And why was he so touchy about his job, anyway? Men. Oh, well, she had plenty to do.

Later, in bed, Mary wondered if all men fell asleep after sex. Her eyes followed the curve of Timothy's relaxed arm, its aggressive bulge now smooth and sensuous. She started to run her hand down his arm, but stopped. No. He'd want sex again and she needed to put the meatloaf and potatoes in the oven.

She slipped out of bed and stood there for a second. Good. He was still asleep. She'd have time for a bath before dinner.

She crept quietly down the stairs and put the meatloaf

and potatoes in the oven, then went to start the bath water. After she'd pinned up her hair, she sank into the tub and let the warm water cover her body. Nineteen, and she'd never before known the pleasure of stretching out in a bathtub. She'd had to sit in a round, galvanized washtub on the kitchen floor, after hauling the water from the creek and heating it on the stove. Never again. She had Timothy and his money now, and his body.

Out of the corner of her eye she caught a glimpse of him standing in the doorway. She smiled and flicked water at him.

"Another bath? How many have you had today?"

"Just two."

He picked up her clothes and left the room.

"Timothy, where are you going with my clothes?"

He came back, empty-handed, and leaned against the door jamb. "What clothes?"

"Timothy." She tried to look angry.

"You won't be needing them anyway," he said.

She laughed at him and stood up. "Then hand me that towel, will you, please?"

His eyes caressed her wet body. "What'll you give me for it?"

She licked her lips, her mouth slightly open. "Whatever you want."

He lifted her out of the tub, but her wet body slipped out of his grasp. For a second, arms and legs flew in all directions, then the two of them landed in a heap on the floor.

Mary kept perfectly still, her eyes closed. She whimpered.

"Oh, God, Mary. Are you all right?"

She moaned.

"My darling, are you hurt?"

Her strangled, "Yes," erupted into an uncontrollable giggle. She grabbed him and they rolled together on the floor, laughing.

"This a new one. I've never had sex with a mermaid before," he said.

"Well, you're going to now, right here on the bathroom floor."

She unbuttoned his shirt.

Three days later, Valina set off for work. She enjoyed walking in the early morning. The town, still quiet, softened by a pale mist that rose from the river, had a beauty it lacked later in the heat of the day. When she heard the noise behind her, she felt a wave of panic. Timothy's car. The honeymoon must be over.

"Want a ride to work?" he said.

She kept right on walking. He shifted down and drove along beside her. "No sense holding a grudge. We're family now. Besides, it doesn't have to be over between us, you know."

Outraged, she stopped. He grinned and stepped on the brake. "You stay away from me," she said. "If you think I'd have anything to do with you, you're dead wrong. You're nothing but a slimy, no-good con man."

His face turned deep red. She turned away and stalked down the street.

He called after her, "You'll regret this Valina."

She heard the car lurch forward. Then the motor died. She hurried on, afraid he might come after her on foot. He was a despicable man. If only she could tell Mama and Papa the truth about him.

She hurried into the cafe. It was still hot, sticky from yesterday's heat. She propped open the door and turned on the fan. Precious little help it would be, but at least she could smell the coolness of the river.

She put the coffee on, wishing it tasted as good as it smelled, then called, "I'm here, Mama."

Mama came to the door from the kitchen. "Good morning, dear. Everything's ready for the breakfast crowd." Her hair was already damp from the heat. "It's going to be another scorcher." She turned and went back into the kitchen.

By the time the coffee had perked, the regulars started straggling into the cafe.

"Is it ready yet?" When Herb settled his ample body on a chair, he looked like a hen setting on her eggs. It struck Valina funny and she had to look away to keep from laughing.

"Sure is, Herb." She poured his coffee and took the mug to him. He was still settling himself in the chair. Exactly like a hen. She dragged her eyes away from him and scrutinized her nails.

"Ham and eggs again this morning?" she asked.

"That's right. And here comes Dogie."

"I already know what he wants. You two are in a rut." She went to the kitchen to place their orders. When she came back, Timothy had come in, helped himself to coffee and was sitting with Herb and Dogie. She wanted to go hide, but it wouldn't be the last time he'd come in. He'd do it just to spite her. Well, at least Bertha hadn't shown up yet.

"Good morning, Timothy. What can I get you for break-fast?" She kept her eyes neutral and bared her teeth in a smile.

"Nothing, thanks, little sis. Mary fixed me a great big breakfast. I just wanted to say hello to my friends here."

Again, the following Monday morning, Valina heard his car come up behind her as she walked to work. He didn't try to talk to her, only followed her while the Model A's engine complained at the slow pace. She hoped the car would break down, or a tire might go flat, but she didn't get her wish.

Every time he came back from his trips he followed her, until she was no longer scared, or furious, or disgusted, and finally, she didn't even hear his car. Sometimes Valina forgot he was even in the cafe, and he'd have to remind her.

"While you're filling Herb's cup you might fill mine, too," he'd say. And there he'd be, sitting right next to Herb. But he didn't matter anymore, one way or the other.

The day before Thanksgiving, Paul came into the cafe for lunch. Valina thought something about him seemed differ-ent, but it certainly wasn't his clothes. She grinned. Baggy old cords and a plaid flannel shirt could hardly account for it.

When he sat down at the counter, she said, "Welcome home," and poured him a cup of coffee. "I thought you weren't due to arrive until this evening?"

"I decided to leave sooner. Have a few things I need to take care of. You look wonderful, Valina."

"Why, thanks." She hadn't looked wonderful in the mirror that morning. Suddenly self-conscious, she shoved a menu toward him. "The special is meatloaf, if that appeals to you."

"Sure does. Anything your mother cooks appeals to me. Understand she's bringing the pies for tomorrow's dinner."

"A mince and a pumpkin. We have apple here today. Like a piece?"

He grinned. "You know I would."

Well, at least his appetite hadn't changed. Was it his posture, or his manner that seemed different? She nudged the cream and sugar toward him, and went to place his order.

When she came back, she said, "Catherine's been counting the days until you got home. I can't understand why she's so fond of you, but Doc says it's just a minor aberration."

He laughed. "They're great people. I've been very lucky."

"So have they, Paul."

His expression sobered. He held her glance with his for a moment. "You still get off at four?"

"Uh-huh. That's the best thing about this job." Her feet, hot and swollen, felt as if she'd been standing in boiling water all morning. She'd take off her shoes but she knew she'd never get them back on.

"Mind if I stop by and walk you home?" he asked.

"Why would I mind?"

"You mean to say there's no special fellow who might get jealous?" His eyes probed hers.

"Nope."

"I can hardly believe there isn't." His smile lit up his whole face. "But I'm sure not unhappy about it."

Just then, Mama came in from the kitchen and put Paul's order in front of him. "This has been sitting on the shelf getting cold. You're neglecting this young man, Valina."

"Sorry, Paul."

"My fault," he said. "I've been taking up your time."

Mama patted his hand. "Nice to have you home." She smiled at Valina and went back to the kitchen.

Valina checked out the other customers, filled their coffee cups, then came back to the counter to watch Paul eat. He could consume more food and not gain weight than anyone else in Pine Bluff or the surrounding area. That part had definitely not changed.

"So, how's business?" she asked.

"Considering the state of our economy, we're holding our own, I'm happy to say."

"Seems like all anyone talks about now is the crash on Wall Street, that and unemployment. I suppose you heard about the mill closing. It's sure made a difference in our business here at the cafe."

"That's a shame. Uncle Charles told me that some of his patients are paying him with chickens or home-canned fruit. He hates to take food from them, but they insist. He'd treat people for nothing. He has, many times."

"Mama told Catherine that Pine Bluff's been blessed with a medical angel. Later Mama heard that Doc had a fit when he heard it."

Paul almost choked. "I'll bet. He doesn't exactly see himself that way."

When he handed her the money for his lunch, their eyes locked for a second.

Valina drew in a quick breath and blinked.

Then he smiled. "See you at four."

"Okay." There was definitely something different about Paul.

As he walked her home that afternoon, she had to struggle to keep up with his long stride.

"You'd like Portland," he said. "It's a beautiful city with green lawns and lots of trees. And people raise so many roses that they have a big parade when they bloom. Maybe you could come over on the train with Aunt Catherine to see it in the spring."

"Really?"

"Sure. I'd like to have you, and I know Aunt Catherine would appreciate your company."

"The only parade I've ever seen is the Mule Days Parade. Why would anyone want to parade a mule?"

Paul grinned. "It's fun being with you, Valina. I'm serious about you coming to Portland with Aunt Catherine."

To ride on a train and visit a beautiful city and see a parade? It would be heaven. "Well, I'll see if I can get the time off. How much do you think it would cost, Paul?"

"Nothing. My treat."

She bit her lip. "No. I can't do that. It wouldn't be right." But, oh, how she would love it.

"Well, we'll argue about that later," he said. "Would you consider going to the dance with me Saturday night?"

"Sure, I'd like to." But what if Mary and Timothy were at the dance? Well, Mary wouldn't dare make a scene. She was married now.

Paul stopped at the steps of her cabin.

"Well," Valina said awkwardly. She couldn't understand

why. She'd known Paul since she was a little girl. "I'll see you at dinner tomorrow. And thanks for walking me home."

Paul grinned and said, "It was a pleasure." He kissed her on the cheek and whistled as he walked back toward town. Valina put her hand on her cheek. He'd never done that before.

The next day, Thanksgiving, Paul picked up the Addison family in his new Hupmobile sedan. Papa sat up in front with Paul. "This is a mighty fine car," Papa said. "It's bigger than Timothy's Model A." He patted the seat beside him. "More comfortable, too."

When they drove up to the Bradford house, Timothy and Mary had just arrived. Valina wondered if anyone else noticed the envious look on Mary's face when she saw Paul's car. She almost felt sorry for Mary. It must be awful to be eaten up with jealousy.

Paul shook Timothy's hand, but just nodded at Mary. "Congratulations on your marriage."

Only a nod? Valina could tell Mary was miffed, and Timothy didn't look happy, either. Maybe he was jealous of Paul. Wouldn't that be ironic?

Rachel, who'd been holding the mince pie on her lap, balanced it carefully as she climbed out of the car.

"Can I help you with that pie, Rachel?" Paul asked.

"Nope. I can manage just fine, thank you."

Paul grinned as he watched Rachel march up the porch steps. "I'm sure she can." He turned to Valina. "Don't suppose you need any help, either."

She grinned at him. "I wouldn't trust you with this pie. It'd be half-eaten by the time you got to the kitchen."

He laughed, then took her elbow and helped her up the steps.

The smell of turkey and sage and spiced cider greeted Valina as she walked into the house. Catherine handed her a cup of cider and took the pie to the kitchen, while Valina stood by the fireplace warming her hands. She heard Mama ask Mary how she liked her house — a little dig — since none of the family had seen the place yet, which suited Valina just fine.

"I'm delighted with it, of course. You must come by and see it," Mary said, as if Mama were just a casual neighbor.

As she walked away from Mary, Mama said, "I will, when I'm invited."

Valina choked on her cider. That silly Mary had actually thought she could put on airs with Mama.

Paul came across the room and stood beside Valina. "You okay?"

"Sure. I just swallowed the wrong way."

"Other than that, you're sort of quiet today." he said.

"I'm enjoying the cider and the fire." Out of the corner of her eye, she saw Mary watching them.

Just then, Catherine came back into the room with Aunt Matilda right behind her. "Surprise! I talked Matilda down off her mountain."

"She promised me a decent meal and good company," Aunt Matilda said. "I know Catherine's a great cook, but I'm kind of dubious about the company."

Valina grinned at Paul, who chuckled.

Aunt Matilda wore what she always wore to town, the

same old buckskin culottes, boots, and plaid shirt. Valina felt certain that her aunt considered the outfit to be her Sunday best, since she always wore men's coveralls at the ranch. No one had ever seen her in a dress.

"I have another surprise for all of you," Catherine announced. She led Rachel to the piano. "Rachel's going to play Beethoven's 'Moonlight Sonata' for you."

Rachel settled herself on the piano stool and played with the confidence of an adult. Of course she would, Valina thought. But imagine the little twerp having such talent. Valina glanced around the room. Mary looked stunned, Mama was crying, and Papa was beaming. And Valina'd never seen Aunt Matilda's face look soft and tender before.

When she finished, Rachel stood up and took a bow, then turned to Timothy. "Did you bring your ukulele?"

"No, thank God. Me and my ukulele wouldn't hold a candle to you and that piano."

Everyone laughed.

During dinner, Valina was relieved to be sitting between Papa and Paul. If she had sat beside Timothy, she could imagine him caressing her leg, or some other obscene thing. Catherine had put him between Mary and Rachel, the only two females who had any use for him.

Suddenly she clenched her fists in her lap. Would he bother Rachel? Of course he would. Maybe not now, but eventually. Oh, Lord, she might have to tell Mama about him. She felt sick.

"Before we bring out the pies, I have something else for all of you." Catherine headed for the kitchen.

She came back carrying a cake with candles on it. "Since your birthday is just three days off, I thought it would be nice to have a cake for you, Valina."

Doc stood up, his water glass in his hand. "Ladies and gentlemen, a toast to Valina, who will be eighteen on Sunday."

"Thank you, Catherine, and you, too, Doc." They were such special people. Everyone sang "Happy Birthday" and she blew out the candles.

Paul hadn't come in for lunch the next day, so Valina was surprised when she found him outside at four o'clock. As they walked through town, Paul said, "I've been waiting for you to be eighteen."

"Why's that?"

He didn't answer.

"Is there some eighteen-year-old birthday ritual that I don't know about?" she laughed.

"Birthday rituals do have to be observed." He grinned at her.

She looked up at him, her eyes narrowed. "Am I going to like this?"

He shrugged. "Hard to say."

"You're not going to tell me a blessed thing, are you?"

"Nope."

"Could I ask you a question?" She hesitated. "It's kind of personal."

"Go ahead."

"Were you and Mary ever serious about each other?" For some reason she had to know.

He shook his head. "Lord, no. That was just gossip."

"You mean she didn't even flirt with you?"

He shrugged. "Not that I could tell. Why?"

"Well . . ." She wished she hadn't started this. "She was very upset that you told me, instead of her, that you were leaving town."

He stopped walking and stared at her. "That's hard to believe. We weren't even friends. Mary's not my type. You're the kind of girl I like."

He'd practically said he was interested in her. If he was, why couldn't he come right out and say so? Though she tried, she couldn't figure out a way to pull it out of him. Frustrated, she stood on the cabin steps and watched him walk back down the road to town. Maybe she was just imagining it. She didn't know what to think.

When Mary walked into the cafe the next morning, Valina almost dropped a plate of ham and eggs. What a surprise. Mary hated associating with what she called, "the riffraff who hang out in the cafe".

"I'll have some coffee," Mary said, her words clipped and hard.

"This is an honor." Valina didn't even try to keep the sarcasm out of her voice. "We don't often see you in here."

Mary leaned toward Valina. "You really think you're something, don't you, cozying up to Paul the way you are."

Even though she had known this would happen, Valina was shocked. "It's a good thing you're keeping your voice down, otherwise the customers would have a juicy piece of gossip to spread around. Paul shouldn't matter to you now. You're married, remember?"

"That has nothing to do with it."

"Oh? Then what does?"

"You acting like such a hussy."

"I warn you, if you start in on that again, I'm going to go get Mama. Just one more word, and that's it."

Mary glared at her, but said nothing. Valina could feel the curious eyes of the regulars watching them.

"Would you like a doughnut to go with your coffee?" Valina raised her voice so the others would hear it.

"I never eat doughnuts. You know that," Mary muttered.

Valina leaned closer to Mary and quietly said, "Excuse me. I thought, since you are a married lady now that you might have changed, but I see you haven't."

When Mary left the cafe, she made a quick stop at Edgerton's for a sack of sugar, then hurried home. She hadn't counted on Timothy being the jealous type. The minute they left the Bradford's after Thanksgiving dinner, he'd sniped at her about Paul. Well, it did show how much he loved her, but she'd have to be very careful.

Just as she got to the front door, Timothy opened it. "Where have you been?"

"I stopped in and had a cup of coffee with Valina."

"I suppose Paul Bradford was there?"

"No. I thought you wanted me to patch things up with the family. That's why I went there." She handed him the sugar and took off her coat, stalling for time. She mustn't let her anger show, but she had no intention of being accused of an affair every time she went out of the house.

"Why don't you trust me, Timothy? I was a virgin when you married me, so you know I haven't been fooling around. You're the one who's had a lot of experience, but you don't hear me complaining, do you?"

She reached up and put her arms around his neck. "I get weak all over when you make love to me. How could I possibly want another man?"

"I'm sorry, baby. It's all happened so fast, I guess I can't believe you're really mine."

She kissed him. "Take me to bed, Timothy."

"Tell me you love me, first."

"I not only love you, I'm yours and yours alone." She gave him an arch look. "Now tell me you believe me."

He picked her up and carried her upstairs without saying a word.

CHAPTER 9

J-Bar-J Ranch — 1969

A couple of raucous crows yakking away in the maple tree outside my window woke me up at dawn. Once those black devils get going, they keep cawing until each one thinks it's had the last word. I was tempted to settle their argument with a well-aimed shotgun blast, but I got dressed and went downstairs, instead. Oscar was already sitting at the kitchen table drinking coffee.

"You're up early," I said.

He just grunted and took another sip of his coffee.

I poured myself a cup and sat down with him. Something was wrong. "What's eating you?"

When he started to fidget with his cup and look anywhere but at me, I knew what he'd been up to. "You spent the night patrolling the fences, didn't you?" His glance skidded around the table and finally lit on my shoulder. "Not the whole night," he said.

"Oh? Well, did you find the culprit?"

"Came close." This time Oscar looked me smack in the eye. "I heard a horse ride off just as I got to the north pasture."

That shook me up a bit. "I'll be damned."

He leaned toward me. "Mattie, you've got to call the sheriff about this guy."

"What in hell could he do about it? He doesn't have the skill, or the luck, to catch that vandal in the act."

"If we had a few extra men, I bet we could trap him."

"We'd need a few hundred men to patrol all our fences."

He glared at me and shrugged. "Well, don't bitch at me if we have to spend all our time mending those fences."

God, he could be obstinate. I knew there'd be no peace until I let him have his way.

"Okay. If you want them so bad, you call the sheriff." I'd caught him off guard with that one. He stood up, but he didn't go to the phone. He headed for the door.

"Got some chores to do first," he said.

Big phony. He hadn't expected me to give him the responsibility. He wanted to think about it for a spell.

Wasn't a half-hour later, he came back and headed for the phone, shoulders back, jaw firm. He was all business.

Lucky for him the line wasn't busy. He might have lost his nerve if it had been.

"Nettie? This is Oscar. Let me speak to Sheriff Jackson, please. If anyone could get him through to that worthless sheriff, Nettie could. She's Oscar's niece.

"Hi, Sheriff. We have a problem up here at Matilda's place. Some bastard is deliberately cutting our fences. Yes, I know you don't have the manpower, but it's pretty hard for just the three of us to catch the guy. I'm sure you're busy, but do you know a few men we could hire to help us? They don't have to know how to read or write, just how to ride. Okay. I'd appreciate it, Sheriff."

Oscar hung up and said, "He thinks he may be able to find some men for us. I'll go clean the bunkhouse."

Sheriff Jackson phoned just as I was dishing up dinner. Oscar was still out in the bunkhouse.

"I found three men for you, Matilda. They'll be there day after tomorrow."

"Thanks, Sheriff."

"That's what I'm here for, Matilda." I hung up fast. His sanctimonious tone of voice just about ruined my appetite. I finished dishing up and rang the dinner bell for the men.

When we got to dessert, I told them about the three men coming up to help patrol fences.

"Why would anybody go to the trouble of cutting fences?" Jimmy asked.

Oscar snorted. "That's a good question."

"Yeah," I said, "but one we don't have an answer for."

After breakfast the next morning, Oscar stayed at the table while Buck and George left to go see if any more fences had been cut. I wouldn't admit it to Oscar, but he was right. Too much of our time was being spent on those fences.

Jimmy, as antsy as spit on a hot stove, paced the floor. Oscar had promised to take him out for some target practice. Pretty soon he stopped pacing and started whining. "Aren't you through yet?"

I watched a red flush climb from Oscar's neck up to his face, but he didn't say a word. I thought that was a good idea, considering what he might say. He stood up and walked to the door. Didn't even finish his coffee.

"Bet I hit a bullseye today," Jimmy said. He practically pushed Oscar out the door.

I didn't quite approve of the shooting lessons, but I was sure happy to see Jimmy's butt go out the door. He could be such a pain. But what did I know about being a parent?

The phone rang just as I'd settled in my chair with a cup of coffee. Wouldn't you know, Jessica Marie again.

"Jimmy's out working with Oscar." I didn't tell her about the target practice. Afraid she'd have a stroke. "He's rarely here during the day." You'd think she'd have figured that out for herself by now. "Why don't you call him after dinner?"

She was quiet for a long minute, then said, "That wouldn't be convenient."

Now, why in hell wouldn't it be, if she was so set on talking to her boy? Then I figured it out. Bob would be home. She didn't want him to hear what she planned on saying to Jimmy. Fool woman.

"Well, then, I'll tell him you called," I said.

"Please do that." She hesitated. "Is he getting my letters?"

"Of course he is. This isn't Siberia. One of my men drives into town every few days to pick up the mail."

"Are you saying that it isn't delivered to your home?"

The hoity-toity way she said it made me want to spit up. "No, the Pony Express doesn't come through here anymore." I said.

She got a little huffy. "I'm terribly sorry if I bothered you."

"No bother. I'll tell him you called."

"Thank you."

I spent the next few minutes wondering if counseling could possibly help someone like Jessica. Not likely. Suddenly, the thought of sending Jimmy back to troubled parents bothered me. I went to the counter and measured flour for bread.

Making bread always brings me back to my senses. Not that I get off track very often.

Jimmy was damned near unbearable at dinner. He fancied himself to be an expert with a rifle, since he'd hit fifteen bullseyes out of twenty.

"Man, I really hit those targets. Dead center, every time. You guys should've seen it." He ran on and on about it.

I didn't think we'd ever get through that meal. The bragging got so bad that Buck and George left the table without having dessert, a first, let me tell you. But Jimmy didn't even notice them leave.

"I'll bet I could get that coyote that's been hanging around the chicken yard," Jimmy said.

Oscar shook his head. "You don't want to try it. You haven't had any experience with live critters yet."

"I don't see what difference that makes." Jimmy stuck out his jaw like he was daring Oscar to hit him. I was sure Oscar would have enjoyed doing exactly that.

Oscar's eyes took on a glazed look. I felt a pang of guilt for what he must've gone through with the boy.

"Your targets weren't moving," I said.

Jimmy looked at me, a sneer on his face. "So what?"

Lord, he was impossible. "Ever hear the expression, 'Pride goeth before a fall'?" I asked.

"Nope."

"Well, it's time you did. And it's also time for you to gather the eggs and milk Daisy." I started clearing off the table.

He grumbled as he left. "Milk the cow, gather the eggs. Do this, do that . . ."

At about eleven that night, after we were all in bed, a

ruckus started out in the chicken coop. And then the dogs set up a fuss. I was struggling into my robe when I heard someone thump down the stairs. That someone had to be Jimmy. Not two minutes later, the blast of a shotgun startled me. I did a little hurrying, myself.

When I got there, Jimmy stood in the chicken yard, barefoot, wearing only his undershorts, and holding a shotgun.

"What in hell do you think you're doing?" I could have strangled that kid.

He wouldn't look at me, just kept his eyes on the gun. "Shooting the coyote." His voice cracked when he said it, and suddenly my anger died. All I wanted to do was laugh, but I couldn't. Wouldn't do to treat it like a joke.

Meanwhile, Oscar came out with the big flashlight. He looked around the whole area with it. "I don't see any dead bodies, but you wounded something. There's blood over here." He gestured with the flashlight. "Hope it isn't human blood." He bent down and peered at it.

Jimmy sort of mumbled, nothing you could understand, while Oscar continued to sweep the light over the whole area.

"Well, you managed to shoot holes in the watering can, and I see we'll have something to remember you by over there, on the wall of the shop."

"What?" Jimmy's voice cracked again.

"If you look close," Oscar said, "you can see where the shot sprayed the metal wall. Little dents all over it. Maybe a hole or two, as well. Have to examine it in the daylight in order to tell." Oscar didn't look at the kid, but he turned and rolled his eyes at me.

Jimmy's Adam's apple bobbed up and down. Believe it or not, I was beginning to feel a little sorry for him. There he stood, in his BVD's, barefoot in the chicken shit, about ready to cry.

Oscar peered inside the coop. "At least you didn't kill any of the chickens. Can't believe we'll have any more trouble tonight." He stopped short and looked over at Jimmy, then at me. "Well, we might, at that." He took the shotgun from Jimmy and headed for the house, leaving me with the boy. I didn't blame him.

"I don't know about you, but I'm not very sleepy," I said. "Hose off your feet before you come in the house, and then go put on some clothes. I'll fix us a cup of hot chocolate."

He didn't make a sound, just walked over to the hose, turned it on, and washed his feet. Then, red-faced, he slipped through the kitchen toward the hall, like he wished he could make himself disappear.

Oscar had waited for me in the kitchen. "I didn't see any coyotes tracks by that blood."

"Why don't you go back to bed, Oscar? I want to talk to Jimmy."

"Sure." He put the shotgun in the storeroom behind the kitchen and went upstairs.

A few minutes later, the young boy who sat at the kitchen table with me, slowly sipping his chocolate, was much humbler than the one who had sat there at dinner.

I got serious. "You ever used a shotgun before tonight?"

He kept his eyes focused on the chocolate in his cup. "No."

"I don't want you to take things into your own hands,

Jimmy. You could hurt yourself, or someone else, or one of my animals."

"My folks will pay for the damage."

God, that made me mad. "You think I'd allow them to cover for you? You did it, and you'll work it off."

He winced.

"Mistakes are damned hard to own up to, aren't they?"

"Yeah."

"You get a mouth full of feathers when you have to eat crow. I do hate looking stupid, don't you?"

He nodded.

I figured we'd just about wrung the most we could out of that incident, so I poured him another cup of chocolate. If I wasn't going to sleep, he wasn't going to either.

Late Friday morning, three men rode into the yard. Men? More like three apes. That damned sheriff had sent us Gill Cramer, Cappie Benson and Rod Elmo, a trio of the most worthless bums in town. Gill's the town drunk, Cappie's retarded, and we won't even discuss Rod.

Gill spoke right up. "Mornin', Mrs. Jacobsen. Sheriff said you needed help, and here we are."

"Mm-hmm." I could hardly unclench my jaw. "So I see."

The other two just sat there with silly grins on their faces.

I was so damned mad, I about rang the dinner bell off its hook. Oscar came running. Oh, how his eyes bugged out when he saw those three clowns. He knew he was in deep trouble.

"They're your responsibility," I said.

I motioned for him to follow me into the house, then shut the door behind us.

"You and your damned ideas. If that idiot sheriff had told me who he was sending, I'd have told him exactly where to put them."

Oscar commenced to shuffle his feet, then cleared his throat. "I know they're not much, Mattie, but we need some help. At least Gill can shoot if he has to."

"Yeah, if he's sober. And what about Cappie and Rod?"

Oscar sighed. "They'd at least be warm bodies out there. That vandal won't know any different."

"They stay three nights. That's all. You got the bunkhouse cleaned up?"

"Yeah."

"That's good," I snapped, "because those bums sure can't stay in the house with us."

His face got bright red. "I'll cook their meals, too. Will that make you happy?"

I just glared at him. "Just keep them away from Jimmy. You hear me?"

His eyes narrowed. "Trying to protect him, Mattie?"

If I'd been a man, I'd have hit him. "If one damned thing goes wrong, it'll be on your back."

"Don't I know it," he snarled. Then he stomped out the door, slamming it behind him.

That night we ate in two shifts. First, George, Buck, Jimmy and me, then Oscar and his three stooges.

"Why can't they eat with us?" Jimmy asked.

George nudged him and gave him a warning look, but Jimmy didn't catch on.

"Well, why can't they?"

"Because I couldn't enjoy my food with them at the same table," I said. "I saw the way they eat when I was in the cafe in town. Enough to turn your stomach." That was only partly true, but I had to give him some reason.

Wasn't long after I went to bed, that I heard Oscar and his patrol ride off. I could just see them out in the pasture milling around in the dark, running into each other. The thought made me chuckle.

But I wasn't laughing when I woke up at 3:00 a.m. with someone pounding on my bedroom door.

I put on my robe and pulled the door open a crack.

Oscar stood there looking for all the world like he'd just swallowed a cup full of lye. "Need you to sew up Cappie's leg," he growled.

"He get shot?"

"No. He tangled with some barbed wire."

"How's his horse?"

Oscar gazed at the ceiling like he wanted a little help from the Almighty. "Wasn't on the horse. He walked into the barbed wire."

"What the hell was he doing on foot?"

"Thought he saw the vandal."

"Mm-hmm." It took all the grit I had to keep my mouth shut, but I didn't need to help Oscar hang himself. He was doing a fine job of it all by his lonesome.

I went downstairs and cleaned up Cappie's wound. When he looked at me with those scared, simple eyes of his, I felt sorry for him. He can't help that he's retarded. Fool sheriff had no business sending him up here. And Oscar should've sent him right back to town the minute he saw him.

After I sewed up his leg, I figured that was the end of any action for that night. I went back to bed.

Oscar made sure they weren't underfoot he next morning, much to my relief.

CHAPTER 10

Pine Bluff—1929

At the grange hall on Saturday night, the Mohaten County Fiddlers started their first set with a waltz. Paul steered Valina out onto the floor, but they didn't get far before they were interrupted by first one couple, then another. Everyone wanted to welcome Paul home. It got so bad they both laughed.

"I'll bet you didn't know you were this popular, did you?" she said.

"Am I popular with you? That's all that really matters."

Again, the hint that he cared about her more than just as a friend. "Of course. Why, when I was little, I wanted to . . . " She had started to say she'd wanted to marry him when she grew up. She could feel her face get red.

He pulled her closer. "I think I can guess, but tell me, do you still want the same thing?"

"Paul, I'm not sure I understand."

He grabbed her hand and started for the door. "Then it's high time I explained it to you."

She tugged at his sleeve. "Our coats."

"Stay here and I'll get them."

When he helped her with her coat his hands rested on her shoulders for a few seconds. She could feel the warmth of them even through her heavy coat. He walked her to his car, opened the passenger door for her, then got in the driver's side. He drove up to a wide spot by the river, where he parked and turned to look at her.

"I remember when you were eight and I was twelve. You were the pluckiest, prettiest little thing I'd ever seen. You still are. I realized I loved you when I was a senior in high school and you were a freshman, but seniors didn't date freshmen."

Valina, stunned, couldn't seem to breathe. He loved her? If only he'd spoken up sooner.

"And by the time you were sixteen, I was away at college," he said. "I dated quite a few girls there, but always found myself comparing them to you. It finally dawned on me that I loved you. When I came home last summer, I worried that some other man might win your heart before I had a chance. Still, I was so sure that I had to get established in the business before I could ask you to marry me. I realize now that I was wrong. You needed to know I loved you. Pretty stupid. Right?"

Valina choked back a sob.

"I did it all wrong." Paul shook his head. "I panicked when I got to Portland, worried that I could lose you. And I hadn't even told you how I felt about you. I'm saying it now. I love you — and I hope to earn your love one day."

"Oh, Paul." Hot tears wet her cheeks.

He pulled her close and wiped the tears with his handkerchief. "Please don't cry. Is there someone else?"

She shook her head. "No, no one. I'm overwhelmed, that's all."

"Thank God." He leaned forward and pulled her into his arms. At first, his lips merely brushed hers, but just as she wanted to beg for more, he took her mouth with a deep devouring kiss. When they finally drew apart, her body was so limp she had to lean against his shoulder.

He stroked her hair. "I wanted to give you your birthday present tonight while we were alone." He turned on the overhead light and took an envelope out of his pocket.

She opened the envelope and gasped. It was a round-trip train ticket to Portland, Oregon.

"I'll come home at Christmas and Easter, and as many times in between as I can, but you need to see Portland." His hand gently stroked her cheek. "Will you come see my parade?"

"Well, yes." She didn't have a chance to say anything else. She was busy with his kiss, so deep and passionate she had to hang onto his shoulders for dear life. She was still numb when he took her home.

After he drove away, she put a big chunk of wood in the stove. Maybe a cup of tea would calm her. How could she sleep when there were so many things whirling around in her head? Paul Bradford loved her, but how did she feel about him? Yes, she'd wanted to marry him when she was little. She'd thought he was smart and kind and handsome, like a god. Dear heaven, he still was. She needed to talk to Mama. She was absently sipping tea when the family came home.

"You and Paul didn't stay long," Mama said. "Did you have a misunderstanding?"

"No."

"Some other kind of problem?"

"No, but I need to talk to you, Mama."

Papa glanced uncertainly at Mama. She nodded toward the bedroom and he left. "Rachel, you get on up to bed," she said.

Rachel took her time climbing the ladder, grumbling all the way. "I never get to hear any of the good stuff."

Mama fixed herself a cup of tea and sat by Valina at the table. "What is it, dear? You look upset."

"I'm not exactly upset, I think I'm stunned. Paul told me he's in love with me."

"My stars!" Mama almost spilled her tea. Carefully, she put down the cup and peered at Valina. "How do you feel about him?"

"When I was younger, I adored him, but when everyone assumed he and Mary would get married, I didn't let myself think that way about him anymore. There'll be trouble when she gets wind of this."

"Why, Valina." Mama looked indignant. "That's ridiculous. She's married."

"But she came into the cafe yesterday and called me a hussy. She claimed I was making a play for Paul."

Mama gasped. "No!"

"I'm sorry, Mama. I know that hurts you, but I'm afraid of what she'll do, especially after she hears about the birthday gift."

"What birthday gift?"

"He gave me a train ticket to Portland. He wants Catherine and me to visit him in the spring. I said I would, but I don't know. Should I keep the ticket, Mama? Would it be proper?"

"How do you mean, proper?"

"He's going to be coming home as often as he can so we can be together, but if I accept the ticket, I feel like I'm saying I'll marry him when I'm not sure yet."

"I see. Well, why don't you tell him that?"

"Because I think I've always loved him. I just need time to get used to the idea."

"Of course you do, so tell him that, too. How long has he felt this way about you?"

"Since he was a senior in high school."

"My land. If only we'd known."

"That's what I say."

This would be the perfect time to tell Mama about Timothy and warn her about Rachel. But the words wouldn't come. Valina didn't hear any of Reverend Howard's sermon the next morning. Paul sat right across the aisle from her, with Catherine and Doc. He kept glancing at her, his warm eyes loving her, caressing her.

Would he still love her, in spite of what happened with Timothy? Wouldn't it be better to confess before the trip? She had to talk to someone. Catherine? No. She was Mama's best friend. That wouldn't be fair. But, doctors weren't supposed to divulge secrets. How could she see Doc without Mama knowing? And how could she get by Minnie? It was too complicated. She could never have dreamed that her eighteenth birthday would have turned out this way.

After the service, Catherine insisted that they all come to lunch. She squeezed Valina's hand and said, "I understand you and I will be going to Portland in the spring. I'm so happy to hear it."

She smiled at Catherine, but felt that things were going too fast. Somehow, she had to talk to Doc.

When Minnie came into the cafe the next afternoon, Valina felt that God had intervened.

"Minnie, I have a sore foot. I think maybe I sprained it." Now she'd have to remember to limp. "Do you suppose Doc could look at it?"

"Sure. Come by when you get off work. And bring him a piece of pie. Try to get him to sit down for a few minutes, will you?" Minnie picked up the coffee she'd ordered for Doc and hurried out the door.

By the time Valina got to Doc's office later that afternoon, the palms of her hands were wet. She shifted the pie and wiped one hand at a time on her skirt, but it didn't help. How could she bring herself to say it? Doc could be her in-law, if she kept her mouth shut. But she had to protect Rachel if she could.

Minnie ushered her into Doc's office, grabbed the pie, and put it on his desk. "Make him sit down. He'll be here in just a minute. Take your shoe off. How'd you do it, anyway?"

For an awful second Valina couldn't make sense of what Minnie was saying. "Oh. I just stepped on a rock the wrong way when I put the garbage out at the cafe."

Minnie wrote something on a piece of paper on Doc's desk, then left the room.

Valina looked at the one painting on the wall, a mother and child. Mama would be mortified if she knew what Doc was about to hear.

When he came in, Doc said, "So. Sprained your foot, I

hear." He sat on a stool beside her and reached for her foot. "Let's have a look."

"That isn't the real reason I came in, Doc."

He looked at her intently, then lowered his hand and sat back. "Something pretty serious on your mind?"

"I'm afraid so." She started to cry. "Oh, Doc, I have to talk to someone."

"Then you've come to the right person. I have to keep my mouth shut, and I've already heard everything there is to hear in this old world."

She swallowed hard. "You know that Paul wants to marry me?"

"He told us Sunday morning, and we're stark-raving happy about it."

"You may not be when you hear." She couldn't look at him. "I thought Timothy loved me. He acted like he did. I had sex with him."

"And then he eloped with Mary? Why, that miserable scoundrel. He moves fast, doesn't he?"

"I'll say."

Doc patted her on the shoulder. "You were seduced, Valina. Don't even think of it as being your fault."

"I don't know what to do." Tears ran down her cheeks. "I have to tell Paul, don't I? But then he might not love me anymore. I never could have dreamed that he would." She bit her lip to keep from crying.

"Paul's a bright, compassionate young man, Valina. Don't underestimate his love for you."

"I loved him when I was younger, but I thought he belonged to Mary, so I pushed him out of my heart."

Doc shook his head. "Damned gossips in this town cause so much miserable trouble. But, listen to me, now. You were innocent and vulnerable. Timothy took advantage of that."

"I was so dumb, I actually thought he'd marry me."

"That bastard!" He stood up and paced the floor. "Well, I don't suppose you'll be able to handle this unless Paul knows. Would you like me to tell him?"

"No. I'm not that much of a coward."

Doc stopped in front of her. "You are not a coward in any sense of the word. You're a fine young woman. Catherine and I will be overjoyed to have you marry Paul."

"But he's educated. I'm only a waitress. What do I have to offer him?"

"Yourself. Your sensitive, loving self."

"There's something else. After Mary and Timothy were married, he had the nerve to tell me it didn't have to be over between us." She shuddered. "And on Thanksgiving, watching him sit there next to Rachel, it hit me that he might do things to her. She adores him. I'm afraid for her, Doc, but I can't tell Mama what he's really like."

Doc sat down and absently started eating the pie. "Emma may not know what that scum did to you, but your mother's no dummy. Let me warn her. She already knows what type he is. I'll simply agree with her and point out that maybe Rachel should never be alone with him." He took a handkerchief out of his pocket and wiped his mouth. "Don't worry. Your mother will see to it. Does she know you're here?"

"Yes. I made up the foot thing when Minnie came into the cafe this afternoon. I'd been trying to figure out a way to get in here so I could talk to you, and there she was."

"Providence. I believe in that. Tell your mother that you came in, in case Minnie says something. And let me wrap that foot so you'll remember to limp." He opened a drawer in the metal cabinet behind him and took out a bandage. After he had wrapped it around her foot, he grinned at her. "I didn't put it on very tight, just enough to help you remember to limp a little. Wear it today, take it off tonight, and tomorrow morning remark on the fact that it is all healed."

Tears welled up in her eyes again. "You're so good to me."

"And why in hell shouldn't I be? Remember, now, you're the one who's been wronged. Don't let needless guilt ruin your life."

"I'll tell Paul when he comes home for Christmas, first thing."

"Do that. I think you'll be surprised at how little it will matter to him. The thing is, it mustn't matter to you. Now, wear this bandage and come back in a couple of days."

"Thanks, doc."

He waited while she put her shoe back on, and then he put his arm around her shoulders as he led her to the office door. "Smile as you leave. You have every reason to be happy."

"Okay." She grinned as she limped by Minnie. "Doc says I should come back in a couple of days."

"Fine. Did he sit down when he ate his pie?"

"He sure did."

She started limping toward home. She felt better.

Christmas was only a month away. She could hardly wait to get it over with.

Emma stopped by Mary's house on her way home from work Monday evening. If Mary heard about Paul and Valina from someone else, she might embarrass herself, or ruin her marriage. Not that Emma would shed a tear if the marriage broke up, but Paul shouldn't be the cause of it. Even more important, Mary had no right to make her sister's life miserable. Valina deserved Paul's love.

Emma prayed as she climbed the front steps of Mary's house. "Dear Lord, please help me say the right thing."

When Mary opened the door, she just stood there, as if she had no intention of letting her mother come inside. Emma waited. After an awkward silence, Mary said, "Well, come on in." She stayed standing just inside the door.

The hostile invitation saddened Emma. To think she wasn't welcome in her own daughter's home. "I have something to tell you, Mary."

Mary just stood there with her arms folded across her chest.

"May I sit down? I've been on my feet all day." It hurt to have to ask.

Mary didn't answer, she just pointed at a chair.

"I thought it would be best if you heard this from me. Paul has asked Valina to marry him." She put out her hand to ward off Mary's retort. "Valina was stunned. She had no idea he loved her, but he says that he has ever since he was a senior in high school."

Mary's face fell.

"Paul told that to Catherine and Doc, as well as Valina." Emma braced herself for an angry outburst.

"But she was making a play for him." The words flew out on Mary's spit.

Her voice calm, Emma said, "I'm very worried about you, dear. If you loved Timothy enough to marry him, then why all this fuss about Paul?"

Mary glowered but said nothing.

"Are you jealous of Valina? Is that it?"

Mary stalked away from the door and stood over Emma. "That's an insulting question. Why on earth would I be jealous of her?"

"Jealousy is never rational. But if it's not jealousy, then your actions indicate that you're in love with both Timothy and Paul."

Mute, Mary stared at her mother.

"That's what Timothy might think if he found out how you feel about Paul."

"But I don't care about Paul," Mary said.

"I know that now. That's what concerns me about this. Why such rage, Mary?"

Mary's eyes filled with tears. "I don't know."

Emma stood up. She'd made her point. "Well, if you need me, I'm usually alone in the kitchen at the cafe."

Right after her mother left, Mary went upstairs to her bedroom closet and pulled out a bright green dress she'd never worn. Mrs. Sampson gave it to her because it hadn't sold. She had to pretend to be grateful, not that she'd ever wear the garish thing. Lucky she had taken it, though. Zoe Adams bought that awful red satin dress last spring, so how could she resist this green thing?

Mary burst into tears. Zoe was the only person she knew who could tell her where to go for an abortion. She couldn't deny it any longer. She'd missed her period, her breasts were swollen and sore, and nausea greeted her every morning. She was pregnant. Well, she'd be damned if she'd look like a walking mountain. She had told Timothy she didn't want children right away. Maybe he'd done it deliberately. He was so sure she was playing around, maybe he had. Mama was right. She'd have to avoid Paul.

Damn it. She was the one who was supposed to move to a city, not her sister. Valina didn't hate Pine Bluff the way she did. But Timothy wouldn't even tell her what he did for a living, much less how he planned to support them in San Francisco, or when. She took a pillow off the bed and threw it at the door. Had Timothy rented a four-bedroom house because he secretly planned on filling it with children, in spite of his wife's wishes? Oh, Lord, she had to stop thinking about it.

She went downstairs, fixed a cup of tea and wandered into the living room. She gazed out the window. How could she contact Zoe? People would talk if she went to her house.

Then she remembered the gossip about Zoe's worthless father, Cooley Adams. He often ate dinner at the cafe. Everyone said Zoe's money paid for it. Well, with Timothy out of town she had a perfect excuse to eat out.

When she got to the cafe, Mary swore under her breath. Bertha Wilcox sat at the corner table. Damned busybody.

Mary ordered fried chicken but when Ben brought it to her, just the smell made her squeamish. She picked at it. Nothing had tasted good for a week now. Since Cooley hadn't shown up yet, she ordered a piece of lemon pie. He might still come in.

Ben frowned at the food left on her plate. "I know that chicken is delicious because I had some myself. Aren't you feeling well? You look a little peaked."

Lord, if he didn't sound like an old lady. "I'm just lonesome for Timothy, that's all."

"Oh." Ben patted her hand. "Must be hard for you two newlyweds, him being away so much of the time."

She looked up at the sound of the door. Cooley Adams had finally arrived. When Ben brought her the pie, she forced herself to eat most of it, praying she wouldn't vomit, then paid her bill and stopped by Cooley's table.

"Seeing you here, Mr. Adams, reminds me that I have a dress Zoe might like. Would you ask her to come see me about it? I'd like to give it to her."

Cooley stared at her, his fork suspended between the plate and his mouth. "Why, that's right nice of you. Mrs. O'Callahan. I'll tell her what you said."

"And tell her it's a pretty shade of green, sort of like the red one she bought at Sampson's. That's where it came from, in fact."

Out of the corner of her eye she saw Bertha taking it all in. There'd be gossip circulating though the whole town by breakfast tomorrow morning. She had to get away from this dreadful town. Those high mountains Papa loved so much were nothing but prison walls.

Zoe showed up two days later, a guarded look on her face. "My pa said you wanted to see me."

"Yes. Do come in, Zoe." Mary could hear herself gushing, but she couldn't stop. "I have a dress I'd like to give you, if you want it, that is." She hurried Zoe up the stairs. "You can try it on. I'm sure it will fit you."

So far, Zoe hadn't responded, not with a word or a smile or a nod. Nothing. Mary couldn't believe a woman like Zoe could make her feel so uncomfortable.

"Here it is." Mary held out the shiny green dress. "Mrs. Sampson gave it to me but I've never had an occasion to wear it. When I saw it in the closet the other day, I immediately thought of you." Why in the world wasn't Zoe more enthusiastic? The dress couldn't be more perfect for her, considering the way she lived. "Do you like it?"

"What do you want from me?" Zoe asked.

Mary stared at her. Slowly, she sat down on the bed. Oh, God, she couldn't ask Zoe about an abortionist. It would sound awful. And Zoe would probably be more than happy to tell on her. She hadn't thought of that. She couldn't face Zoe's scorn, much less the town's. If only she lived in a city where no one would find out.

"I just wanted to give you the dress," Mary said. "I thought you'd like it. But, since we've never been what you'd call friends, I can see it would seem odd to you,"

Zoe just stood there, measuring her. "That all you wanted?"

"Yes." Mary's chin rose. Zoe mustn't see how she felt.

Zoe hesitated, her eyes narrowed.

"If you feel I've insulted you, Zoe, I'm sorry." Why didn't she just take the damned dress and leave?

"Well, I ain't gonna hang around, that's for sure. I don't want the dress. Thanks just the same."

Mary had to rush to catch up with her on the stairs. She started to apologize again but thought better of it. Zoe would know it wasn't sincere.

When she shut the door behind Zoe, she sobbed, deep sobs that hurt her chest. She didn't want to be a matron with a baby. She paced the floor and howled, "No . . . no."

She continued that way for three days. By Friday, she had a plan. Timothy would have to take her to a town where she could have an abortion.

Friday morning she drank some tea and ate a few soda crackers, then took a bath and got dressed. She made a chocolate cake, his favorite, and put a beef roast in the oven.

When she heard his car she hurried to meet him, but she didn't tell him right away. After dinner they sat on the sofa, their hands clasped.

"You hardly ate a bite of dinner, little love." Timothy pulled her toward him. "You don't look so good, either. Are you sick?"

"No." She swallowed hard but couldn't hold back the tears.

"What's wrong, Mary?"

"I'm pregnant."

Timothy beamed as he cradled her in his arms. "That's great. You mustn't cry. Why are you so upset about it?"

She jerked away form him. "Why? Because I told you I didn't want a baby right away that's why."

He smiled. "Sometimes rubbers fail."

She wanted to rake her nails down his face, make him bleed. "You didn't tell me that."

"I thought you knew at least that much about it."

"And just how would I have known? I was a virgin, remember?"

He grinned at her. "I sure do."

He reached for her, but she pushed him away. "I'm not carrying this baby," she said. "You can just take me to some town where no one knows us and I'll have an abortion."

"Just like that?"

"That's right."

"What makes you think I'd know where to go, or who to go to, for that matter?"

She didn't believe a man of his experience hadn't heard things. Maybe his damned rubbers had failed with some other woman. "You'd know who to ask. Don't try to tell me you wouldn't. A person like you?" Too late, she realized how nasty that sounded.

He grabbed her wrist. "I like the thought of you being pregnant. You won't be so appealing to Paul Bradford, will you?"

"Paul has proposed to Valina. Now let go of my wrist. You're hurting me."

His fingers relaxed. He didn't seem as angry, but the look on his face puzzled her.

"Valina? That's a surprise."

"I don't care about Valina or Paul. I just want an abortion. You've got to help me. We agreed."

He laughed at her. "We didn't agree on anything. I'm Catholic. We Catholics like children, lots of them."

"I see." Furious, Mary mocked his sarcasm. "But we didn't have a Catholic ceremony, so we aren't really married, are we?"

He was about as religious as Cooley Adams. Her stomach rolled and she dashed to the bathroom.

He waited in the doorway watching her vomit. When it was over and she tried to get by him, he picked her up and carried her to the sofa.

"But we are married in the eyes of your church, and by law, so you're legally mine."

Mary closed her eyes and let him take off her clothes. She knew he'd have his way, no matter what she did or said. She tried to close her mind, as well as her eyes, but her traitorous body responded to his skillful tongue and clever fingers.

Later that afternoon, Emma looked up from her baking to see Mary standing in the doorway. Hesitant, Mary said, "Is it all right if I come in?"

"Of course it is." Emma had had an uneasy feeling about Mary ever since she'd told her about Paul and Valina. And now there were dark circles under Mary's eyes, as if she were ill, or there'd been trouble. "What's wrong, dear?"

Mary sank into a chair and burst into tears. "I'm pregnant."

Emma wasn't surprised, but she fervently prayed that Mary would be able to accept the responsibility of being a mother. Maybe she'd grow up because of the child. Some people did. "Why, I'm delighted. I'm going to be a grandmother."

"Well, I'm not delighted. I don't want to be pregnant." Mary sniffed, then blew her nose.

"It doesn't last forever, dear. And you're given such a precious gift at the end of nine months. I'll bet three or four of those months have already passed. Am I right?"

Mary nodded. "Doc says it's due toward the end of May."

"A perfect time of year to have a baby, and you have only a little over five months left. Why don't you come home for dinner tonight? We can surprise the family and start planning a layette."

"Maybe I will." Mary stood up, and took an anxious peek at her abdomen as she smoothed her dress. "I'd better let you get back to work." But she didn't leave. She just stood there in the center of the room.

Emma went over and put her arms around her daughter. "Everything will be all right. Don't worry. You'll get used to the idea."

If Mary couldn't handle this, how could she survive a real problem, Emma wondered. If only she hadn't married Timothy. Emma swallowed hard and blinked. She was sure Mary had already shed enough tears for both of them.

Valina shuddered when she saw Timothy come into the cabin with Mary. Mama had invited Mary for dinner, but Timothy was supposed to be out of town.

"I came home early because of the snow." Timothy said.

Just my luck, Valina thought. She wished she could be anywhere but in the same room with him.

"I didn't think I'd make it those last twenty-five miles," he said. "Almost slid over the edge once, and got stuck twice. I'll take the train next trip out. Of course the trains won't run if we get snowed in." He smiled at Mary. "But, I wouldn't mind it a bit if I got to spend more time with my pretty little mother-to-be."

Mary scowled at him. "I wish you'd keep this to yourself until I start to show," she said.

Mary, of all people, pregnant. It was easy to see she wasn't happy about it. Valina couldn't imagine Mary taking care of a child. She had always avoided it when Rachel was little.

Timothy grinned at Mary. "Hey, the sooner you show, the better I'll like it. Emma, don't you think she's too thin?"

Mama just smiled at him. Valina knew Mama would never take sides with Timothy against one of her own children.

"What do you think you'll have, a boy or a girl?" Rachel asked.

"Well, I don't know about Mary, but I'd like a boy." Timothy patted Mary's hand.

"But you'll be happy if it's a girl, won't you?" Papa said, his voice louder than usual.

Timothy actually blushed at Papa's firm declaration. Valina thought Papa was sweet to stick up for girls. Most of the men in town were absolutely tiresome about wanting sons. She'd never understood the big to-do about having a boy. "What names have you picked out, Mary?" she asked.

Timothy interrupted again. "It'll be Timothy O'Callahan, Jr., if it's a boy."

"Don't you mean Timothy Daniel O'Callahan?" Mary said, her jaw set in an all-too-familiar firm line.

"Well, yeah. That would be all right. Yes, indeed."

Papa's face lit up. It would be nice for him to have a grandson after three girls, Valina thought.

"What will you call it if it's a girl?" Rachel asked.

Before Timothy could answer, Mary said, "We haven't decided yet."

"How about Rachel?" Rachel said.

Valina laughed. "Sure. Or, how about Emma, or Mary, or Valina? And there's always Matilda."

Everyone laughed but Mary. "It's going to be a very special name, but I haven't decided yet." She glared at Timothy, as if daring him to utter a sound.

Valina thought Timothy might wish he were dead by the time the baby was born. Knowing Mary, her disposition would get worse in proportion to her size.

During the whole evening, the subject of Paul's proposal wasn't mentioned. It amazed Valina that even little blabber-mouth Rachel hadn't said one word about it. Did Mama warn her? No, Rachel was just excited about the baby. Too bad Mary wasn't.

CHAPTER 11

J-Bar-J Ranch — 1969

At mid-morning it was cooler than usual. I stood on the porch just breathing it in for a moment. But then Buck came out of the barn and hustled over to me. The angry look on his face told me something was wrong.

"Tools missing," he said.

I started to go to the barn, but turned back. This was Oscar's problem right now, and I would just add to the trouble if I got mixed up in it.

"Well, Oscar will handle it, Buck." He just grunted and went back to the barn.

Thank heaven we'd have at least one good extra worker. I had given Oscar permission to hire Orville, so he could help us with the fences. Orville also wanted to help trap the trouble maker who was cutting them. He said he needed the money. And God knows, we could use the help.

I went back into the house where Jimmy sat in a kitchen chair, his elbows resting on the table. He looked pitifully bored. I just shook my head. "Did you remember that you need to milk Daisy and feed the chickens.?" I asked. The kid hurried out.

I wasn't hungry, but I heated up some leftover stew for Buck and George and Jimmy. I sat with them and drank a cup of coffee while they ate. Orville would be eating with Oscar and his bunk house crew.

"Those three men gonna be here long?" George asked.

"Nope. They'll go home Monday morning," I assured him.

"Good thing."

Buck grunted, which meant he agreed with George.

"They causing you trouble?" I asked.

"Nah," George said. "They're just fools."

Jimmy frowned. "Well, I feel kind of sorry for those guys, the way everybody's treating them."

"They're getting paid," I said,

"Yeah, but they're being treated like scumbags."

"Scumbags." It was a word I hadn't heard before. "Good description of those three."

Jimmy rolled his eyes and gave up.

I went over to the barn to make sure things were in order there. Stalls had been cleaned, and the horses groomed. Good. Nothing wrong there.

But when I went back to the front porch, Cappie was there handing Roscoe a chicken bone.

"Don't do that!" I scared Cappie almost to death when I grabbed that bone out of his hand. "Don't ever give a chicken bone to a dog," I said.

Cappie shrank away from me. "I'm sorry, Mrs. Jacobsen."

Hell, he didn't mean any harm, but Roscoe would eat ground glass if you handed it to him. "I'm sorry I scared you, Cappie, but chicken bones splinter. They can kill a dog."

He hung his head and mumbled, "Oh. I didn't know that."

"Well, now you do." I turned and went back into the house. Oscar was wiping the dishes from the meal he'd cooked for himself and the extra helpers.

"You don't need to repeat yourself," he grumbled. "I heard what you said to him."

"They leave Monday morning."

He glared at me. "Yes, damn it."

I went upstairs and got ready for bed. It was early, but it'd been a long day and I was weary. Much as I wanted that vandal caught, I hoped it could be a peaceful night.

It was peaceful, all right. I slept until seven the next morning. Couldn't believe my eyes when I saw what time it was. Doubt I'd ever slept that late before.

When I went downstairs to fix breakfast, Jimmy was waiting for me, a scowl on his face.

"Buck and George were worried about you. Are you all right?"

"Of course I am."

"Oh. Well, they said to tell you they've already had breakfast. And I've eaten, too. I'd better go feed the chickens and milk Daisy." The screen door banged as he left.

He'd made it pretty clear that he'd been worried about me. My, my. And waiting for me to get up, too. Quite a change.

I was just finishing my second cup of coffee, when Oscar came in to fix breakfast for himself and the clowns.

"How'd it go last night?" I asked.

"We didn't find him." He spat out the words, like he could hardly wait to get the nasty taste out of his mouth.

Poor Oscar. I almost felt sorry for him, but he'd asked for it.

"Did you find the tools?"

"Nope."

I didn't ask him any more questions. Things weren't going very well for him. No need to rub it in.

Just then the phone rang. It was Bob Tuttle.

"Are you alone?" he asked.

"No, but I can arrange to be." I put my hand over the mouthpiece. "Oscar, this is a personal call."

You'd have thought I stabbed him. Huffy? He marched out the door and kicked it shut.

"Okay, I'm alone, Bob. What's up?"

"I had a long talk with Jessica over the weekend. I told her I didn't think we'd accomplished much with the counseling, especially in regard to the way we handle Jimmy. I also told her that if we can't find some meeting ground by the time Jimmy comes home, I will leave her and take him with me."

"Oof! How'd she react?"

"Predictably. She claimed I couldn't give him the advantages she could. I swear to God she was nursed on money, not mother's milk."

I couldn't help but chuckle. "There's a lot of truth in that."

"So I told her that my attorney and I had already discussed it, and he maintains that money can't take the place of a father, especially for a boy. That seemed to scare her a little."

"I hope it scared her enough."

"We have another session this afternoon."

"I sure hope it works out. Thanks for letting me know what's going on, not that it's any of my business."

"After what you've done for our son? Of course it is. I'm not kidding myself, Matilda. There isn't much hope for our marriage. It's Jimmy I'm concerned about."

"That's as it should be. Good luck. Keep me posted."

"Thanks," he said. "I will."

I warmed my coffee and sat down to think a spell. Could Jessica change? I doubted it. And poor Jimmy would be caught in the crossfire if his folks divorced. The thought of it turned my stomach sour. Jessica and Marie would manipulate the kid with their damned money, sure as fate. Well, if that happened, I'd at least call in my chips with Mary. I still had a few straws left in my broom.

There was the money she had borrowed from me, but never once offered to pay back. And the trouble she made for her sisters over the pittance Daniel and Emma left when they died. Marie was as rich as Midas, and still hungering for more. Wonder how she'd like it if those little items got loose in the gossip columns of the Frisco papers. At least I could threaten her with it.

Out of the kitchen window, I saw Jimmy chewing on a blade of grass, taking his time coming back to the house. Probably been fooling around with Mattie's Boy. He stopped to pet Angus and talk to him for a bit. Then he came into the house, a big smile on his face.

"What can I do now, aunt Matilda?"

"You can hoe the garden and pick a mess of beans," I said.

I walked over and peered through the screen door. Oscar was sitting in the old rocker, looking like a storm about to bust open.

"Kitchen's all yours, Oscar. I'll be upstairs changing beds."

No way I'd stay in the same room with him and his three bums.

Later, when I went back downstairs, Oscar and his men were gone, thank God. I started making lunch for Buck and George. This business of eating in shifts had me way off schedule.

About then, Jimmy brought in the beans. I was still tired from yesterday. Maybe Jimmy could take the lunches to the men. I surprised the heck out of him, as well as myself, by handing him the key to the jeep.

"What's this for?" he asked.

"It's for taking lunch out to Buck and George. I'm too busy to do it myself."

"You mean I'll be driving alone?"

"Yep. Now, get a move on. They'll be hungry enough to eat those metal fence posts Oscar's so taken with."

His grin damned near broke his face in two. "I won't be long."

"Your lunch will be waiting for you." I figured that would bring him back right away.

The minute he drove off, anxiety started plaguing me. What if he got hurt? Oh, hell, what was wrong with me? Oscar had been letting him drive alone for some time. Besides, Jimmy'd had enough mollycoddling.

He was gone longer than he should've been, though. I was about ready to ride out there and look for him, when I heard a horse come into the yard. I walked up to the screen door to see who it was. Buddy.

"Well, hi, Buddy, come in and have a cup of coffee."

"Sounds good." He took off his hat as he walked into the kitchen.

"How are those two Dobermans coming along?"

"Better than I thought they would." He sat down at the table. "I got them just in time."

I didn't like the sound of that. "What happened?"

"They made such a racket about a week ago, I thought that prowler of ours might be outside. I let the dogs loose and waited to see what would happen. Wasn't long before I heard a man scream, then a horse take off, fast."

"Hmm. Think they bit someone?"

He grinned. "Well, there was blood on the ground."

"That's a coincidence." I poured him a cup of coffee and told him about Jimmy's big night in the chicken yard with the shotgun and the blood on the ground. "Your dogs' bites must have been more painful than Jimmy's bullet. The man didn't scream."

Buddy's huge laugh fairly bounced off the kitchen walls. "I bet that man won't come near our two ranches again."

"He won't if he has any brains," I said.

He was still chuckling when he handed me a thick sheet of paper with an eagle's feather attached to it. "I came over to give you this invitation to our wedding."

The date, time, and place were printed on the paper in calligraphy: September 9th at 10:00 a.m. at his place.

"Now, that's a fine wedding invitation," I said. He beamed. "Lynette made it."

"She's not only beautiful, she's talented. You've got yourself a real prize in that girl."

"Don't I know it." A big grin lit up his face.

"Well, consider your wedding invitation accepted. I wouldn't miss it for anything."

His face turned serious. "Your presence will add a special meaning to our wedding."

I hardly knew what to say. Fortunately, just then Jimmy came in and saved me from embarrassing myself.

The screen door squeaked as he sauntered in, looking like he'd rolled in the dirt.

"What happened to you?" I asked.

"Had a flat tire." He strutted across the room. "But it's okay now. I fixed it."

He grabbed the sandwich I'd made for him, wrapped the cookie jar in a big hug, sat down at the table with us, and said, "Hi, Buddy. Want a cookie?" He even had the good manners to push the jar over to Buddy.

Buddy helped himself, and said, "Thanks. Say, did I tell you that I lived in San Francisco for a while?"

Jimmy's eyes lit up. "Cool."

"Yeah, for a couple of years. I worked at one of the markets on Fisherman's Wharf."

"Why'd you leave?" Jimmy asked.

Buddy grinned. "Linette."

Jimmy's eyebrows skidded toward the ceiling. "Yeah, man."

"You don't have family around here, do you Buddy?" I asked.

"No, we didn't come from here. But my family's all gone anyway. My mother was the last to go. Died of tuberculosis about two years ago."

"And no one else, huh?"

"Only the one brother I told you about. He was killed in a rodeo. Horse fell on him. That's when I quit the rodeo circuit."

Jimmy's eyes bugged out. "You've been in a rodeo? Like the ones I've seen on TV?"

"Yep. I've been in lots of them. Sort of gets in your blood but, sooner or later, your body gets tired of the beating it takes. And, after my brother . . . well, I said to hell with it."

I poured Buddy another cup of coffee and sliced him some banana bread.

He took a bite and smacked his lips, then grinned at me. "You're a great cook, Matilda."

"Years of practice," I said.

Some time later, after the banana bread was gone, Buddy got up to leave. When he held out his hand to Jimmy, the kid stood up and shook hands like a real man. It was foolish of me, but I felt proud of the boy.

"I'll see you later, Matilda."

After Buddy left, Jimmy said, "Why do Indians have such funny names?"

"Indian names have something to say. By the way, what does Tuttle mean?"

He laughed. "Well, at least I didn't make some smart remark the first time I heard "Fast Buffalo Horse.""

"Only because I glared at you."

He snickered. "Yeah, man!"

I handed him the basket of green beans and a pan. "Here, make yourself useful."

He scowled up at me. "What am I supposed to do with these?"

Lord help us, I even had to show him how to snap green beans. "What in the world do you do with your time in The City?"

"Lots of things."

"Nothing practical, that's for sure."

He just shrugged and started off on another tack. "I suppose you'll be happy to get rid of those guys tomorrow." He peered at me out of the corner of his eye.

Since tomorrow would be Monday, when the clowns would definitely leave, I was feeling a little better about things. "Yep. They'll leave first thing in the morning."

"Is Orville still going to stay and help with the fences?"

"Yes, he is. He also wants to help us find the bastard who's cutting them."

"I'll bet Oscar's happy about that."

"Sure. And best of all, Orville is a step above the three stooges."

"Yeah, he knows a lot about ranching, How come he doesn't have his own?"

"It takes a lot of money, to not only buy the land, but to buy the cattle, build a house and a barn, and then hire people to help run the whole thing."

"Yeah, but how did you and your husband do all that? Did you have the money?"

"Jacob had enough to give us a start, but it was spent in no time. Neither of us knew just how much sweat we'd have to put into it."

I thought it was about time for me to fix poor Oscar a decent dinner. I'd been giving him a real hard time. I went out to kill a chicken. Oscar loves chicken and dumplings.

Jimmy came with me. "Thought I'd give the chickens some fresh water," he said.

But when I picked up one of the chickens and wrung its neck, and then another one, as well, Jimmy just about tossed his cookies.

"Why the hell did you do that?" His voice slid up into a screech.

"You don't mean to tell me you thought the chickens you've eaten on my ranch came sealed in a package?"

He looked like he'd smelled a goat. "I hadn't thought about it." He turned and went back to the house.

Poor little city boy.

I had decided I should at least cook enough food for the three stooges, but they'd still have to eat in the bunk house.

The next morning, I swear that new half-baked rooster of mine crowed long before sunrise. Maybe the heat had addled what little brains he had. It sure wasn't doing much for mine. Just then, I heard horses leaving the ranch. I smiled. Finally, the sheriff's three "helpers" were going back to town.

I got dressed and went downstairs to fix breakfast. Just as I finished mixing up the pancake batter, Oscar walked in. I didn't say a thing about the helpers. Neither did he. He just sort of grunted when he came in the kitchen, then poured himself a cup of coffee and sat at the table. I knew he was uneasy by the way he kept adjusting his chair, as if he couldn't get it quite right. I wondered what had gone wrong now.

Pretty soon, he blurted out, "Last night, I told Jimmy he could take the salt lick to the upper pasture today."

I couldn't believe I'd heard him right. "You mean drive the jeep up that mountain by himself?"

"Well, he won't really be alone. I'll be behind him on Dusty."

He knew he had overstepped his bounds, and here he was, up to his neck in trouble again. Hadn't even been twenty-four hours since his last pack of trouble. By golly, he could be almost as hard to handle as Jimmy.

"And I'll be right behind you on Sally," I said.

Oscar gawked at me for a bit, then shook his head and said, "I'll saddle her up for you." He disappeared, fast.

I wasn't really as upset as I'd let on, but he should have asked me about it before saying anything to Jimmy. That kid driving on a steep cow trail? Why, the jeep could turn over, even roll on him. Jimmy was too puffed up about his driving expertise. That was the problem.

About then, George and Buck came downstairs, and just as they started stuffing their faces, here came Jimmy. He didn't want to look at me, though I tried to catch his eye.

Oh, he said good morning. So did I. But he still wouldn't look at me. Well, he had a big surprise ahead of him.

When Oscar came in and gave the keys to Jimmy, you'd have thought he'd been given the keys to the kingdom, instead of a beat-up old jeep.

Jimmy looked over at me, guilt written all over his face. Then he bounded over to the door and said, "Come on, Oscar. Let's get going."

"Just hang onto your puckering string and let me get my boots on," I said.

He was one shocked kid. Out of the corner of my eye I saw him mouth, "Is she coming?" at Oscar. His jaw dropped when Oscar nodded.

Jimmy stood by the back door, shifting from one foot to the other, as if his boots were on fire, but I wasn't impressed. I took my time. He needed to squirm.

When he got behind the wheel of the jeep, his face lit up so bright, if it had been dark outside he wouldn't have needed the headlights.

Before Jimmy had a chance to turn the key, Oscar put a warning hand on his arm. "You be careful, or both you and me are dead men."

Jimmy flicked a glance at me, then looked back at Oscar. "You don't need to worry." He turned on the key and shifted gears.

I began to pray. No doubt Oscar did, too. The jeep was soon out of sight.

We took Aussie with us and checked the cattle along the way. They all looked fine, so Aussie relaxed and chased a squirrel up a tree.

We were about a hundred feet below the upper pasture when we caught up with Jimmy. The jeep had slid into a boulder. Dented the right front fender a good one. Sweat dripped off the kid's face as he tried to pull the fender away from the tire. Apparently he thought cussing and grunting would help.

"You can't do that with your hands, boy," Oscar said. He got the tire iron out of the back of the jeep and showed Jimmy how to use it, then stood back and let him try it. The kid did move it some, but it was slow work.

That's when Oscar said, "You're doing great. It needs just one more pry." He took the tire iron and, with one easy motion, moved the fender further than Jimmy had in several tries.

"There we are," Oscar said. "Now, you get on Dusty and I'll take it from here. I know the jeep pretty well. It might get some strange notions about now."

"Yeah," Jimmy muttered. He was sitting on the ground, his face on his knees.

I nodded at Oscar to go on ahead, then dismounted and sat down by the boy. He didn't look up.

"Why does everything always happen to me?" he groaned.

"Hey, you're not doing that bad. You just don't have a lot of experience."

"Yeah, sure."

"Well, you almost made it to the top. And you had the right idea about the fender."

"I should've thought about using the tire iron." His voice cracked and he slammed his fist into the dirt.

"Come on, where's you sense of humor?" I said.

He sat up and looked me in the eye. "You're not going to yell at Oscar and me?"

"I don't think so. No point in having a tizzy fit on a hot day like this. Not worth the effort."

We sat there, waiting for Oscar, watching that crazy Aussie chase two chipmunks that had ganged up on him. Over and over again, they'd come right up to him then run off in different directions, tails twitching. Aussie never did come close to catching either one of those scamps but he sure as hell tried. Jimmy smiled in spite of himself. Good sign, I thought.

But then he started in again. "I suppose I've ruined the jeep," he said.

"You saw it drive off, so don't give me that." I looked over at Aussie sitting on his haunches, tongue hanging out the side of his mouth. "You know what I admire most about animals? They accept life just as it comes to them. Look at Aussie. He's finally realized that those two chipmunks have made an ass out of him. Does he care? Hell, no. He's had a great old time."

Just then, I heard the jeep edging its way down into the meadow. Oscar drove up and parked beside us. "Everything's fine up above," he said. "Still plenty of grass left for grazing, though I don't know why, what with the hot summer we're having. But there is a bit of shade up there."

He glanced at Jimmy, who lowered his head again and rested it on his knees. Oscar looked at me and raised his eyebrows. I mouthed, "sorry for himself," and Oscar nodded.

I got the thermos out of the jeep and poured some coffee, while Oscar sat down to rest a spell.

Jimmy looked up at me. "You aren't going to tell Buck and George, are you?"

"Damned right I am. Anyone who makes a mistake on this ranch gets ribbed about it." I looked at Oscar. "Don't they?"

He laughed. "Looks like we're in for it, Jimmy."

"I'm sorry, Oscar," Jimmy said.

"Forget it, kid." He reached over and yanked Jimmy's hat down over his face.

When Oscar started down the mountain, we followed, just to make sure the jeep didn't give him any trouble. We took it pretty slow, me pointing out the fresh elk tracks on the road, Aussie chasing another squirrel.

You know that eerie feeling you get when you know some unseen person or thing is watching you? That's what came over me right about then. Was that vandalizing bastard tailing us?

I slipped the thirty-eight out of its holster and gave a slight tug on the reins. Sally stopped. Slowly, I turned and peered into the woods. And then I saw it . . . a bobcat sitting on a stump, partially hidden by some brush. Aussie had followed the squirrel quite a ways down the road. No wonder he hadn't warned us.

By then, Jimmy had stopped his horse, too.

"Turn slowly," I whispered, "and look at the bobcat over on the stump at my left."

When Jimmy turned, the bobcat stood up, giving the boy a full-length view of himself, then disappeared into the brush.

"Now isn't that something," I said. "Not many people get a chance to see a cute little devil like him up close."

"It looked like just an ordinary cat, only bigger," Jimmy said.

"Well, they are in the cat family, but don't ever try to pick one up. Daniel did that when he was about eight-years-old. The bobcat let him carry him clear to our house, but when Mama saw what her baby was carrying, she let out a scream. That scared the bobcat, and it damned near severed an artery in Daniel's arm. Their claws are big and fierce."

"He must've bled a lot," Jimmy said.

"Sure did. Fortunately, Papa learned a lot about wounds in World War I. I can still hear poor little Daniel screaming in pain. You can bet he never picked up another bobcat."

We'd ridden a ways, when Jimmy said, "Your father was in World War I?"

"That's right. Come to think of it, he was just fifteen when he became a soldier."

Jimmy stared at me. "Fifteen?"

"Yep. Just your age. People grew up sooner back then."

"All the World War I stuff is ancient history."

I had a hard time keeping a straight face.

"Must be a shock to find yourself spending the summer with a woman whose father was actually in World War I. If you live to be old, time will have a different meaning for you than it does now."

We rode along in silence. Jimmy's eyebrows were all scrunched together. I figured he must be pondering over the weighty subject of time.

Up on the third pasture there's a place by the road where you can see the valley below. The ground falls away abruptly, and you look down on the tender shoots of the tops of the trees. Normally, I'd stop and admire my spread off there in the distance, but not that day. We rode on. God, it was hot. Must've been over a hundred degrees, and it wasn't quite noon yet. The dust swirled around the horses' hooves and drifted upward. Jimmy sneezed a few times, but he didn't say a word.

We finally caught up with Oscar down in the lower pasture, his head buried under the hood of the jeep.

When he heard us he stood up, wiped his greasy hands on a rag, and said, "I hope you brought a lunch. This jeep needs some new spark plugs."

"Want me to ride to the ranch and get them for you?" Jimmy asked. He was dying to do something to show how competent he could be.

"No need," Oscar said. "I always have a spare set in the jeep, and I've sure needed them often enough."

"Why don't you buy a new jeep, Aunt Matilda?" Jimmy asked. "This one looks pretty bad." He blushed, remembering that he'd just added a new dent.

"Why bother?" I said. "In one year's time it would be in the same shape this one's in."

"Even the upholstery?" Jimmy said.

"I'm so used to the cracks and rips in those seats that my butt wouldn't know what to do without them. See that long slit there on the driver's side?"

Oscar let out a whoop. "Woman's got a mind like a beaver trap. Once she finds out something, she won't let it go. I should never have admitted that I did it. 'Course there's that long scratch on the back fender there. You see it, Jimmy?"

"Did you do that, too?"

"Nope. Your Aunt Matilda did."

"You two are just trying to make me feel better," Jimmy said.

He was still upset about that fool dent. I handed him a chicken sandwich and a cup of coffee. Maybe some food would help. But, by God, if he didn't take the sandwich apart and study it, like he thought it might be poisoned.

"It's not rattlesnake meat, it's chicken." I started to bristle, but thought better of it. Lord, how that kid could get to me.

Later that evening, Jimmy went out to feed the chickens. He hadn't been gone two minutes when he staggered back in, his eyes wide and scared.

"What is it, Jimmy?"

"The rooster . . ." He stopped to swallow.

"What about him?"

His Adam's apple bobbed up and down. "Somebody strangled him and hung him on the fence."

Goosebumps raised on my arms. Sandy had known something about all this. Why hadn't I listened to him? I went to the phone and called the sheriff. Time to get serious.

But the sheriff wasn't in his office. What else is new? So I left a message for him to call me.

When I got off the phone, I could see that the kid was all strung out. I tried to calm him down with a piece of my apple pie and a glass of milk.

CHAPTER 12

Pine Bluff—1929

Valina waited on the platform where the train would stop to let out passengers. Her heart pounded when she heard its whistle. Dry powdery snow swirled around her as the train pulled in. Paul was the first person to get off.

He leaped over the stepping stool and ran to her, a happy grin on his face. "God, I've missed you."

How would he look after she told him? She closed her eyes and melted into his arms. It could be the last time he would want to hold her. He brushed her cheek with his lips.

"Let's drop off my suitcase and say hello to Aunt Catherine," he said. "Then I'll walk you home."

Later, when he walked her home through the woods, the forest's whispers and sighs were muffled by the snow. No bird calls, no rustling branches, no skittering wildlife, just the squeaking sound of their boots on the frozen crust. When they reached the cabin, she thought it looked pristine, pure and untouched, hidden in the snow the way it was.

But inside, it was shabby and worn, just like her.

Paul had to brush the deep snow off the steps so they could get in the door.

The fire had gone out hours before and moisture on the windows had frozen into opaque slabs of ice. An eery blue light filled the room. Valina shivered. When she started to build a fire, Paul took the wood out of her hands.

"You've been on your feet all day. Let me do it."

After he'd finished, she pushed the two good chairs up close to the stove. They sat down and she said, "I have something to tell you."

He smiled, but when he saw her face his smile faded.

She lowered her gaze, then swallowed and took a deep breath. "About a month before Timothy eloped with Mary, he convinced me that I was the one he loved." Out of the corner of her eye she saw Paul stiffen. She gnawed on her lip. "He rented the Carter place and asked me to fix it up." She glanced quickly at Paul.

"Yes, go on," he said, but he didn't look at her.

"Well, when he came back the next time," she gasped for breath, "I showed him what I'd done to the cabin ... and he ... " Her voice cracked. Paul was staring at her. Dear God, she couldn't say the words.

"Are you trying to tell me that he made love to you?"

"Y... yes," she sobbed.

Paul just stared straight ahead.

She wanted to crawl to him, beg his forgiveness, but that would only embarrass him.

"Don't cry."

She caught her breath when he turned and reached for her hand but she couldn't look at him. If only she'd known he had had feelings for her, she thought.

"It's all right, Valina." He pulled her over onto his lap and cradled her in his arms. "It's my fault. I should have spoken up sooner."

She rubbed her aching temples. "I'm so ashamed."

"He's the one who should be ashamed, not you. You didn't know how evil he was."

She pulled back, her face still turned away from his. "But I found out when he eloped with Mary."

"The son of a bitch," Paul muttered.

"What I did was a sin. I have no right to expect you to forgive me. How could you possibly stand to be around someone like me?"

"You think I haven't sinned? I had sex with a couple of girls at college. But something was missing. You. I love you, Valina. I always have and I always will."

Slowly, she turned and looked in his eyes. He meant it. He really meant it. "Oh, Paul, I want to believe that." She shook her head. "But you don't owe me your love. I'm not worthy of it."

"Okay, now that's ridiculous. You can't tell me whether I can love you or not. These are my feelings. And I've been a complete fool waiting so long to tell you." He tucked her head on his shoulder. They sat that way by the fire, neither one saying another word.

The next evening, Paul picked her up in doc's car and drove to the Bradford house. "We have so little time to be alone. I mentioned it to Aunt Catherine and she said we could have the living room to ourselves tonight."

When they went inside, there was a welcoming fire in the

fireplace. Valina and Paul sat on the sofa in front of it. Catherine had put a plate of Christmas cookies on a small antique table. Valina nibbled on one and admired the crèche scene on the mantel.

"I love this house," she said. "Catherine shines out of every room."

"She's quite a woman." He took her hand in his. "So are you."

"I'm just an ordinary person. You know that. You've known me since I was four years old."

He took her chin in his hand and looked into her eyes. "And I've loved you ever since. You're so special, and you don't even know it." He suddenly knelt down on the floor on one knee. She giggled. "What are you doing down there?"

"It's time to make this official. Valina, will you marry me?"

"Oh, Paul." How dear he was. She waited for him to take her in his arms, but he didn't move. "You can get up off the floor now."

"I won't get up until you say yes."

She blinked back tears, and smiled instead. "All right. Yes, I'll marry you. Now get up."

He grinned. "Not until I've given you your Christmas present." He took her left hand in his, reached into his coat pocket, and drew out a diamond ring which he slid onto her finger. "I hope you like it."

She gasped. She'd never seen such a big diamond. "It's beautiful!" The large diamond glittered in the firelight. "But it must have cost a fortune."

"Let me worry about that. There's another part to the present." He pulled a long gold chain out of his pocket and put it around her neck. "You can wear the ring on this, hidden under your clothes, until tomorrow night, when we surprise the family."

"I guess I can stand it till then." She leaned forward and kissed him, wondering how much more happiness she could bear.

Christmas Eve dinner was to be held at Catherine and Doc's house. Valina had gone over early to help Catherine, something she'd done every Christmas Eve for the last seven years. It always made her feel guilty when Catherine told everyone what a help she'd been. The truth was, she enjoyed just touching the elegant linens and china and silverware.

Earlier in the day, she'd arranged a bowl of pine cones and greens for the centerpiece on the dining room table. She stood back, assessed her work, then moved two of the cones just a fraction of an inch. Yes, that looked better.

"You're sure that's perfect, now?"

She jumped. "Doc."

"You look mighty happy. Did you have a talk with Paul?"

"Yes, and it turned out just as you said it would."

"I could tell that by the look on your face."

"I hope you won't get a call from a patient this evening." She could remember only one Christmas Eve when he'd been able to actually finish his dinner.

"Well, I've delivered all the babies that were due, and I told everyone who came in this week that they'd have to be damned sick for me to leave home tonight. They promised to behave."

She laughed. "I'll bet they did."

Just before the guests were due, Valina went upstairs and changed into her new dress, a blue wool challis she'd bought the day before at Osborne's. Her first brand new, store-bought dress. She took the ring off the necklace and put it on her finger, then primped in the mirror over the dresser, pleased with herself. At the sound of voices, she started downstairs. Paul had just come in the room. Mama, beaming at Valina, sat on the sofa beside Rachel.

When Mary and Timothy came in, Paul stood close to Valina. She could feel his body tense. She squeezed his hand and he relaxed a little. He'd promised her he wouldn't confront Timothy, but she could tell it was hard for him. Portland sounded better each day.

Doc handed frothy eggnog to each of them, muttering. "This damned prohibition has taken the glow out of these, but I guess we'll survive."

And then Paul cleared his throat. "If I could have the floor for a moment, Valina and I have an announcement to make." He held up her hand so everyone could see the ring. "We're engaged to be married."

Catherine and Mama began to cry. Valina turned to Paul. "What did I tell you? I knew they'd cry."

"I hope this means they're happy about it," he said.

Doc roared with laughter and Catherine sniffing, said, "Of course we are."

But even Papa's eyes looked brighter than usual. His voice

was hoarse when he congratulated Paul. "You have good taste, young man."

An unfortunate choice of words, Valina thought, when she saw Mary's angry face.

"I just wish Portland weren't so far away," Mama said.

Paul smiled at her. "We'll expect you to visit us whenever you can. I've rented a large house, so we'll have plenty of room. Besides, you haven't seen the last of us in Pine Bluff."

"Do I get to be your bridesmaid?" Rachel asked.

"One of them." Valina smiled at Mary.

"If you're thinking about me being a matron of honor, it will depend on when you get married," Mary said.

"We haven't set a date, yet, but it will be after your baby's born." Valina firmly pushed away the sorrow she felt when she saw the bitter look on Mary's face. This wasn't a night for sorrow.

"I think it's time for a toast," Doc said. He held up his cup of eggnog. "To Valina and Paul. May their love bring them more happiness each year." Quickly, he added, "And to Mary and Timothy's baby. Catherine and I hope you two will think of us as the other set of grandparents."

When there was no response from Mary, Mama immediately stood up and came over to see Valina's ring.

Rachel looked at it first. "Gee, it's pretty. Can I try it on?"

Valina shook her head. "Sorry. I won't take it off."

"Oh." Rachel frowned. "Never?"

Mama put her hand on Rachel's shoulder. "Would you like a little more eggnog?"

"You mean I should shut up?" Rachel said.

Mama nodded and everyone laughed.

Then Paul put his arm around his aunt's shoulders. "Everything smells so good. I'm starved, Aunt Catherine."

"Good thing dinner's ready," Catherine said. "I wouldn't want you fainting from hunger." She led them into the dining room.

Valina was hungry, too, and no wonder. The rich aroma of garlic mingled with sugary spices and evergreens was enough to madden the senses. Roast beef, Yorkshire pudding, and plum pudding with hard sauce had never been served at the Addison table. Now that they were practically in-laws, maybe Catherine would teach her the secret of her hard sauce.

As usual, after dinner the men sat in the living room while the women cleaned up the dishes, though Mary wasn't much help. It depressed Valina just to look at her. Someone should tell her she wasn't pretty with that sullen look on her face. But even Rachel looked glum.

Valina stopped her at the dining room door. "What's wrong, Rachel?"

"Well, gee whiz, I'm going to miss you."

"I'll miss you, too."

"Yeah, but now I'll have to do all the work you've always done."

"What?" Valina shook her head. Rachel could be so blunt. "I don't think you'll suffer too much. There won't be as many of you. Besides, you'll be an only child, a spoiled one, at that." She tugged one of Rachel's pigtails. "You'll get to come see us, you know. Maybe even spend a week or two in the summer."

The glum look on Rachel's face vanished.

"But I'll have to clear that with Paul, first," Valina said. "Do you suppose he could stand to have you around that long?"

"I'll go ask him."

"Don't you dare."

"Rachel." Mama called. "Come dry the dishes."

"You see? It's starting already," Rachel said.

Valina laughed. "Well, I'll wash. How would that be?"

"When you get married, everyone in the family but us will have a sink with running water," Rachel moaned.

"Don't complain, little girl," Mama said. "We're not listening to your woes tonight. It's Christmas Eve, a time to rejoice."

After the dishes were done, they all sang carols while Catherine accompanied them on the piano. They were still singing, "O Come All Ye Faithful," as they walked to the midnight service at the church.

For an awful moment after the service, Timothy and Valina were separated from the others. He'd maneuvered her into a corner. She shuddered. What did he have in mind?

"You really think you're something, don't you?" Timothy kept his voice low. "He wouldn't marry you if he knew."

So that was it. "Yes, he would." She smiled at him. "I told him all about it."

Timothy's lip curled and he turned away with an angry snarl. But before he turned, his hate-filled eyes raked down her body like the claws of a wild animal.

During the next week, when Mary first felt the baby move, it unnerved her. It wasn't natural having another creature move around inside you. She tried to calm herself by walking around the room, but it moved again. She went to the kitchen and made herself a cup of tea, Mama's remedy for every kind of problem.

Timothy was gone, of course. Besides, he'd just laugh at her. How could a man understand how she felt, anyway? Too bad they didn't carry the babies. She smirked at a mental image of Timothy, pregnant.

She had enjoyed sex, but she wasn't a cow to be bred each year. After the baby was born, she wouldn't have sex with Timothy again unless they moved to San Francisco.

She walked over to Edgerton's and bought the least repulsive of the maternity patterns, then stopped at the cafe for a creme soda. A true measure of her boredom, she thought. Imagine, Mary Addison O'Callahan reduced to associating with those bone-headed regulars and that nasty Bertha Wilcox.

"Here's our little mother." Mary's skin prickled at the sound of Bertha's voice. Wretched old bat.

"Hi, Mary," Valina said. "Want a crème soda?"

Mary nodded, angry at the sight of Valina and her vulgar engagement ring. What a fool she'd been to let Timothy talk her into eloping. She could have had an engagement ring and a nice wedding, too. But, at least she'd be moving to San Francisco, a real city, not just a big town like Portland.

Before going home, Mary went back to the kitchen to see Mama.

"How are you feeling, dear?" Mama asked.

"'Oh, I'm okay. I felt the baby move today."

"That's an awe-inspiring moment, isn't it?"

Mary shrugged. "I suppose so."

Mama gave her a strange look. "Sit down. We need to talk."

Here it comes, Mary thought. The motherhood lecture. Just what she needed, but she sat down at the table.

Mama sat down across from her. "I know you were unhappy when you first got pregnant, but you still don't want the baby, do you?"

"Where did you get that idea?" It wasn't any of Mama's business.

"You're depressed and sullen, and you've never shown the slightest interest in the baby. The layette, for instance. Are you sewing anything for it?"

"There's plenty of time yet."

"Little ones don't do well if they aren't loved or wanted," Mama said. "I'm very worried about your baby. It needs your love, even now, while it's developing."

"Oh, that's just an old wives' tale." Honestly, how could Mama repeat that drivel?

"Is that right?" Mama's eyes snapped. "Well, the 'old wives' know a lot more about babies than you do. If you don't love your baby now, just what kind of mother do you think you'll be?"

Mary bristled. "I don't need to stay here and be insulted." She stood up.

But Mama came over and stood in front of her. "One more thing before you go. You need to know that you're not beautiful anymore. It has nothing to do with being pregnant. It has everything to do with that sullen pout on your face. It's time you grew up." Mama turned her back and walked over to the sink.

Mary gasped, then marched out the door and headed for home. The minute she got there she went into the bathroom and looked in the mirror. She did look unhappy. She tried to smile but it turned into an unpleasant grimace. She felt a wave of panic. Maybe her face had changed permanently. She picked up her hairbrush, threw it at the wall, and burst into tears.

By the time Timothy came home on Friday, she had cut and hemmed flannel for six dozen diapers and made four little sacks. They were folded in a neat pile on the table next to the chair where she sat knitting a tiny sweater.

She looked up at him and wondered, for the first time, what kind of father he'd be. True, he seemed to want children, but he was gone most of the time. All the more reason to live in San Francisco. The traveling had to stop.

Maybe if they moved she'd finally discover what Timothy's mysterious job was. She felt like a fool not knowing. What was he trying to hide?

He picked up one of the sacks and grinned. "With your talent for sewing, our kid will be the best dressed kid in the whole state of Idaho."

"Why, thank you, Timothy." His remark surprised her. He'd never noticed her talent before, only her looks. It felt kind of nice. She patted the sofa. "Sit down a minute, I've picked out a girl's name."

"Oh?"

"It's Jessica Marie. What do you think?"

"Jessica Marie O'Callahan. I like the way it rolls off the tongue." He nuzzled her neck. "Any name you pick out is fine with me, darling."

"How was your trip?"

"So-so." He took a sheaf of bills out of his pocket. "Here's the household money."

The money was nice, very nice, but what could she spend it on in Pine Bluff? She'd saved most of it for when they'd move to San Francisco. She could hardly wait to shop there.

He cuddled her breast in his hand and kissed her neck. Better have sex first, and then bring up the subject of moving.

She waited until after dinner before she mentioned it. "Timothy, I'm worried that our baby will have a daddy only on weekends. Are you going to be happy with that?"

"No. But for the time being I'll have to be. Don't think I haven't given it some thought. I'll put out feelers about San Francisco this next trip, I promise."

What luck. She didn't even have to make a scene.

On Monday, Mary went back to Edgerton's to buy more flannel, this time for little nightgowns. She also thumbed through the maternity patterns again, but soon gave up. She'd create her own design. If only they had a better selection of fabrics. Resigned, she bought a length of printed cotton and one of navy faille, then went to the cafe to show the fabrics to Mama.

"After I make these dresses, I'm going to sew some nighties for the baby. How many should I make?" she asked.

Mama looked relieved. "About seven or eight. You'll be washing every day for a while, so that should be enough. Make a few larger ones, too. Babies grow pretty fast."

"Okay. I made six dozen diapers. Will that be enough?"

"I'd say so." Mama sat down at the table with Mary and said, "You look better."

Mary hated it when Mama did that. She might just as well say I told you so. "I'm feeling fine, thank you." She stood up. "Think I'll go have a creme soda."

"I hope you're drinking enough milk."

Oh, God, Mama never gave up. "Yes, I am, much as I hate it."

When Mary walked into the other room, Bertha Wilcox turned to Herb Johnson, and said, "I understand Timothy O'Callahan's been seen coming out of the speakeasy over in Wickicum." She raised her eyebrows. "And we all know what goes on in that place."

Shocked, Mary stayed by the counter.

"For Christ's sake, Bertha," Herb said, "maybe he just went in there for a drink." He turned to Mary. "Don't pay any attention to her. Some people like to make other people's lives miserable."

"Better believe I know what I'm talking about." Bertha stood up and huffed her way out the door.

"Thanks, Herb," Valina said. "Let's hope we won't see her again for a while."

"She reminds me of a rattlesnake," Dogie said. "Nasty old bitch."

"I'm surprised her husband didn't kill her before he left." Herb shook his head. "I wish to God he had."

Mary walked out the door, fast. Zoe Adams hung out at the speakeasy. Everyone said that was where she picked up her customers.

By Friday, Mary's rage had simmered so long that the words came out of her mouth the minute Timothy opened the door. "I understand you've been visiting the speakeasy over in Wickicum."

He just looked at her for a second, then said, "Yes, I've been there on business."

Mary hissed through gritted teeth. "And what kind of business might that be?"

"I sold them their liquor. I'm a bootlegger, at least I was."

"A bootlegger?" Her legs got weak and she sat down. She'd married a criminal.

"Oh, come on, what are you so shocked about? Where'd you think all that money came from? You never gave it much thought, did you? Just so I handed you a fistful of it every Friday."

She glared at him. "That's not true. I asked you several times about your job, but you wouldn't tell me."

"Well, I'm telling you now. I've been dealing on the fringes of the mob, but now a new man has taken over."

Mary's heart pounded. "The mob!"

"That's right. And this man isn't just connected to the mob, he is the mob. He wants me out, far away from the Canadian border. It's either get out or get killed."

Mary's eyes wouldn't focus. The room floated around her. When she came to, he was kneeling beside her.

"Mary, I'll get a job. We'll be all right. Please trust me."

"You want me to trust a man who's lied to me all this time?" She tried to sit up but she was still dizzy. And then it hit her. She'd be stuck in Pine Bluff for the rest of her life. He was no use to her at all, now.

"Mary, don't look at me like that. I love you."

She felt the baby kick as she sobbed. Maybe the old wives were right, after all. The poor little thing had a criminal for a father. Thank heaven Timothy didn't know about the money she'd saved.

When Spike Washburn came into the cafe the next morning he announced, for all to hear, that Timothy O'Callahan was a bootlegger.

"Bootlegger?" Valina gasped. Her hands tightened on the edge of the counter. Poor Mary.

"Yep," Spike said. "There was many a Friday at the speakeasy when I helped him bring in the booze. But yesterday he told me he'd been forced out by the mob. And him with a pregnant wife. Helluva note."

Valina's mouth tightened as the cafe buzzed with gossip. She thought Spike's concern was pretty hollow, considering he was the one who'd just spread the bad news. Odd that he hadn't said anything about it until now. No doubt Timothy had paid him to keep quiet.

Even though she knew better than anyone what a louse Timothy was, the news stunned her. What on earth would happen to Mary? She might think she had to stay married to him, being pregnant. Valina suddenly felt guilty about her own happiness.

As soon as she could, she hurried into the kitchen. Mama mustn't hear this from some gossipy old biddy. "I have something to tell you, Mama." She led her over to a chair.

"What is it?"

"You know how everyone wondered what Timothy's job

was? Well, he was a bootlegger. He's out of work now because gangsters have taken over his contacts."

Mama sank into the chair. "Oh, my Lord!"

"I didn't want you to hear it from someone else. Spike Washburn just came in and blabbed it to everyone out there." Mama looked pale. "Are you all right?"

"I guess so. It shouldn't be such a surprise. I've always wondered how he made all that money."

"You saw through him right away, didn't you?"

Mama nodded. "Yes."

"Do you think Mary knows yet?"

"If she doesn't, she'll find out soon enough." Mama rubbed her eyes.

That damned Timothy. Valina took two plates of pancakes off the order rack. "I'd better deliver these before they get cold." When she went back into the other room, all conversation stopped. She put the plates in front of Herb and Dogie, then turned to Spike. "What would you like?"

He ducked his head. "Just coffee."

Most of the breakfast crowd had evaporated, probably in a hurry to tell the world about Timothy. Well, one phone call would do it. Dottie Harper thought her job as the town's telephone operator included dispatching gossip. Papa always said they didn't call her information for nothing.

Ben Hillyard had left Valina's salary in the cash box the night before. She put the envelope in her pocket. Since Papa had gone to work at the courthouse, she'd been saving most of her salary. Every week she put money away in a cigar box that she'd hidden up in the attic. It wouldn't be much, but at least she wouldn't go to Paul empty handed.

She was setting tables for the lunch crowd when she heard Papa's voice in the kitchen. She went in to see how he was taking the news about Timothy.

"Yes, Daniel, I've already heard about it," Mama said. "How did you find out?"

"Herb Johnson. He thought he ought to warn me. It's hard for me to believe Timothy would bootleg," Papa said. "But I know he'll get a real job now. The man could sell anything."

"Yes, can't he, though?" Mama turned away from Papa and rolled her eyes toward the ceiling.

Valina'd never seen her do that before. They didn't even know she was in the room. She couldn't decide whether to leave or stay put.

Papa went right on. "This is a terrible thing for Mary and the baby. What can we do to help, Emma?"

"I don't know, but I'm afraid Mary won't take this very well." Mama took a hankie out of her apron pocket and dabbed her eyes with it.

"Well, how are we going to handle it?" Papa paced the floor. "Just sit at home and wait for them to come to us?"

Valina moved so they could see her. Mama jumped. "Rachel's so crazy about Timothy, she'll be very upset. What are we going to tell her?"

"Oh, dear." Mama looked at Papa who just shook his head and shrugged.

Valina pushed for an answer. "Well, if I see her before you do, what do you want me to say?"

Mama sighed. "I wish I knew."

"What's really needed here," Papa said, "is a family conference."

"I agree. Timothy ought to have to explain it to Rachel himself." There was an edge of bitterness in Mama's voice.

"Now, Emma, that's asking a lot."

Valina couldn't stand it. "He'd just lie to Rachel, anyway. He's nothing but a no-good criminal."

"Well, now, prohibition's made criminals out of a lot of people," Papa said.

Mama looked like she wanted to slap Papa. "I can't believe you said that, Daniel."

Valina couldn't either. "Papa, those people chose to be criminals."

"Now, wait a minute. Timothy hasn't murdered anybody." Papa gnawed on his lip and glanced at Mama.

"Not that we know about," Mama said.

"Emma, we've got to stop haggling. Our concern should be for Mary and her baby, and Rachel."

Mama sighed. "Of course."

"We all need to get back to work, so I guess we'll have to wait until this evening," Papa said.

"Except there's Rachel," Valina reminded them.

"There's no way in the world we can make it easy for her," Mama said. "I wish there were. We hardly know what to think, ourselves. I guess that's all we can tell her."

Papa bent down and kissed Mama. "You're right, darling. Now I've got to go."

Though she was tempted to avoid a scene with Rachel by

staying in town until Mama's shift ended, Valina went home after work. She'd just taken a pan of sugar cookies out of the oven, when Rachel threw open the door.

"It's not true, is it?" Rachel's dress was torn and one pigtail had come undone.

"What in the world happened to you?"

"I beat up Roy Bailey. He said Timothy was a bootlegger."

Valina devoutly wished she had stayed in town.

Rachel scowled. "Timothy wouldn't do a thing like that, would he?"

"Rachel, I don't know, but you'd better get cleaned up before Mama and Papa get home."

Rachel grabbed two of the cookies and stuffed one in her mouth. "That Roy Bailey's nothing but a dumb bunny," she mumbled.

"Why don't you get out of that dress so I can mend it? And bring the hairbrush when you come back. Your hair looks funny with one side braided and the other flying all over the place."

Later, when Mama and Papa came home, Valina said, "Dinner's ready. Let's eat before it gets cold." She quickly dished up the food, glad that nothing had been said about Timothy just yet.

During dinner, Mama peered at Rachel. "I heard from Mrs. Bailey again today."

Valina groaned.

Rachel said nothing, just made a face.

"Seems you gave Roy quite a beating. Is that true?"

"He said a bad thing."

"And what was that?" Mama asked.

Rachel wouldn't look at Mama. "He said Timothy is a bootlegger. Roy's nothing but a rotten liar."

Mama sighed. "There is a rumor going around about Timothy and, frankly, we don't know what to think."

Rachel stared at Mama.

"I'm more concerned about your temper, right now," Mama said. "You can't just beat up on people when you differ with them."

Rachel's lower lip drooped. "I don't beat up on anybody but Roy."

"Well, I insist you stop it. I never again want to be embarrassed because you've done something wicked to Roy. I'm very upset with you. After we've finished dinner, you will clear off the table, then wash and dry the dishes."

Rachel looked at Papa.

"You heard your mother," he said.

Valina's stomach ached. She wished the subject hadn't come up at dinner. The whole thing was Timothy's fault, though she had to agree that Rachel should quit tormenting Roy, even though he was a miserable brat.

Not five minutes later, someone knocked on the door. When Papa opened it, there stood Timothy and Mary. They came in the cabin and stood just inside the door, while everyone stared at them. Timothy finally broke the uncomfortable silence.

"We won't sit down," he said. "I came to apologize for the pain I've brought to this family. I'm sure you've heard that I was a bootlegger. I feel terrible about hurting all of you, especially Mary. I'll make up for it, I swear. As a matter of fact, I already have a job selling farm equipment. I got a call this evening from Harland's over in Wickicum. I applied there on my way home."

Valina couldn't bear to listen to Timothy's pretended remorse. She concentrated on Mary, but couldn't tell what Mary might be feeling. Her face looked blank, almost like death. Valina shivered.

"That's all I have to say." Timothy turned to Mary. "Let's go home." And Mary, who hadn't said a word, followed him.

The family stared at the door. The only sound in the room was the crackling of the fire in the stove, until Rachel spoke up. "The Bible says we're supposed to forgive."

"That's true." Papa said.

Valina wondered if Papa would be so forgiving if he knew what Timothy had done to her.

"It's just as I thought it would be. He's already got a job," Papa said. "The man made a mistake, but Mary and her baby need us to forgive him."

Mama sighed, and in a low voice, said, "Thy will be done." Then she turned to Rachel. "With your vast knowledge of the Bible, I hope you remember that it also says we should turn the other cheek. Think about that the next time you see Roy."

"Yes, Mama. I guess I'll finish the dishes."

"An excellent idea," Papa said.

Valina turned to Mama, and in a low voice, said, "Mary didn't look good, did she?"

Mama shook her head. "I'm very worried about her."

Before a month had passed, Mary found out that Timothy

had to sell equipment or he wouldn't get paid. Since no one was buying farm equipment, he hadn't earned a cent. He was nothing but a failure, just like Papa, only much worse. Timothy was an out-and-out criminal, and he'd even failed at that.

She hated him. He had deliberately misled her. And now he was even pretending to go to work each morning. She knew he had no work to go to, but she couldn't bear to have him in the house all day.

The night he came home with whiskey on his breath, she started making plans. She'd divorce him as soon as the baby was born. She knew Mama and Papa would help her, but she had a fierce desire to show everyone that she could manage by herself.

Within days, she rented out two of the bedrooms, one to Alice Furman, the home-economics teacher at the high school, the other to Miss Furman's brother, Gunther, a six-foot-four hulk of a man who worked at the feed and seed store. When Timothy came home and found them moving in, he grabbed Mary's arm and shoved her out onto the side porch. "What do you think you're doing, renting out rooms behind my back? I don't want strangers living in my home." His bloodshot eyes bulged with anger.

"What would you suggest I do?" she asked. "I'm having a baby. I can't live out in the woods and there isn't room for us at Mama and Papa's. We do have to eat and pay the rent."

"You're deliberately trying to humiliate me, aren't you?" Timothy clenched his fists.

For just a second, she thought he might strike her.

"I'm carrying your child." He turned away. She was glad a big man like Gunther was living there now.

Mary had spent so much time alone that she found she enjoyed having people around. Gunther, who got up at five each morning, fixed his own breakfast and even chopped the wood and started a fire in the fireplace.

"Any time you need a chore done, you be sure to let me know, Mrs. O'Callahan."

He blushed every time he talked to her, though that wasn't often. Strange such a huge man could be so gentle and shy.

His sister was the talker. When Mary had taken Miss Furman's home-economics class, she'd been her pet. "Amazing talent," Miss Furman told anyone who'd listen. Mary had grown weary of hearing it. Besides, the other girls hated her for it. But now it was nice to have her company.

Just then, Miss Furman came in the room. "I'd really like you to call me Alice, if you don't mind. And I want you to know that Gunther and I are very pleased to be here, though I do worry about you working so hard."

"Why, I'd be bored to death without something to do."

"Well, at least you're young and healthy. And I've been wanting to ask you, did you design the dress you're wearing?"

"Yes, I did."

A triumphant smile lit up Alice Furman's face. "I just knew it. In all the years I've taught sewing, I've never had another student with talent like yours."

There she goes again, Mary thought. "Thank you, Alice." But Mary didn't think the competition she'd had in the backwoods high school had been a good measure of talent.

"It's true, you know. Why, you could teach me things."

Mary knew she could. Alice Furman made all of her dresses out of the same pattern, always in navy or gray, with never a variation. Her one capitulation to fashion had been a haircut and marcel. Mary thought it was pitiful. She yearned to design a dress for her. Well, if Alice would pay for the fabric, why not?

When Timothy came home late that night, Alice and Gunther had already gone to bed.

"It's nice to be alone," he said, and leaned forward to kiss her.

She backed away. "When you start supporting us again maybe I'll feel like having sex. Until then, why don't you make an arrangement with Zoe Adams?"

She turned away from the pain in his eyes. If he tried again, she'd tell him that Doc had said it was best to abstain because of the baby. He'd be too humiliated to check with Doc about it.

Her own humiliation intensified on the morning she finally ventured into the cafe for a creme soda. Just as she walked in, Dogie told Bertha, "Saw Timothy O'Callahan again last night. Drunk, of course. Spike says he's always at the speakeasy now."

"I'm not surprised," Bertha replied. "I knew what kind he was the minute I saw him."

Mary couldn't believe she'd done this to herself, coming to this stupid cafe.

When Dogie saw her, his neck and ears turned red, but Bertha looked straight at her, a malevolent smirk on her face.

Valina stood behind the counter, a bottle of creme soda in her hand. "The usual?" she asked, chewing on her lip.

Without a word, Mary took the bottle from her and went into the kitchen. Valina followed her.

Mama peered at Mary, then asked, "What's wrong?"

Valina rolled her eyes. "Dogie and Bertha."

"What it amounts to is that I'm stuck in my house, unless I want to hear people gossip about Timothy," Mary said. "Not much of a choice is it?" It was the first time she'd spoken to them about Timothy's fall from grace.

"They'll go on to something else pretty soon," Valina said. "They always do."

"Not with such a juicy bit of dirt. I suppose you've heard about my two boarders."

"Yes," Mama said, "but isn't it going to be too much for you, the extra work and all?"

"I don't have much choice in that either, do I?" Mary thought Mama should have figured that out for herself. "At least they're company."

Mama nodded. "I'm glad of that. You know we'll do all we can to help you, dear."

"I'll be fine, Mama." Mary put the creme soda on the table. "Right now I'm designing a dress for Alice Furman. It'll be fun, and she insists on paying me for it."

"You're the one person who could get her out of those uniforms of hers," Valina said. "I can hardly wait to see it."

"It will be tailored, of course. She's too conservative to change much. I've got to go over to Edgerton's now and pick out the fabric." Best to leave while Mama and Valina looked a little happier. Next time she'd keep her mouth shut about Timothy. She didn't need Mama fussing over her.

Doris Wemberly and her mother were at Edgerton's. Doris and Mary had graduated at the same time. Mr. Wemberly owned the town's one car agency, and though Doris could have had all the clothes she wanted, she'd always coveted those that Mary wore, a fact that still gave Mary satisfaction.

"Look who's here, Doris," Mrs. Wemberly said, "An answer to our prayers. Mary, we're going on a trip and we need some traveling clothes. Are you too busy to help us out?"

"Depends on when you'll need them."

"Not until next month."

Mary knew they were doing her a favor. Three other women had brought patterns to her just this week. Well, no use denying that she could use the money. "Come over at ten tomorrow, and we'll talk about what you'll need."

One night when she couldn't sleep, Mary fretted about when she ought to kick Timothy out. Right now? Or after the baby was born? Since the time she'd told Timothy to make an arrangement with Zoe Adams, he'd stayed out almost every night, which suited her just fine. And no doubt Alice and Gunther were spreading the word about his behavior. She almost hoped they were.

She'd wait, but she'd like to know how he paid for his liquor and sex. She'd had to dip into some of the money she'd saved in order to pay the rent, but most everything else had come out of her dressmaking money. Imagine her supporting Timothy. Still, she'd wait a few more weeks.

The very next day, Mrs. Sampson came to call. Mary

cringed at the memory of how stupid she'd been, quitting her job at Osborne's without giving any notice. She could use that job now.

Mrs. Sampson took off her galoshes and left them on the porch. "Don't you just hate spring thaw? Snow's all covered with dirt, and mud's running down the road. I wish we had paved streets like they do over in Wickicum."

"Would you like a cup of coffee, or some tea?" What did the woman want, anyway?

"Nothing, thanks. I have to get back to the store, so I'll get right to the point. When you left Osborne's the way you did, I was very angry. You put us in a terrible spot. But the truth is, we still need you. Now, I realize you're pregnant, but could you do a few alterations for us here at home?"

"Well, that's a real surprise."

"We understand that you'd be limited for a while," Mrs. Sampson said.

"Yes, I would."

"But by the time your baby's, say two months old, you might be able to do most of our alterations right out of your home, don't you think?"

"We could certainly try it."

"Good. I'll tell Mr. Osborne. We'll call ahead when we send a customer to you, and don't hesitate to set yourself some limits, at least for the time being."

"All right. Thank you, Mrs. Sampson."

Mary could hardly wait for her to leave so she could crow and laugh and sing. But after she'd shut the door behind Mrs. Sampson, all she could do was sob.

CHAPTER 13

J-Bar-J Ranch — 1969

Sheriff Jackson called me back, all right, but he had the nerve to laugh when I told him about the rooster. "Wrung its neck and hung it on the fence, huh?" He gasped for breath, then laughed some more. If he'd been in the room, I'd have wrung his neck. Right then and there, I decided to donate money to his opponent in the next election. "Before you expire from all that laughter, Sheriff, I have a few other details to add." I told him about the vandalism at both my place and Buddy's.

"Oh, probably just some boys letting off steam," he said. "Happens every summer."

"Never happened on my place before, or Sandy's either. I'd say we're just a little out of the way for kids. But since you don't want to be bothered, we'll handle it ourselves."

"Now, hold on there, Matilda."

"Go to hell, Sheriff." I hung up with a bang and turned to Oscar and Jimmy. "The son of a bitch laughed. We're on our own."

"Then we'll start guarding the place in shifts," Oscar said. He went into the storeroom behind the kitchen and brought out his favorite hunting rifle, a Winchester 308. "Want me to bring out your Remington, Mattie?"

"No. I'll just keep my 38 handy."

"Which rifle can I use?" Jimmy asked.

Oscar gave me a look that said the responsibility for that decision belonged to me. And he was right. "I can't allow you to be on guard duty, Jimmy. I'm accountable to your parents for your safety."

Jimmy plopped down in a chair and slapped the kitchen table with his hand. "Shit!"

"That's what my name would be if anything happened to you," I said.

Oscar was cleaning his rifle. "I'll have George take the first shift from seven to eleven, Buck can take it form eleven to three, and I'll take it from three to seven."

In all the years I'd lived there, we'd never had prowlers or vandals. Damn that sheriff. I wasn't exactly the type to cry wolf. "How are you going to go about this, Oscar? One man can guard only so much property."

"Guess we'll have to concentrate on the house and out-buildings." He shook his head. "Wish we had some deputies to help us. But since we don't, we'll just have to do the best we can."

Jimmy started setting the table. He hadn't done that before without being asked. I put slices of cold roast beef, cheddar cheese, and tomatoes on the table.

"Sit down and start in. This rye bread is still warm." I got the applesauce and pickled watermelon out of the refrigerator and put them on the table, too. Then I remembered there was still some chocolate cake, so I put it on the table with a butcher knife. They could help themselves.

I made myself some oatmeal.

The next day, as Oscar walked out the door after lunch, he said, "Jimmy, when you get through eating, come over to the barn. It's time for Mattie's Boy to get his diploma."

Jimmy looked at me out of the corner of his eye. "Want to come and watch?"

He was dying for me to see how much he'd taught Mattie's Boy. "I think I will, by golly."

He started toward the door but turned back. "I almost forgot. I have to call Mom before I go. I'll call her collect."

"No need to do that." I went out on the porch so he could have some privacy, and so I could eavesdrop without being too obvious.

Jimmy got through to her real fast. "Mom?" he said. "Yeah, I'm fine. Look, I've got to hurry. I just wanted to tell you not to bother sending me money anymore."

I sat on the porch, itching to know what Jessica Marie said about that.

"There's no place to spend it up here." Jimmy lowered his voice. "Besides, I don't want it. You've got to quit treating me like a little kid."

Another long silence.

"Mom . . . Oscar's waiting for me. I've got to go. See you later. Goodbye." And he hung up.

When he came out on the porch, he said, "You ready to go, Aunt Matilda?"

"I expect so." I stood up and walked with him over to

the barn. Oscar was waiting with Mattie's Boy, who was all saddled up and ready for his big moment.

"Sorry I took so long, Oscar, but I had to call my mom," Jimmy said.

"No trouble. I'll go send a cow into the corral now."

That poor cow didn't have a chance against Jimmy and the horse. They made her move every which way. And Jimmy made every move count. You'd have thought he and Mattie's Boy had cut cattle together for years.

Oscar walked up beside me. "I'm real proud of that boy. He hasn't made a single mistake."

I slapped him on the back. "You did a good job, Oscar."

"Aw, go on."

"Don't give me that modest stuff, you old fart."

Oscar snorted, then yelled at Jimmy. "That's about enough. You'll wear that cow down to gristle and bone."

Jimmy rode over to us, his face split in a big grin. "How was that?"

"Pretty damned good, I'd say, wouldn't you Oscar?"

"Yep. Sure would. You'd better take Mattie's Boy into the barn now, Jimmy, and take care of him. He really worked up a lather. Wipe some fly spray all over him, too."

When Jimmy rode away, I told Oscar about the phone call. "He actually told his mother not to send him any more money."

"Well, well. Looks like you got through to him, after all," Oscar said.

I grinned at him and started toward the house.

Right after dinner, I got a call from Buddy. "The survey's done, Matilda. Could we go over the property some time soon?"

"That'd be fine. You free tomorrow?"

"Sure am," he said. "I'll be there about ten, if that's okay."

"See you then." I turned to the men. "Buddy's survey is done. I'll be riding the property with him tomorrow." Oscar gave me a worried look, but I pretended I hadn't seen it.

"Can I go with you?" Jimmy asked, his face wreathed in an eager grin.

"I guess so."

I left the dishes for the men to do and went to bed. Tomorrow would be a big day.

Oscar came in the house shortly after seven the next morning, looking mighty downhearted. "No sign of the bastard last night." He sat down at the table across from Jimmy and started shoveling in the breakfast I'd set in front of him.

After a bit, he gazed idly out the window. "Maybe we should turn off the outside lights tonight."

"What do you think that will accomplish?" I asked.

"Well, we'd see him. He'd have to use some kind of light."

"So would you, for God's sake."

He groaned. "There has to be some way to catch him."

Jimmy was quick to take advantage of the situation. "If you had another person helping you out there . . ."

I interrupted him. "No. And that's final."

The kid blushed and zippered his mouth. Probably didn't want to risk being left behind when I rode off with Buddy.

I went into the storeroom and got my lightweight jacket and a pair of gloves. I'd need those on the ride. But when Oscar saw them he gave me fits.

"Damn it, Mattie, you can't be riding all over those two hundred acres with Buddy."

My dander sizzled. "Why the hell not?"

"Because you're in your seventies, for crissake. When in tarnation are you gonna start acting your age?"

"When I'm dead and buried, that's when. And until then, no one tells me what I can or can't do. You got that?"

Oscar just growled, "Might as well talk to that mountain out there."

We glared at each other. Oscar's face was so red I got a little worried about him. He was frustrated to the breaking point over the vandal, and he hadn't had enough rest. How long could the men hold up, what with all the work on the place and too few hours of sleep?

Oscar motioned to Jimmy. "Let's go saddle up the horses," Oscar said. He grabbed his hat and stomped out the door. Jimmy scampered right behind him, a silly grin on his face.

Jimmy had just brought the horses into the front yard, when Buddy rode in. He and Buddy talked for a bit and then came in the house.

"Things are getting serious, aren't they?" Buddy said, a worried frown on his face. "Jimmy told me about the rooster."

"Did he tell you about the sheriff's reaction?" I asked.

"Yeah. Sheriff Jackson's a moron."

"That's for sure. You had any more incidents at your place?"

"Not lately."

"Good. Let's get a move on," I said. "We have a new boundary line to ride."

Buddy and Jimmy and I headed out, leaving Oscar in

charge of the ranch. Hell, after our little discussion, he wouldn't have come with us at gunpoint.

Now, I know damned well how old I am. There isn't a minute of the day that I don't have to battle with these old bones of mine. And they fight back, believe me. But I sure don't intend to let anyone see the war. Sure, I cut a few corners now and then like not riding over the whole two hundred acres with Buddy. Never intended to.

"We'll just ride the new boundary line between your place and mine, Buddy. You can go over the acreage on your own time."

"You sure this won't be too much for you?" Buddy asked.

Jimmy answered for me. "Doesn't pay to say things like that to Aunt Matilda. She might skin you alive."

Buddy's eyebrows shot up. Then he just grinned and bowed at me from the waist. I knew all along that he had brains.

We rode till we came to the wide, deep canyon that's a natural property line on the southern part of both my ranch and Sandy's, now Buddy's. Buddy was in the lead on his sorrel. When he suddenly reined up fast, I thought he might have come across a rattler, but he just sat there, real still. As Jimmy and I started to pull up alongside him, Buddy put out his hands to stop us from going any further.

"Quiet," he whispered.

For a second, I couldn't figure out what was going on. But then I realized that Buddy was staring through the veil of tree branches and undergrowth at someone across the wide canyon. Though I couldn't make out details, I could tell it was a man.

Dear God, what we saw then. That man lifted the limp body of another man and tossed him over the edge. I could hear the rocks scatter as the poor soul bounced off the walls of the canyon. Then a hollow thump echoed as the body landed at the bottom. No way on earth a person could live through that.

Jimmy gasped.

"Hush," Buddy hissed.

We sat on our horses, stone quiet, till the murdering swine turned and disappeared through the tall bushes and trees on the other side.

Then Buddy got off his horse, walked to the rim of the canyon, and peered through his binoculars at the other side where the man had stood.

"Those plants across there look like they could be marijuana," he said. Then he aimed his binoculars at the floor of the canyon.

Jimmy started to get off his horse, but I grabbed his arm and held him back. Didn't want him shot by that murdering son of a bitch. "You stay here beside me." I kept my voice low.

"But the guy isn't there now."

"You don't know that for sure."

He scowled and rolled back in his saddle.

"We need to get the sheriff up here, right away," I said. "He can't ignore murder."

We didn't speak a word on the ride back. When we got to the house, I hurried to the phone. The line was free, thank heaven. I didn't waste time with formalities when Nettie answered. "This is Matilda Jacobsen. Let me talk to the sheriff. There's been a murder up here."

While waiting for the sheriff, I heard Buddy and Jimmy tell Oscar what had happened.

About then, Sheriff Jackson came on the line, sputtering. "Did you say murder?"

"That's right." I told him what we'd seen. "Could be the poor guy stumbled onto a marijuana farm and got caught. Those growers are a mean lot."

"Getting down into that canyon could be a problem. I'll need to get hold of some special equipment. Might be a couple of days before it arrives."

"When you do get the body out, would you let me know who it is?"

"I'll take your request under advisement, Matilda. The person's identity could turn out to be confidential information."

He hung up before I could give him hell for that last remark. What a jackass.

I turned to the others. "The sheriff didn't laugh this time," I said, "but he got very official about needing special equipment to get down in the canyon."

"What?" Oscar said.

"Yep. Has to order it special. May take a couple of days. Not only that, the identity of the murdered man may be confidential."

Oscar groaned. "Ah, come on. He didn't say that, did he?"

"He did."

Oscar put his head in his hands. "A man that dumb, he'll never find the murderer."

"If he does arrest anybody, better remind him to look for buckshot scars," Buddy grinned at Jimmy. "And maybe even signs of a dog bite."

"Good point," I said.

Jimmy's face turned brick red.

"Well, I'd better get back to my ranch," Buddy said. "Let me know if you hear anything."

After Buddy left, I told Jimmy to go feed the chickens and turn the eggs in the incubator. "Carefully," I said.

He sighed and rolled his eyes. "I break one egg and she never forgets it." He headed for the chicken coop, grumbling all the way.

But I hadn't told him to bring in the fresh-laid eggs. Would he think of it himself? I doubted it. So I went out to make sure.

He'd just gone into the chicken yard. I went in and stood beside him. Should've known better than to go in just then. The new rooster started attacking the kid. A sight to see, I'll tell you, Jimmy hotfooting it around the chicken yard, and the rooster hell bent on pecking him to death.

"What's wrong with him?" Jimmy yelled, dancing from one foot to the other. The rooster pecked at Jimmy's legs and squawked as if he were putting a curse on him.

"He thinks I'm one of his hens and that you're a rival for my affections." I couldn't help but laugh.

"I don't think it's so damned funny." He raised his foot to kick the rooster.

"Don't you do it," I warned. "We just bought him, and he's mighty important around here."

"Then get him off me," he bellered. He finally sidled and hopped his way over to the gate and slipped out just in time. That devil rooster threw himself at the gate as it closed. The silly thing stood there kind of uncertain for a bit, then gave up and stalked away. I'm sure he thought he'd done a good job of protecting his harem.

"That's the last time I'm going in there," Jimmy snarled.

"No, it isn't. You'll be all right as long as I'm not in there with you. Being new here, the rooster had to establish the pecking order."

"Funny, real funny," Jimmy said.

"I'm serious. I'll bet you five dollars that if I leave right now he'll let you come in and gather eggs from his hens, just as if he'd never tried to kill you."

"The hell you say." Jimmy was already on his way to the house. I was left to gather the eggs. Served me right for laughing at him.

Just as I got back, Buck drove up in the jeep. He'd gone down to town to get the mail. He crawled out of the jeep and came over and handed it to me.

I started sorting it. I got the phone and electric bills, and Oscar had a package, the part he'd ordered for the tractor, no doubt. And another letter for Jimmy from his mother, sure to contain another twenty-dollar bill. "Jessica Marie, you ought to be ashamed of yourself," I muttered.

Buck grunted and I looked up from the mail. "Something else?"

True to form, Buck grunted again and handed me a strange looking envelope. My name was printed on it in big childish letters, just my name, not even a box number. Inside was a small sheet of crumpled paper. Printed on it in the same crude fashion, were four words: BACK OFF OR ELSE.

A chill ran up my spine. Had the murderer sent it? Or was it the vandal? Were they one and the same?

At dinner that night, I showed it to everyone.

"Back off?" Oscar roared. "He's the one who should back off. Hell, we haven't exactly chased the bastard."

"So you think it's from the vandal?" I asked.

He gawked at me. "Who else?"

"It couldn't be from the murderer," Jimmy said. "He wouldn't have had enough time."

"What's to say it isn't the same person?" I asked.

Silence filled the room. We all looked at each other.

"Naw," Oscar said.

"Why not? A lot of strange things have been going on. A dead cow, fences cut, tools stolen from Buddy, tools missing from here, and the rooster . . . that was evil and vicious."

"Either way, we're dealing with a madman," Oscar said.

I'd had enough. "The sheriff will have to take this seriously now. And it will be in his and his deputies hands, not ours." I gave Oscar a stern look.

He looked me straight in the eye. "We'll still do guard duty, until the sheriff and his men convince me we'll have some protection up here," Oscar said.

"Oh, all right." I stood up. "I'm going to sit on the porch and watch the sunset. Need to clear my brain."

After he and Oscar did the dishes, Jimmy came out and sat in the chair next to mine.

"Feels strange to be doing regular chores after what we saw today," he said.

"That's exactly why work is good for people. Helps them get their mind off the dark side of life."

"Did Daniel and Emma ever fight?" he asked.

"No, I don't think they did." His question surprised me. But then I saw that he had the letter from his mother clutched in his hand. "Oh, Emma told him off that one time when she insisted he get a permanent job. But he didn't really argue with her about it. He knew he'd been wrong. They were deeply in love, those two."

"My parents fight a lot," he said.

Things must've been even worse than Bob had let on. "That so?" I didn't know what else to say.

"Yeah. They had a real bad fight about me coming up here, and about the car. You know, the deal I made with Dad."

"They didn't agree about it?"

"Mom cried and yelled a lot, but Dad just got red in the face and told me to go to bed."

"Hmm." I didn't want to pry, but I didn't want to shut Jimmy out, either.

"A lot of my friends, their parents are divorced, but they still fight, anyway. I hope that doesn't happen to Mom and Dad."

"Well, even if it did, you'd survive," I said. "You have a good head on your shoulders."

He looked surprised.

"Well, you do. You've grown up a lot this summer. Why, every little thing on this ranch has been a challenge for you, hasn't it?"

"Well, yeah."

"And you've met the challenges head on, sometimes literally." I couldn't help but smile. "We can all survive just about anything if we really want to, unless we start looking for a crutch of some kind. But you wouldn't do that."

Jimmy straightened up in his chair and grinned at me. I grinned back at him.

The sun sank behind the mountain. The sky was filled with shades of purple and pink and orange and gold. The glory of it lasted such a short time, but a person can live quite a while on the memory of it.

CHAPTER 14

Pine Bluff—1930

A few days later, Rachel came into the kitchen of the cafe. Her face looked splotchy, as if she'd been crying. Valina, who had just placed an order, hoped the problem wasn't another attack on Roy.

Mama knelt down by Rachel. "What is it, dear?"

"Roy." Rachel sniffed.

Mama sighed. "Did you beat up on him again?"

Rachel shook her head. "No. Roy told me Timothy's drunk all the time. I didn't hit him, Mama. I turned the other cheek, but, oh, it hurts."

Valina had to blink back her own tears. That miserable Timothy. He broke Rachel's heart, too.

Mama folded Rachel in her arms. "I'm sorry, dear, but I'm afraid what Roy said is true."

Rachel's face crumpled. "Why would Timothy do that?"

"I can't see into his heart," Mama said, "but he doesn't have a job now. Maybe that's part of it."

Rachel made a face. "Yeah, but what about Mary and the baby?"

"We'll look out for them, won't we?" To the unspoken question on Rachel's face, Mama said, "God will show us the way."

Rachel dropped into a chair. "I don't feel like practicing at Catherine's today. Can I stay here and walk home with you? Please?"

"All right. Valina would you stop by Catherine's on your way home and tell her Rachel won't be there?"

"Sure." Valina left the cafe, delivered the message to Catherine, then walked on up the street to Mary's house.

When Mary opened the front door her face looked drawn, and when she smoothed her hair with a jerky, anxious gesture, Valina knew it must be terrible for a vain person like Mary to be pregnant.

"Come on in," Mary said. "Don't worry. Timothy isn't here. He rarely is."

"Does he treat you all right? I mean, he doesn't hit you, or anything, does he?"

"No. He wouldn't dare with Gunther here."

"Herb Johnson said to tell you that if you need money, he'll loan it to you without interest."

"Herb said that?" Mary's eyes brimmed with tears.

"He meant it, but he doesn't want Timothy to know about it. How long are you going to put up with this situation, Mary? Now that Osborne's has hired you and you have the boarders, maybe you could make it on your own. I know Mama and Papa would do all they could to help you. And Herb's offer is good."

"I'm going to divorce Timothy, but I need to talk to Mama, first."

"What's Mama got to do with it?"

"I can't discuss it right now."

Frustrated, Valina left and walked home, where she found Aunt Matilda cooking dinner. Her aunt wore bib overalls and a man's plaid shirt. It looked like her salt and pepper hair had been twisted into a bun and pinned up hours before. The spikes of errant hair and loose bobby pins reminded Valina of a porcupine. She stifled a giggle.

"Well, hello, Aunt Matilda."

"Hello, yourself."

"Do Mama and Papa know you're here?"

"Yep. Your mother talked me into staying overnight. I told her I'd cook dinner. Got to pay for my keep, somehow."

Valina wondered why Mama hadn't mentioned it. She couldn't imagine her forgetting Aunt Matilda, but she did have a lot on her mind.

When she set the table, the sight of the cracked mismatched pottery depressed Valina. That was the first thing she'd pick out in Portland, a set of dishes. But how could she enjoy them when Mama had nothing, and Mary's situation was so gloomy? She sighed.

"Something wrong?" Aunt Matilda asked.

"No. Just thinking about how lucky I am."

"Well good God. Why aren't you happy about?"

"I am. But Mama deserves better, and Mary . . ."

"To hell with that. Now, you listen to me. We all have our burdens. You'll get your share, believe me. You'd better learn to savor the taste of joy while you have it."

"For once, I agree with my sister." Papa's voice. "That's good advice."

Valina turned to see Papa, Mama and Rachel standing in the doorway.

"Well, get in here, you slowpokes," Aunt Matilda said. "Dinner's ready, and nothing makes me madder than people who let the food get cold."

After Papa said grace, and the food was passed around, Aunt Matilda said, "We've got a plague of coyotes up at the ranch. I bought some traps today, but those damned animals are smart."

"Why don't you just shoot them?" Papa said.

"Hell, we've tried, but by the time we hear the ruckus and get out to the chicken coop, the rascals are gone, along with a chicken or two."

"I'll come up some weekend and take care of them for you," Papa said.

Aunt Matilda's eyebrows shot up. "Oh? How're you going to do it? Sit in the hen house all night? Why, they might cart you off."

Valina giggled.

"You've forgotten what a good shot I am."

"I sure have. Remember that six-point buck you missed?"

"Can we please change the subject?" Mama said. "I don't think I can take one of your discussions tonight."

That surprised Valina. She thought the wrangling between Papa and Aunt Matilda was funny. They loved to needle each other.

They ate in silence, until Aunt Matilda said, "How long is Mary going to put up with that man? I can help her out if she needs money."

"Herb Johnson offered to loan her some money today."
Valina gave Papa a meaningful look. "But he doesn't want
Timothy to know."

"Herb?" Papa stared at her. "Herb Johnson actually offered
to loan Mary money?"

Valina wondered why that should surprise him. "Herb's a
real nice person, Papa."

"I know that, but he's tighter than a muscle cramp. Has he
ever left you a tip?"

"No, of course not. No one does."

Aunt Matilda grunted. "The only thing the people in this
town are generous with is gossip. Has Mary said anything
about leaving the bastard?"

Rachel giggled, but she stopped when she saw Mama's
warning glance.

"I asked her today," Valina said. "She plans to divorce him,
but she has to talk to Mama first."

Mama looked puzzled. "Did she say why?"

"She wouldn't tell me. You know Mary."

"Well," Aunt Matilda said, "when she gets around to telling
you, Emma, let her know she can come to me if she needs
money."

"Maybe she's waiting till after the baby's born," Mama said.
"Might be easier for her then."

"Maybe she wants you to be there when she tells him,
Mama." Valina didn't think Timothy would agree to a divorce
without a fight.

Mama looked at Papa. "You don't think he'd beat her, do
you?"

"Of course not," Papa said.

Valina interrupted. "I asked her and she said he hadn't."

Later, after Rachel had gone to bed, Papa brought up the subject again. "I'm very disappointed in Timothy. I tried to talk to him yesterday, but I might as well have talked to that stove over there." He shook his head. "What can we do, Emma?"

"I've been thinking about it. If she divorces him, maybe we could move in with her. There's still one extra bedroom, and Valina and Rachel could sleep in that sunroom downstairs. We could fit in somehow."

Aunt Matilda nodded. "Sounds like a good idea to me."

"Me too," Valina said. "And you'd have electricity and running water."

"And an indoor toilet," Rachel yelled from the attic.

Papa walked over to the ladder and raised his voice. "Rachel, you get to sleep."

"Yes, Papa."

Several days later at the cafe, Valina went in the kitchen to pick up an order and found Mary in there with Mama. "Well, hello. How are you feeling?"

"Fat."

"Oh." She could tell that she'd interrupted them, so she took the order and hurried out. When she hadn't heard voices for a few minutes, she went in to see if Mary had left.

"Curious?" Mama said.

"Yes. What happened?"

"Well, she plans to divorce him after the baby's born, and then she wants us to move in with her."

"So she liked your idea."

"No. She'd thought of it before I did. Isn't that something?"

Some of the strain had left Mama's face. She looked almost happy. Valina was pretty happy herself. Things would work out now. Timothy might even leave town. "When does she plan to tell him?"

"She didn't say."

That night, Mary looked up from her sewing to see Timothy standing over her. She drew in a quick breath. "You startled me."

"Just standing here admiring my precious little wife."

His words were slurred, but the menace in his voice was clear enough.

"Have you had dinner?"

"I don't remember. I'm drunk." He pulled a flask out of his pocket. "And I'm going to get drunker, so you needn't trouble yourself about me."

At that point, Alice came in the room. She nodded at Timothy, sat down in the chair next to Mary, and started embroidering a baby's sack. "What do you think of the color of this thread, Mary?"

"I like it." She sent a grateful glance at Alice.

"It's a fine thing when a man doesn't get any attention in his own home." Timothy said. "But I wouldn't want to bother you. I have friends who'll take me in for the night."

When he left, Alice said, "You've probably noticed that Gunther and I have taken the liberty of being nearby when your husband comes home. I hate to say it, but he's so belligerent, we're afraid for you."

"I'm not too comfortable, myself, but I'd like to wait until after the baby's born before I divorce him."

"Then you are . . ."

"Yes I am, but it mustn't get back to him. Who knows what he'd do if he found out before I told him?"

"Indeed. Rest assured, no one will hear it from us."

Two nights later, Mary walked home with Alice from the baby shower Catherine had given her. She felt happy for the first time in months. Everyone had been kind to her. Papa had made a cradle for the baby and the guests had piled it high with gifts, delicate, pretty things. Crocheted sweaters and blankets, with little booties and hats to match, and sheets and soakers, even a baby pillow and pillowslip edged with tatting. And Mama had made a beautiful christening dress. Everything a baby needed, hers had now.

When they got home, Alice insisted on displaying all the presents on the dining room table. Gunther had gone to Catherine's to get the cradle.

Mary slowly unpacked the gifts, enjoying them even more than she had at the party.

"Look at the beautiful tatting on this little sack and nightgown." Mary held it up for Alice to see. "Mrs. Bailey made it. I'm surprised she'd bother, the way my little sister treats her son."

"I'm sure she wouldn't hold a grudge against you because of that." Alice said.

They took their time arranging all the pink gifts together, then all the blue. After they were done, they stood back to admire their work.

"It was quite a party, wasn't it?" Alice said. "The cake Catherine and your mother made looked exactly like a giant bootie. They did a remarkable job. Best of all, though, you looked happy for a change."

"I realized tonight that it's been a long time since I've felt happy," Mary said.

They heard the front door open. "Gunther, is that you?" Alice called.

"No. It's the master of the house." Timothy lurched into the doorway of the dining room. "What's all of this?"

"Catherine gave me a baby shower." Oh, Lord. If only they hadn't sent Gunther to get the cradle. Papa could have brought it tomorrow after work.

"Now, isn't that nice? Lady Bountiful and her friends doling out charity to the poor." Timothy picked up a pink bootie. "My son isn't going to wear this pink crap."

Just then Mary heard a noise in the living room.

"Here's the cradle, Mrs. O'Callahan. Where would you like me to put it?"

Thank heaven. Gunther was back. "In the living room, Gunther. I'll show you where I want it." Mary tried to brush past Timothy, but he grabbed her arm. "I'd like to speak to my wife, alone."

She nodded at Alice, who hesitated, but finally left the room. "What is it, Timothy?" Mary asked.

"You think you're better than me, but I sure was good enough to marry, wasn't I? Oh, yeah. My friends tell me you also wanted to marry Paul. Got the wrong one didn't you, honey? I'll bet that's burning a hole in your gut."

He moved in front of her, his face inches from hers. The sour smell of him made her nauseous. He took hold of her arm with one hand and fiddled with her collar with the other. She jerked away, involuntarily.

"Can't stand to have me touch you? Ah, poor little girl. I'll bet you just love carrying my baby." When he grinned, saliva leaked out of the corners of his mouth.

Mary almost gagged.

He suddenly let go of her. "Don't worry. I'm leaving. There are some women who still want me, even if you don't."

When the door closed behind him, she took a deep breath and leaned against the wall. Gunther came in immediately. "Mrs. O'Callahan, I brought some bolts for your front and back doors. I hope that's all right."

"Yes, of course it is. Thank you."

"Would you like me to put them on tonight?"

"Please."

Alice had been watching Timothy out of the front window. "He's gone. Are you all right?"

Mary nodded. "I think I'll go to bed. It's been quite a day."

"I'll help you upstairs."

Alice took Mary's hand. Mary turned to Gunther and said, "Thank you, Gunther, and you too, Alice. You're both very kind."

When Mary stopped at the cafe the next day, Mama looked upset.

"Alice was waiting for me when I got here this morning," she said. "She told me what's been going on over there with Timothy. You've got to kick him out before he hurts you and the baby."

"I know. I'd already planned to tell him tonight. If he comes home, that is."

Mary eased herself down onto one of the chairs.

"I'll send Papa over after work. He'll see that you don't get hurt."

"But Timothy might not come by. Besides, Gunther's always there, and he's bigger and younger than Papa. He could crack Timothy in two with one hand. I think he's been waiting for the chance."

Mama wiped her hands on her apron and sat at the table with Mary. She leaned forward, her voice urgent. "Promise me you'll go over to Ed Garrison's office when you leave here and get him to start the petition for a divorce."

Mary remembered the hateful sneer on Timothy's face last night and shuddered. "I will."

"Ask him to send me the bill," Mama said, "and then you go stay at Catherine's."

"Why should I go to Catherine's? Timothy never comes home during the day."

"What's to keep him from it?"

Mary shrugged. "His hangovers, I imagine."

"Please don't take a chance, Mary. Promise me you'll go to Catherine's."

"All right. Maybe that would be best." She was too tired to argue about it.

When Mary walked into Ed Garrison's office, he was sitting back in his chair clicking his pencil against his thumbnail. Mary thought his shiny black hair and hooked nose made him look more like a criminal than a lawyer. Her head ached and she had to force herself to concentrate on what he was saying.

"It's about time you got rid of that son of a bitch," he said. "I expected you sooner."

His tone of voice infuriated her. "I wanted to wait until the baby was born."

"I've already checked up on any debts he might owe. The furnishings in your house are all paid for, and there don't seem to be any other debts, though I haven't checked out the speakeasy in Wickicum." His face creased in a grin. "Their position, however, is shaky at best."

The gall of the man, assuming he had the right to pry into her affairs before he was asked. That was exactly why she hated Pine Bluff. Everybody minded everybody else's business. If only they would all leave her alone.

"You'll get everything in that house," he said, "and we might as well ask for the car, too. You'll never get child support out of that bastard. Be sure to have Gunther in the room with you when you tell Timothy. And don't hesitate to call the sheriff if you need him."

She stood up. "Is that all for now?"

"Yes. I'll get the papers to you as soon as they're ready." He stood up and opened the door for her. "Be careful."

Mary walked to Catherine's house and found her waiting on the front porch.

"I'm so relieved you got here all right. Your mother's been frantic about you. All of us have been." Catherine opened the screen door and ushered Mary into the living room.

"Is there a single soul in this town who doesn't know every

detail of my life? I hate it, Catherine. When we got married, Timothy promised me we'd move to San Francisco. But now I'm stuck here in this horrid town."

Catherine nodded. "I can appreciate how you feel. I was raised in San Francisco. When Charles decided to settle here, I almost died. If your mother, bless her heart, hadn't offered me her friendship, I might have bolted within a month." She smiled. "As it is, every year, when I go to San Francisco for two weeks, Charles is certain I won't come back."

Mary's head throbbed. "Could I lie down for a while?"

"What's wrong? Should I call Charles?"

"No. It's not the baby. I have a headache."

"No wonder. You can stretch out on that big leather couch in Charles' den, or upstairs in the guest room."

"The den." The sooner she got there, the better. Catherine's chatter felt like a hammer beating on her skull.

When she wakened at 3:15, she wanted to go home. She didn't want to spend the rest of the day with Catherine, much less listen to Rachel practice the piano after school. She found Catherine in the kitchen baking cookies.

"Just in time for some tea," Catherine said. "How's the headache?"

"It's a little better, but I can't stay. I'm going home." She was going no matter what Catherine said.

"Oh, dear. I promised Emma . . ."

"Alice will be there shortly. I'll be all right. Timothy never comes home this early."

Catherine sighed. "Well, if your mind's made up, I guess I can't stop you."

"Thank you for understanding, Catherine."

She was slow walking home. She got more awkward each day, and her swollen feet were getting too big for her shoes.

"Mary?" It was Alice's voice.

"You're early," Mary said. "Are you sick?"

"No, I just left the very minute the bell rang. Our illustrious principal was shocked, I think, but I don't care. Lord knows my wages don't cover all the extra hours I put in at that school." Alice looked intently at Mary. "How are you feeling?"

"I filed for a divorce today."

Alice beamed. "I'm so happy to hear it. Now, maybe he will leave you alone."

When they walked into the house, something didn't feel right to Mary. She looked around the living room. Nothing was out of place, but she heard Alice gasp. Mary turned just in timed to see Timothy stagger in from the kitchen. His bloodshot eyes, wild with anger, impaled her. Dear God. Gunther wouldn't be home for three more hours.

"Why do you have bolts on the doors? Are you trying to lock me out of my own home?"

"Timothy, please."

Alice stepped forward. "It was my brother's and my idea, Mr. O'Callahan. You can be rather intimidating when you are drinking."

"I want you and your damned brother out of my home."

"They're not leaving, Timothy," Mary said.

"Oh? Could it be that Gunther has replaced me in your affections? Is that what's going on here behind my back?"

Mary heard herself laughing. She couldn't stop.

"Don't you dare laugh at me." He lunged forward and slapped her face so hard she stumbled and fell. "Now, you crawl over here and treat me with respect. You hear me?"

Alice grabbed Gunher's gun from the broom closet. "You lay another hand on her and I'll shoot." She stood by the kitchen door holding Gunther's shotgun, aiming the gun at Timothy's heart. "I know how to shoot it, believe me. Mary tell him the news, and then out he goes."

"What news?" Timothy's eyes darted over to Mary.

Painfully, she pulled herself up and walked over to stand by Alice. "I filed for a divorce today. Now, get out and don't ever come back. You can pick up your clothes at Ed Garrison's office."

"Out, Mr. O'Callahan." Alice jabbed the shotgun toward him. "This will make quite a big hole in you, and I'd be delighted to pull the trigger."

Timothy clenchhed his fists. His hate-contorted face flushed a deep red. "Don't think I'll forget this." He walked out the front door and slammed it so hard the windows shook.

When he left, Mary said, "Alice, quick. Bolt the kitchen door while I bolt this one."

Walking home after work, Valina heard something behind her in the woods. She started to turn when a hand closed over her mouth. Terrified, she clawed at the hand and struggled to get away, but the man's other arm wrapped around her like a vise. She couldn't get her breath.

"I told you you'd regret it, little sis."

Timothy. No!

Emma poured Ben Hillyard a cup of coffee while he

complained about the unexpected drop in temperature outside. "I swear to God, we'll have a freeze tonight. I remember when I was a boy, we had ice in April then, too."

"I remember that storm," Emma said. "The freeze lasted for a week."

Just then the kitchen door of the cafe crashed open. Rachel, wild-eyed, dashed over to Emma, grabbed her hand, and tugged.

"Mama, come. Valina's hurt. We've got to get Papa."

Emma's heart thumped against her chest. "What happened?"

"Hurry!"

"Go," Ben said. "I'll take over here."

Emma found Daniel at the office near the front door of the courthouse. "Something's happened to Valina. I can't get the details out of Rachel. She's incoherent. Come with us, quickly!"

Daniel poked his head in the office door. "I have to leave. An emergency."

When they went outside, he knelt beside Rachel, his hands on her shoulders. "Tell us what happened."

Tears coursed down Rachel's cheeks. "I was walking home when I heard something in the bushes. Timothy. On top of Valina." She shuddered. "He got up and kicked her and ran away. I tried to help her," she wailed, "but she wouldn't wake up."

"My God in heaven. Take us to her," Daniel said.

Emma felt as if she were standing outside of herself, watching from a distance through someone else's eyes. They followed Rachel for what seemed like an eternity, to where Valina lay, her dress pulled up to her neck, her left eye swollen, blood trickling from the corner of her mouth.

Emma sank to her knees beside her. "Valina, my little Valina."

When Daniel felt Valina's neck for a pulse, she moaned. "She's alive," he said, tears in his eyes.

"Thank God," Emma whispered. She stood up and took Rachel's hand in hers. "Come, dear. Papa will carry her home. You and I will take care of her while he goes to get Doc." Rachel was close to hysteria. No one, much less a child, should ever have to see such horror, yet what would have happened to Valina if Rachel hadn't found her?

When they got to the cabin, Daniel put Valina on their bed and tenderly kissed her forehead, then hurried to get Doc.

"Get me a basin of water, Rachel, and a washcloth and a bar of soap." Emma tucked an extra blanket over Valina. Should she wash her face? It might hurt her. Had he broken her jaw? She'd wait and ask Doc.

"Mama, what did you want me to get?"

Rachel stood in the doorway looking like a pathetic, wounded animal. That monster, Timothy, had wounded all three of her girls. A dull ache filled her chest, the same ache she felt the day her mother died.

"Come here, darling." Emma sat in the rocker and pulled Rachel onto her lap. "You've been through a terrible experience, my little one, but I'm sure you saved Valina's life by finding her. I'm very proud of you, coming to get us the way you did."

Rachel put her head on Emma's shoulder and they rocked until Daniel and Doc came in.

"Daniel, you take Rachel and go into the other room," Doc said. "Emma, you can stay in here with me, but heat some water first. We'll need to clean her up. I'll see if she has any broken bones."

When Emma came back, Doc said, "No broken bones that I can find. He tore her vagina some, but it will heal." He clenched his fists. "That monster. She's bruised all over, Emma. She's in a lot of pain, and she's in shock. I have to warn you . . . a few rape victims remain in a permanent trance-like state. I don't think that will happen to Valina, but she will need someone with her at all times. I brought some sleeping pills. Give one to Rachel when she goes to bed, but don't give any to Valina unless she comes out of it. When she does, give her one of them, as well as one of these pills for pain."

He handed her the two pill bottles and put his arms around her. "I'm so damned sorry, Emma. I'm going over to Mary's right now. I'll send Catherine to let you know how things are over there."

After he left, Emma sat on the bed next to Valina. How helpless a mother was when tragedy struck her child. The only comfort she could give was her love. Could Valina overcome this horrible experience? She was strong, but how would people treat her? Bertha, and a few others like her, would delight in being cruel. And Paul. How would he react?

She wanted to caress Valina's face, but that might hurt her, so she just picked the pine needles out of her hair and talked softly to her unconscious daughter.

"Remember the time your pet chicken was carried off by a coyote? 'Why does God let bad things happen?' you asked. You scowled at me, demanding an answer. Do you remember what I said? 'I don't know why bad things happen, but the important thing is how we react to them.' I still believe that, Valina. You are strong. You will overcome this."

She felt a hand on her shoulder. Catherine. "Paul's on his way, and Mary's all right. When she got home today, Timothy was waiting for her, drunk. Fortunately, Alice was there. When Mary told him about the divorce he got abusive, but Alice threatened him with Gunther's shotgun and he left. Charles thinks Timothy saw Valina and took out his anger on her. How is she doing?"

"Still unconscious. Did Charles tell Mary about Valina?"

"Yes. He said she was stunned. He'll go back later this evening to check up on her, then come here to see how Valina is. And don't worry, Alice and Gunther are taking good care of Mary. When Charles stopped by, Gunther met him at the door with his shotgun. Charles said the sight of that huge fellow with that gun was all the protection Mary needed."

"I'm worried about Daniel, what he might do," Emma whispered.

"Charles called Sheriff Coleman, but he'd just left for Whiskey Creek. Seems two of the Jensen's hired men got into a fight and tried to kill each other."

"Oh, dear, then he won't be back until tomorrow."

"Try not to worry. I'll be in the other room if you need me." She patted Emma's shoulder and left.

Emma gently stroked Valina's hair, but Valina moved, as if

to get away. She opened her eyes and stared. Stared at nothing. Emma shivered. Was this the trance Charles mentioned?

"Valina, it's Mama. Can you hear me?" Still no response. "You're home, darling. You're safe here, safe with the people who love you." Emma fought her own panic by praying.

A few minutes later, Catherine came back in the bedroom. "Is she awake yet?" she whispered.

"Not quite."

Catherine peered at Valina. "Oh."

"How is Rachel?" Emma asked.

"She's quiet, but she ate a few bites of dinner. Where is she going to sleep?"

"On the cot out there." Emma took two blankets out of the cedar chest at the foot of the bed. "I have to give her a pill. Would you stay with Valina? I hate to leave her, but Rachel needs me, too."

"I'll call you if there's the slightest change."

Seeing Rachel withdrawn and listless made Emma heartsick. She gave her a glass of water. "Doc wants you to take this pill, dear. You can sleep on the cot. I'll be nearby in the bedroom."

Rachel stared at the pill. "Is Valina going to die?"

Emma pulled Rachel into her arms. "No, she won't die. It will take her a while to get over this, though."

"Oh." Rachel swallowed the pill, then gave the glass back to Emma.

"Why don't you lie down now?" Emma said.

She tucked the blanket around Rachel's shoulders, then bent down and kissed her cheek. It wasn't long before Rachel fell asleep.

Emma thought Daniel must be outside. She went to the door and opened it. "Daniel?"

"How is Valina?" He was sitting on the bottom step.

"Her eyes are open, but she's not aware of her surroundings yet."

"Oh, Lord."

She could hear the sob in his voice.

"It's all my fault, Emma. I brought Satan himself into our home, against your better judgment. I even saved his life, saved it so he could ruin the lives of our daughters."

"Don't blame yourself."

"I was a fool."

"Daniel, you've given love and joy to each of us. Now please come inside."

"Not yet. Go on in. The girls need you."

"It's freezing out here."

"I have on my heavy wool jacket."

She crept down the steps and kissed him on the cheek, then went in to see how Valina was.

"No change," Catherine said. "I'll go make you a cup of tea."

When Catherine left the room, Emma looked intently at Valina. Were her eyes focusing, or had she imagined it?

"Mama, God punished me."

Emma stared. Had she gone mad? "What?" She listened horrified.

"I thought . . . " Valina's voice wavered . . . "He loved me . . . " She winced and put her hand on her bruised cheek. "He . . . made love to me."

Tears blurred Emma's vision. "Why didn't you tell me?"

"I was too ashamed."

"There's no call for you to feel shame. He's an evil, vicious man who deliberately took advantage of an innocent girl. And, as for God punishing you, He doesn't want to hurt you, Valina. Timothy did that, not God." Emma sat on the bed by Valina and held her hand.

"How can I face people, after this? What will Paul think of me?"

"He'll be here tomorrow, and he can tell you himself. Now, listen to me, darling. This is a terrible thing that's been done to you, but you are still kind, loving, responsible Valina, a worthy person. Say those words to yourself, over and over. They are true, as God is my witness."

Silently, Valina wiped the tears off her cheeks.

How much should I tell Daniel, Emma wondered. If he knew the whole story, dear, Lord, what would he do? She started at the sound of his voice behind her.

"Charles is here to see Valina."

Daniel stood in the doorway. She could tell by the look on his face that he'd heard the whole thing. "Oh, Daniel . . ." He turned and walked away just as Charles came in the room.

"How is our patient?" he asked. His face lit up when he saw Valina. "Good, she's awake. While I'm here, Emma, why don't you go take a break? Walk around, eat something, and shut the door as you leave."

Later, when Charles and Catherine had left, Emma put her arms around Daniel. "You're not going to do anything foolish, are you?"

"What makes you think that, though, I admit I've been

foolish all my life. You need to rest. Why don't you lie down on the bed with Valina for a while?"

He seemed so distant. If only he didn't blame himself. "The sheriff will take care of this," she said.

Daniel patted her arm and nodded. "I'm sure he will."

Reassured, Emma thought maybe she'd been imagining things.

Early the next morning, Emma woke with a jerk. She'd been asleep in the rocker and her neck hurt. She rubbed it and stretched, only to find that she ached all over. When she looked at Valina, she almost wished she hadn't. The poor child looked terrible. But, at least she'd slept through the night, though she had groaned several times, from pain in the spirit as well as the body, Emma feared.

She went into the other room. Rachel was asleep on her stomach, one arm hanging down off the cot. The cabin was bitter cold.

Where was Daniel? Emma opened the front door, slowly, so it wouldn't squeak. He wasn't on the steps, thank goodness. He'd be a block of ice by now. She grabbed a sweater and slipped it on. Maybe he was in the outhouse. She inched her way down the ice-glazed steps.

When she rapped on the outhouse door it opened. He wasn't in there. Maybe he'd gone up in the attic. Of course. He must've slept there. After she had to crawl up the steps into the cabin, she sprinkled the steps with some rock salt.

She glanced at Rachel, who was still asleep, and then she climbed the ladder, up to where she could see the whole attic. Daniel wasn't there. Fear crawled up her spine.

Well, maybe he'd gone to work early, since he'd missed a few hours yesterday. But he wouldn't do that without leaving a note. Oh, God, where had he gone? What could she do? No phone, no close neighbors. She couldn't leave the girls. All she could do was pray. As she crawled back down the ladder, she shivered. She'd have to build a fire even though the noise might disturb Rachel.

But Rachel was already sitting up and yawning. "Do I have to go to school today, Mama?"

"No, dear."

"How's Valina?"

"She's still asleep. Why don't you get dressed and sit with her while I get breakfast?"

Rachel slipped into her clothes and went into the bedroom to see her sister.

Emma hurried with the breakfast, then took a plate of it into Valina. She was awake, thank God. But when Emma got a closer look at her face, she stifled a gasp. It was swollen and blue, the skin of her mouth split and puffy.

"I brought a glass of milk and some scrambled eggs," Emma said. "They might be easier for you to eat."

"Thank you." Valina could hardly move her mouth.

"Rachel, your breakfast is on the table. Don't let it get cold." The sight of her battered daughter and the horror in her littlest one's eyes began to tear at Emma's self-control. But she couldn't succumb to panic. Her girls needed her to be strong. Dear God, it was so hard.

"Just a minute, Rachel," Valina said. "Doc told me you saved my life. Thank you. I love you very much."

Tears filled Rachel's eyes. "I love you, too. I'm sorry about what happened to you."

Emma put her hands on Rachel's shoulders and gently propelled her toward the other room. "Better go eat now."

When Rachel had gone, Emma turned to Valina. "Paul should be here this afternoon."

"I must look terrible." Her eyes questioned Emma.

"Your face is quite swollen. Would you like to have a hot water bottle to put on it? It might ease the pain."

"Please."

"I'll get it for you. Keep trying to eat. I'll give you a pain pill when I come back."

In the kitchen, Rachel sat at the table idly moving the eggs around on her plate with her fork. "Mama, why did Timothy do that to Valina?"

Emma said a quick prayer for guidance. "Well, he was in a drunken rage."

"Why?"

"I don't know. Maybe he hated the turn his life had taken."

"But why hurt Valina?"

"Some people are driven to hurt others when they're angry. We'll never really know what was going on in his mind."

"I can't remember why I used to like him," Rachel said, "but I'm sorry I did."

"You don't need to feel bad about that. Lots of people liked him."

Rachel studied her plate. "I know one thing. I'll never, ever hit Roy Bailey again."

Emma had to swallow twice before she could talk. "That's good, dear."

Just as Emma was filling the hot water bottle, Catherine came in the door. "Good morning. How's Valina?"

"Awake and trying to eat breakfast. She's a pitiful sight."

Catherine took off her coat and hung it on a nail by the door, then glanced at the plate of bacon and eggs across the table from Rachel. "Did you eat your own breakfast?"

"I'll eat as soon as I take this to Valina and give her a pill. Help yourself to the coffee."

Emma wrapped the hot water bottle in a dishtowel and took it into the bedroom.

"Is Mary all right?" Valina asked.

"Yes, she is. Charles tells me that Alice and Gunther are taking very good care of her. Catherine just got here, and Charles will come by to see you later."

Emma handed Valina a pain pill, then watched as Valina tipped her head and tried to pour some milk into her mouth. Some of it dribbled down her chin, but she did manage to swallow the pill.

"That's enough, Mama."

"All right. Rest for a while. We'll check in every now and then to see how you're doing."

When Emma came out of the bedroom, Catherine said, "That breakfast of yours is cold. Can I fix you another egg?"

"I can't eat, Catherine."

"Well then, why don't you go up in the attic and try to get some rest?"

"I'm worried about Daniel," Emma whispered. "He's gone, I don't know where."

"I'm sure he must have gone to work," Catherine said. "Everything will look better if you get some rest. You look like you really need it."

Emma didn't protest. She was tired. It was an effort just to climb the ladder up into the attic. She stretched out on the girls' bed, but she couldn't sleep. Daniel was looking for Timothy, she was sure of that. And it was worse to lie there fretting than it would be to get up. She went back downstairs and did some ironing, while Catherine and Rachel played checkers.

Late in the afternoon, Charles and Paul arrived.

Valina woke with a start. Paul stood beside the bed, tears streaming down his face. Dearest Paul. She reached for his hand.

"I look awful, don't I?" she said.

"Oh, God, Valina." He buried his face in her raised hand.

"I'm so glad you're here," she whispered.

"Nothing could keep me away."

He sat on the bed beside her and gently kissed her forehead. She tried to smile but her mouth hurt.

"How long are you going to stay?" she asked.

"Until we're married. I put someone else in charge of the business while I'm gone."

"You did that for me?"

"I love you. I want so much to hold you in my arms, but I'm afraid I'll hurt you."

Tears filled her eyes. "Paul, I don't care if it does hurt, I need you to hold me."

"Oh, my love." He leaned forward and gently put his arms around her.

She nestled in the curve of his shoulders and closed her eyes.

• • •

Just before dark, Mary went outside when she heard the sound of a horse galloping toward her house. The icy fog shrouding the horse and its rider parted for an instant revealing Papa's head, floating in space. Steam from the horse's nostrils mingled with the fog, again obscuring him, leaving only the brittle crack of hooves hitting frozen ground to indicate his approach.

Mary hugged a woolen scarf closer to her body. She waited.

Gradually, he came into full view, eyebrows and lashes covered with ice, face burned red by the freezing air, dark jacket now a frozen gray canvas. She watched him dismount and come toward her. He stood, mute, until he saw her shiver.

"He's dead, Mary."

She looked past him into the fog. "Where is he?"

"At the mortician's. He walked in front of my rifle just as I shot at a coyote."

Mary nodded, then said, "We weren't divorced yet. I'll have to bury him, won't I?"

"Yes, but I'll make the arrangements. You know about Valina?"

"Doc told me."

He glanced up at Alice standing in the doorway, then back at Mary. "Are you all right?"

"Yes, Papa. Alice and Gunther are taking good care of me."

"Let me help you up those stairs, and then I have to go sign some papers about the accident, and then go break the news to the family."

"Thank you, Papa." She turned and looked him straight in the eye. "Thank you."

He helped her up the steps, kissed her cheek, then left.

She'd been expecting Papa because Gunther had told her what he'd seen at dawn: Papa had taken Timothy out of his car where he was passed out, drunk. Then Papa draped Timothy over the horse like a sack of meal, and rode off into the woods.

Mary sat down in the rocker by the fireplace. She let it move slowly forward, slowly backward, and whispered to herself. "Thank you, Papa."

The Bradfords were still at the cabin when Daniel came in, rifle in hand. "I'm glad you're all here," he said. "I borrowed a couple of horses so Timothy and I could go up to Matilda's place to hunt for those coyotes that were making off with her chickens. Timothy got in the line of fire just as I shot at one. He's dead. I took his body to the mortician's, then went to tell Mary. I'll make all the funeral arrangements."

A heavy silence settled in the room. Emma drew Rachel into the shelter of her arms. Daniel put his rifle in its place by the wood box. And then the silence was broken by a voice at the bedroom door. "Papa?"

Paul got to her first, Daniel and Emma right behind him.

But Valina held out her arms to her father. "Papa, how terrible for you."

Daniel shook his head, his eyes bright with unshed tears. "Nowhere near as terrible as what you've been through my dear child."

Emma could hardly stand up. What would happen to Daniel, to all of them, now?

Later, when Emma and Daniel were alone, she was too exhausted to question him. She knew he had deliberately shot Timothy. Daniel had committed an unforgivable sin. Nevertheless, she prayed that the sheriff would accept his story.

Timothy's funeral was held two days later. Alice and Gunther brought Mary, and Matilda came down from the ranch. Rachel stayed home with Paul and Valina. Among the people attending the service was Sheriff Coleman.

Reverend Howard read some bible verses and said a few prayers while he turned the responsibility for Timothy's soul over to God.

After the service, Sheriff Coleman shook Daniel's hand. "These accidents are unfortunate, but they happen," he said.

Emma said her own silent prayer of thanks.

Late that night, Mary's baby was born.

CHAPTER 15

J-Bar-J Ranch—1969

When I came downstairs the next morning, I went outside and headed straight for the pickle tree. I needed to think about a few things. Imagine my surprise when I found Jimmy sitting at the base of the tree. He looked up at me and grunted.

I sat down beside him. I already knew the answer, but I asked anyway. "How come you're up so early?"

"Couldn't sleep. I kept thinking about what Timothy did to Valina. I don't like having him for a grandfather."

"Can't say I blame you." I'd had a bad night myself. The horrified look on Jimmy's face when I told him about the rape had worried me.

"My mom sure didn't take after him, did she?"

His face, stripped of all its frowns and sneers and grins, had a naked look to it. About broke my heart.

"I should say not. And you're certainly not at all like him."

He glanced at me out of the corner of his eye. Seemed like he needed to know if I'd really meant what I said. Poor kid.

"It's no disgrace to have a black sheep in the family," I said. "Just the nature of things. Why, even the animals I've helped into this world, and there've been plenty of them, have had their own unique personalities right from birth. The majority of them were normal, easy to deal with. But a few were trouble right from the start. People are like that too."

His eyes narrowed. "You think so?"

"I sure do, and I've got years of experience to back it up. Look here, if you're worried about inheriting Timothy's bad qualities, take my word for it, you haven't. I could show you some mighty fine families with a black sheep or two among them. It isn't like one bad apple in a box rotting all the rest. People have a lot more going for them than apples do."

He grinned. "I guess that makes sense."

"Damned right it does. Besides, Timothy let old John Barleycorn mess up his life."

"Who's John Barleycorn? You haven't mentioned him before."

That struck me funny, but I kept a straight face. "Just an old-time way of saying liquor."

"Oh." Jimmy chuckled. "You've sure got some weird expressions."

"So do you." I gave my shoulder a little shove forward the way he always did. "That's cool, man."

I waited 'til Jimmy stopped laughing. "But it wasn't just drink that did it. Timothy's morals left a lot to be desired. Some people get hooked on sex. They think it's more important than anything else in their lives. He had too much of that in his makeup. And he didn't have to be a bootlegger, either. He had an amiable quality that makes for a good salesman. He could've been one of the best."

"I'm glad I never had to know him," he said, "and I'm, glad my mom didn't either."

"Yes, it's just as well."

We sat there, each thinking our own thoughts. I was furious. Here I was, stuck with a big lump of guilt because I'd told Jimmy the truth. And there was more to tell. But should I tell it? I wasn't at all convinced the kid would benefit from knowing all the dark secrets about his family. And it wasn't doing me much good, going back over all those painful memories. Damned depressing.

Jimmy interrupted my concentration. "It's real hard for me to imagine Grandmother Marie being married to someone like Timothy."

"A lot of marriages aren't exactly made in heaven. My marriage to Sandy, for instance."

"That one's hard to believe, too." He shook his head. "Real hard."

"People have a tendency to see what they want to see, particularly when it comes to picking out a mate."

Jimmy gave that some serious thought, at least I think he did.

"You know what the saddest part of Mary and Timothy's marriage was? For a brief period of time, those two came close to really loving each other. But Mary didn't take well to Timothy being a bootlegger, much less knowing she'd be stuck in Pine Bluff for the rest of her life. And Timothy was badly hurt when she rejected him. But he couldn't deal with it like a man. If he had, they might have made it. He destroyed his marriage and his life, and hurt a lot of people in the process."

"Yeah, man, he sure did." Jimmy sighed, then stood up and helped me get to my feet. "I'd better milk Daisy and feed the chickens."

Later, after breakfast, when all the men had left, I went out on the porch to feed the dogs. The breeze felt good on my bare arms. It was cooler than it'd been for a week.

Roscoe and Aussie were sitting by the back door, patiently waiting for the highlight of their day, both of them drooling.

But Angus wasn't there. Where could he be? I'd taken him off of the rope a few days before, and he'd never once offered to run away. I went out in the yard and yelled for him. Couldn't see him anywhere. Well, he'd come back pretty soon, I hoped.

I went in and started washing the dishes. It wasn't long before Jimmy came back with the milk.

He looked around the kitchen. "Where's Angus? He wasn't outside when I left."

"He wasn't there when I went out to feed the dogs, either."

He looked mighty worried. I was concerned, myself, but I wouldn't let him know it. "I don't know where he's gone to. Maybe he's just getting acquainted with his new surroundings. He'll find his way back." I hoped I was right.

Jimmy left, a worried frown on his face. I could hear him calling Angus as he walked to the barn.

After a bit, he came back chuck full of the awful things that could happen to the dog. "He might be in trouble, trapped or hurt. Can't we all go look for him?"

"There are only five of us," I said. "How could we scour twenty thousand acres? It would take weeks."

Jimmy gnawed on his lip. "But what if the vandal got him?"

Oh, God. I hadn't thought of that. I could just imagine poor Angus hanging from a tree. I swallowed hard. "Let's wait till noon before we panic," I said. "His empty belly may steer him home."

"If he can get home," Jimmy muttered.

"Better go clean out the barn. And then help Buck with that bad shoe on the horse. And tell him to come in for lunch when you get through."

I got busy making an applesauce cake. Every little bit, I'd got outside to see if Angus had come back, but no such luck. I couldn't stop thinking about the harm that vandal could do to the dog. But if the bastard had been close to the house, we'd have heard a ruckus from the dogs. Then it hit me. Don't know why I hadn't thought of it sooner. If that dog went anywhere, it'd be back to his home. He needed to go there to finish his mourning.

Jimmy came in just before lunch, still fretting about Angus. "Aren't we at least going to try to find him?" he asked.

"As soon as we eat lunch. I figure he must have gone over to Buddy's place."

Jimmy smiled for the first time that morning. "Why, sure. That's exactly what he'd do."

He went out and yelled for Buck, then came back in and sat down at the table. But he wasn't the least bit interested in food.

"Can we take the jeep?" he said. "That way we could make sure he's with us, coming home."

"Good thinking. Why don't you go check the gas in the jeep while I finish eating?"

Buck came in for lunch just as Jimmy left. "Kid's upset," he said.

"Yeah. We're going over to Sandy's old place to see if Angus is there."

I think I managed to eat a couple of bites before Jimmy came back. After that, I gave up on lunch. I got a rope out of the storeroom, in case Angus wasn't willing to come with us, and we climbed into the jeep. I let Jimmy drive.

He was in a powerful hurry to get to Buddy's place. I held on tight. The way the jeep hit some of those bumps, I was glad I hadn't finished my lunch.

Finally, I said, "Whoa. Slow down a bit. You're rattling these old bones of mine."

He slowed down nice as you please. "I'm sorry, Aunt Matilda. I forgot all about you being old."

I didn't know whether to laugh or cry. His apology hadn't hurt my feelings one little bit, but he didn't word it too well.

It wasn't long before we saw Buddy's house in the distance. We had an awful letdown when we drove into the yard. I think we'd both expected Angus to be sitting by the front door, the way he was the day Sandy died.

"Damn it," Jimmy wailed. "He isn't here."

"Well, now, hang in there. Let's look around the place." I went to the front door and knocked. No answer.

Buddy had built a run for his dogs with a high fence around it. Those two Dobermans were making an awful racket.

"Maybe Buddy put him in with the other dogs," Jimmy said. He peered over the fence, then shook his head. "He isn't there." He looked like he might start bawling any minute.

"I don't think Buddy's here, or he'd have heard us," I said. "But let's go look in the barn."

There wasn't a sign of Buddy or Angus in the barn, but while we were in there, we heard a horse come up and stop right outside. Buddy met us at the open barn door.

"I'm glad you're here," he said. "I came back so I could call you. That dog of Sandy's. I forget it's name."

"Angus," Jimmy's eyes lit up. "Is he here?"

"Yeah. He's right over that rise." Buddy pointed at a rise of ground about thirty feet from us. "He's stretched out on a big rock. I tried to get him to come with me, but he wouldn't budge."

I got a shiver up my back. "That must be the place where Sandy was thrown off his horse."

"I'm sure it is," he said. "There was dried blood there. And I found that piece of barbed wire, there, too. Remember? There also was a marijuana joint that had been flicked in the dirt nearby."

"Marijuana?" I couldn't have heard him right. "Not on Sandy's place."

Buddy hesitated. "Well, you never know about people."

"I know about Sandy. He despised the stuff, along with those who grew and sold it."

"Oh." Buddy's eyes narrowed. "Then that puts a different light on it, doesn't it?"

"I should say it does."

"Think it belonged to our neighborhood vandal?"

"Could be." I needed to think about that for a while.

The three of us walked up the rise. At the top on the large

flat rock, Angus was stretched out on his belly, head resting on his paws.

"He wasn't there when I went out early this morning," Buddy said, "so I've no idea how long he's been there. But he sure hasn't moved since I first laid eyes on him. I kept my dogs fenced in, so they wouldn't bother him."

"He's in mourning," I said. "He needs to say goodbye to Sandy in his own way."

Buddy peered at me, the strangest look on his face.

"What do we do now?" Jimmy asked. "Do you think he'll come with us?"

I was glad Jimmy hadn't rushed up to Angus right off the bat. But there was something about the dog that commanded our respect. We all lowered our voices.

"It's important that we honor his feelings," I said. "He hasn't given us a sign, but he knows we're here." There was another big rock nearby. "Let's just sit down here like part of his family, mindful of his mission."

Buddy peered at me. "Are you part Indian?"

"Not that I know of, but I had a good Indian friend when I was a kid."

Buddy nodded and sat beside me.

During the next half-hour, I tried, but I'll be blessed if I could see that dog take a breath. His concentration was a marvel to behold. When I thought we'd waited long enough, I said, "I'm going over to him now. You two stay here."

I walked slow, just like that Indian, Joe, had taught me to when approaching an animal. And I hummed a tuneless thing he'd made me learn. When I got right up next to Angus,

I slowly stretched out beside him on the ground and talked to him in a low voice about Sandy. Did the words mean anything to him? I doubt it. Maybe the drone of my voice, or my hand on his back, or my body prone on the ground beside his had some effect.

By God, he raised his head and looked me straight in the eye, a look that gave me a chill.

I sat up real slow. "Let's go home, Angus."

Well, can you believe it, the dog stood up, a lot easier than I could. Next thing I knew, Buddy was there helping me to my feet. "That's hard on old bones," I said.

"I won't forget this as long as I live." Buddy passed his hand across my forehead. "You are my Indian grandmother now."

I stared at him, wondering if I'd just been party to some sort of Indian ceremony.

Jimmy, his face wet with tears, had his arms around the dog's neck. He was so fond of that dog, I wondered how in the world he'd be able to say goodbye to him, come September. He sure couldn't take him to The City.

Jimmy looked up at me. "Thanks, Aunt Matilda."

"Animals can teach humans a lot, if we watch and listen."

We all started walking toward the jeep. Angus pranced along beside us, just as if nothing out of the ordinary had happened.

"It was a beautiful memorial service," I said to Angus. "Better than the one we had for Sandy," I said. "You did right by him — he would've been proud."

Buddy kept shaking his head, as if he couldn't believe what he'd seen.

Then Angus trotted right up to the jeep and jumped into the back, slick as you please. So we headed home.

When we got there, Angus ate three bowls of food and drank water till I thought he'd burst. Then, by golly, he played with Aussie and Roscoe, though poor old Roscoe wasn't much of a challenge to him.

"I can't believe it," Jimmy said. "Look at him go. He hasn't run like that since you turned him loose."

"He's finally put Sandy to rest. Now he can go on with his life."

Jimmy looked at me like he'd never seen me before. "That was cool, the way you talked to him." He blushed.

We sat on the porch and watched those goofy dogs run, their ears flying in the breeze. Roscoe was standing off to one side by that time. His old body had had enough for one day. I knew the symptoms well.

Jimmy laughed. "Roscoe's smiling again. Wait'll I tell the guys I met a dog that smiles."

"Reminds me of the first time you saw him."

"I sure was a greenhorn." He snorted. "And George really took advantage of it, didn't he?"

"Yep. But you aren't a greenhorn any more."

He got a silly grin on his face. "You mean it?"

"Damn right I do. Do you think I'd say it if I didn't?"

He chuckled. "No. You never say anything you don't mean."

A few minutes later, who should ride up but Sheriff Jackson and two of his deputies. Now, I'd expected maybe a phone call, but not a personal visit. The sheriff got off his horse and walked over to Jimmy and me.

"I'm sorry to say, I've got some bad news. The fellow who was murdered . . ."

My heart started hammering in my ears. "Yes?"

"Well, it was Cal Lewis."

I fell back in my chair. Couldn't get my breath for a minute. "Oh, no. Not Cal."

"I've had two deputies staked out in that marijuana field ever since we got the body out of the canyon. They almost cornered a man they saw there, but he took off fast."

I flinched when I looked at Jimmy's shocked, gray face. How much more of this real life could the kid survive?

I stood up and rang the dinner bell to call the men in. Oscar and George and Buck arrived in nothing flat. I let Sheriff Jackson tell them the bad news.

Oscar looked at me. "Damn it to hell!"

I nodded.

Buck and George said nothing, just took off their hats.

Strange, but that simple gesture brought tears to my eyes. And then I realized the sheriff was talking to me again.

"We think the man is over here on your spread somewhere."

That struck me as mighty odd. "Why would he go all the way around that canyon and come onto my property, when he could get away by going over the mountain?"

"I don't know," he snapped, "but we sure as hell saw him over here."

"That doesn't make sense."

"Maybe he knows you were right across the canyon when he threw Cal over the edge. I want you and the boy to stay in the house until we flush him out. And I need Buddy Fast

Buffalo Horse to come over here and help me track him down."

"I'll call him." I walked into the kitchen and phoned Buddy. He was in the house, thank God. "Buddy . . ." I got a terrible lump in my throat.

"Is that you, Matilda?"

"Yes. It was Cal Lewis we saw thrown into that canyon."

"Cal? Oh, God, no!"

"Sheriff Jackson and his men are here right now. They think the murderer might be on my spread somewhere. He needs you to help him track down the bastard."

"I'll be right there," he said, and hung up.

I went back out to the porch. "Buddy will be right here."

Sheriff Jackson looked relieved. "Thanks, Matilda."

Now, I'd always had a hard time trusting the sheriff. I knew damned well he'd left out some important details.

"You know who the murderer is, don't you?"

He scowled at me. "Yep, but I ain't sayin', and that's that."

"Well, what if he walks right up to my door? How am I going to know he's the one who has murder on his mind?"

He snorted. "He won't get that close. My men and I will be circling the area, while your men guard the outside of your house." He pointed, with all the authority he could muster, at the two deputies on their horses. "They'll circle around all your outer buildings, separately, of course."

My, he was taken with himself. I wasn't convinced his precautions were necessary, but I sure wanted that murderer caught. "Feel free to use this house as your headquarters, Sheriff. Have you and your men eaten lately?"

He hesitated. "We could use a sandwich and some coffee."

I got busy fixing sandwiches, and Jimmy made a big pot of coffee. The kid hadn't said a blessed word. I didn't know how to help him deal with the horror of it, but I sure knew how to keep him from physical harm. I'd send him home tomorrow.

Just as the sheriff and his men finished eating, Buddy rode up. When I saw him, all I could do was nod at him. I didn't want to cry in front of those men. He nodded in return. I knew he understood. He and the sheriff took off right away, and those two deputies started circling the area. You could tell they felt ridiculous, there in broad daylight going around in circles, but they did as they'd been told.

Oscar scowled and shifted his weight back and forth, like he didn't know which direction to go. "Want George and me to start circling the house?"

"Hell, no. Just keep your guns handy and your eyes open."

He grinned. "Yes, ma'am." He and George went on out to the barn.

Buck stood in the middle of the kitchen. Now, I knew he wasn't about to ask me, so I said, "You might as well go put that shoe on Dusty. Just take your rifle with you."

I put my thirty-eight in the drawer closest to the back door, and turned to the boy. "I'm sorry, Jimmy, but under the circumstances, I'm afraid you'll have to head for home tomorrow."

His eyes almost bugged out of his head. "Why?"

"We may all be in danger. I can't let anything happen to you."

"What about the deal I made with my dad?"

"I'm sure he'll take special circumstances into account."

"But if you make me go home, Mom will be certain that I narrowly escaped death and she and Dad will have a big fight because he sent me up here, and it will be your fault."

Talk about noodle-headed reasoning. Well, he wasn't fooling me. He didn't want to leave because he might miss all the excitement, though that bit about Jessica and Bob sounded plausible, all right. "But what if you were hurt?" I said.

"That isn't going to happen. Look. If you let me stay, I won't leave the house until they find the guy."

"That could be the rest of the summer."

Jimmy clenched his fists and glared at me.

Hell, I didn't know what to do with the kid. "All right. I'll let you stay for a couple of days. But if the murderer hasn't been caught by then, off you go." I hurried to add, "And you're housebound for those days. Understand?"

Jimmy grinned. "Yep."

I felt like an Eskimo with a new refrigerator. I'd been sucked in. That smart-assed kid.

That night, Jimmy fell asleep on the couch in the living room. Oscar and George prowled around the outside of the house, and Buck kept an eye on the inside. I baked bread. About two in the morning, I sat down on my lounger across from Jimmy and dozed. Every little bit, I'd wake with a start, then doze again.

At five-thirty, I was wide awake. That's when Jimmy stood up, stretched, and marched briskly to the kitchen door. Jimmy? Alert at this hour?

"Just a damn minute," I yelled, as I struggled out of the chair. "Where do you think you're going?"

His hand was still on the doorknob when I finally made it to the kitchen. He turned and looked at me with wide eyes. "Isn't it all right if I go milk Daisy and get the eggs? Someone has to do it."

What could I say? Someone did have to do it. "Well, as long as Oscar's nearby."

I went out on the porch and waited until Oscar walked past. "Jimmy's going to milk Daisy and get the eggs."

Oscar nodded. "I'll stand outside the shed until he's through."

Together, they walked toward the cowshed. I started breakfast, growling to myself. "You'd think that sheriff would realize my men need their sleep, for God's sake."

When I heard Buck grunt, I jumped. I'd forgotten he was in the room. Lack of sleep can give a person a serious case of nerves.

I started to pour a cup of coffee for Buck, when I heard a shot. Buck jumped to his feet and I grabbed my thirty-eight out of the drawer.

Buck started for the door. "Be careful," I warned. "We don't know what's going on out there." I edged over to the window and peered out.

I damn near fainted at the sight of Orville Adams holding Jimmy with one arm, while his other arm held a pistol up to Jimmy's temple. And Oscar ... he was sprawled on the ground by Orville's feet. Was he dead?

"Mother of God," I moaned. "Orville's holding Jimmy hostage, and Oscar's down."

Buck scrambled over to the window to see for himself. Then he headed for the door again.

"Stop right there." My voice sounded like a whip, even to me. Buck stopped in his tracks. "If you go out there, Orville might shoot you, or Jimmy."

I didn't have a plan in mind myself, but I went over and eased the door open a crack. And that's when I heard Orville ranting. The voice of a madman. Full of hate, venom, rage. Who was he yelling at?

"Matilda Jacobsen! Get your ass out here, or I'll shoot your precious little boy."

I wasn't going without my gun, but how could I hide it from Orville? I had an idea.

"Get Oscar's windbreaker out of the storeroom, Buck. And hurry."

When Buck handed it to me, I put the huge thing on, cocked the thirty-eight and stuck it in the right hand pocket. Buck tried to get out the door first, but I yanked him away.

"Orville wants to talk to me," I said. "You go out the other side of the house and circle around behind him. Maybe we can confuse the bastard so one of us can shoot him. We've got to try."

Buck nodded and I stepped out on the porch, my hands hanging limp at my sides.

"It's about time," Orville snarled.

He was almost twenty feet from me. Slowly, I started walking toward him. I could feel Jimmy's eyes on me, but didn't dare look at him. That would give Orville an edge.

"You can walk faster than that, you old bitch!"

I stopped. "Why don't you let the boy go so we can talk?"

The sound of his laughter made my skin crawl.

"Why should I? He shot me." Slowly, he caressed Jimmy's face with the muzzle of his gun.

I choked back a scream. Somehow we had to kill him before he killed the boy. I gauged Orville's height — he was at least four inches taller than Jimmy. Maybe with me as a decoy, Buck could shoot him in the head. But would he think of it in time? And could he do it before Orville pulled the trigger and killed Jimmy?

I needed to keep him talking. "Why are you holding the boy?"

"Got your attention, didn't I?" He looked at Jimmy, his lip curling. "This little boy means a lot to you doesn't he? But don't worry. The sheriff won't risk shooting, not when I'm holding someone who's so important to the great Matilda Jacobsen." His eyes glittered.

He hated my guts, no doubt of that. But why? All those times he helped with our haying there'd been no sign of it.

"Did you like your dead rooster, Matilda?"

I gasped. "You're the one . . ."

"That's right." He pushed the muzzle up under Jimmy's chin and grinned at me.

I took a deep breath to ward off a wave of nausea.

He chuckled. "And that dead cow. You thought it was just a poacher, didn't you?"

"Guess I did, at that." What else would he confess to?

"You're slowing down, old woman."

"Afraid so."

He sneered at me. "But I sure kept your men busy with all those cut fences."

I nodded. "That's for sure."

"And you didn't even catch on." His finger teased the trigger of his revolver. "Not even about Sandy."

The words tumbled out of my mouth. "You killed Sandy?"

His vicious laughter made the bile rise to my throat.

"Both Sandy and Cal made a big mistake when they found my marijuana field." Orville's voice got louder, angrier. "You've been making a big mistake, too, treating me like dirt all these years."

"I didn't realize I had. I'm sorry." His laughter had a maniacal edge to it this time, a sound that almost curdled my soul.

"I never got any recognition from you." He was almost screaming. "Not a kind word, or an offer of help. My mother and me, we could've starved to death, for all of you. But I came from scum, didn't I? Wasn't good enough for the likes of you."

"Orville, if it's money you want, I'll give you plenty. Just let the boy go."

He bent his head toward Jimmy. "You didn't like me, but when this little boy came along, you couldn't do enough for him."

My God, he was jealous. My legs wobbled at the sight of his malicious sneer.

At that instant, Buck coughed. Orville's head snapped to his left. His arm, the one around Jimmy, must've relaxed, because Jimmy suddenly hit the dirt and started crawling behind Orville.

I whipped out my thirty-eight. Orville's head snapped back to me. Two shots rang out.

My bullet hit Orville right between the eyes. The second shot, meant for me, went astray.

I sank to the ground.

When I could focus my eyes again, I looked up at a group of men peering down at me. Someone was on the ground beside me, hanging onto my arms with a grip so strong it hurt.

"Aunt Matilda. Are you all right?"

"I think so. Haven't shot anybody in a while. Wasn't sure my old eyes and hand could do the trick." And then Jimmy's face swam into focus. "Oh, God, Jimmy. Are you all right?"

He grinned, but he had tears in his eyes. "I'm fine, thanks to you."

There was a big to-do after that. Buck, the sheriff, and his two deputies helped me up off the ground.

Buck and George tended to Oscar, who was alive, thank God. When they helped him stand up, I walked over and held tight to his hand. "I thought you were dead, Oscar."

"Nope, it's just a flesh wound." Someone had given him a handkerchief he was holding up to his shoulder. "I moved just as Orville shot me. Seems he was hiding in the cowshed."

"Yeah," Jimmy said. "When I went into the shed, Oscar stayed outside. Orville grabbed me, then snuck up behind Oscar and ..."

I could see him swallow hard. Poor Jimmy couldn't say the awful words, and I didn't want to hear them. Besides, in my numb state, all I could think about was the big meal I'd have to cook for those men.

Well, it didn't turn out that way. Buddy showed up and did the cooking while I dressed Oscar's wound. Then we drank up my whole supply of raspberry cordial. Even Jimmy had a snort.

As soon as the meal was over, the sheriff's deputies rode

for town. Sheriff Jackson, true to form, came riding in and commandeered George to drive Orville's body down to Pine Bluff.

"Feel like a damned undertaker," George grumbled.

Without a word of thanks, Sheriff Jackson got in the jeep and they drove off. I had to chuckle. "Don't think Sheriff Jackson was too happy with me."

"No," Buddy said. "You stole his thunder." He gave me a big hug. "Lord, I'm glad you and Jimmy are still with us. You are some kind of woman, Matilda Jacobsen." He kissed me on the forehead and grinned. "I'd better go take care of my animals, but you call if you need me. Okay?"

I nodded. "Get on home you smooth talker, you."

He gave me a salute and left.

Buck went out to check things in the barn. About then, Jimmy went upstairs to take a shower. Oscar and I sat at the table drinking coffee.

"I wasn't unconscious after Orville shot me," he said. "I was trying to figure out a way to disarm him, yet keep Jimmy from getting killed." He got a funny look on his face. "Good thing Orville couldn't shoot worth a damn, or you'd have been a goner," he said.

"I have a hunch you had something to do with his bad aim." I grinned at him.

"Nope. Jimmy kicked him."

"Well, I'll be damned."

Oscar stood up and went to the door. "Better go help Buck," he said.

"The hell you will. You get on upstairs and go to bed."

"Aw, Matilda . . ."

"Who's boss around here, anyway?" I demanded.

"Can't win."

He grumbled all the way up the stairs, but I wasn't impressed.

Later, when Jimmy came back down, I asked him if he wanted a cup of hot chocolate.

"Now?"

"Can you think of a better time?"

"Well, no." He sat down at the table.

He was mighty quiet. When I set the cup of chocolate in front of him, he just gave me a weak smile.

I sat down across from him. "We've had a pretty bad time of it today. Don't know about you, but I was really scared."

"You were? I sure couldn't tell." He kept his eyes on the table. "I was scared, too. I didn't want to die."

He swallowed hard, then peered up at me. "Thanks for saving me, Aunt Matilda." He blushed as he wiped his eyes with the back of his hands.

I wiped away my own tears. "I couldn't have stood it if anything had happened to you, Jimmy. And I need to thank you, too. I understand you're the reason I'm still alive."

He stared at me. "What are you talking about?"

"You ruined Orville's aim when you kicked him."

"Oh." His Adam's apple bounced up and down. "Well, I sure didn't want him to kill you."

We were quiet for a spell, just drinking our hot chocolate. I figured we'd said enough about the incident, at least for now. There might be a nightmare or two to deal with later.

But after a bit, he said, "Could I ask you something?"

"Sure."

"Why don't you like my grandmother?"

Now that sure came out of the blue. Not at all what I expected. "It isn't a matter of liking, so much as it's a different way of living."

Jimmy nodded. "Yeah, I understand that."

"I'm not sure you do. I could never fault Mary for the strength she had. She rose from ashes to glory by being a shrewd, talented businesswoman. I respect her for that."

"Well, yeah, but you don't like her."

God, what could I say? "In all our lives, there are people we're close to, and others we don't feel comfortable with. Mary and I don't feel comfortable with each other. Never did. We have nothing in common. That doesn't mean we hate each other. But can you see Mary living here on this ranch, wearing the clothes I wear?"

Jimmy grinned. "Nope. She wouldn't even make it up here in the jeep."

"Okay," I said. "Now, can you see me living in The City, wearing designer dresses, getting my hair done?"

Jimmy snickered. "I see what you mean."

We sat back in our chairs and sipped our chocolate.

Pretty soon Jimmy spoke up again. "Are you through with the family story?"

Oh, Lord. After the day we'd had, did I really have to go into all this? "Actually, I wish I could forget the rest of it."

"Why? What happened to Valina, anyway? Was she all right?"

"Not exactly. Wasn't too long before she found out she was pregnant."

"Timothy's baby?" He gasped.

"Of course."

"Oh, shit."

CHAPTER 16

Pine Bluff—1930

Jessica Marie O'Callahan looked exactly like Mary, much to her mother's relief. If the baby had looked like Timothy, she couldn't have loved it. Fortunately, the delicate little beauty was an exact replica of herself. Before Jessica was old enough to understand the gossip about her father, Mary was determined to leave Pine Bluff. She bent down and tucked the blanket around little Jessica. "Thank heaven you're a good baby. Your mother will be very busy making a living."

Mary walked over to the front window and pulled back the lace curtain. Just the sight of the Model A parked out in front of the house upset her. She would never marry again, much less have another child. The whole ordeal, from Timothy's downfall to the painful birth, had only served to strengthen her resolve. She and Jessica Marie needed a fresh start, just the two of them, in a city where no one knew about Timothy's degradation of the Addison family. Fat chance this backward town would ever forget the high drama of a rape and a killing.

The very idea of Timothy beating and raping Valina. But her sister would get over it. She had Paul. She wouldn't have to work to support herself and a baby, either.

Alice came into the room. "I'm leaving now," she said. "Do you want me to wait until Catherine gets here?"

"No." Mary turned away from the window. "I'll be fine."

"You're sure?"

"Alice, it's been two weeks, after all. You've already done too much for me. Now, get on to school before the principal hands you a warning slip."

Alice pursed her lips in a wry smile. "I suppose I'd better." She waved as she left.

Mary had had someone with her every minute since Jessica's birth, Catherine during the day, until Alice came home, then Mama came after work with their dinner.

Well, today she'd tell both Catherine and Mama that she could manage by herself now. She went over to her sewing machine to examine a dress she'd finished just last night for Ed Garrison's wife, Molly. But she was interrupted by Catherine's arrival.

"Should you be sewing so soon after the baby?" Catherine asked.

Mary shrugged. "Why not? I feel fine. You've been a great help, Catherine, and I appreciate everything you've done for me, but this is your last day."

"Oh. Well, I guess you know best." Catherine walked over to Mary and picked up Molly Garrison's dress. "You do such beautiful work. You should be a designer."

"I wish I could be, in a big city a thousand miles from here. I'm even more determined, now, to move away."

"But you'll need your family."

Mary bristled. "But what about little Jessica when she's

old enough to understand what people are saying about her father? A gossip like Bertha Wilcox, or a brat like Roy Bailey, would be only too happy to tell her every last lurid detail."

Catherine frowned and put down the dress. "That's probably true."

"Do you think I could make a living with my sewing, perhaps in San Francisco? Jessica wouldn't have to know about her father, if we lived that far away."

"But your parents would be devastated. Besides, children need loving grandparents."

"But both Jessica and I need to get away from here. I have to put it all behind me." She choked back a sob. "Valina's going to move away. Why can't I?"

Catherine put her hand on Mary's shoulder. "Please, I didn't mean to upset you. I really do see your point."

"I know Aunt Matilda would loan me money to get started. I'd need a decent apartment in a good area, and I'd have to advertise."

"What you'd need would be a few happy customers, wealthy ones, with friends. They'd do your advertising for you." Catherine looked thoughtful. "If you can make three outfits for me before Paul and Valina and I make that trip to Portland I might be able to help you."

Mary bounced out of her chair. "That's only two weeks off, but I can do it." She held her breath.

"I have two wealthy friends who live in San Francisco. If I can persuade them to meet me in Portland, your creations will sell themselves. But don't get your hopes up until I call them. I'll do that tonight."

"Oh, Catherine . . ."

"Wait, now. It may not work out right away. These women are very busy and they travel quite often. And Jessica won't understand for quite some time."

"But I understand, all too well." How could Catherine tantalize her like that, and then pull back so abruptly?

"If it doesn't work out this time, I promise I'll find a way, eventually. But remember, these are society women. They often don't give a thought to another person's schedule or need." Catherine looked closely at Mary. "Could you work with women like that?"

Mary stood up straighter. "Indeed I could."

Catherine smiled. "I believe you. But not a word to anyone until it's certain. I don't want Emma's heart broken before it's absolutely necessary."

"Of course not." At least she had something to hang onto now.

When the telephone rang later that evening, Mary rushed to answer it. It was Catherine. "Mary, my friends can't meet me in Portland. They are about to leave for Paris."

"Oh." Hot tears filled Mary's eyes.

"But there's a good chance they'll be in San Francisco in October. If so, you could come with me and meet them."

"Really?"

"Yes. And I'll get some of that marvelous wool from Paul's mill when I go to Portland. You can make fall suits for the two of us to wear."

"Wonderful."

"I'm almost sure it will work out, Mary."

"I'll try to be patient. Thank you, Catherine."

"You're very welcome."

Slowly, Mary hung up the receiver. Would Catherine's friends laugh at her designs after seeing what the French designers did?

She went over to the sewing machine, picked up Mrs. Garrison's dress and scrutinized every seam, every detail. No, they wouldn't laugh. She'd start sketching her designs and then work them out in muslin. She'd have more time now to get prepared. It would also give her time to get her figure back in shape, though it didn't look as bad as she'd feared it would. Her own outfit, as well as Catherine's would be stunning. She laughed. Women always believed they'd be as beautiful as the model, if only they had the model's dress.

Mary waited until Gunther and Alice had gone to bed at nine o'clock, before she called Aunt Matilda. How could she word it so Dottie and the neighbors on the line wouldn't catch on?

When she gave Dottie the phone number, Dottie said, "Oh, you're calling your Aunt Matilda."

Mary tried to keep the irritation out of her voice. "That's right."

When someone answered, Mary asked, "Is that you, Aunt Matilda?"

A grumpy voice said, "Who else were you expecting?"

"I hope I didn't wake you. This is Mary. I wanted to know when you're coming down to see my baby." That ought to placate the eavesdroppers.

"So happens I'm coming down tomorrow."

"Good. You can stay here. I have an extra bedroom."

"Might take you up on that."

"Then I'll see you tomorrow," Mary said.

She hung up the phone and smiled. When Aunt Matilda saw Jessica Marie, she'd understand why they had to leave Pine Bluff.

Aunt Matilda got there right after Gunther and Alice left for work the next morning. Mary cringed when she saw her aunt's same old culottes and man's shirt. To think she wanted to borrow money to set up a dressmaking business from a woman who'd never been seen in a dress. "Have you had breakfast?" Mary asked.

"I'd like a cup of coffee and a piece of bread and butter, if you have it." Aunt Matilda walked over to the cradle and peered at Jessica Marie. "My God, that baby looks exactly like you did. Good thing, isn't it?"

Aunt Matilda's words caught Mary by surprise, but her aunt's blunt manner had never failed to catch her off-guard. Well, she could be blunt, too. "I couldn't mention what I wanted to talk to you about on the phone last night."

"I figured that out."

Mary led Aunt Matilda into the kitchen. She poured a cup of coffee and began buttering two slices of bread. "You said you'd loan me money if I needed it."

Aunt Matilda sat down at the breakfast table, leaned back in the chair and said, "That's right. How much?"

Mary put the cup of coffee and a plate of bread on the table. "I want to set myself up as a couturier in San Francisco."

"What the hell is that?"

Mary sat down across from her aunt. "A fashionable dressmaker, a creative one." She hurried to add, "I want to get Jessica out of this town before she's old enough to be hurt by the gossip."

"And you're eager to leave, too."

"I've wanted to get out of here ever since I can remember. Now, more than ever. I need to put all of it behind me. Catherine has some wealthy friends in San Francisco, and she's going to try to get me started through them — though it may take a little time."

"Do you know how much you'll need?"

"Not yet. I just need to know if you'll help me?"

"I said I would, didn't I?"

"Yes, you did, and I appreciate it. Catherine didn't think we should tell Mama and Papa until it's all accomplished. I know they'll be unhappy."

"Yes, but I think they'll understand."

"I won't come back, not even for a visit."

"They'll know that. Even so, they might think it's best for both of you. And I'll send them to see you once in a while; they'll need to know Jessica Marie."

Aunt Matilda took a last gulp of coffee, and stood up. "Think I'll pick up my supplies and drop by the courthouse to see Daniel. And I'll have lunch at the cafe so I can check up on Emma and Valina. See you later."

When Aunt Matilda rode out of sight, Mary let out an exultant yell. Jessica Marie began to cry.

"Did I scare you, little one?" She picked up the baby and waltzed around the room. "I'll be free to do what I please. And when you get big enough, you and I will go to the theater and shop in the best stores and have hot chocolate in ritzy restaurants. Our lives will be glorious. Just you wait and see."

Valina had the same nightmare every night. First, a jolt of terror at a sound right behind her, then a hand clamped over her mouth and nose. Screaming into the hand, she struggled for breath, fought the arm that dragged her into the bushes, gasped as her jaw felt the crush of his fist. A scream, her own, always ended the dream but never her torment.

Rachel's worried face floated into focus. "Valina, wake up. It's just a nightmare."

"I'm sorry. I keep you awake every night, don't I?"

Rachel's eyes shifted to the quilt on the bed. "I go right back to sleep. You okay now?"

"Sure. Go back to bed." Valina crawled out of her side of the sweat-drenched bed, shivering in her damp nightgown. They were all pretending a serenity they didn't feel. Was that the way to survive? She didn't know. She knew only that she'd never be the same. She didn't even feel the same about Paul. Dear kind Paul. He deserved better. But she couldn't imagine having sex with any man now. She didn't want to get back in bed. If she went to sleep she might dream again.

Early the next morning, when Valina went out to get some water, she found Paul sitting on the front steps. "I thought you might like to go for a little walk," he said. "It's cooler early in the morning." His voice sounded cheery, but there were worry lines between his eyes.

"A walk would be nice."

He took the pail from her and filled it with water from the tub by the door.

She smiled when he stood up. That stubborn lock of hair hung down on his forehead again.

"Wait here," he said. "I'll take this inside."

When he came back, he steered her toward town but she stopped him. Her hand shook on his arm. "I don't want to go that way. Let's go down to the creek."

He peered at her, the worry lines deepening. "Okay."

She'd have to go by the place eventually. There was no other way out of there. When they got to the creek, she remembered the day she'd stretched out in the water to cool off, the day Timothy had seen her in her wet nightgown. Would things have been different if he hadn't seen her that way? Why couldn't she stop thinking about it?

"Do you think I'm going crazy?" she asked.

He put his arm around her. "Of course not. You've been through a dreadful experience. You can't expect to get over it all at once."

"That's what concerns me. There's no way to know if I'll ever feel normal again. I don't even know if I should marry you. You'd be taking a terrible risk. What if I couldn't bear to have sex?"

"Valina, don't."

"I'm glad you're here, but ..."

"I'm here because I love you." He took her chin in his hand and gazed into her eyes. "You can't begin to know how much."

She bit her lip. "But you're disrupting your life."

He moved his hand up to her hair and stroked it. "And your life hasn't been disrupted? What happens to you happens to me. That's all there is to it."

She wanted him to go home, but how could she tell him such a thing? "I'm going to go back to work on Monday."

He smiled. "Good. I'll be there with you."

"You're going to sit in the cafe all day?" She wanted to scream at him to leave her alone. Instead, she sat down on the bank and patted the ground beside her. He sat down next to her.

"I can't predict when I'll be ready to get married," she said. "You can't stay here indefinitely. I love you, but I don't want our relationship to be one where I'm dependent on you for every little thing."

She hugged her knees and looked at him out of the corner of her eye. He was staring at the creek. "Your love and support have meant more than I can put into words, Paul, but I want you to go back to Portland."

He kept his eyes on the creek.

"There are some things that I have to live through on my own. I won't get better unless I do. Can you understand?"

"I've been overprotective, is that it?"

"You've been wonderful. It's just that now I need to see if I can be alone with it. If I can't, then we shouldn't marry."

He turned to face her. "You're not cancelling the trip to Portland, are you?"

"Well, no. You've made plans, and we've all counted on it for a long time. I'm sure it would be good for me to get away. I just thought you could stay there when Catherine and I go home."

He looked hurt. She'd done it all wrong. "Try to understand. I need to get up right now and walk by the spot where it happened. I have to do it before I go back to work again, and I want you with me, desperately. But, eventually, I have to go by there alone. As long as you're here, I'll lean on you."

"I see what you mean. Okay. I'll stay in Portland after the trip, and I won't hang around quite so much until then." He reached for her hand and pulled her up off the ground.

"I'm sorry, Paul. Your help was just what I needed, and now I've made it sound like I don't appreciate all you've done for me."

"I really do understand, darling. But this first time you walk by the place, I insist on being with you."

"Yes. Maybe I do need you with me." She paused, embarrassed. Perhaps she was going crazy. "That sounds ridiculous after all I've said."

He took her hand in his. "Never mind. Let's go."

When they stood by the spot where the underbrush was bent and the weeds had been flattened, she couldn't control her loud wailing sobs. She clung to Paul, her sobs mingling with the silent tears that streamed down his face.

Finally, her sobs quieted, and still clinging to each other, they walked back to the cabin.

He took her to work Monday morning. At least driving by the place wasn't as bad as walking by it. When she stood outside the door of the cafe, she wanted to run right back to his car, but she turned and waved at him. How would the regulars react? Her face was still bruised, but everyone knew, anyway. But what if Bertha came in?

Her back was to the door when the first customer entered. Her heart lurched. Was it Bertha, or Spike?

"Good morning, Valina. It's nice to have you back."

Herb Johnson. Thank God. She turned to face him, but he didn't seem to notice her bruises.

He sat down and said, "I'll have the usual. So will Dogie. He'll be right here."

When Valina placed the orders, Mama searched her face. "Everything all right?"

"So far."

When she went back into the other room, Dogie waved from his chair next to Herb. "Glad you're back, Valina."

He, too, hadn't paid a bit of attention to the bruises. Maybe they weren't as noticeable as she'd thought. Or maybe they were just being kind.

By eleven-thirty, she was glad Paul had talked her into working only a half-day. She had a pain in her stomach. It had been an awful strain. Everyone had been kind, but they hadn't acted natural either. She could hardly wait to leave.

Tillie had just started to take over for Valina, when Bertha Wilcox walked in.

"You're not leaving already are you, Valina?" Bertha said. "Surely you've recovered by now. 'Course I can still see the bruises on your face. He must've smacked you a good one."

The room quieted. Herb and Dogie glared at Bertha.

"Oh, come on." Bertha looked around the room. "We all know that any girl who's been raped has asked for it."

Valina's body sagged against the counter. She couldn't faint. Bertha would love that. The room whirled for an instant,

but she concentrated on breathing deeply. Suddenly she realized that Herb was pulling Bertha out of her chair.

"It's a damned shame that you came in the door." He
dragged her up onto her feet.

"You get your hands off me," Bertha snarled.

"Gladly, if you'll leave this very moment," Herb said.

"I'll do nothing of the sort. Tillie, make this maniac leave
me alone."

"Not on your life," Tillie said. "Ben and I decided that if
you pulled a stunt like this, you could just get out and stay out."

Bertha's face turned purple. "You can't do that to me. This
is a public place."

"We own this public place. You're not welcome here,
Bertha. Don't try to come back or we'll get Sheriff Coleman
to help us get rid of you for disturbing the peace, which you
certainly do very well."

Herb pushed a loudly protesting Bertha out the door.

Valina could see Paul in the roadster parked across the
street in front of the feed store. She turned to Tillie. "I'm
going to leave now. Thank you. And please thank Ben for me,
too. I'll be here all day tomorrow."

"Okay, if you think you can manage." Tillie put her arm
around Valina's shoulders. "But I'll check in once in a while to
see if you need me."

"Don't let Bertha upset you," Herb said, when Valina
started for the door.

Dogie nodded. "That's right. At least we've seen the last of
the old witch in here."

Valina smiled at them and shut the door behind her.

She walked across the street and started to get in Paul's car, but stopped. "Do you mind if we walk?"

"Good idea. I can get the car on my way back." He took her hand and they started walking up the street. "What happened in there? Was I imagining it, or did I see Herb kick Bertha out of the cafe?"

When she told him what had happened, he grinned at her. "Feel better, now that the thing you dreaded most about your first day is behind you?"

"How did you know?"

"Didn't take a mind-reader," Paul said. "I was dreading it, too, but you handled it beautifully."

"You mean Tillie and Herb handled it."

"Quit underestimating yourself. Did you faint or have hysterics? No. Some people never recover from such an experience, but here you are, back at work, surviving a nasty attack by Bertha. You're much stronger than you think, Valina."

"Would I have been so strong if Tillie and Herb hadn't stopped her, or if you hadn't been with me through the worst of all this?"

"I'm certain that you would. But what's wrong with having people help you?"

She hesitated. "I'm not sure."

Paul put his arm around her shoulders protectively. "Maybe we should stop talking about this. We're coming into the woods now. You want me to leave you here so you can go in alone?"

She wanted to throw herself into the comfort of his embrace, to beg him to go with her, but she said, "Yes."

She walked on without him, blinded by tears. Why had she been so perverse? Why couldn't she admit she wanted him with her? Dear God, please help me. Please. What was that noise? She whirled around. Nothing. Not even a bird or a squirrel. She rubbed the goose bumps on her arms. She had to get control of herself. Timothy was dead, not behind her on the path. No one was going to hurt her. Her mouth was dry. She kept swallowing, but it didn't help. There it was, the place where . . . hysteria rose in her throat. She ran the rest of the way to the cabin, past it, and on to the creek, where she drank water from the cup of her hand. She was washing her face when she heard Paul's voice.

"Valina, where are you?"

"By the creek."

He hurried into the clearing. "I had to know if you were all right."

She went into his open arms. "I'm so glad you're here. It was awful."

He gently kissed her. "But you did it."

"I thought I heard him behind me. Isn't that crazy? He's dead."

Paul caressed her cheek, then held her closer. "After a while the memory of it will fade. I promise you it will."

Three weeks before the trip to Portland, Valina went to see Doc Bradley. She hadn't told anyone, but she was terrified she might be pregnant. She hadn't had a period since the rape and her breasts were sore.

After he examined her, Doc asked her to get dressed and come into his office. Her fingers trembled so hard she could hardly fasten her skirt. When she tried to walk across the hall to his office, her legs felt like lead weights. She had to stop and take a deep breath before she could even open the door. When she went in, the pained look on his face told her that her fear was justified.

"Valina, I'm sorry. You are pregnant. Damn it to hell." He pounded his fist on his desk. "It's against the law for me to help you get rid of it, but if I ever saw a case where it was justified, it's yours. I wish to God I could help you."

The room whirled. Timothy's baby. No. It was horrible, impossible. Her whole life was ruined. There was no way in the world she could marry Paul now.

"Have you talked to your mother about this?" Doc asked.

"No. No one." She had tried hard to convince herself it wasn't true.

"You're very pale. I think you'd better lie down on the couch for a little while."

She shook her head. She just wanted to leave, to run.

"I insist." He led her to the couch. "You wait here while I go get Emma. I won't be long."

She stretched out on the couch so he'd go away. She wanted to scream at him when he hesitated. But just then, Minnie stuck her head inside the door.

"Emergency, Doc," she said. "One of the Anderson boys cut his arm real bad. He's in the infirmary." Minnie disappeared into the next room.

Doc frowned. She knew he didn't want to leave her.

"You stay here and rest until I get back," he said, as he hurried off.

The instant he left, Valina got up and went to the door.

She opened it just enough to see that no one was in the outer office. Carefully, she tiptoed through it and slipped out the front door. From there, she ran all the way to the cabin.

When she got there, she paced the floor. She couldn't stand still. What had Doc expected Mama to do about it, anyway? Talking with Mama wouldn't help. No words could take away the harm. God did punish me for having sex with Timothy. She shuddered. Timothy's baby. No. Never. She would die, instead.

But how would she manage it? She hadn't let herself think about suicide until now. She'd hung on desperately to the hope that she wasn't pregnant. Well, there was no hope. What could she use? She walked over to Papa's rifle, ran her hand down the smooth stock, fingered the trigger. But she let her hand drop. She didn't know how to shoot, didn't even know how to load a gun, and the rifle was too long for her to aim it at herself. She could go to the river, put rocks in her pockets and drown herself. But she'd always been afraid of drowning. Wasn't there an easier way? The sleeping pills! Yes. There were more of them. Lots of them. In Mama's dresser.

She went into the bedroom and pawed through the top drawer. Her hand closed on the bottle. She took off the lid. How many would it take? She counted them out in the palm of her hand. Nine. That should be enough. Before she could change her mind, she went out the front door, got a dipper of water out of the tub and swallowed all of them. For just a second, a wave of panic swept through her. But she could not, would not, have Timothy's baby. All her plans — to marry Paul and live in Portland and have his children — all gone.

She walked back into the cabin and looked around her.

Such ordinary things that she would never see again. The wood stove, the decrepit chairs, the cot with the old army blanket on it . . . they all looked like home, crude as it was. Mustn't think about it.

Where should she be when she died? On the bed? She looked again at the old army blanket, then sat down on the cot and wrapped the blanket around her body.

Mama's apron hung on a nail beside the stove. She'd made it out of flour sacking. Valina could see the worn spot where Mama's round tummy stuck out. Poor Mama. But surely she would understand. Not Timothy's baby. No. Oh, God, why couldn't it be Paul's baby? Paul, please understand. I love you, but there won't be a wedding now, my darling.

Wedding. The money in the attic. Mama wouldn't know it was there. She had to get it for her. When she stood up, she felt light-headed. How much time was left? Tears streamed down her face. She walked over to the ladder, lifted her foot up to the first rung, then the next. Such an effort. Mama . . . the money.

When the kitchen door of the cafe crashed open, and Doc ran in, Emma panicked at the frantic look on his face. "What's wrong? In the name of God, what is it?"

"Come with me." He grabbed her arm and pulled. "Right now!"

"Go on, Emma." Tillie said.

When the door shut behind them, Emma flared. "Tell me this instant." She heard only two words. Pregnant. Timothy. "No. Oh, no. My poor Valina."

"Emma, I know this is a shock," Doc said, "but we have to hurry."

"Where is she?"

"I left her in my office, with orders to stay there on the couch until I got back. But she's gone. I'm very worried about her . . . about what she'll do."

A sob caught in Emma's throat. "Dear God, how much more?"

"Minnie's over in the infirmary. She might have seen Valina," Doc said. "Let's go ask her."

When they got to the infirmary, Minnie was putting clean sheets on one of the beds. Doc grabbed her by the arm. "Have you seen Valina?"

"Not since I told you about the Anderson boy," Minnie said. "What's going on? Something wrong with her?"

Doc spun around to face Emma. "Quick. Where would she go?"

Too frightened to think, Emma just shook her head.

Doc wasted no time. "Minnie, find Paul. I think he's fishing at that hole just above the cafe. See if he knows any place she might go. We'll be at the Addison's cabin. Come on, Emma, the car's out front."

It seemed to Emma that the drive took forever. She could have sworn they passed the same trees, the same bushes, over and over again, until, through tears, she saw just a blur of green.

When they finally got to the cabin and went inside, they found Valina on the floor at the base of the ladder. Doc bent down and felt her neck for a pulse.

Emma sank to her knees next to Valina. No. Please, no.

"She's alive," Doc's voice cracked. "By God, she's alive." Carefully, he felt Valina's arms and legs. "Her wrist is broken,

but everything else seems intact. Must've fallen off the ladder."
He picked her up, carried her to the bedroom, and laid her on
the bed.

Emma, followed him and saw the empty pill bottle on the
dresser. "The pills," she gasped. "She took the sleeping pills."
Emma showed him the bottle. "Those pills you gave me for
her and Rachel. The bottle's empty."

"I gave you twelve pills."

Emma gulped for breath. "And we only used three of them."

Doc let out a loud breath. "Well, that's not enough to kill
her. She'll sleep for a long time, twenty-four hours or more. I
think she'll be all right, though. Her pulse is steady and her
breathing is normal. Would you get me a dishtowel or a rag so
I can bind her wrist?"

Emma brought Doc the towel and some scissors. Not
trusting her wobbly legs, she leaned against the dresser while
Doc wrapped Valina's wrist. How could they make Valina
want to live? God in heaven, what could they do?

"Since she's going to pull a Rip Van Winkle on us, we
might as well make her comfortable," Doc said.

Emma, in a daze, took a nightgown out of the dresser
drawer and began to take off Valina's clothes. When she
started to remove the teddie, Doc had to help hold Valina's
broken wrist.

That was when Emma saw the blood on the crotch of the
teddie. She looked at Doc, her eyes questioning him.

"Praise the Lord," he said. "Looks like she's miscarried."

Emma slumped onto the bed and sobbed. She felt Doc's
hand on her shoulder. "I'm sorry, Charles. I shouldn't break
down like this."

"Go right ahead. I feel like bawling, myself. There's been an awful lot of suffering in this family. Enough to snap a body in two."

Emma sat up and wiped her eyes. "You've been wonderful through all this horror."

"Your family means a great deal to Catherine and me." He patted Emma's shoulder. "I'll have to take Valina to the infirmary now. She needs a D & C. Let's get that nightgown on her, and then you'll need to help me get her in the car. She'll stay at the infirmary, so Minnie and I can monitor her breathing and blood pressure."

"You mean overnight?" Emma didn't want Valina to be there alone. What if she woke up and didn't know where she was, or that she wasn't pregnant any more?

"You can sleep in one of the beds in the room, Emma. And I'm sure Paul won't want to leave her, either."

Emma pulled the nightgown over Valina's head while Doc protected the broken wrist. It was a struggle getting Valina's limp body off the bed and draped over Doc's shoulder. Emma held Valina's wrist to keep it from swinging or bumping into something. Getting her into the back seat of the car was even harder, but they managed. Before Doc could start the car, Paul drove up, slammed on his brakes, and dashed over to them. "What happened?" That's when he saw Valina stretched out on the back seat, unconscious, her head in Emma's lap. "My God, is she . . . ?"

"She's going to be all right," Doc said. "Emma can explain it to you when we get to the infirmary. Meet us there."

While Doc and Minnie took care of Valina, Emma took Paul outside and told him what had happened. She put her arm around him when she saw his stricken face. "It's like a nightmare, isn't it?"

"How much more can she stand, Emma? Will she be all right? All those sleeping pills . . . "

Your uncle said she'll sleep for maybe twenty-four hours. He and Minnie will check on her. I'm going to stay here with her, too."

"So am I," he said. "Nothing could keep me away."

"I have to run over to Catherine's to ask her to take care of Rachel," Emma said. "If you see your uncle before I get back, will you tell him, please? I'll hurry."

"Sure."

Emma watched as he slowly lowered his body onto the top step of the infirmary and put his head in his hands. Paul had suffered agonies, too. They all had.

As she hurried to Catherine's house, Emma wondered how Daniel would react. He hadn't been the same ever since that awful night. Who had? But his burden was greater. She prayed that time would give him some comfort.

She had to see about Rachel's care first, then she'd find Daniel. When she stepped onto Catherine's front porch, she could hear Rachel practicing the piano. Catherine was in the kitchen.

"I just finished baking oatmeal cookies," Catherine said. "Would you like one?"

"No thanks. I'm here to ask a favor of you."

Catherine's face blanched when Emma told her what had happened. "Poor Valina. Surely this is the end of it."

"Let's hope so," Emma said. "Would you keep Rachel overnight? I have to go find Daniel and get back to Valina."

"l will be happy to."

"I'll stop in the music room and tell her that Valina's had a little setback."

"That's a good idea. You can explain later."

Valina finally wakened the next afternoon. Emma, seeing the panic in her daughter's eyes, said, "Everything's all right, now, dear."

Valina's eyes filled with tears. "But I don't want to live."

"Yes you do," Emma said. "You miscarried. You're not pregnant anymore."

Valina grabbed Emma's arm. "You're sure?"

"Absolutely positive."

Valina looked around the room. "Is Paul here?"

"He took our lunch dishes to Catherine. He'll be right back. And we'll send for Papa. Doc assured us that you'd be all right, so Papa decided he'd go to work this morning. I thought he might be better off there."

Doc came into the room. Minnie had gone to get him the instant Valina opened her eyes.

"Welcome back, Valina," he said. "You must have climbed up the ladder. Am I right?"

"Yes. I wanted to get my wedding money out, so Mama could pay for the funeral."

Emma gasped.

"I'm sorry, Mama."

Doc broke in, "You probably fell off the ladder, and the fall not only broke your wrist, it more than likely caused the miscarriage."

Valina glanced down at her bandaged wrist. "I didn't even know it was broken," she said.

"I want you to stay here another day so I can keep track of your temperature and any possible bleeding," Doc said. "We also need to put a cast on that wrist, now that you're awake." He took her other hand and squeezed it. "You're a lucky girl. Now, I've got to get back to my office."

He bumped into Paul as he went out the door. "You're just in time," Doc said. "She's awake."

Paul knelt by the bed, speechless. He just held Valina's hand.

Emma put her hand on Paul's shoulder. "I must get back to work. You can have her to yourself for the rest of the day, Paul, but I need to have a few minutes alone with my daughter right now. Would you mind terribly?"

"Of course not." Paul stood up and walked to the door. "I'll be out front."

Minnie, who'd been standing in the background, quietly went into the other room.

Emma settled herself in the chair beside Valina's bed. "God gave you a second chance. Show Him how grateful you are, Valina. He doesn't take kindly to His children taking their own lives. That's His job. Promise me that you will never do this again, no matter what happens."

"I promise, Mama."

"You've been through fire and brimstone. Those of us who love you have been through it too. Paul's love for you is a gift that needs cherishing. Yes, you deserve it, but you'd better really treasure it. Not all men would stand behind you the way he has."

"I know, Mama."

"Are you ready to allow yourself to be happy?"

"Oh, yes. Yes, Mama."

"Good." Emma kissed Valina's cheek. "I must go back to work. It's Paul's turn now." She went to the door.

"I love you, Mama."

"And I love you, my darling." Emma, standing at the open door, blew her daughter a kiss, then held the door open so Paul could go in.

Valina found it hard to look at Paul. "I'm sorry," she whispered.

"No, don't apologize." He kissed her cheek, then knelt on the floor beside the bed and took her hand in his. "Knowing you were pregnant with his child must have been the ultimate hell for you. You'd already gone through more than should be expected of any woman. But it's over now. Really over."

"Yes, but I'm not sure I can go on our trip. At least not so soon."

"We'll just delay it until you can."

He looked exhausted. She ran her hand over his stubble of beard. "But you won't get to see your parade."

"There'll be another one next year." He reached up and moved a strand of her hair away from her cheek. "We'll see many parades together."

"I think it would be a good idea if we could be married before we go on that trip," Valina said.

Paul's hand tightened on hers. "You mean it?"

"Yes I do. We can get married just as soon as Doc says I'm able."

He picked up her hand and held it against his cheek. "Ah, Valina."

She knew she would always remember the way he looked at her at that moment.

CHAPTER 17

J-Bar-J Ranch—1969

I woke up with a feeling of dread. It was Jimmy's last day at the ranch. I glanced at the clock on my bedside table. Four in the morning had become the usual time for me to get up. I got dressed, made coffee, and took a cup of it out to the barn. I needed to talk to Daniel's spirit in a place where no one could overhear me making an ass of myself.

The minute I got there, I started right in. "Daniel, I wouldn't have given a nickel for your great-grandson when I first laid eyes on him. Now it hurts to see him go. He's the closest thing I've ever had to a child of my own."

Old Roscoe had followed me into the barn. He pushed his muzzle against my hand. Sweet old fellow knew I was hurting. I rubbed his ear and scratched under his neck, then got back to my conversation with Daniel.

"You remember Jimmy's dad. He called to ask if he should come up and get the boy, or let him come home by himself. The man has far too much faith in my judgment. Never thought you'd hear me say a thing like that, did you, Daniel? Well, if it gives you any comfort, I still can't keep my mouth shut. I told Bob I thought Jimmy might need some private time on the train to sort things out, though he really should ask Jimmy. Damned if the kid didn't give him the same answer I did when he talked to him. I wish you could see how good Jimmy looks now. No more skinny, defensive brat. No, sir. He's developed the muscles of a man, and the heart of one, too."

"Yes, Daniel, I know. I'm just feeling sorry for myself. You've probably got better things to do than listen to me whine. I'll get out of your hair now. Give my love to Emma." As I walked to the house, the rooster crowed. The sky had turned light while I was in the barn.

Oscar was sitting on the porch when I got there. "It'll be tough to see the kid leave, won't it?" he said. "Are you gonna tell him about Orville before he goes?"

"No. Jimmy's had enough lumps this summer."

"Yeah, he has." Oscar scratched the day's growth of beard on his chin. "Mattie, I've been wanting to talk to you about something."

"Go ahead."

"I hope you aren't fretting about those vile things Orville said to you. Too bad he didn't know the truth. Zoe must not have told him about the money you gave her each month."

"Well, it wasn't a huge amount."

"But it wasn't owed to her, either. Wasn't your fault she had Timothy's baby."

A loud gasp stopped us cold. I turned toward the sound. Jimmy stood looking at us through the screen door. Damn.

"Come out and sit down, Jimmy."

He sat in the chair next to mine, a guarded look on his face.

What could I say to the kid? While I was trying to figure that out, he took a deep, shaky breath, and said, "Timothy was Orville's father?"

"It's possible he was."

"Then what relation was he to me?"

"He may not have been related to you at all. But, Zoe Adams swore that Orville was Timothy's baby. And he may have been. She had him five months after Timothy died. But she also slept with a lot of other men."

"She was the town whore," Oscar said.

I frowned at him.

He frowned right back at me. "Zoe knew she could get you to help her if you thought that baby was Timothy's. She probably didn't even know who the father was."

I sighed. "That's true. But even if Timothy wasn't the father, Zoe and the baby needed help."

Oscar turned to Jimmy. "Orville never knew how much your Aunt Matilda did for him and his mother."

"That's too bad," Jimmy said. "He might not have been so mean if he'd known someone cared enough to help out."

My God, that kid had grown up. "That's a mighty wise observation, Jimmy."

"Damned right," Oscar said. He stood up. "I forgot to shave," he said, and quickly went inside.

I looked over at Jimmy. "You hungry?"

He laughed. "Since the second morning I was here, have you heard me say I wasn't hungry?"

"Breakfast in twenty minutes." I stood up. "Thought you might like to go fishing, since it's your last day."

"But what about work?"

"The men can do it. They'll have to anyway, when you're gone."

"At least I'd better milk Daisy and feed the chickens," he said.

"Good idea."

While he was gone, I fixed a special breakfast for the occasion. I got out my old waffle iron and made Daniel's favorite, chocolate waffles with whipped cream. Then I baked eggs with grated cheese on them. And, of course, we had applesauce, cinnamon rolls, fresh pears with nutmeg and cream, and lots of good black coffee.

Jimmy kept saying, "Man, this is great," then he'd ask for another chocolate waffle. Between him and the men, they kept me and that waffle iron busy for a solid hour.

When I told the men that Jimmy was going fishing with me, you should have heard them moan. Now they'd have to do the work he'd been doing. 'Course they did it just to tease Jimmy, and it did tickle the boy.

"You guys are full of beans," Jimmy said.

After breakfast, the two of us rode up to a place on the river that we call Big Bend. There's a deep pool on one side where large trout hang low in the water. It's beside a grassy knoll under the branches of a weeping willow tree.

"This is cool," Jimmy said.

I handed him the metal box with the flies in it. "Which one should I use?" he asked.

"Doesn't matter. Those trout will nibble on anything. I brought some worms, too."

He looked in the worm can. "Think I'll use these. I feel like sitting and talking."

So that was it. "Fine." I thought I'd split laughing at the way he flexed his muscle after he threw out his line. I could tell he was expecting me to comment. "Quite a set of muscles you've developed this summer."

He shined a big grin at me. "Yeah. I'm going to work out with weights when I get home so I won't lose them."

I put my line in the water and we settled back onto a couple of rocks. He got out the thermos and poured each of us a cup of coffee. About then, a mouse darted past us heading for a hole by the base of the willow.

"My mother would faint if she saw that mouse," Jimmy said. "I wish she could be more like you. I bet she'd be a lot happier if she was."

He felt that way about me? "That's very flattering, Jimmy, but your mother's world is different from mine. She can't help that."

We watched a dragonfly sun itself on a warm rock, while a pair of crows yakked their heads off in a nearby fir tree.

"That's Harry and Larry," I said.

"Who? The crows?"

"Yep. They think they own the place, but I don't see them paying any taxes."

The crows flew off and peace descended again.

We sat there lazing away the time, just as if we had forever.

The river at the bend spreads wide around the curve, its fierce energy just one hundred yards upstream slowed by the resistance of an outcropping of massive rocks. But below the bend the river narrows and flings itself at the rocks in its path, daring them to hold it back.

"I never come here without remembering Jacob," I said. "He discovered this fishing hole. He even planted the willow tree. You can see that most of the original tree is gnarled and half-rotted, but it's still there." Just like me, I thought. We'll both topple one of these days.

Suddenly Jimmy's line dipped and he let out a whoop. "I've got the first fish."

"Not until it's on land." I said.

That trout gave Jimmy a real fight. Time and again it whipped up out of the water, just to show us how pretty it was, with its silver fins glittering in the sunlight. That went on for some time before Jimmy finally landed it.

"Bet you five dollars I catch more fish than you do," he said. "And bigger ones, too."

"You're on."

He sat down and said, "How come Rachel and Roy got married, anyway? They sure didn't like each other much."

"Well, they changed as they grew up. She quit beating up on him, for one thing. And he got big and muscular, so whenever she got feisty he'd just laugh at her. They still tease each other, but now it's funny. I think they make a good pair."

"You've never said what happened to Emma and Daniel. Why not?"

"Too much else to tell you, I guess. After Valina and Paul were married, Emma and Daniel moved in with Mary. And when Mary left a few months later, they stayed in the house. Alice and Gunther stayed with them until Emma died ten years ago."

"What did she die of?" he asked.

"Cancer. At the end, that last month of her misery, both Valina and Rachel came and stayed with her. Worked in shifts taking care of their mama."

Jimmy frowned. "Ten years ago? I don't remember that."

"You were only five years old then. Can't expect to remember things at that age." I'd been afraid this would come up.

"But I remember when my Grandpa Tuttle died, and I was only four then," he said.

"Probably it didn't make an impression on you because you hadn't seen Emma and Daniel very often."

"But I would've known that Marie had gone to the funeral."

I tried to say it as gently as I could. "Marie didn't come over for the funeral."

He looked really upset. Damn. "Now, wait a minute before you jump to any conclusions. Marie had vowed she'd never come back to Pine Bluff. You have to realize how hard it would've been on her."

"Well, what about Valina? It would've been hard on her, too, but she came back."

"She and Paul had come back often to visit their families. Actually, I think it helped Valina to put what had happened with Timothy in perspective. What's more, she had Paul's love and strength behind her. Marie's situation was different. It's best not to waste your energy judging others, son. Each of us has our own weaknesses and strengths.

"Well, if anything happened to you, I'd manage to get here in a hurry."

His words didn't register for a second, but when they did . . . "That's mighty comforting to hear. I thank you for that."

"You saved my life."

"You saved mine, too."

He was silent for quite a spell. Then he asked, "What did Daniel do after Emma died?"

"Daniel was so broken up about it, that I got him to come live with me. We both missed Emma something fierce, but we had some good days together after the grief lessened a bit. Four years later he up and died, sitting in the rocker on the porch. Had a heart attack. One minute he was laughing, the next he was gone. I didn't even have a chance to say goodbye."

He thought a minute, then said, "Marie didn't come back for his funeral, either, did she?"

"Nope." I poured some more coffee for us. "You've been through some pretty heavy stuff this summer, Jimmy. Things I would never have wanted to happen to you, not for anything. Sandy's death, and Cal's and then Orville . . ."

"You forgot Mattie's Lady."

"So I did. What I'm trying to say is how proud I am of the way you came through it all. You're quite a guy."

He grinned. "Wish I had a recording of that."

"Fat chance," I said.

"I've been meaning to ask you something," He paused and nudged a rock with the toe of his boot. "Since you think so highly of me, could I come back next summer?"

Good thing I had my mouth shut or my upper plate might've landed on the ground. I swallowed hard. "Happy to have you, if I'm still here, that is."

He stared at me, an anxious look on his face. "Are you going to sell the ranch?"

"No, it's just that I'm old, and we never know."

He grinned at me. "Oscar says you're too ornery to die."

"Oh, he does, does he? Well, to tell you the truth, I'm kind of curious about what's on the other side, aren't you?"

He rolled his eyes. "Not especially."

"Never know. When the time comes, I might get to see Jacob and Daniel and Emma. If I do, I'll tell them you said hello."

"You do that. You won't be seeing Timothy up there, that's for sure."

"Timothy still bothers you, doesn't he?" I said.

"Yeah, I guess so. My biology teacher claimed that family traits skip a generation."

"Hogwash. You can't inherit bad deeds, for God's sake. That thought isn't even worthy of brain space."

Jimmy snickered. "Thanks. I'll remember that."

The next morning I told him I wasn't going to ride down to town with him, that I'd rather say goodbye at the house.

"That's okay," he said. "I know you don't like that train platform."

When breakfast was over, he went up and got his things. Oscar brought the jeep around and Buck and George helped Jimmy carry everything out. I was pretty much rooted to the spot, trying to keep my cool, as the kid would say.

Buck shook his hand and said, "See you next year." Jimmy's mouth dropped open a foot. He probably hadn't heard Buck say that many words in a row all summer.

Then George patted the kid on the back and said, "Been great, son."

"We'd better get going," Oscar hollered from the jeep.

Jimmy came up on the porch and stood in front of me. "Just a minute," he yelled. "Gotta say goodbye."

"Trains don't wait."

That Oscar. He was having as hard a time as I was.

"Calm down, Oscar. You have plenty of time." I handed Jimmy a sack lunch. "We've appreciated your help around here, and enjoyed your company, as well. Say hello to your folks for me." I bent down and kissed him on the cheek.

His eyes flew open wide and his Adam's apple began to bob up and down again. He cleared his throat. "It's been cool. See you next year." He bent down to tell Angus goodbye, then turned and walked quickly toward the pickup.

"You tell Oscar he'd better watch his step or you'll be replacing him as head man around here," I yelled.

He waved as the pickup drove away. I turned my back on Buck and George, so they couldn't see the fool tears in my eyes, and walked over to the pickle tree.

Hell, just another damned goodbye.

Acknowledgments

To J. Gale Frank, who has shared her numerous talents as well as her editing knowledge.

To Margaret Donsbach Tomlinson, whose critiques during the original creation of this book were invaluable.

To Jennifer Omner, for her amazing skill in the design of this book.

To Mary Usui, who graciously typed a useable copy of the book for me.

And to the late Bill Mathis for all the research he did.

About the Author

Carol Grier was born in 1924 and raised in Yosemite National Park, or paradise, in her opinion. She currently lives in Beaverton, Oregon. Carol has written poetry, newspaper articles, and four books. She is eager to start yet another novel.